King Vortigern said: "A king's stronghold should be built on blood."

"Yes!" Maugan, the High Priest, shouted. "In ancient times no king built a fortress without observing this rite. The blood of a strong man, a warrior, kept the walls standing."

My heart had begun to beat in slow, hard strokes that made the blood tingle in my limbs. I said coldly: "And what has this to do with me? I am no warrior."

"You are no man, neither," said the King harshly. "It has been revealed to me, that I should seek out a lad who never had a father, and slake the foundations with his blood."

I stared at him, then looked round the ring of faces. I could see it in all of them, the death I had smelled ever since I entered the hall. I turned back to the King.

"What rubbish is this, that you talk of blood and human sacrifice?"

"I do not speak of 'human' sacrifice," said Vortigern. "You are the son of no man, Merlin. Remember this."

THE
CRYSTAL
CAVE

by MARY STEWART

FAWCETT CREST • NEW YORK

To the Memory of
MOLLIE CRAIG
with my love

ACKNOWLEDGEMENTS

Edwin Muir's poem "Merlin" is reprinted by permission of Faber and Faber Ltd. from the *Collected Poems, 1921–58.*

The poem on pages 182–183 is a free translation of verses appearing in *Barzaz Briez; Chants Populaires de la Bretagne,* by the Vicomte de la Villemarqué (Paris, 1867).

The Legend of Merlin is based on the translation of Geoffrey of Monmouth's *History of the Kings of Britain* which was first published in the Everyman's Library, Vol. 577, by J. & M. Dent in 1912.

THE CRYSTAL CAVE

THIS BOOK CONTAINS THE COMPLETE TEXT OF THE ORIGINAL HARDCOVER EDITION.

Published by Fawcett Crest Books, a unit of CBS Publications, the Consumer Publishing Division of CBS Inc., by arrangement with William Morrow & Company, Inc.

ISBN: 0-449-24111-4

Selection of The Literary Guild, July 1970
Selection of the Doubleday Bargain Book Club, April 1971

32 31 30 29 28 27 26 25 24 23

CONTENTS

MERLIN

O Merlin in your crystal cave
Deep in the diamond of the day,
Will there ever be a singer
Whose music will smooth away
The furrow drawn by Adam's finger
Across the meadow and the wave?
Or a runner who'll outrun
Man's long shadow driving on,
Burst through the gates of history,
And hang the apple on the tree?
Will your sorcery ever show
The sleeping bride shut in her bower,
The day wreathed in its mound of snow,
And Time locked in his tower?

Edwin Muir

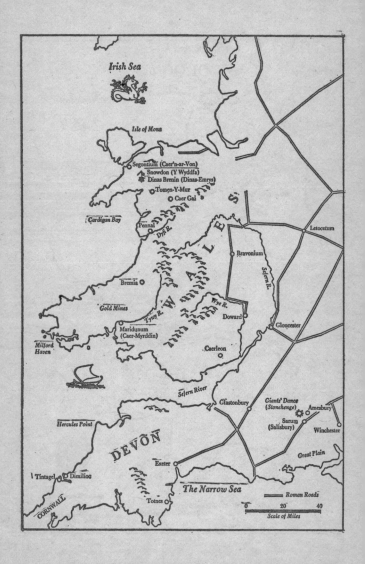

PROLOGUE

THE PRINCE
OF DARKNESS

I am an old man now, but then I was already past my prime when Arthur was crowned King. The years since then seem to me now more dim and faded than the earlier years, as if my life were a growing tree which burst to flower and leaf with him, and now has nothing more to do than yellow to the grave.

This is true of all old men, that the recent past is misted, while distant scenes of memory are clear and brightly coloured. Even the scenes of my far childhood come back to me now sharp and high-coloured and edged with brightness, like the pattern of a fruit tree against a white wall, or banners in sunlight against a sky of storm.

The colours are brighter than they were, of that I am sure. The memories that come back to me here in the dark are seen with the new young eyes of childhood; they are so far gone from me, with their pain no longer present, that they unroll like pictures of something that happened, not to me, not to the bubble of bone that this memory used to inhabit, but to another Merlin as young and light and free of the air and spring winds as the bird she named me for.

With the later memories it is different; they come back, some of them, hot and shadowed, things seen in the fire. For this is where I gather them. This is one of the few trivial tricks—I cannot call it power—left to me now that I am old and stripped at last down to man. I can see still ... not clearly or with the call of trumpets as I once did, but in the child's way of dreams and pictures in the fire. I can still make the flames burn up or die; it is one of the simplest of magics, the most easily learned, the last forgotten. What I cannot recall in dream I see in the flames, the red heart of the fire or the countless mirrors of the crystal cave.

The first memory of all is dark and fireshot. It is not my own memory, but later you will understand how I know these things. You would call it not memory so much as a dream of the past, something in the blood, something recalled from him, it may be, while he still bore me in his body. I believe

10

that such things can be. So it seems to me right that I should start with him who was before me, and who will be again when I am gone.

This is what happened that night. I saw it, and it is a true tale.

It was dark, and the place was cold, but he had lit a small fire of wood, which smoked sullenly but gave a little warmth. It had been raining all day, and from the branches near the mouth of the cave water still dripped, and a steady trickle overflowed the lip of the well, soaking the ground below. Several times, restless, he had left the cave, and now he walked out below the cliff to the grove where his horse stood tethered.

With the coming of dusk the rain had stopped, but a mist had risen, creeping knee-high through the trees so that they stood like ghosts, and the grazing horse floated like a swan. It was a grey, and more than ever ghostly because it grazed so quietly; he had torn up a scarf and wound fragments of cloth round the bit so that no jingle should betray him. The bit was gilded, and the torn strips were of silk, for he was a king's son. If they caught him, they would have killed him. He was just eighteen.

He heard the hoofbeats coming softly up the valley. His head moved, and his breathing quickened. His sword flicked with light as he lifted it. The grey horse paused in its grazing and lifted its head clear of the mist. Its nostrils flickered, but no sound came. The man smiled. The hoofbeats came closer, and then, shoulder-deep in mist, a brown pony trotted out of the dusk. Its rider, small and slight, was wrapped in a dark cloak, muffled from the night air. The pony pulled to a halt, threw up its head, and gave a long, pealing whinny. The rider, with an exclamation of dismay, slipped from its back and grabbed for the bridle to muffle the sound against her cloak. She was a girl, very young, who looked round her anxiously until she saw the young man, sword in hand, at the edge of the trees.

"You sound like a troop of cavalry," he said.

"I was here before I knew it. Everything looks strange in the mist."

"No one saw you? You came safely?"

"Safely enough. It's been impossible the last two days. They were on the roads night and day."

"I guessed it." He smiled. "Well, now you are here. Give

me the bridle." He led the pony in under the trees, and tied it up. Then he kissed her.

After a while she pushed him away. "I ought not to stay. I brought the things, so even if I can't come tomorrow—" She stopped. She had seen the saddle on his horse, the muffled bit, the packed saddle-bag. Her hands moved sharply against his chest, and his own covered them and held her fast. "Ah," she said, "I knew. I knew even in my sleep last night. You're going."

"I must. Tonight."

She was silent for a minute. Then all she said was: "How long?"

He did not pretend to misunderstand her. "We have an hour, two, no more."

She said flatly: "You will come back." Then as he started to speak: "No. Not now, not any more. We have said it all, and now there is no more time. I only meant that you will be safe, and you will come back safely. I tell you, I know these things. I have the Sight. You will come back."

"It hardly needs the Sight to tell me that. I must come back. And then perhaps you will listen to me—"

"No." She stopped him again, almost angrily. "It doesn't matter. What does it matter? We have only an hour, and we are wasting it. Let us go in."

He was already pulling out the jewelled pin that held her cloak together, as he put an arm round her and led her towards the cave.

"Yes, let us go in."

BOOK I

THE DOVE

1

The day my uncle Camlach came home, I was just six years old.

I remember him well as I first saw him, a tall young man, fiery like my grandfather, with the blue eyes and reddish hair that I thought so beautiful in my mother. He came to Maridunum near sunset of a September evening, with a small troop of men. Being only small, I was with the women in the long, old-fashioned room where they did the weaving. My mother was sitting at the loom; I remember the cloth; it was of scarlet, with a narrow pattern of green at the edge. I sat near her on the floor, playing knuckle-bones, right hand against left. The sun slanted through the windows, making oblong pools of bright gold on the cracked mosaics of the floor; bees droned in the herbs outside, and even the click and rattle of the loom sounded sleepy. The women were talking among themselves over the spindles, but softly, heads together, and Moravik, my nurse, was frankly asleep on her stool in one of the pools of sunlight.

When the clatter, and then the shouts, came from the courtyard, the loom stopped abruptly, and with it the soft chatter from the women. Moravik came awake with a snort and a stare. My mother was sitting very straight, head lifted, listening. She had dropped her shuttle. I saw her eyes meet Moravik's.

I was halfway to the window when Moravik called to me sharply, and there was something in her voice that made me stop and go back to her without protest. She began to fuss with my clothing, pulling my tunic straight and smoothing my hair, so that I understood the visitor to be someone of importance. I felt excitement, and also surprise that apparently I was to be presented to him; I was used to being kept out of the way in those days. I stood patiently while Moravik dragged the comb through my hair, and over my head she and my mother exchanged some quick, breathless talk which, hardly heeding, I did not understand. I was listening to the tramp of horses in the yard and the shouting of men, words

14

here and there coming clearly in a language neither Welsh nor Latin, but Celtic with some accent like the one of Less Britain, which I understood because my nurse, Moravik, was a Breton, and her language came to me as readily as my own.

I heard my grandfather's great laugh, and another voice replying. Then he must have swept the newcomer indoors with him, for the voices receded, leaving only the jingle and stamp of the horses being led to the stables.

I broke from Moravik and ran to my mother.

"Who is it?"

"My brother Camlach, the King's son." She did not look at me, but pointed to the fallen shuttle. I picked it up and handed it to her. Slowly, and rather mechanically, she set the loom moving again.

"Is the war over, then?"

"The war has been over a long time. Your uncle has been with the High King in the south."

"And now he has to come home because my uncle Dyved died?" Dyved had been the heir, the King's eldest son. He had died suddenly, and in great pain, of cramps in the stomach, and Elen his widow, who was childless, had gone back to her father. Naturally there had been the usual talk of poison, but nobody took it seriously; Dyved had been well liked, a tough fighter and a careful man, but generous where it suited. "They say he'll have to marry. Will he, Mother?" I was excited, important at knowing so much, thinking of the wedding feast. "Will he marry Keridwen, now that my uncle Dyved—"

"What?" The shuttle stopped, and she swung round, startled. But what she saw in my face appeased her, for the anger went out of her voice, though she still frowned, and I heard Moravik clucking and fussing behind me. "Where in the world did you get that? You hear too much, whether you understand it or not. Forget such matters, and hold your tongue." The shuttle moved again, slowly. "Listen to me, Merlin. When they come to see you, you will do well to keep quiet. Do you understand me?"

"Yes, Mother." I understood very well. I was well accustomed to keeping out of the King's way. "But will they come to see me? Why me?"

She said, with a thin bitterness that made her look all at once older, almost as old as Moravik: "Why do you think?"

The loom clacked again, fiercely. She was feeding in the

green thread, and I could see that she was making a mistake, but it looked pretty, so I said nothing, watching her and staying close, till at length the curtain at the doorway was pushed aside, and the two men came in.

They seemed to fill the room, the red head and the grey within a foot of the beams. My grandfather wore blue, periwinkle colour with a gold border. Camlach was in black. Later I was to discover that he always wore black; he had jewels on his hands and at his shoulder, and beside his father he looked lightly built and young, but as sharp and whippy as a fox.

My mother stood up. She was wearing a house-robe of dark brown, the colour of peat, and against it her hair shone like corn-silk. But neither of the two men glanced at her. You would have thought there was no one in the room but I, small as I was, by the loom.

My grandfather jerked his head and said one word: "Out," and the women hurried in a rustling, silent group from the chamber. Moravik stood her ground, puffed up with bravery like a partridge, but the fierce blue eyes flicked to her for a second, and she went. A sniff as she passed them was all that she dared. The eyes came back to me.

"Your sister's bastard," said the King. "There he is. Six years old this month, grown like a weed, and no more like any of us than a damned devil's whelp would be. Look at him! Black hair, black eyes, and as scared of cold iron as a changeling from the hollow hills. You tell me the devil himself got that one, and I'll believe you!"

My uncle said only one word, straight to her: "Whose?"

"You think we didn't ask, you fool?" said my grandfather. "She was whipped till the women said she'd miscarry, but never a word from her. Better if she had, perhaps—some nonsense they were talking, old wives' tales of devils coming in the dark to lie with young maids—and from the look of him they could be right."

Camlach, six foot and golden, looked down at me. His eyes were blue, clear as my mother's, and his colour was high. The mud had dried yellow on his soft doeskin boots, and a smell of sweat and horses came from him. He had come to look at me before even taking the dirt of travel off. I remember how he stared down at me, while my mother stood silent, and my grandfather glowered under his brows, his breath coming harsh and rapid, as it always did when he had put himself in a passion.

"Come here," said my uncle.

I took half a dozen steps forward. I did not dare go nearer. I stopped. From three paces away he seemed taller than ever. He towered over me to the ceiling beams.

"What's your name?"

"Myrddin Emrys."

"Emrys? Child of light, belonging to the gods ... ? That hardly seems the name for a demon's whelp."

The mildness of his tone encouraged me. "They call me Merlinus," I ventured. "It's a Roman name for a falcon, the *corwalch*."

My grandfather barked, "Falcon!" and made a sound of contempt, shooting his arm-rings till they jingled.

"A small one," I said defensively, then fell silent under my uncle's thoughtful look.

He stroked his chin, then looked at my mother with his brows up. "Strange choices, all of them, for a Christian household. A Roman demon, perhaps, Niniane?"

She put up her chin. "Perhaps. How do I know? It was dark."

I thought a flash of amusement came and went in his face, but the King swept a hand down in a violent gesture. "You see? That's all you'll get—lies, tales of sorcery, insolence! Get back to your work, girl, and keep your bastard out of my sight! Now that your brother's home, we'll find a man who'll take the pair of you from under my feet and his! Camlach, I hope you see the sense of getting yourself a wife now, and a son or two, since this is all I'm left with!"

"Oh, I'm for it," said Camlach easily. Their attention had lifted from me. They were going, and neither had touched me. I unclenched my hands and moved back softly, half a pace; another. "But you've got yourself a new queen meantime, sir, and they tell me she's pregnant?"

"No matter of that, you should be wed, and soon. I'm an old man, and these are troubled times. As for this boy"—I froze again—"forget him. Whoever sired him, if he hasn't come forward in six years, he'll not do so now. And if it had been Vortigern himself, the High King, he'd have made nothing of him. A sullen brat who skulks alone in corners. Doesn't even play with the other boys, afraid to, likely. Afraid of his own shadow."

He turned away. Camlach's eyes met my mother's, over my head. Some message passed. Then he looked down at me again, and smiled.

I still remember how the room seemed to light up, though the sun had gone now, and its warmth with it. Soon they would be bringing the rushlights.

"Well," said Camlach, "it's but a fledgling falcon after all. Don't be too hard on him, sir; you've frightened better men than he is, in your time."

"Yourself, you mean? Hah!"

"I assure you."

The King, in the doorway, glared briefly at me under his jutting brows, then with a puff of impatient breath settled his mantle over his arm. "Well, well, let be. God's sweet death, but I'm hungry. It's well past supper-time—but I suppose you'll want to go and soak yourself first, in your damned Roman fashion? I warn you, we've never had the furnaces on since you left ..."

He turned with a swirl of the blue cloak and went out, still talking. Behind me I heard my mother's breath go out, and the rustle of her gown as she sat. My uncle put out a hand to me.

"Come, Merlinus, and talk to me while I bathe in your cold Welsh water. We princes must get to know one another."

I stood rooted. I was conscious of my mother's silence, and how still she sat.

"Come," said my uncle, gently, and smiled at me again.

I ran to him.

I went through the hypocaust that night.

This was my own private way, my secret hiding-place where I could escape from the bigger boys and play my own solitary games. My grandfather had been right when he said I "skulked alone in corners," but this was not from fear, though the sons of his nobles followed his lead—as children do—and made me their butt in their rough war-games whenever they could catch me.

At the beginning, it is true, the tunnels of the disused heating-system were a refuge, a secret place where I could hide and be alone; but I soon found a curiously strong pleasure in exploring the great system of dark, earth-smelling chambers under the palace floors.

My grandfather's palace had been, in times past, a vast country-house belonging to some Roman notable who had owned and farmed the land for several miles each way along the river valley. The main part of the house still stood, though badly scarred by time and war, and by at least one disastrous fire, which had destroyed one end of the main block and part of a wing. The old slaves' quarters were still intact round the courtyard where the cooks and house-servants worked, and the bath-house remained, though patched and plastered, and with the roof rough-thatched over the worst bits. I never remember the furnace working; water was heated over the courtyard fires.

The entrance to my secret labyrinth was the stoke-hole in the boiler-house; this was a trap in the wall under the cracked and rusting boiler, barely the height of a grown man's knee, and hidden by docks and nettles and a huge curved metal shard fallen from the boiler itself. Once inside, you could get under the rooms of the bath-house, but this had been out of use for so long that the space under the floors was too cluttered and foul even for me. I went the other way, under the main block of the palace. Here the old hot-air system had been so well built and maintained that. even now the knee-high space under the floors was dry and airy, and plaster still clung to the brick pillars that held up the floors. In places, of course, a pillar had collapsed, or debris had fallen, but the traps which led from one room to another were solidly arched and safe, and I was free to crawl, unseen and unheard, even as far as the King's own chamber.

If they had ever discovered me I think I might have received a worse punishment than whipping: I must have listened, innocently enough, to dozens of secret councils, and certainly to some very private goings-on, but that side of it never occurred to me. And it was natural enough that no-body should give a thought to the dangers of eavesdropping; in the old days the flues had been cleaned by boy-slaves, and nobody much beyond the age of ten could ever have got through some of the workings; there were one or two places where even I was hard put to it to wriggle through. I was only once in danger of discovery: one afternoon when Mora-vik supposed I was playing with the boys and they in turn thought I was safe under her skirts, the red-haired Dinias, my chief tormentor, gave a younger boy such a shove from the roof-tree where they were playing that the latter fell and broke a leg, and set up such a howling that Moravik, running to the scene, discovered me absent and set the palace by the ears. I heard the noise, and emerged breathless and dirty from under the boiler, just as she started a hunt through the bath-house wing. I lied my way out of it, and got off with boxed ears and a scolding, but it was a warning; I never went into the hypocaust again by daylight, only at night before Moravik came to bed, or once or twice when I was wakeful and she was already abed and snoring. Most of the palace would be abed, too, but when there was a feast, or when my grandfather had guests, I would listen to the noise of voices and the singing; and sometimes I would creep as far as my mother's chamber, to hear the sound of her voice as she talked with her women. But one night I heard her praying, aloud, as one does sometimes when alone, and in the prayer was my name, "Emrys," and then her tears. After that I went another way, past the Queen's rooms, where almost every evening Olwen, the young Queen, sang to her harp among her ladies, until the King's tread came heavily down the corridor, and the music stopped.

But it was for none of these things that I went. What mattered to me—I see it clearly now—was to be alone in the secret dark, where a man is his own master, except for death.

Mostly I went to what I called my "cave." This had been part of some main chimney-shaft, and the top of it had crumbled, so that one could see the sky. It had held magic for me since the day I had looked up at midday and had seen, faint but unmistakable, a star. Now when I went in at night I would curl up on my bed of stolen stable-straw and watch the stars wheeling slowly across, and make my own bet with heaven, which was, if the moon should show over the shaft while I was there, the next day would bring me my heart's desire.

The moon was there that night. Full and shining, she stood clear in the center of the shaft, her light pouring down on my upturned face so white and pure that it seemed I drank it in like water. I did not move till she had gone, and the little star that dogs her.

On the way back I passed under a room that had been empty before, but which now held voices.

Camlach's room, of course. He and another man whose name I did not know, but who, from his accent, was one of those who had ridden in that day; I had found that they came from Cornwall. He had one of those thick, rumbling voices of which I caught only a word here and there as I crawled quickly through, worming my way between the pillars, concerned only not to be heard.

I was right at the end wall, and feeling along it for the arched gap to the next chamber, when my shoulder struck a broken section of flue pipe, and a loose piece of fireclay fell with a rattle.

The Cornishman's voice stopped abruptly. "What's that?"

Then my uncle's voice, so clear down the broken flue that you would have thought he spoke in my ear.

"Nothing. A rat. It came from under the floor. I tell you, the place is falling to pieces." There was the sound of a chair scraping back, and footsteps going across the room, away from me. His voice receded. I thought I heard the chink and gurgle of a drink being poured. I began slowly, slowly, to edge along the wall towards the trap.

He was coming back.

. . . "And even if she does refuse him, it will hardly matter. She won't stay here—at any rate, no longer than my father can fight the bishop off and keep her by him. I tell you, with her mind set on what she calls a higher court, I've nothing to fear, even if he came himself."

"As long as you believe her."

"Oh, I believe her. I've been asking here and there, and everyone says the same." He laughed. "Who knows, we may be thankful yet to have a voice at that heavenly court of hers before this game's played out. And she's devout enough to save the lot of us, they tell me, if she'll only put her mind to it."

"You may need it yet," said the Cornishman.

"I may."

"And the boy?"

"The boy?" repeated my uncle. He paused, then the soft footsteps resumed their pacing. I strained to hear. I had to hear. Why it should have mattered I hardly knew. It did not worry me overmuch to be called bastard, or coward, or devil's whelp. But tonight there had been that full moon.

He had turned. His voice carried clearly, careless, indulgent even.

"Ah, yes, the boy. A clever child, at a guess, with more there than they give him credit for . . . and nice enough, if one speaks him fair. I shall keep him close to me. Remember that, Alun; I like the boy . . ."

He called a servant in then to replenish the wine-jug, and under cover of this, I crept away.

That was the beginning of it. For days I followed him

everywhere, and he tolerated, even encouraged me, and it never occurred to me that a man of twenty-one would not always welcome a puppy of six for ever trotting at his heels. Moravik scolded, when she could get hold of me, but my mother seemed pleased and relieved, and bade her let me be.

2

It had been a hot summer, and there was peace that year, so for the first few days of his homecoming Camlach idled, resting or riding out with his father or the men through the harvest fields and the valleys where the apples already dropped ripe from the trees.

South Wales is a lovely country, with green hills and deep valleys, flat water-meadows yellow with flowers where cattle grow sleek, oak forests full of deer, and the high blue uplands where the cuckoo shouts in springtime, but where, come winter, the wolves run, and I have seen lightning even with the snow.

Maridunum lies where the estuary opens to the sea, on the river which is marked Tobius on the military maps, but which the Welsh call Tywy. Here the valley is flat and wide, and the Tywy runs in a deep and placid meander through bog and water-meadow between the gentle hills. The town stands on the rising ground of the north bank, where the land is drained and dry; it is served inland by the military road from Caerleon, and from the south by a good stone bridge with three spans, from which a paved street leads straight uphill past the King's house, and into the square. Apart from my grandfather's house, and the barrack buildings of the Roman-built fortress where he quartered his soldiers and which he kept in good repair, the best building in Maridunum was the Christian nunnery near the palace on the river's bank. A few holy women lived there, calling themselves the Community of St. Peter, though most of the townspeople called the place Tyr Myrddin, from the old shrine of the god which had stood time out of mind under an oak not far from St. Peter's gate. Even when I was a child, I heard the town itself called Caer-Myrddin*: it is not true (as they say now) that men call it after me. The fact is that I, like the town and

---

* dd is pronounced th as in thus. Myrddin is, roughly, Murthin. Caer-Myrddin is the modern Carmarthen.

the hill behind it with the sacred spring, was called after the god who is worshipped in high places. Since the events which I shall tell of, the name of the town has been publicly changed in my honour, but the god was there first, and if I have his hill now, it is because he shares it with me.

My grandfather's house was set among its orchards right beside the river. If you climbed—by way of a leaning appletree—to the top of the wall, you could sit high over the towpath and watch the river-bridge for people riding in from the south, or for the ships that came up with the tide.

Though I was not allowed to climb the trees for apples—being forced to content myself with the windfalls—Moravik never stopped me from climbing to the top of the wall. To have me posted there as sentry meant that she got wind of new arrivals sooner than anyone else in the palace. There was a little raised terrace at the orchard's end, with a curved brick wall at the back and a stone seat protected from the wind, and she would sit there by the hour, dozing over her spindle, while the sun beat into the corner so hotly that lizards would steal out to lie on the stones, and I called out my reports from the wall.

One hot afternoon, about eight days after Camlach's coming to Maridunum, I was at my post as usual. There was no coming and going on the bridge or the road up the valley, only a local grain-barge loading at the wharf, watched by a scatter of idlers, and an old man in a hooded cloak who loitered, picking up windfalls along under the wall.

I looked over my shoulder towards Moravik's corner. She was asleep, her spindle drooping on her knee, looking, with the white fluffy wool, like a burst bulrush. I threw down the bitten windfall I had been eating, and tilted my head to study the forbidden tree-top boughs where yellow globes hung clustered against the sky. There was one I thought I could reach. The fruit was round and glossy, ripening almost visibly in the hot sun. My mouth watered. I reached for a foothold and began to climb.

I was two branches away from the fruit when a shout from the direction of the bridge, followed by the quick tramp of hoofs and the jingle of metal, brought me up short. Clinging like a monkey, I made sure of my feet, then reached with one hand to push the leaves aside, peering down towards the bridge. A troop of men was riding over it, towards the town. One man rode alone in front, bare-headed, on a big brown horse.

Not Camlach, or my grandfather; and not one of the nobles, for the men wore colours I did not know. Then as they reached the nearer end of the bridge I saw that the leader was a stranger, black-haired and black-bearded, with a foreign-looking set to his clothes, and a flash of gold on his breast. His wristguards were golden, too, and a span deep. His troop, as I judged, was about fifty strong.

King Gorlan of Lanascol. Where the name sprang from, clear beyond mistake, I had no idea. Something heard from my labyrinth, perhaps? A word spoken carelessly in a child's hearing? A dream, even? The shields and spear-tips, catching the sun, flashed into my eyes. Gorlan of Lanascol. A king. Come to marry my mother and take me with him overseas. She would be a queen. And I . . .

He was already setting his horse at the hill. I began to half-slither, half-scramble, down the tree.

And if she refuses him? I recognized that voice; it was the Cornishman's. And after him my uncle's: *Even if she does, it will hardly matter . . . I've nothing to fear, so even if he came himself . . .*

The troop was riding at ease across the bridge. The jingle of arms and the hammering of hoofs rang in the still sunlight.

He had come himself. He was here.

A foot above the wall-top I missed my footing and almost fell. Luckily my grip held, and I slithered safely to the coping in a shower of leaves and lichen just as my nurse's voice called shrilly:

"Merlin? Merlin? Save us, where's the boy?"

"Here—here, Moravik—just coming down."

I landed in the long grass. She had left her spindle and, kilting up her skirts, came running.

"What's the to-do on the river road? I heard horses, a whole troop by the noise— Saints alive, child, look at your clothes! If I didn't mend that tunic only this week, and now look at it! A tear you could put a fist through, and dirt from head to foot like a beggar's brat!"

I dodged as she reached for me. "I fell. I'm sorry. I was climbing down to tell you. It's a troop of horse—foreigners! Moravik, it's King Gorlan from Lanascol! He has a red cloak and a black beard!"

"Gorlan of Lanascol? Why, that's barely twenty miles from where I was born! What's he here for, I wonder?"

I stared. "Didn't you know? He's come to marry my mother."

"Nonsense."

"It's true!"

"Of course it's not true! Do you think I wouldn't know? You must not say these things, Merlin, it could mean trouble. Where did you get it?"

"I don't remember. Someone told me. My mother, I think."

"That's not true and you know it."

"Then I must have heard something."

"Heard something, heard something. Young pigs have long ears, they say. Yours must be for ever to the ground, you hear so much! What are you smiling at?"

"Nothing."

She set her hands on her hips. "You've been listening to things you shouldn't. I've told you about this before. No wonder people say what they say."

I usually gave up and edged away from dangerous ground when I had given too much away, but excitement had made me reckless. "It's true, you'll find it's true! Does it matter where I heard it? I really can't remember now, but I know it's true! Moravik—"

"What?"

"King Gorlan's my father, my real one."

"*What?*" This time the syllable was edged like the tooth of a saw.

"Didn't you know? Not even you?"

"No, I did not. And no more do you. And if you so much as breathe this to anyone— How do you know the name, even?" She took me by the shoulders and gave me a sharp little shake. "How do you even know this is King Gorlan? There's been nothing said of his coming, even to me."

"I told you. I don't remember what I heard, or where. I just heard his name somewhere, that's all, and I know he's coming to see the King about my mother. We'll go to Less Britain, Moravik, and you can come with us. You'll like that, won't you? It's your home. Perhaps we'll be near—"

Her grip tightened, and I stopped. With relief I saw one of the King's body-servants hurrying towards us through the apple-trees. He came up panting.

"He's to go before the King. The boy. In the great hall. And hurry."

"Who is it?" demanded Moravik.

"The King said to hurry. I've been looking everywhere for the boy—"

"*Who is it?*"

"King Gorlan from Brittany."

She gave a little hiss, like a startled goose, and dropped her hands. "What's his business with the boy?"

"How do I know?" The man was breathless—it was a hot day and he was stout—and curt with Moravik, whose status as my nurse was only a little higher with the servants than my own. "All I know is, the Lady Niniane is sent for, and the boy, and there'll be a beating for someone, by my reckoning, if he's not there by the time the King's looking round for him. He's been in a rare taking since the outriders came in, that I can tell you."

"All right, all right. Get back and say we'll be there in a few minutes."

The man hurried off. She whirled on me and grabbed at my arm. "All the sweet saints in heaven!" Moravik had the biggest collection of charms and talismans of anyone in Maridunum, and I had never known her pass a wayside shrine without paying her respects to whatever image inhabited it, but officially she was a Christian and, when in trouble, a devout one. "Sweet cherubim! And the child has to choose this afternoon to be in rags! Hurry, now, or there'll be trouble for both of us." She hustled me up the path towards the house, busily calling on her saints and exhorting me to hurry, determinedly refusing even to comment on the fact that I had been right about the newcomer. "Dear, dear St. Peter, why did I eat those eels for dinner and then sleep so sound? Today of all days! Here"—she pushed me in front of her into my room—"get out of those rags and into your good tunic, and we'll know soon enough what the Lord has sent for you. Hurry, child!"

The room I shared with Moravik was a small one, dark, and next to the servants' quarters. It always smelt of cooking smells from the kitchen, but I liked this, as I liked the old lichened pear tree that hung close outside the window, where the birds swung singing in the summer mornings. My bed stood right under this window. The bed was nothing but plain planks set across wooden blocks, no carving, not even a head or foot board. I had heard Moravik grumble to the other servants when she thought I wasn't listening, that it was hardly a fit place to house a king's grandson, but to me she said merely that it was convenient for her to be near the other servants; and indeed I was comfortable enough, for she saw to it that I had a clean straw mattress, and a coverlet of wool every bit as good as those on my mother's bed in the big room next to my grandfather. Moravik herself had a pallet on the floor near the door, and this was sometimes shared by the big wolfhound who fidgeted and scratched for fleas beside her feet, and sometimes by Cerdic, one of the grooms, a Saxon who had been taken in a raid long since, and had settled down to marry one of the local girls. She had died in childbed a year later, and the child with her, but he stayed on, apparently quite content. I once asked Moravik why she allowed the dog to sleep in the room, when she grumbled so much about the smell and the fleas; I forget what she answered, but I knew without being told that he was there to give warning if anyone came into the room during the night. Cerdic, of course, was the exception; the dog accepted him with no more fuss than the beating of his tail upon the floor, and vacated the bed for him. In a way, I suppose, Cerdic fulfilled the same function as the watchdog, and others besides. Moravik never mentioned him, and neither did I. A small child is supposed to sleep very soundly, but even then, young as I was, I would wake sometimes in the middle of the night, and lie quite still, watching the stars through the window beside me, caught like sparkling silver fish in the net of the pear tree's boughs. What passed between Cerdic and Moravik meant no more to me than that he helped to guard my nights, as she my days.

My clothes were kept in a wooden chest which stood against the wall. This was very old, with panels painted with scenes of gods and goddesses, and I think originally it had come from Rome itself. Now the paint was dirty and rubbed and flaking, but still on the lid you could see, like shadows, a scene taking place in what looked like a cave; there was a bull, and a man with a knife, and someone holding a sheaf of corn, and over in the corner some figure, rubbed almost away, with rays round his head like the sun, and a stick in his hand. The chest was lined with cedarwood, and Moravik washed my clothes herself, and laid them away with sweet herbs from the garden.

She threw the lid up now, so roughly that it banged against the wall, and pulled out the better of my two good tunics, the green one with the scarlet border. She shouted for water, and one of the maids brought it, running, and was scolded for spilling it on the floor.

The fat servant came panting again to tell us that we should hurry, and got snapped at for his pains, but in a very short time I was hustled once more along the colonnade, and through the big arched doorway into the main part of the house.

The hall where the King received visitors was a long, high room with a floor of black and white stone framing a mosaic of a god with a leopard. This had been badly scarred and broken by the dragging of heavy furniture and the constant passing of booted feet. One side of the room was open to the colonnade, and here in winter a fire was kindled on the bare floor, within a loose frame of stones. The floor and pillars near it were blackened with the smoke. At the far end of the room stood the dais with my grandfather's big chair, and beside it the smaller one for his Queen.

He was sitting there now, with Camlach standing on his right, and his wife, Olwen, seated at his left. She was his third wife, and younger than my mother, a dark, silent, rather stupid girl with a skin like new milk and braids down to her knees, who could sing like a bird, and do fine needlework, but very little else. My mother, I think, both liked and despised her. At any rate, against all expectation, they got along tolerably well together, and I had heard Moravik say that life for my mother had been a great deal easier since the King's second wife, Gwynneth, had died a year ago, and within the month Olwen had taken her place in the King's bed. Even if Olwen had cuffed me and sneered at me as Gwynneth did I should have liked her for her music, but she was always kind to me in her vague, placid way, and when the King was out of the way had taught me my notes, and even let me use her harp till I could play after a fashion. I had a feeling for it, she said, but we both knew what the King would say to such folly, so her kindness was secret, even from my mother.

She did not notice me now. Nobody did, except my cousin Dinias, who stood by Olwen's chair on the dais. Dinias was a bastard of my grandfather's by a slave-woman. He was a big boy of seven, with his father's red hair and high temper; he was strong for his age and quite fearless, and had enjoyed the King's favour since the day he had, at the age of five, stolen a ride on one of his father's horses, a wild brown colt that had bolted with him through the town and only got rid of him when he rode it straight at a breast-high bank. His father had thrashed him with his own hands, and afterwards given him a dagger with a gilded hilt. Dinias claimed the title of Prince—at any rate among the rest of the children—from then on, and treated his fellow-bastard, myself, with the utmost contempt. He stared at me now as expressionless as a stone, but his left hand—the one away from his father—made a rude sign, and then chopped silently, expressively, downwards.

I had paused in the doorway, and behind me my nurse's hand twitched my tunic into place and then gave me a push between the shoulder-blades. "Go on now. Straighten your back. He won't eat you." As if to give the lie to this, I heard the click of charms and the start of a muttered prayer.

The room was full of people. Many of them I knew, but there were strangers there who must be the party I had seen ride in. Their leader sat near the King's right, surrounded by his own men. He was the big dark man I had seen on the bridge, full-bearded, with a fierce beak of a nose and thick limbs shrouded in a scarlet cloak. On the King's other side, but standing below the dais, was my mother, with two of her women. I loved to see her as she was now, dressed like a princess, her long robe of creamy wool hanging straight to the floor as if carved of new wood. Her hair was unbraided, and fell down her back like rain. She had a blue mantle with a copper clasp. Her face was colourless, and very still.

I was so busy with my own fears—the gesture from Dinias, the averted face and downcast eyes of my mother, the silence of the people, and the empty middle of the floor over which I must walk—that I had not even looked at my grandfather. I had taken a step forward, still unnoticed, when suddenly, with a crash like a horse kicking, he slammed both hands down on the wooden arms of his chair, and thrust himself to his feet so violently that the heavy chair went back a pace, its feet scoring the oak planks of the platform.

"By the light!" His face was mottled scarlet, and the reddish brows jutted in knots of flesh above his furious little blue eyes. He glared down at my mother, and drew a breath to speak that could be heard clear to the door where I had paused, afraid. Then the bearded man, who had risen with him, said something in some accent I didn't catch, and at the same moment Camlach touched his arm, whispering. The King paused, then said thickly, "As you will. Later. Get them out of here." Then clearly, to my mother: "This is not the end of it, Niniane, I promise you. Six years. It is enough, by God! Come, my lord."

He swept his cloak up over one arm, jerked his head to his son, and, stepping down from the dais, took the bearded man by the arm, and strode with him towards the door. After him, meek as milk, trailed his wife Olwen with her women, and after her Dinias, smiling. My mother never moved. The King went by her without a word or a look, and the crowd parted between him and the door like a stubble-field under the share.

It left me standing alone, rooted and staring, three paces in from the door. As the King bore down on me I came to myself and turned to escape into the anteroom, but not quickly enough.

He stopped abruptly, releasing Gorlan's arm, and swung round on me. The blue cloak swirled, and a corner of the cloth caught my eye and brought the tears to it. I blinked up at him. Gorlan had paused beside him. He was younger than my uncle Dyved had been. He was angry, too, but hiding it, and the anger was not for me. He looked surprised when the King stopped, and said: "Who's this?"

"Her son, that your grace would have given a name to," said my grandfather, and the gold flashed on his armlet as he swung his big hand up and knocked me flat to the floor as easily as a boy would flatten a fly. Then the blue cloak swept by me, and the King's booted feet, and Gorlan's after him with barely a pause. Olwen said something in her pretty voice and stooped over me, but the King called to her, angrily, and her hand withdrew and she hurried after him with the rest.

I picked myself up from the floor and looked round for Moravik, but she was not there. She had gone straight to my mother, and had not even seen. I began to push my way towards them through the hubbub of the hall, but before I could reach my mother the women, in a tight and silent group round her, left the hall by the other door. None of them looked back.

Someone spoke to me, but I did not answer. I ran out through the colonnade, across the main court, and out again into the quiet sunlight of the orchard.

My uncle found me on Moravik's terrace.

I was lying on my belly on the hot flagstones, watching a lizard. Of all that day, this is my most vivid recollection; the lizard, flat on the hot stone within a foot of my face, its body still as green bronze but for the pulsing throat. It had small dark eyes, no brighter than slate, and the inside of its mouth was the colour of melons. It had a long, sharp tongue, which flicked out quick as a whip, and its feet made a tiny rustling noise on the stones as it ran across my finger and vanished down a crack in the flags.

I turned my head. My uncle Camlach was coming down through the orchard.

He mounted the three shallow steps to the terrace, soft-footed in his elegant laced sandals and stood looking down. I looked away. The moss between the stones had tiny white flowers no bigger than the lizard's eyes, each one perfect as a carved cup. To this day I remember the design on them as well as if I had carved it myself.

"Let me see," he said.

I didn't move. He crossed to the stone bench and sat down facing me, knees apart, clasped hands between them.

"Look at me, Merlin."

I obeyed him. He studied me in silence for a while.

"I'm always being told that you will not play rough games, that you run away from Dinias, that you will never make a soldier or even a man. Yet when the King strikes you down with a blow which would have sent one of his deerhounds yelping to kennel, you make no sound and shed no tear."

I said nothing.

"I think perhaps you are not quite what they deem you, Merlin."

Still nothing.

"Do you know why Gorlan came today?"

I thought it better to lie. "No."

"He came to ask for your mother's hand. If she had consented you would have gone with him to Brittany."

I touched one of the moss-cups with a forefinger. It crumbled like a puff-ball and vanished. Experimentally, I touched another. Camlach said, more sharply than he usually spoke to me: "Are you listening?"

"Yes. But if she's refused him it will hardly matter." I looked up. "Will it?"

"You mean you don't want to go? I would have thought . . ." He knitted the fair brows so like my grandfather's. "You would be treated honourably, and be a prince."

"I am a prince now. As much a prince as I can ever be."

"What do you mean by that?"

"If she has refused him," I said, "he cannot be my father. I thought he was. I thought that was why he had come."

"What made you think so?"

"I don't know. It seemed—" I stopped. I could not explain to Camlach about the flash of light in which Gorlan's name had come to me. "I just thought he must be."

"Only because you have been waiting for him all this time." His voice was calm. "Such waiting is foolish, Merlin. It's time you faced the truth. Your father is dead."

I put my hand down on the tuft of moss, crushing it. I watched the flesh of the fingers whiten with the pressure. "She told you that?"

"No." He lifted his shoulders. "But had he been still alive he would have been here long since. You must know that."

I was silent.

"And if he is not dead," pursued my uncle, watching me, "and still has never come, it can surely not be a matter for great grief on anyone's part?"

"No, except that however base he may be, it might have saved my mother something. And me." As I moved my hand, the moss slowly unfurled again, as if growing. But the tiny flowers had gone.

My uncle nodded. "She would have been wiser, perhaps, to have accepted Gorlan, or some other prince."

"What will happen to us?" I asked.

"Your mother wants to go into St. Peter's. And you—you are quick and clever, and I am told you can read a little. You could be a priest."

"No!"

His brows came down again over the thin-bridged nose. "It's a good enough life. You're not warrior stock, that's certain. Why not take a life that will suit you, and where you'd be safe?"

"I don't need to be a warrior to want to stay free! To be shut up in a place like St. Peter's—that's not the way—" I broke off. I had spoken hotly, but found the words failing me. I could not explain something I did not know myself. I looked up eagerly: "I'll stay with you. If you cannot use me I—I'll run away to serve some other prince. But I would rather stay with you."

"Well, it's early yet to speak of things like that. You're very young." He got to his feet. "Does your face hurt you?"

"No."

"You should have it seen to. Come with me now."

He put out a hand, and I went with him. He led me up through the orchard, then in through the arch that led to my grandfather's private garden.

I hung back against his hand. "I'm not allowed in there."

"Surely, with me? Your grandfather's with his guests, he'll not see you. Come along. I've got something better for you than your windfall apples. They've been gathering the apricots, and I saved the best aside out of the baskets as I came down."

He trod forward, with that graceful cat's stride of his, through the bergamot and lavender, to where the apricot and peach trees stood crucified against the high wall in the sun. The place smelt drowsy with herbs and fruit, and the doves were crooning from the dove-house. At my feet a ripe apricot lay, velvet in the sun. I pushed it with my toe until it rolled over, and there in the back of it was the great rotten hole, with wasps crawling. A shadow fell over it. My uncle stood above me, with an apricot in each hand.

"I told you I'd got something better than windfalls. Here." He handed me one. "And if they beat you for stealing, they'll have to beat me as well." He grinned, and bit into the fruit he held.

I stood still, with the big bright apricot cupped in the palm of my hand. The garden was very hot, and very still, and quiet except for the humming of insects. The fruit glowed like gold, and smelt of sunshine and sweet juice. Its skin felt like the fur of a golden bee. I could feel my mouth watering.

"What is it?" asked my uncle. He sounded edgy and impatient. The juice of his apricot was running down his chin. "Don't stand there staring at it, boy! Eat it! There's nothing wrong with it, is there?"

I looked up. The blue eyes, fierce as a fox, stared down into mine. I held it out to him. "I don't want it. It's black inside. Look, you can see right through."

He took his breath in sharply, as if to speak. Then voices came from the other side of the wall; the gardeners, probably, bringing the empty fruit-baskets down ready for morning. My uncle, stooping, snatched the fruit from my hand and threw it from him, hard against the wall. It burst in a golden splash of flesh against the brick, and the juice ran down. A wasp, disturbed from the tree, droned past between us. Camlach flapped at it with a queer, abrupt gesture, and said to me in a voice that was suddenly all venom:

"Keep away from me after this, you devil's brat. Do you hear me? Just keep away."

He dashed the back of his hand across his mouth, and went from me in long strides towards the house.

I stood where I was, watching the juice of the apricot trickle down the hot wall. A wasp alighted on it, crawled stickily, then suddenly fell, buzzing on its back to the ground. Its body jack-knifed, the buzz rose to a whine as it struggled, then it lay still.

I hardly saw it, because something had swelled in my throat till I thought I would choke, and the golden evening swam, brilliant, into tears. This was the first time in my life that I remember weeping.

The gardeners were coming down past the roses, with baskets on their heads. I turned and ran out of the garden.

3

My room was empty even of the wolfhound. I climbed on my bed and leaned my elbows on the windowsill, and stayed there a long while alone, while outside in the pear tree's boughs the thrush sang, and from the courtyard beyond the shut door came the monotonous clink of the smith's hammer and the creak of the windlass as the mule plodded round the well.

Memory fails me here. I cannot remember how long it was before the clatter and the buzz of voices told me that the evening meal was being prepared. Nor can I remember how badly I was hurt, but when Cerdic, the groom, pushed the door open and I turned my head, he stopped dead and said: "Lord have mercy upon us. What have you been doing? Playing in the bull-shed?"

"I fell down."

"Oh, aye, you fell down. I wonder why the floor's always twice as hard for you as for anyone else? Who was it? That little sucking-boar Dinias?"

When I did not answer he came across to the bed. He was a small man, with bowed legs and a seamed brown face and a thatch of light-coloured hair. Standing on my bed as I was, my eyes were almost on a level with his.

"Tell you what," he said. "When you're a mite larger I'll teach you a thing or two. You don't have to be big to win a fight. I've a trick or two worth knowing, I can tell you. Got to have, when you're wren-size. I tell you, I can tumble a fellow twice my weight—and a woman too, come to that." He laughed, turned his head to spit, remembered where he was, and cleared his throat instead. "Not that you'll need my tricks once you're grown, a tall lad like you, nor with the girls neither. But you'd best look to that face of yours if you're not to scare them silly. Looks as if it might make a scar." He jerked his head at Moravik's empty pallet. "Where is she?"

"She went with my mother."

"Then you'd best come with me. I'll fix it up."

So it was that the cut on my cheek-bone was dressed with horse-liniment, and I shared Cerdic's supper in the stables, sitting on straw, while a brown mare nosed round me for fodder, and my own fat slug of a pony, at the full end of his rope, watched every mouthful we ate. Cerdic must have had methods of his own in the kitchens, too; the barm-cakes were fresh, there was half a chicken-leg each as well as the salt bacon, and the beer was full-flavoured and cool.

When he came back with the food I knew from his look that he had heard it all. The whole palace must be buzzing. But he said nothing, just handing me the food and sitting down beside me on the straw.

"They told you?" I asked.

He nodded, chewing, then added through a mouthful of bread and meat: "He has a heavy hand."

"He was angry because she refused to wed Gorlan. He wants her wed because of me, but till now she has refused to wed any man. And now, since my uncle Dyved is dead, and Camlach is the only one left, they asked Gorlan from Less Britain. I think my uncle Camlach persuaded my grandfather to ask him, because he is afraid that if she marries a prince in Wales—"

He interrupted at that, looking both startled and scared. "Whist ye now, child! How do you know all this? I'll be bound your elders don't tattle of these high matters in front of you? If it's Moravik who talks when she shouldn't—"

"No. Not Moravik. But I know it's true."

"How in the Thunderer's name do you know any such thing? Slaves' gossip?"

I fed the last bite of my bread to the mare. "If you swear by heathen gods, Cerdic, it's you who'll be in trouble, with Moravik."

"Oh, aye. That kind of trouble's easy enough to come by. Come on, who's been talking to you?"

"Nobody. I know, that's all. I—I can't explain how ... And when she refused Gorlan my uncle Camlach was as angry as my grandfather. He's afraid my father will come back and marry her, and drive him out. He doesn't admit this to my grandfather, of course."

"Of course." He was staring, even forgetting to chew, so that saliva dribbled from the corner of his open mouth. He swallowed hastily. "The gods know—God knows where you got all this, but it could be true. Well, go on."

The brown mare was pushing at me, snuffing sweet breath at my neck. I handed her away. "That's all. Gorlan is angry, but they'll give him something. And my mother will go in the end to St. Peter's. You'll see."

There was a short silence. Cerdic swallowed his meat and threw the bone out of the door, where a couple of the stableyard curs pounced on it and raced off in a snarling wrangle.

"Merlin—"

"Yes?"

"You'd be wise if you said no more of this to anyone. Not to anyone. Do you understand?"

I said nothing.

"These are matters that a child doesn't understand. High matters. Oh, some of it's common talk, I grant you, but this about Prince Camlach—" He dropped a hand to my knee, and gripped and shook it. "I tell you, he's dangerous, that one. Leave it be, and stay out of sight. I'll tell no one, trust me for that. But you, you must say no more. Bad enough if you were rightwise a prince born, or even in the King's favour like that red whelp Dinias, but for you . . ." He shook the knee again. "Do you heed me, Merlin? For your skin's sake, keep silent and stay out of their way. And tell me who told you all this."

I thought of the dark cave in the hypocaust, and the sky remote at the top of the shaft. "No one told me. I swear it." When he made a sound of impatience and worry I looked straight at him and told him as much of the truth as I dared. "I have heard things, I admit it. And sometimes people talk over your head, not noticing you're there, or not thinking you understand. But at other times"—I paused—"it's as if something spoke to me, as if I saw things . . . And sometimes the stars tell me . . . and there is music, and voices in the dark. Like dreams."

His hand went up in a gesture of protection. I thought he was crossing himself, then saw the sign against the evil eye. He looked shamefaced at that, and dropped the hand.

"Dreams, that's what it is; you're right. You've been asleep in some corner, likely, and they've talked across you when they shouldn't, and you've heard things you shouldn't. I was forgetting you're nothing but a child. When you look with those eyes—" He broke off, and shrugged. "But you'll promise me you'll say no more of what you've heard?"

"All right, Cerdic. I promise you. If you'll promise to tell me something in return."

"What's that?"

"Who my father was."

He choked over his beer, then with deliberation wiped the foam away, set down the horn, and regarded me with exasperation. "Now how in middle-earth do you think I know that?"

"I thought Moravik might have told you."

"Does she know?" He sounded so surprised that I knew he was telling the truth.

"When I asked her she just said there were some things it was better not to talk about."

"She's right at that. But if you ask me, that's her way of saying she's no wiser than the next one. And if you do ask me, young Merlin, though you don't, that's another thing you'd best keep clear of. If your lady mother wanted you to know, she'd tell you. You'll find out soon enough, I doubt."

I saw that he was making the sign again, though this time he hid the hand. I opened my mouth to ask if he believed the stories, but he picked up the drinking horn, and got to his feet.

"I've had your promise. Remember?"

"Yes."

"I've watched you. You go your own way, and sometimes I think you're nearer to the wild things than to men. You know she called you for the falcon?"

I nodded.

"Well, here's something for you to think about. You'd best be forgetting falcons for the time being. There's plenty of them around, too many, if truth be told. Have you watched the ring-doves, Merlin?"

"The ones that drink from the fountain with the white doves, then fly away free? Of course I have. I feed them in winter, along with the doves."

"They used to say in my country, the ring-dove has many enemies, because her flesh is sweet and her eggs are good to eat. But she lives and she prospers, because she runs away.

The Lady Niniane may have called you her little falcon, but
you're not a falcon yet, young Merlin. You're only a dove.
Remember that. Live by keeping quiet, and by running away.
Mark my words." He nodded at me, and put a hand down to
pull me to my feet. "Does the cut still hurt?"

"It stings."

"Then it's on the mend. The bruise is nought to worry you,
it'll go soon enough."

It did, indeed, heal cleanly, and left no mark. But I
remember how it stung that night, and kept me awake, so
that Cerdic and Moravik kept silent in the other corner of
the room, for fear, I suppose, that it had been from some of
their mutterings that I had pieced together my information.

After they slept I crept out, stepped past the grinning
wolfhound, and ran along to the hypocaust.

But tonight I heard nothing to remember, except Olwen's
voice, mellow as an ousel's, singing some song I had not
heard before, about a wild goose, and a hunter with a golden
net.

4

After this, life settled back into its peaceful rut, and I think
that my grandfather must eventually have accepted my
mother's refusal to marry. Things were strained between
them for a week or so, but with Camlach home, and settling
down as if he had never left the place—and with a good
hunting season coming up—the King forgot his rancour, and
things went back to normal.

Except possibly for me. After the incident in the orchard,
Camlach no longer went out of his way to favour me, nor I
to follow him. But he was not unkind to me, and once or
twice defended me in some petty rough-and-tumble with the
other boys, even taking my part against Dinias, who had
supplanted me in his favour.

But I no longer needed that kind of protection. That
September day had taught me other lessons besides Cerdic's
of the ring-dove. I dealt with Dinias myself. One night,
creeping beneath his bedchamber on the way to my "cave," I
chanced to hear him and his pack-follower Brys laughing
over a foray of that afternoon when the pair of them had
followed Camlach's friend Alun to his tryst with one of the

servant-girls, and had stayed hidden, watching and listening, to the sweet end. When Dinias waylaid me next morning I stood my ground and—quoting a sentence or so—asked if he had seen Alun yet that day. He stared, went red and then white (for Alun had a hard hand and a temper to match it) and then sidled away, making the sign behind his back. If he liked to think it was magic rather than simple blackmail, I let him. After that, if the High King himself had ridden in claiming parentage for me, none of the children would have believed him. They left me alone.

Which was just as well, for during that winter part of the floor of the bath-house fell in, my grandfather judged the whole thing dangerous, and had it filled in and poison laid for the rats. So like a cub smoked from its earth, I had to fend for myself above ground.

About six months after Gorlan's visit, as we were coming through a cold February into the first budding days of March, Camlach began to insist, first to my mother and then to my grandfather, that I should be taught to read and write. My mother, I think, was grateful for this evidence of his interest in me; I myself was pleased and took good care to show it, though after the incident in the orchard I could have no illusions about his motives. But it did no harm to let Camlach think that my feelings about the priesthood had undergone a change. My mother's declaration that she would never marry, coupled with her increased withdrawal among her women and her frequent visits to St. Peter's to talk with the Abbess and such priests as visited the community, re- moved his worst fears—either that she would marry a Welsh prince who could hope to take over the kingdom in her right, or that my unknown father would come to claim her and legitimate me, and prove to be a man of rank and power who might supplant him forcibly. It did not matter to Cam- lach that in either event I was not much of a danger to him, and less than ever now, for he had taken a wife before Christmas, and already at the beginning of March it seemed that she was pregnant. Even Olwen's increasingly obvious pregnancy was no threat to him, for Camlach stood high in his father's favour, and it was not likely that a brother so much younger would ever present a serious danger. There could be no question; Camlach had a good fighting record, knew how to make men like him, and had ruthlessness and common sense. The ruthlessness showed in what he had tried to do to me in the orchard; the common sense showed in his indifferent kindness once my mother's decision removed the threat to him. But I have noticed this about ambitious men, or men in power—they fear even the slightest and least likely threat to it. He would never rest until he saw me priested and safely out of the palace.

Whatever his motives, I was pleased when my tutor came; he was a Greek who had been a scribe in Massilia until he drank himself into debt and ensuing slavery; now he was assigned to me, and because he was grateful for the change in status and the relief from manual work, taught me well and without the religious bias which had constricted the teaching I had picked up from my mother's priests. Demetrius was a pleasant, ineffectually clever man who had a genius for languages, and whose only recreations were dice and (when he won) drink. Occasionally, when he had won enough, I would find him happily and incapably asleep over his books. I never told anyone of these occasions, and indeed was glad of the chance to go about my own affairs; he was grateful for my silence, and in his turn, when I once or twice played truant, held his tongue and made no attempt to find out where I had been. I was quick to catch up with my studies and showed more than enough progress to satisfy my mother and Camlach, so Demetrius and I respected one another's secrets and got along tolerably well.

One day in August, almost a year after the coming of Gorlan to my grandfather's court, I left Demetrius placidly sleeping it off, and rode up alone into the hills behind the town.

I had been this way several times before. It was quicker to go up past the barrack walls and then out by the military road which led eastwards through the hills to Caerleon, but this meant riding through the town, and possibly being seen, and questions being asked. The way I took was along the river-bank. There was a gateway, not much used, leading straight out from our stableyard to the broad flat path where the horses went that towed the barges, and the path followed the river for quite a long way, past St. Peter's and then along the placid curves of the Tywy to the mill, which was as far as the barges went. I had never been beyond this point, but there was a pathway leading up past the mill-house and over the road, and then by the valley of the tributary stream that helped to serve the mill.

It was a hot, drowsy day, full of the smell of bracken. Blue dragonflies darted and glimmered over the river, and the meadowsweet was thick as curds under the humming clouds of flies.

My pony's neat hoofs tapped along the baked clay of the towpath. We met a big dapple grey bringing an empty barge down from the mill with the tide, taking it easy. The boy perched on its withers called a greeting, and the barge-man lifted a hand.

When I reached the mill there was no one in sight. Grain-sacks, newly unloaded, were piled on the narrow wharf. By them the miller's dog lay sprawled in the hot sun, hardly troubling to open an eye as I drew rein in the shade of the buildings. Above me, the long straight stretch of the military road was empty. The stream tumbled through a culvert beneath it, and I saw a trout leap and flash in the foam.

It would be hours before I could be missed. I put the pony at the bank up to the road, won the brief battle when he tried to turn for home, then kicked him to a canter along the path which led upstream into the hills.

The path twisted and turned at first, climbing the steep stream-side, then led out of the thorns and thin oaks that filled the gully, and went north in a smooth level curve along the open slope.

Here the townsfolk graze their sheep and cattle, so the grass is smooth and shorn. I passed one shepherd boy, drowsy under a hawthorn bush, with his sheep at hand; he was simple, and only stared vacantly at me as I trotted past, fingering the pile of stones with which he herded his sheep. As we passed him he picked up one of them, a smooth green pebble, and I wondered if he was going to throw it at me, but he lobbed it instead to turn some fat grazing lambs which were straying too far, then went back to his slumbers. There were black cattle further afield, down nearer the river where the grass was longer, but I could not see the herdsman. Away at the foot of the hill, tiny beside a tiny hut, I saw a girl with a flock of geese.

Presently the path began to climb again, and my pony slowed to a walk, picking his way through scattered trees. Hazel-nuts were thick in the coppices, mountain ash and brier grew from tumbles of mossed rock, and the bracken was breast-high. Rabbits ran everywhere, scuttering through the fern, and a pair of jays scolded a fox from the safety of a swinging hornbeam. The ground was too hard, I supposed, to bear tracks well, but I could see no sign, either of crushed bracken or broken twigs, that any other horseman had recently been this way.

The sun was high. A little breeze swept through the hawthorns, rattling the green, hard fruit. I urged the pony on. Now among the oaks and hollies were pine trees, their stems reddish in the sunlight. The ground grew rougher as the path climbed, with bare grey stone outcropping through the thin turf, and a honeycombing of rabbit burrows. I did not know where the path led, I knew nothing but that I was alone, and free. There was nothing to tell me what sort of day this was, or what way-star was leading me up into the hill. This was in the days before the future became clear to me.

The pony hesitated, and I came to myself. There was a fork in the track, with nothing to indicate which would be the best way to go. To left, to right, it led away round the two sides of a thicket.

The pony turned decisively to the left, this being downhill. I would have let him go, but that at that moment a bird flew low across the path in front of me, left to right, and vanished beyond the trees. Sharp wings, a flash of rust and slate-blue, the fierce dark eye and curved beak of a merlin. For no reason, except that this was better than no reason, I turned the pony's head after it, and dug my heels in.

The path climbed in a shallow curve, leaving the wood on the left. This was a stand mainly of pines, thickly clustered and dark, and so heavily grown that you could only have hacked your way in through the dead stuff with an axe. I heard the clap of wings as a ring-dove fled from shelter, dropping invisibly out of the far side of the trees. It had gone to the left. This time I followed the falcon.

We were now well out of sight of the river valley and the town. The pony picked his way along one side of a shallow valley, at the foot of which ran a narrow, tumbling stream. On the far side of the stream the long slopes of turf went bare up to the scree, and above this were the rocks, blue and grey in the sunlight. The slope where I rode was scattered with hawthorn brakes throwing pools of slanted shadow, and above them again, scree, and a cliff hung with ivy where choughs wheeled and called in the bright air. Apart from their busy sound, the valley held the most complete and echo-less stillness.

The pony's hoofs sounded loud on the baked earth. It was hot, and I was thirsty. Now the track ran along under a low cliff, perhaps twenty feet high, and at its foot a grove of hawthorns cast a pool of shade across the path. Somewhere, close above me, I could hear the trickle of water.

I stopped the pony and slid off. I led him into the shade of the grove and made him fast, then looked about me for the source of the water.

The rock by the path was dry, and below the path was no sign of any water running down to swell the stream at the foot of the valley. But the sound of running water was steady and unmistakable. I left the path and scrambled up the grass at the side of the rock, to find myself on a small flat patch of turf, a little dry lawn scattered with rabbits' droppings, and at the back of it another face of cliff.

In the face of the rock was a cave. The rounded opening was smallish and very regular, almost like a made arch. To one side of this, the right as I stood looking, was a slope of grass-grown stones long ago fallen from above, and overgrown with oak and rowan, whose branches overhung the cave with shadow. To the other side, and only a few feet from the archway, was the spring.

I approached it. It was very small, a little shining movement of water oozing out of a crack in the face of the rock, and falling with a steady trickle into a round basin of stone. There was no outflow. Presumably the water sprang from the rock, gathered in the basin, and drained away through another crack, eventually to join the stream below. Through the clear water I could see every pebble, every grain of sand at the bottom of the basin. Hart's-tongue fern grew above it, and there was moss at the lip, and below it green, moist grass.

I knelt on the grass, and had put my mouth to the water, when I saw there was a cup. This stood in a tiny niche among the ferns. It was a handspan high, and made of brown horn. As I lifted it down I saw above it, half-hidden by the ferns, the small, carved figure of a wooden god. I recognized him. I had seen him under the oak at Tyr Myrddin. Here he was in his own hill-top place, under the open sky.

I filled the cup and drank, pouring a few drops on the ground for the god.

Then I went into the cave.

5

This was bigger than had appeared from outside. Only a couple of paces inside the archway—and my paces were very short—the cave opened out into a seemingly vast chamber whose top was lost in shadow. It was dark, but—though at first I neither noticed this nor looked for its cause—with some source of extra light that gave a vague illumination, showing the floor smooth and clear of obstacles. I made my way slowly forward, straining my eyes, with deep inside me the beginning of that surge of excitement that caves have always started in me. Some men experience this with water; some, I know, on high places; some create fire for the same pleasure: with me it has always been the depths of the forest, or the depths of the earth. Now, I know why; but then, I only knew that I was a boy who had found somewhere new, something he could perhaps make his own in a world where he owned nothing.

Next moment I stopped short, brought up by a shock which spilled the excitement through my bowels like water. Something had moved in the murk, just to my right.

I froze still, straining my eyes to see. There was no movement. I held my breath, listening. There was no sound. I flared my nostrils, testing the air cautiously round me. There was no smell, animal or human; the cave smelt, I thought, of smoke and damp rock and the earth itself, and of a queer musty scent I couldn't identify. I knew, without putting it into words, that had there been any other creature near me the air would have felt different, less empty. There was no one there.

I tried a word, softly, in Welsh. "Greetings." The whisper came straight back at me in an echo so quick that I knew I was very near the wall of the cave, then it lost itself, hissing, in the roof.

There was movement there—at first, I thought, only an intensifying of the echoed whisper, then the rustling grew and grew like the rustling of a woman's dress, or a curtain stirring in the draught. Something went past my cheek, with a shrill, bloodless cry just on the edge of sound. Another followed, and after them flake after flake of shrill shadow, pouring down from the roof like leaves down a stream of

wind, or fish down a fall. It was the bats, disturbed from
their lodging in the top of the cave, streaming out now into
the daylight valley. They would be pouring out of the low
archway like a plume of smoke.

I stood quite still, wondering if it was these that had made
the curious musty smell. I thought I could smell them as they
passed, but it wasn't the same. I had no fear that they would
touch me; in darkness or light, whatever their speed, bats will
touch nothing. They are so much creatures of the air, I
believe, that as the air parts in front of an obstacle the bat is
swept aside with it, like a petal carried downstream. They
poured past, a shrill tide of them between me and the wall.
Childlike, to see what the stream would do—how it would
divert itself—I took a step nearer to the wall. Nothing
touched me. The stream divided and poured on, the shrill air
brushing both my cheeks. It was as if I did not exist. But at
the same moment when I moved, the creature that I had
seen moved, too. Then my outstretched hand met, not rock,
but metal, and I knew what the creature was. It was my own
reflection.

Hanging against the wall was a sheet of metal, burnished
to a dull sheen. This, then, was the source of the diffused
light within the cave; the mirror's silky surface caught,
obliquely, the light from the cave's mouth, and sent it on
into the darkness. I could see myself moving in it like a
ghost, as I recoiled and let fall the hand which had leapt to
the knife at my hip.

Behind me the flow of bats had ceased, and the cave was
still. Reassured, I stayed where I was, studying myself with
interest in the mirror. My mother had had one once, an
antique from Egypt, but then, deeming such things to be
vanity, she had locked it away. Of course I had often seen
my face reflected in water, but never my body mirrored, till
now. I saw a dark boy, wary, all eyes with curiosity, nerves,
and excitement. In that light my eyes looked quite black; my
hair was black, too, thick and clean, but worse cut and
groomed than my pony's; my tunic and sandals were a
disgrace. I grinned, and the mirror flashed a sudden smile
that changed the picture completely and at once, from a
sullen young animal poised to run or fight, to something
quick and gentle and approachable; something, I knew even
then, that few people had ever seen.

Then it vanished, and the wary animal was back, as I
leaned forward to run a hand over the metal. It was cold and

smooth and freshly burnished. Whoever had hung it—and he must be the same person who used the cup of horn outside—had either been here very recently, or he still lived here, and might come back at any moment to find me.

I was not particularly frightened. I had pricked to caution when I saw the cup, but one learns very young to take care of oneself, and the times I had been brought up in were peaceful enough, at any rate in our valley; but there are always wild men and rough men and the lawless and vagabonds to be reckoned with, and any boy who likes his own company, as I did, must be prepared to defend his skin. I was wiry, and strong for my age, and I had my dagger. That I was barely seven years old never entered my head; I was Merlin, and, bastard or not, the King's grandson. I went on exploring.

The next thing I found, a pace along the wall, was a box, and on top of it shapes which my hands identified immediately as flint and iron and tinderbox, and a big, roughly made candle of what smelled like sheep's tallow. Beside these objects lay a shape which—incredulously and inch by inch—I identified as the skull of a horned sheep. There were nails driven into the top of the box here and there, apparently holding down fragments of leather. But when I felt these, carefully, I found in the withered leather frameworks of delicate bone; they were dead bats, stretched and nailed on the wood.

This was a treasure cave indeed. No find of gold or weapons could have excited me more. Full of curiosity, I reached for the tinderbox.

Then I heard him coming back.

My first thought was that he must have seen my pony, then I realized he was coming from further up the hill. I could hear the rattling and scaling of small stones as he came down the scree above the cave. One of them splashed into the spring outside, and then it was too late. I heard him jump down on to the flat grass beside the water.

It was time for the ring-dove again; the falcon was forgotten. I ran deeper into the cave. As he swept aside the boughs that darkened the entrance, the light grew momentarily, enough to show me my way. At the back of the cave was a slope and jut of rock, and, at twice my height, a widish ledge. A quick flash of sunlight from the mirror caught a wedge of shadow in the rock above the ledge, big enough to hide me. Soundless in my scuffed sandals, I swarmed on to the ledge, and crammed my body into that wedge of shadow, to find it was in fact a gap in the rock, giving apparently on to another, smaller cave. I slithered in through the gap like an otter into the river-bank.

It seemed that he had heard nothing. The light was cut off again as the boughs sprang back into place behind him, and he came into the cave. It was a man's tread, measured and slow.

If I had thought about it at all, I suppose I would have assumed that the cave would be uninhabited at least until sunset, that whoever owned the place would be away hunting, or about his other business, and would return only at nightfall. There was no point in wasting candles when the sun was blazing outside. Perhaps he was here now only to bring home his kill, and he would go again and leave me the chance to get out. I hoped he would not see my pony tethered in the hawthorn brake.

Then I heard him moving, with the sure tread of someone who knows his way blindfold, towards the candle and the tinderbox.

Even now I had no room for apprehension, no room, indeed, for any but the one thought or sensation—the extreme discomfort of the cave into which I had crawled. It was apparently small, not much bigger than the large round vats they use for dyeing, and much the same shape. Floor, wall and ceiling hugged me round in a continuous curve. It was like being inside a large globe; moreover, a globe studded with nails, or with its inner surface stuck all over with small pieces of jagged stone. There seemed no inch of surface not bristling like a bed of strewn flints, and it was only my light weight, I think, that saved me from being cut, as I quested about blindly to find some clear space to lie on. I found a place smoother than the rest and curled there, as small as I could, watching the faintly defined opening, and inching my dagger silently from its sheath into my hand.

I heard the quick hiss and chime of flint and iron, and then the flare of light, intense in the darkness, as the tinder caught hold. Then the steady, waxing glow as he lit the candle.

Or rather, it should have been the slow-growing beam of a candle flame that I saw, but instead there was a flash, a sparkle, a conflagration as if a whole pitch-soaked beacon was roaring up in flames. Light poured and flashed, crimson, golden, white, red, intolerable into my cave. I winced back from it, frightened now, heedless of pain and cut flesh as I shrank against the sharp walls. The whole globe where I lay seemed to be full of flame.

It was indeed a globe, a round chamber floored, roofed, lined with crystals. They were fine as glass, and smooth as glass, but clearer than any glass I had ever seen, brilliant as diamonds. This, in fact, to my childish mind, was what they first seemed to be. I was in a globe lined with diamonds, a million burning diamonds, each face of each gem wincing with the light, shooting it to and fro, diamond to diamond and back again, with rainbows and rivers and bursting stars and a shape like a crimson dragon clawing up the wall, while below it a girl's face swam faintly with closed eyes, and the light drove right into my body as if it would break me open.

I shut my eyes. When I opened them again I saw that the golden light had shrunk and was concentrated on one part of the wall no bigger than my head, and from this, empty of visions, rayed the broken, brilliant beams.

There was silence from the cave below. He had not stirred. I had not even heard the rustle of his clothes.

Then the light moved. The flashing disc began to slide, slowly, across the crystal wall. I was shaking. I huddled closer to the sharp stones, trying to escape it. There was nowhere to go. It advanced slowly round the curve. It touched my shoulder, my head, and I ducked, cringing. The shadow of my movement rushed across the globe, like a wind-eddy over a pool.

The light stopped, retreated, fixed glittering in its place. Then it went out. But the glow of the candle, strangely, remained; an ordinary steady yellow glow beyond the gap in the wall of my refuge.

"Come out." The man's voice, not loud, not raised with shouted orders like my grandfather's, was clear and brief with all the mystery of command. It never occurred to me to disobey. I crept forward over the sharp crystals, and through the gap. Then I slowly pulled myself upright on the ledge, my back against the wall of the outer cave, the dagger ready in my right hand, and looked down.

6

He stood between me and the candle, a hugely tall figure (or so it seemed to me) in a long robe of some brown homespun stuff. The candle made a nimbus of his hair, which seemed to be grey, and he was bearded. I could not see his expression, and his right hand was hidden in the folds of his robe.

I waited, poised warily.

He spoke again, in the same tone. "Put up your dagger and come down."

"When I see your right hand," I said.

He showed it, palm up. It was empty. He said gravely: "I am unarmed."

"Then stand out of my way," I said, and jumped. The cave was wide, and he was standing to one side of it. My leap carried me three or four paces down the cave, and I was past him and near the entrance before he could have moved more than a step. But in fact he never moved at all. As I reached the mouth of the cave and swept aside the hanging branches I heard him laughing.

The sound brought me up short. I turned.

From here, in the light which now filled the cave, I saw him clearly. He was old, with grey hair thinning on top and hanging lank over his ears, and a straight growth of grey beard, roughly trimmed. His hands were calloused and grained with dirt, but had been fine, with long fingers. Now the old man's veins crawled and knotted on them, distended like worms. But it was his face which held me; it was thin, cavernous almost as a skull, with a high domed forehead and bushy grey brows which came down jutting over eyes where I could see no trace of age at all. These were closely set, large, and of a curiously clear and swimming grey. His nose was a thin beak; his mouth, lipless now, stretched wide with his laughter over astonishingly good teeth.

"Come back. There's no need to be afraid."

"I'm not afraid." I dropped the boughs back into place, and not without bravado walked towards him. I stopped a few paces away. "Why should I be afraid of you? Do you know who I am?"

He regarded me for a moment, seeming to muse. "Let me see you. Dark hair, dark eyes, the body of a dancer and the manners of a young wolf ... or should I say a young falcon?"

My dagger sank to my side. "Then you do know me?"

"Shall I say I knew you would come some day, and today I knew there was someone here. What do you think brought me back so early?"

"How did you know there was someone here? Oh, of course, you saw the bats."

"Perhaps."

"Do they always go up like that?"

"Only for strangers. Your dagger, sir."

I put it back in my belt. "Nobody calls me sir. I'm a bastard. That means I belong to myself, no one else. My name's Merlin, but you knew that."

"And mine is Galapas. Are you hungry?"

"Yes." But I said it dubiously, thinking of the skull and the dead bats.

Disconcertingly, he understood. The grey eyes twinkled. "Fruit and honey cakes? And sweet water from the spring? What better fare would you get, even in the King's house?"

"I wouldn't get that in the King's house at this hour of the day," I said frankly. "Thank you, sir, I'll be glad to eat with you."

He smiled. "Nobody calls me sir. And I belong to no man, either. Go out and sit down in the sun, and I'll bring the food."

The fruit was apples, which looked and tasted exactly like the ones from my grandfather's orchard, so that I stole a sideways glance at my host, scanning him by daylight, wondering if I had ever seen him on the river-bank, or anywhere in the town.

"Do you have a wife?" I asked. "Who makes the honey cakes? They're very good."

"No wife. I told you I belonged to no man, and to no woman either. You will see, Merlin, how all your life men, and women too, will try to put bars round you, but you will escape those bars, or bend them, or melt them at your will, until, of your will, you take them round you, and sleep behind them in their shadow. ... I get the honey cakes from the shepherd's wife, she makes enough for three, and is good enough to spare some for charity."

"Are you a hermit, then? A holy man?"

"Do I look like a holy man?"

"No." This was true. The only people I remember being afraid of at that time were the solitary holy men who sometimes wandered, preaching and begging, into the town; queer, arrogant, noisy men, with a mad look in their eyes, and a smell about them which I associated with the heaps of offal outside the slaughter-pens. It was sometimes hard to know which god they professed to serve. Some of them, it was whispered, were druids, who were still officially outside the law, though in Wales in the country places they still practiced without much interference. Many were followers of the old gods—the local deities—and since these varied in popularity according to season, their priests tended to switch allegiance from time to time where the pickings were richest. Even the Christian ones did this sometimes, but you could usually tell the real Christians, because they were the dirtiest. The Roman gods and their priests stayed solidly enshrined in their crumbling temples, but did very well on offerings likewise. The Church frowned on the lot, but could not do much about it. "There was a god at the spring outside," I ventured.

"Yes. Myrddin. He lends me his spring, and his hollow hill, and his heaven of woven light, and in return I give him his due. It does not do to neglect the gods of a place, whoever they may be. In the end, they are all one."

"If you're not a hermit, then, what are you?"

"At the moment, a teacher."

"I have a tutor. He comes from Massilia, but he's actually been to Rome. Who do you teach?"

"Until now, nobody. I'm old and tired, and I came to live here alone and study."

"Why do you have the dead bats in there, on the box?"

"I was studying them."

I stared at him. "Studying bats? How can you study bats?"

"I study the way they are made, and the way they fly, and mate, and feed. The way they live. Not only bats, but beasts and fish and plants and birds, as many as I see."

"But that's not studying!" I regarded him with wonder. "Demetrius—that's my tutor—tells me that watching lizards and birds is dreaming, and a waste of time. Though Cerdic—that's a friend—told me to study the ring-doves."

"Why?"

"Because they're quick, and quiet, and keep out of the way. Because they only lay two eggs, but still though everybody hunts them, men and beasts and hawks, there are still more ring-doves than anything else."

"And they don't put them in cages." He drank some water, regarding me. "So you have a tutor. Then you can read?"

"Of course."

"Can you read Greek?"

"A little."

"Then come with me."

He got up and went into the cave. I followed him. He lit

the candle once more—he had put it out to save tallow—and by its light lifted the lid of the box. In it I saw the rolled shapes of books, more books together than I had ever imagined there were in the world. I watched as he selected one, closed the lid carefully, and unrolled the book.

"There."

With delight, I saw what it was. A drawing, spidery but definite, of the skeleton of a bat. And alongside it, in neat, crabbed Greek letters, phrases which I immediately, forgetting even Galapas' presence, began to spell out to myself.

In a minute or two his hand came over my shoulder. "Bring it outside." He pulled out the nails holding one of the dried leathery bodies to the box-lid, and lifted it carefully in his palm. "Blow out the candle. We'll look at this together."

And so, with no more question, and no more ceremony, began my first lesson with Galapas.

It was only when the sun, low over one wing of the valley, sent a long shadow creeping up the slope, that I remembered the other life that waited for me, and how far I had to go. I jumped to my feet.

"I'll have to go! Demetrius won't say anything, but if I'm late for supper they'll ask why."

"And you don't intend to tell them?"

"No, or they'd stop me coming again."

He smiled, making no comment. I doubt if I noticed then the calm assumptions on which the interview had been based; he had neither asked how I had come, nor why. And because I was only a child I took it for granted, too, though for politeness' sake I asked him:

"I may come again, mayn't I?"

"Of course."

"I—it's hard to say when. I never know when I'll get away—I mean, when I'll be free."

"Don't worry. I shall know when you are coming. And I shall be here."

"How can you know?"

He was rolling up the book with those long, neat fingers. "The same way I knew today."

"Oh! I was forgetting. You mean I go into the cave and send the bats out?"

"If you like."

I laughed with pleasure. "I've never met anyone like you!

To make smoke signals with bats! If I told them they'd never believe me, even Cerdic."

"You won't tell even Cerdic."

I nodded. "That's right. Nobody at all. Now I must go. Goodbye, Galapas."

"Goodbye."

And so it was in the days, and in the months, that followed. Whenever I could, once and sometimes twice in the week, I rode up the valley to the cave. He certainly seemed to know when I was coming, for as often as not he was there waiting for me, with the books laid out; but when there was no sign of him I did as we had arranged and sent out the bats as a smoke signal to bring him in. As the weeks went by they got used to me, and it took two or three well-aimed stones sent up into the roof to get them out; but after a while this grew unnecessary; people at the palace grew accustomed to my absences, and ceased to question them, and it became possible to make arrangements with Galapas for meeting from day to day.

Moravik had let me go more and more my own way since Olwen's baby had been born at the end of May, and when Camlach's son arrived in September she established herself firmly in the royal nursery as its official ruler, abandoning me as suddenly as a bird deserting the nest. I saw less and less of my mother, who seemed content to spend her time with her women, so I was left pretty much to Demetrius and Cerdic between them. Demetrius had his own reasons for welcoming a day off now and again, and Cerdic was my friend. He would unsaddle the muddy and sweating pony without question, or with a wink and a lewd remark about where I had been that was meant as a joke, and was taken as such. I had my room to myself now, except for the wolfhound; he spent the nights with me for old times' sake, but whether he was any safeguard I have no idea. I suspect not; I was safe enough. The country was at peace, except for the perennial rumours of invasion from Less Britain; Camlach and his father were in accord; I was to all appearances heading willingly and at high speed for the prison of the priesthood, and so, when my lessons with Demetrius were officially done, was free to go where I wished.

I never saw anyone else in the valley. The shepherd only lived there in summer, in a poor hut below the wood. There were no other dwellings there, and beyond Galapas' cave the track was used only by sheep and deer. It led nowhere.

He was a good teacher, and I was quick, but in fact I hardly thought of my time with him as lessons. We left languages and geometry to Demetrius, and religion to my mother's priests; with Galapas to begin with it was only like listening to a story-teller. He had travelled when young to the other side of the earth, Aethiopia and Greece and Germany and all around the Middle Sea, and seen and learned strange things. He taught me practical things, too; how to gather herbs and dry them to keep, how to use them for medicines, and how to distil certain subtle drugs, even poisons. He made me study the beasts and birds, and—with the dead birds and sheep we found on the hills, and once with a dead deer—I learnt about the organs and bones of the body. He taught me how to stop bleeding, how to set a broken bone, how to cut bad flesh away and cleanse the place so that it heals cleanly; even—though this came later—how to draw flesh and sinews into place with thread while the beast is stunned with fumes. I remember that the first spell he taught me was the charming of warts; this is so easy that a woman can do it.

One day he took a book out of the box and unrolled it. "Do you know what this is?"

I was used to diagrams and drawings, but this was a drawing of nothing I could recognize. The writing was in Latin, and I saw the words *Aethiopia* and *Fortunate Islands*, and then right out in a corner, *Britannia*. The lines seemed to be scrawled everywhere, and all over the picture were trails of mounds drawn in, like a field where moles have been at work.

"Those, are they mountains?"

"Yes."

"Then it's a picture of the world?"

"A map."

I had never seen a map before. At first I could not see how it worked, but in a while, as he talked, I saw how the world lay there as a bird sees it, with roads and rivers like the radials of a spider's web, or the guidelines that lead the bee into the flower. As a man finds a stream he knows, and follows it through the wild moors, so, with a map, it is possible to ride from Rome to Massilia, or London to Caerleon, without once asking the way or looking for the milestones. This art was discovered by the Greek Anaximander, though some say the Egyptians knew it first. The map that

Galapas showed me was a copy from a book by Ptolemy of Alexandria. After he had explained, and we had studied the map together, he bade me get out my tablet and make a map for myself, of my own country.

When I had done he looked at it. "This in the center, what is it?"

"Maridunum," I said in surprise. "See, there is the bridge, and the river, and this is the road through the market place, and the barrack gates are here."

"I see that. I did not say your town, Merlin, I said your country."

"The whole of Wales? How do I know what lies north of the hills? I've never been further than this."

"I will show you."

He put aside the tablet, and taking a sharp stick, began to draw in the dust, explaining as he did so. What he drew for me was a map shaped like a big triangle, not Wales only, but the whole of Britain, even the wild land beyond the Wall where the savages live. He showed me the mountains and rivers and roads and towns, London and Calleva and the places that cluster thick in the south, to the towns and fortresses at the ends of the web of roads, Segontium and Caerleon and Eboracum and the towns along the Wall itself. He spoke as if it were all one country, though I could have told him the names of the kings of a dozen places that he mentioned. I only remember this because of what came after.

Soon after this, when winter came and the stars were out early, he taught me their names and their powers, and how a man could map them as one would map the roads and townships. They made music, he said, as they moved. He himself did not know music, but when he found that Olwen had taught me, he helped me to make myself a harp. This was a rude enough affair, I suppose, and small, made of hornbeam, with the curve and fore-pillar of red sallow from the Tywy, and strung with hair from my pony's tail, where the harp of a prince (said Galapas) should have been strung with gold and silver wire. But I made the string-shoes out of pierced copper coins, the key and tuning-pins of polished bone, then carved a merlin on the sounding-board, and thought it a finer instrument than Olwen's. Indeed it was as true as hers, having a kind of sweet whispering note which seemed to pluck songs from the air itself. I kept it in the cave: though Dinias left me alone these days, being a warrior while I was only a sucking clerk, I would not have kept anything I treasured in the palace, unless I could lock it in my clothes-chest, and the harp was too big for that. At home for music I had the birds in the pear tree, and Olwen still sang sometimes. And when the birds were silent, and the night sky was frosted with light, I listened for the music of the stars. But I never heard it.

Then one day, when I was twelve years old, Galapas spoke of the crystal cave.

7

It is common knowledge that, with children, those things which are most important often go unmentioned. It is as if the child recognizes, by instinct, things which are too big for him, and keeps them in his mind, feeding them with his imagination till they assume proportions distended or grotesque which can become equally the stuff of magic or of nightmare.

So it was with the crystal cave.

I had never mentioned to Galapas my first experience there. Even to myself I had hardly admitted what came sometimes with light and fire; dreams, I had told myself, memories from below memory, figments of the brain only, like the voice which had told me of Gorlan, or the sight of the poison in the apricot. And when I found that Galapas never mentioned the inner cave, and that the mirror was kept covered whenever I was there, I said nothing.

I rode up to see him one day in winter when frost made the ground glitter and ring, and my pony puffed out steam like a dragon. He went fast, tossing his head and dragging at the bit, and breaking into a canter as soon as I turned him away from the wood and along the high valley. I had at length grown out of the gentle, cream-coloured pony of my childhood, but was proud of my little Welsh grey, which I called Aster. There is a breed of Welsh mountain pony, hardy, swift, and very beautiful, with a fine narrow head and small ears, and a strong arch to the neck. They run wild in the hills, and in past times interbred with horses the Romans brought from the East. Aster had been caught and broken for my cousin Dinias, who had overridden him for a couple of years and then discarded him for a real war-horse. I found him hard to manage, with rough manners and a ruined mouth, but his paces were silken after the jogging I was used to, and once he got over his fear of me he was affectionate.

I had long since contrived a shelter for my pony when I came here in winter. The hawthorn brake grew right up against the cliff below the cave, and deep in the thickest part of it Galapas and I had carried stones to make a pen of which the back wall was the cliff itself. When we had laid dead boughs against the walls and across the top, and had carried a few armfuls of bracken, the pen was not only a warm, solid shelter, but invisible to the casual eye. This need for secrecy was another of the things that had never been openly discussed; I understood without being told that Galapas in some way was helping me to run counter to Camlach's plans for me, so—even though as time went on I was left more completely to my own devices—I took every precaution to avoid discovery, finding half a dozen different ways to approach the valley, and a score of stories to account for the time I spent there.

I led Aster into the pen, took off his saddle and bridle and hung them up, then threw down fodder from a saddle-bag, barred the entrance with a stout branch, and walked briskly up to the cave.

Galapas was not there, but that he had gone only recently was attested by the fact that the brazier which stood inside the cave mouth had been banked down to a glow. I stirred it till the flames leapt, then settled near it with a book. I had not come today by arrangement, but had plenty of time, so left the bats alone, and read peacefully for a while.

I don't know what made me, that day out of all the days I had been there alone, suddenly put the book aside, and walk back past the veiled mirror to look up at the cleft through which I had fled five years ago. I told myself that I was only curious to see if it was as I had remembered it, or if the crystals, like the visions, were figments of my imagination; whatever the reason, I climbed quickly to the ledge, and dropping on my hands and knees by the gap, peered in.

The inner cave was dead and dark, no glimmer reaching it from the fire. I crawled forward cautiously, till my hands met the sharp crystals. They were all too real. Even now not admitting to myself why I hurried, with one eye on the mouth of the main cave and an ear open for Galapas' return, I slithered down from the ledge, snatched up the leather riding jerkin which I had discarded and, hurrying back, thrust it in front of me through the gap. Then I crawled after.

With the leather jerkin spread on the floor, the globe was comparatively comfortable. I lay still. The silence was complete. As my eyes grew accustomed to the darkness, I could see the faintest grey glimmer from the crystals, but of the magic that the light had brought there was no sign.

There must have been some crack open to the air, for even in that dark confine there was a slight current, a cold thread of a draught. And with it came the sound I was listening for, the footsteps of someone approaching over the frosty rock . . .

When Galapas came into the cave a few minutes later I was sitting by the fire, my jerkin rolled up beside me, poring over the book.

Half an hour before dusk we put our books aside. But still I made no move to go. The fire was blazing now, filling the cave with warmth and flickering light. We sat for a while in silence.

"Galapas, there's something I want to ask you."

"Yes?"

"Do you remember the first day I came here?"

"Very clearly."

"You knew I was coming. You were expecting me."

"Did I say so?"

"You know you did. How did you know I would be here?"

"I saw you in the crystal cave."

"Oh, that, yes. You moved the mirror so that the candle-light caught me, and you saw my shadow. But that's not what I was asking you. I meant, how did you know I was going to come up the valley that day?"

"That was the question I answered, Merlin. I knew you were coming up the valley that day, because, before you came, I saw you in the cave."

We looked at one another in silence. The flames glowed and muttered between us, flattened by the little draught that carried the smoke out of the cave. I don't think I answered him at first, I just nodded. It was something I had known. After a while I said, merely: "Will you show me?"

He regarded me for a moment more, then got to his feet. "It is time. Light the candle."

I obeyed him. The little light grew golden, reaching among the shadows cast by the flickering of the fire.

"Take the rug off the mirror."

I pulled at it and it fell off into my arms in a huddle of wool. I dropped it on his bed beside the wall.

"Now go up on the ledge, and lie down."

"On the ledge?"

"Yes. Lie on your belly, with your head towards the cleft, so that you can see in."

"Don't you want me to go right in?"

"And take your jerkin to lie on?"

I was halfway up to the ledge. I whipped round, to see him smiling.

"It's no use, Galapas, you know everything."

"Some day you will go where even with the Sight I cannot follow you. Now lie still, and watch."

I lay down on the ledge. It was wide and flat and held me comfortably enough, prone, with my head pillowed on my bent arms, and turned towards the cleft.

Below me, Galapas said softly: "Think of nothing. I have the reins in my hand; it is not for you yet. Watch only."

I heard him move back across the cave towards the mirror.

The cave was bigger than I had imagined. It stretched upwards further than I could see, and the floor was worn smooth. I had even been wrong about the crystals; the glimmer that reflected the torchlight came only from puddles on the floor, and a place on one wall where a thin slither of moisture betrayed a spring somewhere above.

The torches, jammed into cracks in the cave wall, were cheap ones, of rag stuffed into cracked horns—the rejects from the workshops. They burned sullenly in the bad air. Though the place was cold, the men worked naked save for loincloths, and sweat ran over their backs as they hacked at the rock-face, steady ceaseless tapping blows that made no noise, but you could see the muscles clench and jar under the torchlit sweat. Beneath a knee-high overhang at the base of the wall, flat on their backs in a pool of seepage, two men hammered upwards with shortened, painful blows at rock within inches of their faces. On the wrist of one of them I saw the shiny pucker of an old brand.

One of the hewers at the face doubled up, coughing, then with a glance over his shoulder stifled the cough and got back to work. Light was growing in the cave, coming from a square opening like a doorway, which gave on a curved tunnel down which a fresh torch—a good one—came.

Four boys appeared, filthy with dust and naked like the others, carrying deep baskets, and behind them came a man dressed in a brown tunic smudged with damp. He had the torch in one hand and in the other a tablet which he stood studying with frowning brows while the boys ran with their baskets to the rock-face and began to shovel the fallen rock into them. After a while the foreman went forward to the face and studied it, holding his torch high. The men drew back, thankful it seemed for the respite, and one of them spoke to the foreman, pointing first at the workings, then at the seeping damp at the far side of the cave.

The boys had shovelled and scrabbled their baskets full, and dragged them back from the face. The foreman, with a shrug and a grin, took a silver coin from his pouch and, with the gambler's practiced flick, tossed it. The workmen craned to see. Then the man who had spoken turned back to the face and drove the pick in.

The crack widened, and dust rushed down, blotting out the light. Then in the wake of the dust came the water.

"Drink this," said Galapas.

"What is it?"

"One of my brews, not yours; it's quite safe. Drink it."

"Thanks. Galapas, the cave *is* crystal still. I—dreamed it differently."

"Never mind that now. How do you feel?"

"Odd . . . I can't explain. I feel all right, only a headache, but—empty, like a shell with the snail out of it. No, like a reed with the pith pulled out."

"A whistle for the winds. Yes. Come down to the brazier."

When I sat in my old place, with a cup of mulled wine in my hands, he asked: "Where were you?"

I told him what I had seen, but when I began to ask what it meant, and what he knew, he shook his head. "I think this has already gone past me. I do not know. All I know is that you must finish that wine quickly and go home. Do you realize how long you lay there dreaming? The moon is up."

I started to my feet. "Already? It must be well past suppertime. If they're looking for me—"

"They will not be looking for you. Other things are happening. Go and find out for yourself—and make sure you are part of them."

"What do you mean?"

"Only what I say. Whatever means you have to use, go

with the King. Here, don't forget this." He thrust my jerkin into my arms.

I took it blindly, staring. "He's leaving Maridunum?"

"Yes. Only for a while. I don't know how long."

"He'll never take me."

"That's for you to say. The gods only go with you, Myrddin Emrys, if you put yourself in their path. And that takes courage. Put your jerkin on before you go out, it's cold."

I shoved a hand into the sleeve, glowering. "You've seen all this, something that's really happening, and I—I was looking into the crystals with the fire, and here I've got a hellish headache, and all for nothing . . . Some silly dream of slaves in an old mine. Galapas, when will you teach me to see as you do?"

"For a start, I can see the wolves eating you and Aster, if you don't hurry home."

He was laughing to himself as if he had made a great jest, as I ran out of the cave and down to saddle the pony.

8

It was a quarter moon, which gave just enough light to show the way. The pony danced to warm his blood, and pulled harder than ever, his ears pricked towards home, scenting his supper. I had to fight to hold him in, because the way was icy, and I was afraid of a fall, but I confess that—with Galapas' last remark echoing uncomfortably in my head—I let him go downhill through the trees a good deal too fast for safety, until we reached the mill and the level of the towpath.

There it was possible to see clearly. I dug my heels in and galloped him the rest of the way.

As soon as we came in sight of town I could see that something was up. The towpath was deserted—the town gates would have been locked long since—but the town was full of lights. Inside the walls torches seemed to be flaring everywhere, and there was shouting and the tramp of feet. I slipped from the saddle at the stableyard gate, fully prepared to find myself locked out, but even as I reached to try it the gate opened, and Cerdic, with a shaded lantern in his hand, beckoned me in.

"I heard you coming. Been listening all evening. Where've you been, lover-boy? She must have been good tonight."

"Oh, she was. Have they been asking for me? Have they missed me?"

"Not that I know of. They've got more to think about tonight than you. Give me the bridle, we'll put him in the barn for now. There's too much coming and going in the big yard."

"Why, what's going on? I heard the noise a mile off. Is it a war?"

"No, more's the pity, though it may end up that way. There's a message come this afternoon, the High King's coming to Segontium, and he'll lie there for a week or two. Your grandfather's riding up tomorrow, so everything's to be got ready mighty sharp."

"I see." I followed him into the barn, and stood watching him unsaddle, while half-absently I pulled straw from the pile and twisted a wisp for him. I handed this across the pony's withers. "King Vortigern at Segontium? Why?"

"Counting heads, they say." He gave a snort of laughter as he began to work the pony over.

"Calling in his allies, do you mean? Then there is talk of war?"

"There'll always be talk of war, so long as yon Ambrosius sits there in Less Britain with King Budec at his back, and men remember things that's better not spoken of."

I nodded. I could not remember precisely when I had been told, since nobody said it aloud, but everyone knew the story of how the High King had claimed the throne. He had been regent for the young King Constantius who had died suddenly, and the King's younger brothers had not waited to prove whether the rumours of murder were true or false; they had fled to their cousin Budec in Less Britain, leaving the kingdom to the Wolf and his sons. Every year or so the rumours sprang up again; that King Budec was arming the two young princes; that Ambrosius had gone to Rome; that Uther was a mercenary in the service of the Emperor of the East, or that he had married the King of Persia's daughter; that the two brothers had an army four hundred thousand strong and were going to invade and burn Greater Britain from end to end; or that they would come in peace, like archangels, and drive the Saxons out of the eastern shores without a blow. But more than twenty years had gone by, and the thing had not happened. The coming of Ambrosius was spoken of now as if it were accomplished, and already a legend, as men spoke of the coming of Brut and the Trojans four generations after the fall of Troy, or Joseph's journey to Thorny Hill near Avalon. Or like the Second Coming of Christ—though when I had once repeated this to my mother she had been so angry that I had never tried the joke again.

"Oh, yes," I said, "Ambrosius coming again, is he? Seriously, Cerdic, why is the High King coming to North Wales?"

"I told you. Doing the rounds, drumming up a bit of support before spring, him and that Saxon Queen of his." And he spat on the floor.

"Why do you do that? You're a Saxon yourself."

"That's a long time ago. I live here now. Wasn't it that flaxen bitch that made Vortigern sell out in the first place? Or at any rate you know as well as I do that since she's been in the High King's bed the Northmen have been loose over the land like a heath fire, till he can neither fight them nor buy them off. And if she's what men say she is, you can be sure none of the King's true-born sons'll live to wear the crown." He had been speaking softly, but at this he looked over his shoulder and spat again, making the sign. "Well, you know all this—or you would, that is, if you listened to your betters more often, instead of spending your time with books and such like, or chasing round with the People from the hollow hills."

"Is that where you think I go?"

"It's what people say. I'm not asking questions. I don't want to know. Come up, you." This to the pony as he moved over and started work, hissing, on the other flank. "There's talk that the Saxons have landed again north of Rutupiæ, and they're asking too much this time even for Vortigern to stomach. He'll have to fight, come spring."

"And my grandfather with him?"

"That's what he's hoping, I'll be bound. Well, you'd best run along if you want your supper. No one'll notice you. There was all hell going on in the kitchens when I tried to get a bite an hour back."

"Where's my grandfather?"

"How do I know?" He cocked his head at me, over the pony's rump. "Now what's to do?"

"I want to go with them."

"Hah!" he said, and threw the chopped feed down for the pony. It was not an encouraging sound.

I said stubbornly: "I've a fancy to see Segontium."

"Who hasn't? I've a fancy to see it myself. But if you're thinking of asking the King . . ." He let it hang. "Not but what it's time you got out of the place and saw a thing or two, shake you a bit out of yourself, it's what you need, but I can't say I see it happening. You'll never go to the King?"

"Why not? All he can do is refuse."

"All he can do—? Jupiter's balls, listen to the boy. Take my advice and get your supper and go to bed. And don't try Camlach, neither. He's had a right stand-up fight with that wife of his and he's like a stoat with the toothache. —You can't be serious?"

"The gods only go with you, Cerdic, if you put yourself in their path."

"Well, all right, but some of them have got mighty big hoofs to walk over you with. Do you want Christian burial?"

"I don't really mind. I suppose I'll work my way up to Christian baptism fairly soon, if the bishop has his way, but till then I've not signed on officially for anyone."

He laughed. "I hope they'll give me the flames when my turn comes. It's a cleaner way to go. Well, if you won't listen, you won't listen, but don't face him on an empty belly, that's all."

"I'll promise you that," I said, and went to forage for supper. After I had eaten, and changed into a decent tunic, I went to look for my grandfather.

To my relief Camlach was not with him. The King was in his bedchamber, sprawled at ease in his big chair before a roaring log fire, with his two hounds asleep at his feet. At first I thought the woman in the high-backed chair on the other side of the hearth was Olwen, the Queen, but then I saw it was my mother. She had been sewing, but her hands had dropped idle in her lap, and the white stuff lay still over the brown robe. She turned and smiled at me, but with a look of surprise. One of the wolfhounds beat his tail on the floor, and the other opened an eye and rolled it round and closed it again. My grandfather glowered at me from under his brows, but said kindly enough: "Well, boy, don't stand there. Come in, come in, there's a cursed draught. Shut the door."

I obeyed, approaching the fire.

"May I see you, sir?"

"You're seeing me. What do you want? Get a stool and sit down."

There was one near my mother's chair. I pulled it away, to

show I was not sitting in her shadow, and sat down between them.

"Well? Haven't seen you for some time, have I? Been at your books?"

"Yes, sir." On the principle that it is better to attack than to defend, I went straight to the point. "I ... I had leave this afternoon, and I went out riding, so I—"

"Where to?"

"Along the river path. Nowhere special, only to improve my horsemanship, so—"

"It could do with it."

"Yes, sir. So I missed the messenger. They tell me you ride out tomorrow, sir."

"What's that to you?"

"Only that I would like to come with you."

"You would like? You would like? What's this, all of a sudden?"

A dozen answers all sounding equally well jostled in my head for expression. I thought I saw my mother watching me with pity, and I knew that my grandfather waited with indifference and impatience only faintly tempered with amusement. I told the simple truth. "Because I am more than twelve years old, and have never been out of Maridunum. Because I know that if my uncle has his way, I shall soon be shut up, in this valley or elsewhere, to study as a clerk, and before that happens—"

The terrifying brows came down. "Are you trying to tell me you don't want to study?"

"No. It's what I want more than anything in the world. But study means more if one has seen just a little of the world—indeed, sir, it does. If you would allow me to go with you—"

"I'm going to Segontium, did they tell you that? It's not a feast-day hunting-party, it's a long ride and a hard one, and no quarter given for poor riders."

It was like lifting a heavy weight, to keep my eyes level on that fierce blue glare. "I've been practicing, sir, and I've a good pony now."

"Ha, yes, Dinias' breakdown. Well, that's about your measure. No, Merlin, I don't take children."

"Then you're leaving Dinias behind?"

I heard my mother gasp, and my grandfather's head, already turned away, jerked back to me. I saw his fists clench on the chair arm, but he did not hit me. "Dinias is a man."

"Then do Mael and Duach go with you, sir?" They were his two pages, younger than myself, and went everywhere with him.

My mother began to speak, in a breathless rush, but my grandfather moved a hand to stop her. There was an arrested look in the fierce eyes under the scowling brows. "Mael and Duach are some use to me. What use are you?"

I looked at him calmly. "Till now, of very little. But have they not told you that I speak Saxon as well as Welsh, and can read Greek, and that my Latin is better than yours?"

"Merlin—" began my mother, but I ignored her.

"I would have added Breton and Cornish, but I doubt if you will have much use for these at Segontium."

"And can you give me one good reason," said my grandfather dryly, "why I should speak to King Vortigern in any other language but Welsh, seeing that he comes from Guent?"

I knew from his tone that I had won. Letting my gaze fall from his was like retreating with relief from the battlefield. I drew a breath, and said, very meekly: "No, sir."

He gave his great bark of laughter, and thrust out a foot to roll one of the dogs over. "Well, perhaps there's a bit of the family in you after all, in spite of your looks. At least you've got the guts to beard the old dog in his den when it suits you. All right, you can come. Who attends you?"

"Cerdic."

"The Saxon? Tell him to get your gear ready. We leave at first light. Well, what are you waiting for?"

"To say good night to my mother." I rose from my stool and went to kiss her. I did not often do this, and she looked surprised.

Behind me, my grandfather said abruptly: "You're not going to war. You'll be back inside three weeks. Get out."

"Yes, sir. Thank you. Good night."

Outside the door I stood still for a full half minute, leaning against the wall, while my blood-beat steadied slowly, and the sickness cleared from my throat. *The gods only go with you if you put yourself in their path. And that takes courage.*

I swallowed the sickness, wiped the sweat off my palms, and ran to find Cerdic.

9

So it was that I first left Maridunum. At that time it seemed like the greatest adventure in the world, to ride out in the chill of dawn, when stars were still in the sky, and make one of the jostling, companionable group of men who followed Camlach and the King. To begin with, most of the men were surly and half asleep, and we rode pretty well in silence, breath smoking in the icy air, and the horses' hoofs striking sparks from the slaty road. Even the jingle of harness sounded cold, and I was so numb that I could hardly feel the reins, and could think of nothing else but how to stay on the excited pony and not get myself sent home in disgrace before we had gone a mile.

Our excursion to Segontium lasted eighteen days. It was my first sight of King Vortigern, who had at this time been High King of Britain for more than twenty years. Be sure I had heard plenty about him, truth and tales alike. He was a hard man, as one must be who had taken his throne by murder and held it with blood; but he was a strong king in a time when there was need for strength, and it was not altogether his fault that his stratagem of calling in the Saxons as mercenaries to help him had twisted in his hand like an edged sword slipping, and cut it to the bone. He had paid, and paid again, and then had fought; and now he spent a great part of every year fighting like a wolf to keep the ranging hordes contained along the Saxon Shore. Men spoke of him—with respect—as a fierce and bloodthirsty tyrant, and of his Saxon Queen, Rowena, with hatred as a witch; but though I had been fed from childhood on the tales of the kitchen slaves, I was looking forward to seeing them with more curiosity than fear.

In any event, I need not have been afraid; I saw the High King only from a distance. My grandfather's leniency had extended only to letting me go in his train; once there, I was of no more account—in fact of much less—than his pages Mael and Duach. I was left to fend for myself among the anonymous rabble of boys and servants, and, because my ways had made me no friends among my contemporaries, was left to myself. I was later to be thankful for the fact that, on the few occasions when I was in the crowd surrounding the two Kings, Vortigern did not lay eyes on me, and neither my grandfather nor Camlach remembered my existence.

We lay a week at Segontium, which the Welsh call Caer-yn-ar-Von, because it lies just across the strait from Mona, the druids' isle. The town is set, like Maridunum, on the banks of an estuary, where the Seint River meets the sea. It has a splendid harbour, and a fortress placed on the rising ground above this, perhaps half a mile away. The fortress was built by the Romans to protect the harbour and the town, but had lain derelict for over a hundred years until Vortigern put part of it into repair. A little lower down the hill stood another more recent strong-point, built, I believe, by Macsen, grandfather of the murdered Constantius, against the Irish raiders.

The country here was grander than in South Wales, but to my eyes forbidding rather than beautiful. Perhaps in summer the land may be green and gentle along the estuary, but when I saw it first, that winter, the hills rose behind the town like storm-clouds, their skirts grey with the bare and whistling forests, and their crests slate blue and hooded with snow. Behind and beyond them all towers the great cloudy top of Moel-y-Wyddfa, which now the Saxons call Snow Hill, or Snowdon. It is the highest mountain in all Britain, and is the home of gods.

Vortigern lay, ghosts or no ghosts, in Macsen's Tower. His army—he never moved in those days with less than a thousand fighting men—was quartered in the fort. Of my grandfather's party, the nobles were with the King in the tower, while his train, of which I was one, was housed well enough, if a trifle coldly, near the west gate of the fort. We were treated with honour; not only was Vortigern a distant kinsman of my grandfather's, but it seemed to be true that the High King was—in Cerdic's phrase—"drumming up support." He was a big dark man, with a broad fleshy face and black hair as thick and bristled as a boar's, growing grey. There were black hairs on the back of his hands, and sprouting from his nostrils. The Queen was not with him; Cerdic whispered to me that he had not dared bring her where Saxons were so little welcome. When I retorted that he was only welcome himself because he had forgotten his Saxon and turned into good Welsh, he laughed and cuffed my ear. I suppose it was not my fault that I was never very royal.

The pattern of our days was simple. Most of the day was spent hunting, till at dusk we would return to fires and drink and a full meal, and then the kings and their advisers turned to talk, and their trains to dicing, wenching, quarrelling, and whatever other sports they might choose.

I had not been hunting before; as a sport it was foreign to my nature, and here everyone rode out hurly-burly in a crowd, which was something I disliked. It was also dangerous: there was plenty of game in the foothills, and there were some wild rides with necks for sale; but I saw no other chance of seeing the country, and besides, I had to find out why Galapas had insisted on my coming to Segontium. So I went out every day. I had a few falls, but got nothing worse than bruises, and managed to attract no attention, good or bad, from anyone who mattered. Nor did I find what I was looking for; I saw nothing, and nothing happened except that my horsemanship improved, and Aster's manners along with it.

On the eighth day of our stay we set off for home, and the High King himself, with an escort a hundred strong, went with us to set us on our road.

The first part of the way lay along a wooded gorge where a river ran fast and deep, and where the horses had to go singly or two abreast between the cliffs and the water. There was no danger for so large a party, so we went at ease, the gorge ringing with the sound of hoofs and bridle-chains and men's voices, and the occasional croak overhead as the ravens sailed off the cliffs to watch us. These birds do not wait, as some say, for the noise of battle; I have seen them follow armed bands of men for miles, waiting for the clash and the kill.

But that day we went safely, and near midday we came to the place where the High King was to part from us and ride back. This was where the two rivers met, and the gorge opened out into a wider valley, with forbidding icebound crags of slate to either side, and the big river running south, brown and swollen with melting snow. There is a ford at the watersmeet, and leading south from this a good road which goes dry and straight over high ground towards Tomen-y-Mur.

We halted just north of the ford. Our leaders turned aside into a sheltered hollow which was cupped on three sides by thickly wooded slopes. Clumps of bare alder and thick reeds showed that in summer the hollow would be marsh-land; on

that December day it was solidly frostbound, but protected
from the wind, and the sun came warmly. Here the party
stopped to eat and rest. The kings sat apart, talking, and near
them the rest of the royal party. I noticed that it included
Dinias. I, as usual, finding myself not of the royal group, nor
with the men-at-arms, nor yet the servants, handed Aster to
Cerdic, then went apart, climbing a short way among the
trees to a wooded dell where I could sit alone and out of
sight of the others. At my back was a rock thawed by the
sun, and from the other side of this came, muffled, the jingle
of bits as horses grazed, the men's voices talking, and an
occasional guffaw, then the rhythmic silences and mutterings
that told me the dice had come out to pass the time till the
kings completed their farewell. A kite tilted and swung above
me in the cold air, the sun striking bronze from its wings. I
thought of Galapas, and the bronze mirror flashing, and
wondered why I had come.

King Vortigern's voice said suddenly, just behind me:
"This way. You can tell me what you think."

I had whipped round, startled, before I realized that he,
and the man he was speaking to, were on the other side of
the rock that sheltered me.

"Five miles, they tell me, in either direction . . ." The High
King's voice dwindled as he turned away. I heard footsteps
on the frosty ground, dead leaves crackling, and the jar of
nailed boots on stone. They were moving off. I stood up,
taking it carefully, and peered over the rock. Vortigern and
my grandfather were walking up through the wood together,
deep in talk.

I remember that I hesitated. What, after all, could they
have to say that could not already have been said in the
privacy of Macsen's Tower? I could not believe that Galapas
had sent me merely as a spy on their conference. But why
else? Perhaps the god in whose way I had put myself had
sent me here alone, today, for this. Reluctantly, I turned to
follow them.

As I took the first step after them a hand caught my arm,
not gently. "And where do you think you're going?" demanded Cerdic under his breath.

I shook him off violently. "Damn you, Cerdic, you nearly
made me jump out of my skin! What does it matter to you
where I'm going?"

"I'm here to look after you, remember?"

"Only because I brought you. No one tells you to look

after me, these days. Or do they?" I looked at him sharply. "Have you followed me before?"

He grinned. "To tell you the truth, I never troubled. Should I have?"

But I persisted. "Did anyone tell you to watch me today?"

"No. But didn't you see who went this way? It was Vortigern and your grandfather. If you'd any idea of wandering after them, I'd think again if I was you."

"I wasn't going 'after them,'" I lied. "I was merely taking a look round."

"Then I'd do it elsewhere. They said special that the escort had to wait down here. I came to make sure you knew it, that's all. Very special about it, they was."

I sat down again. "All right, you've made sure. Now leave me again, please. You can come and tell me when we're due to move off."

"And have you belting off the minute my back's turned?"

I felt the blood rise to my cheeks. "Cerdic, I told you to go."

He said doggedly: "Look, I know you, and I know when you look like that. I don't know what's in your mind, but when you get that look in your eye there's trouble for somebody, and it's usually for you. What's to do?"

I said furiously: "The trouble's for you this time, if you don't do as I say."

"Don't go all royal on me," he said. "I was only trying to save you a beating."

"I know that. Forgive me. I had—something on my mind."

"You can tell me, can't you? I knew there'd been something biting you this last few days. What is it?"

"Nothing that I know of," I said truthfully. "Nothing you can help with. Forget it. Look, did the kings say where they were going? They could have talked their fill at Segontium, surely, or on the ride here?"

"They've gone to the top of the crag. There's a place up there at the end of the ridge where you can look right up and down the valley, all ways. There used to be an old tower there, they say. They call it Dinas Brenin."

"King's Fort? How big's the tower?"

"There's nothing there now but a tumble of stones. Why?"

"I—nothing. When do we ride home, I wonder?"

"Another hour, they said. Look, why don't you come down, and I'll cut you in on a dice game."

I grinned. "Thanks for nothing. Have I kept you out of your game, too? I'm sorry."

"Don't mention it. I was losing anyway. All right, I'll leave you alone, but you wouldn't think of doing anything silly now, would you? No sense in sticking your neck out. Remember what I told you about the ring-dove."

And at that exact moment, a ring-dove went by like an arrow, with a clap and whistle of wings that sent up a flurry of frost like a wake. Close behind her, a little above, ready to strike, went a merlin.

The dove rose a fraction as she met the slope, skimming up as a gull skims a rising wave, hurtling towards a thicket near the lip of the dell. She was barely a foot from the ground, and for the falcon to strike her was dangerous, but he must have been starving, for, just as she reached the edge of the thicket, he struck.

A scream, a fierce *kwik-ik-ik* from the falcon, a flurry of crashing twigs, then nothing. A few feathers drifted lazily down, like snow.

I started forward, and ran up the bank. "He got her!" It was obvious what had happened; both birds, locked together, had hurtled on into the thicket and crashed to the ground. From the silence, it was probable that they both now lay there, stunned.

The thicket was a steep tangle almost covering one side of the dell. I thrust the boughs aside and pushed my way through. The trail of feathers showed me my way. Then I found them. The dove lay dead, breast downwards, wings still spread as she had struck the stones, and with blood smearing bright over the iris of her neck feathers. On her lay the merlin. The steel ripping-claws were buried deep in the dove's back, the cruel beak half driven in by the crash. He was still alive. As I bent over them his wings stirred, and the bluish eyelids dropped, disclosing the fierce dark eye.

Cerdic arrived, panting, at my shoulder. "Don't touch him. He'll tear your hands. Let me."

I straightened. "So much for your ring-dove, Cerdic. It's time we forgot her, isn't it? No, leave them. They'll be here when we come back."

"Come back? Where from?"

I pointed silently to what showed ahead, directly in the path the birds had been taking. A square black gap like a door in the steep ground behind the thicket; an entrance hidden from casual sight, only to be seen if, for some reason, one pushed one's way in among the tangled branches.

"What of it?" asked Cerdic. "That's an old mine adit, by the look of it."

"Yes. That's what I came to see. Strike a light, and come along."

He began to protest, but I cut him short. "You can come or not, as you please. But give me a light. And hurry, there isn't much time." As I began to push my way towards the adit I heard him, muttering still, dragging up handfuls of dry stuff to make a torch.

Just inside the adit there was a pile of debris and fallen stone where the timber props had rotted away, but beyond this the shaft was smooth enough, leading more or less levelly into the heart of the hill. I could walk pretty nearly upright, and Cerdic, who was small, had to stoop only slightly. The flare of the makeshift torch threw our shadows grotesquely in front of us. It showed the grooves in the floor where loads had been dragged to daylight, and on walls and roof the marks of the picks and chisels that had made the tunnel.

"Where the hell do you think you're going?" Cerdic's voice, behind me, was sharp with nerves. "Look, let's get back. These places aren't safe. That roof could come in."

"It won't. Keep that torch going," I said curtly, and went on.

The tunnel bent to the right, and began to curve gently downhill. Underground one loses all sense of direction; there is not even the drift of wind on one's cheek that gives direction even on the blackest night; but I guessed that we must be winding our way deep into the heart of the hill on which had stood the old king's tower. Now and again smaller tunnels led off to left and right, but there was no danger of losing our way; we were in the main gallery, and the rock seemed reasonably good. Here and there had been falls from roof or wall, and once I was brought to a halt by a fall of rubble which almost blocked the way, but I climbed through, and the tunnel was clear beyond.

Cerdic had stopped at the barrier of rubble. He advanced the torch and peered after me. "Hey, look, Merlin, come back, for pity's sake! This is beyond any kind of folly. I tell you, these places are dangerous, and we're getting down into the very guts of the rock. The gods alone know what lives down here. Come back, boy."

"Don't be a coward, Cerdic, there's plenty of room for you. Come on through. Quickly."

"That I won't. If you don't come out this minute, I swear I'll go back and tell the King."

"Look," I said, "this is important. Don't ask me why. But I swear to you there's no danger. If you're afraid, then give me that torch, and get back."

"You know I can't do that."

"Yes, I know. You wouldn't dare go back to tell him, would you? And if you did leave me, and anything happened, what do you suppose would happen to you?"

"They say right when they say you're a devil's spawn," said Cerdic.

I laughed. "You can say what you like to me when we're back in daylight, but hurry now, Cerdic, please. You're safe, I promise you. There's no harm in the air today, and you saw how the merlin showed us the door."

He came, of course. Poor Cerdic, he could afford to do nothing else. But as he stood beside me again, with the torch held up, I saw him looking at me sideways, and his left hand was making the sign against the evil eye.

"Don't be long," he said, "that's all."

Twenty paces further, round a curve, the tunnel led into the cavern.

I made a sign to him to lift the torch. I could not have spoken. This vast hollow, right in the hill's heart, this darkness hardly touched by the torch's flare, this dead stillness of air where I could hear and feel my own blood beating—this, of course, was the place. I recognized every mark of the workings, the face seamed and split by the axes, and smashed open by the water. There was the domed roof disappearing into darkness, there in a corner some rusty metal where the pump had stood. There the shining moisture on the wall, no longer a ribbon, but a curtain of gleaming damp. And there where the puddles had lain, and the seepage under the overhang, a wide, still pool. Fully a third of the floor was under water.

The air had a strange smell all its own, the breath of the water and the living rock. Somewhere above, water dripped, each tap clear like a small hammer on metal. I took the smouldering faggot from Cerdic's hand, and went to the water's edge. I held the light as high as I could, out over the water, and gazed down. There was nothing to see. The light glanced back from a surface as hard as metal. I waited. The light ran, and gleamed, and drowned in darkness. There was nothing there but my own reflection, like the ghost in Galapas' mirror.

I gave the torch back to Cerdic. He hadn't spoken. He was watching me all the time with that sidelong, white-eyed look.

I touched his arm. "We can go back now. This thing's nearly out anyway. Come on."

We didn't speak as we made our way back along the curving gallery, past the rubble, through the adit and out into the frosty afternoon. The sky was a pale, milky blue. The winter trees stood brittle and quiet against it, the birches white as bone. From below a horn called, urgent, in the still metallic air.

"They're going." Cerdic drove the torch down into the frozen ground to extinguish it. I scrambled down through the thicket. The dove still lay there, cold, and stiff already. The merlin was there too; it had withdrawn from the body of its kill, and sat near it on a stone, hunched and motionless, even when I approached. I picked up the ring-dove and threw it to Cerdic. "Shove it in your saddle-bag. I don't have to tell you to say nothing of this, do I?"

"You do not. What are you doing?"

"He's stunned. If we leave him here he'll freeze to death in an hour. I'm taking him."

"Take care! That's a grown falcon—"

"He'll not hurt me." I picked up the merlin; he had fluffed his feathers out against the cold, and felt soft as a young owl in my hands. I pulled my leather sleeve down over my left wrist, and he took hold of this, gripping fiercely. The eyelids were fully open now, and the wild dark eyes watched me. But he sat still, with shut wings. I heard Cerdic muttering to himself as he bent to retrieve my things from the place where I had taken my meal. Then he added something I had never heard from him before. "Come on then, young master."

The merlin stayed docile on my wrist as I fell in at the back of my grandfather's train for the ride home to Maridunum.

10

Nor did it attempt to leave me when we reached home. I found, on examining it, that some of its wing feathers had been damaged in that hurtling crash after the ring-dove, so I mended them as Galapas had taught me, and after that it sat in the pear tree outside my window, accepting the food I gave it, and making no attempt to fly away.

I took it with me when next I went to see Galapas.

This was on the first day of February, and the frost had broken the night before, in rain. It was a grey leaden day, with low cloud and a bitter little wind among the rain. Draughts whistled everywhere in the palace, and curtains were fast drawn across the doors, while people kept on their woollen cloaks and huddled over the braziers. It seemed to me that a grey and leaden silence hung also over the palace; I had hardly seen my grandfather since we had returned to Maridunum, but he and the nobles sat together in council for hours, and there were rumours of quarrelling and raised voices when he and Camlach were closeted together. Once when I went to my mother's room I was told she was at her prayers and could not see me. I caught a glimpse of her through the half-open door, and I could have sworn that as she knelt below the holy image she was weeping.

But in the high valley nothing had changed. Galapas took the merlin, commended my work on its wings, then set it on a sheltered ledge near the cave's entrance, and bade me come to the fire and get warm. He ladled some stew out of the simmering pot, and made me eat it before he would listen to my story. Then I told him everything, up to the quarrels in the palace and my mother's tears.

"It was the same cave, Galapas, that I'll swear! But why? There was nothing there. And nothing else happened, nothing at all. I've asked as best I could, and Cerdic has asked about among the slaves, but nobody knows what the kings discussed, or why my grandfather and Camlach have fallen out. But he did tell me one thing; I am being watched. By Camlach's people. I'd have come to see you sooner, except for that. They've gone out today, Camlach and Alun and the rest, so I said I was going to the water-meadow to train the merlin, and I came up here."

Then as he was still silent, I repeated, worried into urgency: "What's happening, Galapas? What does it all mean?"

"About your dream, and your finding of the cavern, I know nothing. About the trouble in the palace, I can guess. You knew that the High King had sons by his first wife, Vortimer and Katigern and young Pascentius?"

I nodded.

"Were none of them there at Segontium?"

"No."

"I am told that they have broken with their father," said Galapas, "and Vortimer is raising troops of his own. They say he would like to be High King, and that Vortigern looks like having a rebellion on his hands when he can least afford it. The Queen's much hated, you know that; Vortimer's mother was good British, and besides, the young men want a young king."

"Camlach is for Vortimer, then?" I asked quickly, and he smiled.

"It seems so."

I thought about it for a little. "Well, when wolves fall out, don't they say the ravens come into their own?" As I was born in September, under Mercury, the raven was mine.

"Perhaps," said Galapas. "You're more likely to be clapped in your cage sooner than you expected." But he said it absently, as if his mind were elsewhere, and I went back to what concerned me most.

"Galapas, you've said you know nothing about the dream or the cavern. But this—this must have been the hand of the god." I glanced up at the ledge where the merlin sat, broodingly patient, his eyes half shut, slits of firelight.

"It would seem so."

I hesitated. "Can't we find out what he—what it means?"

"Do you want to go into the crystal cave again?"

"N-no, I don't. But I think perhaps I should. Surely you can tell me that?"

He said heavily, after a few moments: "I think you must go in, yes. But first, I must teach you something more. You must make the fire for yourself this time. Not like that—" smiling, as I reached for a branch to stir the embers. "Put that down. You asked me before you went away to show you something real. This is all I have left to show you. I hadn't realized . . . Well, let that go. It's time. No, sit still, you have no more need of books, child. Watch now."

Of the next thing, I shall not write. It was all the art he taught me, apart from certain tricks of healing. But as I have said, it was the first magic to come to me, and will be the last to go. I found it easy, even to make the ice-cold fire and the wild fire, and the fire that goes like a whip through the dark; which was just as well, because I was young to be taught such things, and it is an art which, if you are unfit or unprepared, can strike you blind.

It was dark outside when we had done. He got to his feet.

"I shall come back in an hour and wake you."

He twitched his cloak down from where it hung shrouding the mirror, put it round him, and went out.

The flames sounded like a horse galloping. One long, bright tongue cracked like a whip. A log fell down with a hiss like a woman's sigh, and then a thousand twigs crackled like people talking, whispering, chattering of news . . .

It faded all into a great brilliant blaze of silence. The mirror flashed. I picked up my cloak, now comfortably dry, and climbed with it into the crystal cave. I folded it and lay down on it, with my eyes fixed on the wall of crystal arching over me. The flames came after me, rank on bright rank, filling the air, till I lay in a globe of light like the inside of a star, growing brighter and ever brighter till suddenly it broke and there was darkness . . .

The galloping hoofs sparked on the gravel of the Roman road. The rider's whip cracked and cracked again, but the horse was already going full tilt, its nostrils wide and scarlet, its breath like steam in the cold air. The rider was Camlach. Far behind him, almost half a mile behind now, were the rest of the young men of his party, and still further behind them, leading his lamed and dripping horse, came the messenger who had taken the news to the King's son.

The town was alive with torches, men running to meet the galloping horse, but Camlach paid no heed to them. He drove the spiked spurs into the horse's sides, and galloped straight through the town, down the steep street, and into the outer yard of the palace. There were torches there, too. They caught the quick glint of his red hair as he swung from the horse and flung the reins into the hands of a waiting slave. The soft riding boots made no sound as he ran up the steps and along the colonnade that led to his father's room. The swift black figure was lost for a moment in shadow under the arch, then he flung the door wide and went through.

The messenger had been right. It had been a quick death. The old man lay on the carved Roman bed, and over him someone had thrown a coverlet of purple silk. They had somehow managed to prop his jaw, for the fierce grey beard jutted ceilingwards, and a little head-rest of baked clay beneath his neck held his head straight, while the body slowly froze iron-hard. There was no sign, the way he lay, that the neck was broken. Already the old face had begun to fall away, to shrink, as death pared the flesh down from the jut of the nose till it would be left simply in planes of cold candlewax. The gold coins that lay on his mouth and shut eyelids glimmered in the light of the torches at the four corners of the bed.

At the foot of the bed, between the torches, stood Niniane. She stood very still and upright, dressed in white, her hands folded quietly in front of her with a crucifix between them, her head bent. When the door opened she did not look up, but kept her eyes fixed on the purple coverlet, not in grief, but almost as if she were too far away for thought.

To her side, swiftly, came her brother, slim in his black clothes, glinting with a kind of furious grace that seemed to shock the room.

He walked right up to the bed and stood over it, staring down at his father. Then he put down a hand and laid it over the dead hands clasped on the purple silk. His hand lingered there for a moment, then drew back. He looked at Niniane. Behind her, a few paces back in the shadows, the little crowd of men, women, servants, shuffled and whispered. Among them, silent and dry-eyed, Mael and Duach stared. Dinias, too, all his attention fixed on Camlach.

Camlach spoke very softly, straight to Niniane. "They told me it was an accident. Is this true?"

She neither moved nor spoke. He stared at her for a moment, then with a gesture of irritation, looked beyond her, and raised his voice.

"One of you, answer me. This was an accident?"

A man stepped forward, one of the King's servants, a man called Mabon. "It's true, my lord." He licked his lips, hesitating.

Camlach showed his teeth. "What in the name of the devils in hell's the matter with you all?" Then he saw where they were staring, and looked down at his right hip, where, sheathless, his short stabbing dagger had been thrust through his belt. It was blood to the hilt. He made a sound of impatience and disgust and, pulling it out, flung it from him, so that it skittered across the floor and came up against the wall with a small clang that sounded loud in the silence.

"Whose blood did you think?" he asked, still with that lifted lip. "Deer's blood, that's all. When the message came, we had just killed. I was twelve miles off, I and my men." He stared at them, as if daring them to comment. No one moved. "Go on, Mabon. He slipped and fell, the man told me. How did it happen?"

The man cleared his throat. "It was a stupid thing, sir, a pure accident. Why, no one was even near him. It was in the small courtyard, the way through to the servants' rooms, where the steps are worn. One of the men had been carrying oil around to fill the lamps. He'd spilt some on the steps, and before he got back to wipe it up the King came through, in a bit of a hurry. He—he hadn't been expected there at the time. Well, my lord, he treads in the oil, and goes straight down on his back, and hits his head on the stone. That's how it happened, my lord. It was seen. There's those that can vouch for it."

"And the man whose fault it was?"

"A slave, my lord."

"He's been dealt with?"

"My lord, he's dead."

While they had been talking, there had been a commotion in the colonnade, as the rest of Camlach's party arrived and came hurrying along to the King's room after him. They had pressed into the room while Mabon was speaking, and now Alun, approaching the prince quietly, touched his arm.

"The news is all round the town, Camlach. There's a crowd gathering outside. A million stories going round—there'll be trouble soon. You'll have to show yourself and talk to them."

Camlach flicked him a glance, and nodded. "Go and see to it, will you? Bran, go with him, and Ruan. Shut the gates. Tell the people I'm coming out soon. And now, the rest of you, out."

The room emptied. Dinias lingered in the doorway, got not even a glance, and followed the rest. The door shut.

"Well, Niniane?"

In all this time she had never looked at him. Now she raised her eyes. "What do you want of me? It's true as Mabon tells you. What he didn't say was that the King had been fooling with a servant-girl and was drunk. But it was an accident, and he's dead ... and you with all your friends were a good twelve miles away. So you're King now, Camlach, and there is no man can point a finger at you and say, 'He wanted his father dead.' "

"No woman can say that to me either, Niniane."

"I have not said it. I'm just telling you that the quarrels here are over. The kingdom's yours—and now it's as Alun says, you had better go and speak to the people."

"To you first. Why do you stand like that, as if you didn't care either way? As if you were scarcely with us here?"

"Perhaps because it's true. What you are, brother, and what you want, does not concern me, except to ask you one thing."

"And that is?"

"That you let me go now. He never would, but I think you will."

"To St. Peter's?"

She bent her head. "I told you nothing here concerned me any more. It has not concerned me for some time, and less than ever now, with all this talk about invasion, and war in the spring, and the rumours about shifts of power and the death of kings. ... Oh, don't look at me like that; I'm not a fool, and my father talked to me. But you need not be afraid of me; nothing I know or can do can ever harm your plans for yourself, brother. I tell you, there is nothing I want out of life now except to be allowed to go in peace, and live in peace, and my son too."

"You said 'one thing.' That makes two."

For the first time something came to life in her eyes; it might have been fear. She said swiftly: "It was always the plan for him, your plan, even before it was my father's. Surely, after the day Gorlan went, you knew that even if Merlin's father could come riding in, sword in hand and with three thousand men at his back, I would not go to him? Merlin can do you no harm, Camlach. He will never be anything but a nameless bastard, and you know he is no warrior. The gods know he can do you no harm at all."

"And even less shut up as a clerk?" Camlach's voice was silky.

"Even less, shut up as a clerk. Camlach, are you playing with me? What's in your mind?"

"This slave who spilt the oil," he said. "Who was he?"

That flicker in her eyes again. Then the lids dropped. "The Saxon. Cerdic."

He didn't move, but the emerald on his breast glittered suddenly against the black as if his heart had jumped.

She said fiercely: "Don't pretend you guessed this! How could you guess it?"

"Not a guess, no. When I rode in the place was humming

with whispers like a smashed harp." He added, in sudden irritation: "You stand there like a ghost with your hands on your belly as if you still had a bastard there to protect."

Surprisingly, she smiled. "But I have." Then as the emerald leapt again: "No, don't be a fool. Where would I get another bastard now? I meant that I cannot go until I know he is safe from you. And that we are both safe from what you propose to do."

"From what I propose to do to *you*? I swear to you there is nothing—"

"I am talking about my father's kingdom. But let it go now. I told you, my only concern is that St. Peter's should be left in peace . . . And it will be."

"You saw this in the crystal?"

"It is unlawful for a Christian to dabble in soothsaying," said Niniane, but her voice was a little over-prim, and he looked sharply at her, then, suddenly restless, took a couple of strides away into the shadows at the side of the room, then back into the light.

"Tell me," he said abruptly. "What of Vortimer?"

"He will die," she said indifferently.

"We shall all die, some day. But you know I am committed to him now. Can you not tell me what will happen this coming spring?"

"I see nothing and I can tell you nothing. But whatever your plans for the kingdom, it will serve no purpose to let even the smallest whisper of murder start, and I can tell you this, you're a fool if you think that the King's death was anything but an accident. Two of the grooms saw it happen, and the girl he'd been with."

"Did the man say anything before they killed him?"

"Cerdic? No. Only that it was an accident. He seemed concerned more for my son than for himself. It was all he said."

"So I heard," said Camlach.

The silence came back. They stared at one another. She said: "You would not."

He didn't answer. They stood there, eyes locked, while a draught crept through the room, making the torches gutter.

Then he smiled, and went. As the door slammed shut behind him a gust of air blew through the room, and tore the flames along from the torches, till shadow and light went reeling.

The flames were dying, and the crystals dim. As I climbed out of the cave and pulled my cloak after me, it tore. The embers in the brazier showed a sullen red. Outside, now, it was quite dark. I stumbled down from the ledge and ran towards the doorway.

"Galapas!" I shouted. "Galapas!"

He was there. His tall, stooping figure detached itself from the darkness outside, and he came forward into the cave. His feet, half-bare in his old sandals, looked blue with cold.

I came to a halt a yard from him, but it was as if I had run straight into his arms, and been folded against his cloak.

"Galapas, they've killed Cerdic."

He said nothing, but his silence was like words or hands of comfort.

I swallowed to shift the ache in my throat. "If I hadn't come up here this afternoon ... I gave him the slip, along with the others. But I could have trusted him, even about you. Galapas, if I'd stayed—if I'd been there—perhaps I could have done something."

"No. You counted for nothing. You know that."

"I'll count for less than nothing now." I put a hand to my head: it was aching fiercely, and my eyes swam, still half-blind. He took me gently by the arm and made me sit down near the fire.

"Why do you say that? A moment, Merlin, tell me what has happened."

"Don't you know?" I said, surprised. "He was filling the lamps in the colonnade, and some oil spilled on the steps, and the King slipped in it and fell and broke his neck. It wasn't Cerdic's fault, Galapas. He spilt the oil, that's all, and he was going back, he was actually going back to clean it up when it happened. So they took him and killed him."

"And now Camlach is King."

I think I stared at him for some time, unseeing with those dream-blinded eyes, my brain for the moment incapable of holding more than the single fact.

He persisted, gently: "And your mother? What of her?"

"What? What did you say?"

The warm shape of a goblet was put into my hand. I could smell the same drink that he had given me before when I dreamed in the cave. "Drink that. You should have slept till I wakened you, then it wouldn't have come like this. Drink it all."

As I drank, the sharp ache in my temples dulled to a

throb, and the swimming shapes round me drew back into focus. And with them, thought.

"I'm sorry. It's all right now, I can think again, I've come back. . . . I'll tell you the rest. My mother's to go into St. Peter's. She tried to make Camlach promise to let me go too, but he wouldn't. I think . . ."

"Yes?"

I said slowly, thinking hard now: "I didn't understand it all. I was thinking about Cerdic. But I believe he's going to kill me. I believe he will use my grandfather's death for this; he'll say that my slave did it . . . Oh, nobody will believe that I could take anything from Camlach, but if he does shut me up in a religious house, and then I die quietly, a little time after, then by that time the whispers will have worked, and nobody will raise a voice about it. And by that time, if my mother is just one of the holy women at St. Peter's, and no longer the King's daughter, she won't have a voice to raise, either." I cupped my hands round the goblet, looking across at him. "Why should anyone fear me so, Galapas?"

He did not answer that, but nodded to the goblet in my hands. "Finish it. Then, my dear, you must go."

"Go? But if I go back, they'll kill me, or shut me up . . . Won't they?"

"If they find you, they will try."

I said eagerly: "If I stayed here with you—nobody knows I come here—even if they found out and came after me, you'd be in no danger! We'd see them coming up the valley for miles, or we'd know they were coming, you and I . . . They'd never find me; I could go in the crystal cave."

He shook his head. "The time for that isn't come. One day, but not now. You can no more be hidden now, than your merlin could go back into its egg."

I glanced back over my shoulder at the ledge where the merlin had sat brooding, still as Athene's owl. There was no bird there. I wiped the back of a hand across my eyes, and blinked, not believing. But it was true. The firelit shadows were empty.

"Galapas, it's gone!"

"Yes."

"Did you see it go?"

"It went by when you called me back into the cave."

"I—which way?"

"South."

I drank the rest of the potion, then turned the goblet up to

spill the last drops for the god. Then I set it down and
reached for my cloak.

"I'll see you again, won't I?"

"Yes. I promise you that."

"Then I shall come back?"

"I promised you that already. Some day, the cave will be
yours, and all that is in it."

Past him, in from the night, came a cold stray breath of
air that stirred my cloak and lifted the hairs on my nape. My
flesh prickled. I got up and swung the cloak round me and
fastened the pin.

"You're going, then?" He was smiling. "You trust me so
much? Where do you plan to go?"

"I don't know. Home, I suppose, to start with. I'll have
time to think on the way there, if I need to. But I'm still in
the god's path. I can feel the wind blowing. Why are you
smiling, Galapas?"

But he would not answer that. He stood up, then pulled
me towards him and stooped and kissed me. His kiss was dry
and light, an old man's kiss, like a dead leaf drifting down to
brush the flesh. Then he pushed me towards the entrance.
"Go. I saddled your pony ready for you."

It was raining still as I rode down the valley. The rain was
cold and small, and soaking; it gathered on my cloak and
dragged at my shoulders, and mixed with the tears that ran
down my face.

This was the second time in my life that I wept.

11

The stableyard gate was locked. This was no more than I had
expected. That day I had gone out openly enough through
the main yard with the merlin, and any other night might
have chanced riding back the same way, with some story of
losing my falcon and riding about till dark to look for it. But
not tonight.

And tonight there would be no one waiting and listening
for me, to let me in.

Though the need for haste was breathing on the back of
my neck, I kept the impatient pony to a walk, and rode

quietly along under the palace wall in the direction of the bridge. This and the road leading to it were alive with people and torches and noise, and twice in the few minutes since I had come in sight of it a horseman went galloping headlong out over the bridge, going south.

Now the wet, bare trees of the orchard overhung the towpath. There was a ditch here below the high wall, and over it the boughs hung, dripping. I slid off the pony's back and led him in under my leaning apple-tree, and tethered him. Then I scrambled back into the saddle, got unsteadily to my feet, balanced for a moment, and jumped for the bough above me.

It was soaking, and one of my hands slipped, but the other held. I swung my legs up, cocked them over the bough, and after that it was only the work of moments to scramble over the wall, and down into the orchard grasses.

There to my left was the high wall which masked my grandfather's garden, to the right the dovecote and the raised terrace where Moravik used to sit with her spinning. Ahead of me was the low sprawl of the servants' quarters. To my relief hardly a light showed. All the light and uproar of the palace was concentrated beyond the wall to my left, in the main building. From even further beyond, and muted by the rain, came the tumult of the streets.

But no light showed in my window. I ran.

What I hadn't reckoned on was that they should have brought him here, to his old place. His pallet lay now, not across the door, but back in the corner, near my bed. There was no purple here, no torches; he lay just as they had flung him down. All I could see in the half-darkness was the ungainly sprawled body, with an arm flung wide and the hand splayed on the cold floor. It was too dark to see how he had died.

I stooped over him and took the hand. It was cold already, and the arm had begun to stiffen. I lifted it gently to the pallet beside his body, then ran to my bed and snatched up the fine woollen coverlet. I spread it over Cerdic, then jerked upright, listening, as a man's voice called something in the distance, and then there were footsteps at the end of the colonnade, and the answer, shouted:

"No. He's not come this way. I've been watching the door. Is the pony in yet?"

"No. No sign." And then, in reply to another shout: "Well,

he can't have ridden far. He's often out till this time. What? Oh, very well . . ."

The footsteps went, rapidly. Silence.

There was a lamp in its stand somewhere along the colonnade. This dealt enough light through the half-open door for me to see what I was doing. I silently lifted the lid of my chest, pulled out the few clothes I had, with my best cloak, and a spare pair of sandals. I bundled these all together in a bag, together with my other possessions, my ivory comb, a couple of brooches, a cornelian clasp. These I could sell. I climbed on the bed and pitched the bag out of the window. Then I ran back to Cerdic, pulled aside the coverlet, and kneeling, fumbled at his hip. They had left his dagger. I tugged at the clasp with fingers that were clumsier even than the darkness made them, and it came undone. I took it, belt and all, a man's dagger, twice as long as my own, and honed to a killing point. Mine I laid beside him on the pallet. He might need it where he had gone, but I doubted it; his hands had always been enough.

I was ready. I stood looking down at him for a moment longer, and saw instead, as in the flashing crystal, how they had laid my grandfather, with the torchlight and the watchers and the purple. Nothing here but darkness, a dog's death. A slave's death.

"Cerdic." I said it half aloud, in the darkness. I wasn't weeping now. That was over. "Cerdic, rest you now. I'll send you the way you wanted, like a king."

I ran to the door, listened for a moment, then slipped through into the deserted colonnade. I lifted the lamp from its bracket. It was heavy, and oil spilled. Of course; he had filled it just that evening.

Back in my own room I carried the lamp over to where he lay. Now—what I had not foreseen—I could see how he had died. They had cut his throat.

Even if I had not intended it, it would have happened. The lamp shook in my hand, and hot oil splashed on the coverlet. A burning fragment broke from the wick, fell, caught, hissed. Then I flung the lamp down on the body, and watched for five long seconds while the flame ran into the oil and burst like blazing spray.

"Go with your gods, Cerdic," I said, and jumped for the window.

I landed on the bundle and went sprawling in the wet grass, then snatched it up and ran for the river wall.

Not to frighten the pony, I made for a place some yards beyond the apple tree, and pitched the bag over the wall into the ditch. Then back to the tree, and up it, to the high coping.

Astride of this, I glanced back. The fire had caught. My window glowed now, red with pulsing light. No alarm had yet been given, but it could only be a matter of moments before the flames were seen, or someone smelled the smoke. I scrambled over, hung by my hands for a moment, then let myself drop. As I got to my feet a shadow, towering, jumped at me and struck.

I went down with a man's heavy body on top of me, pinning me to the muddy grass. A splayed hand came hard down on my face, choking my cry off short. Just near me was a quick footstep, the rasp of drawn metal, and a man's voice saying, urgently, in Breton: "Wait. Make him talk first."

I lay quite still. This was easy to do, for not only had the force of the first man's attack driven the breath right out of my body, but I could feel his knife at my throat. Then as the second man spoke, my captor, with a surprised grunt, shifted his weight from me, and the knife withdrew an inch or two.

He said, in a tone between surprise and disgust: "It's only a boy." Then to me, harshly, in Welsh: "Not a sound out of you, or I'll slit your throat here and now. Understood?"

I nodded. He took his hand from my mouth, and getting up, dragged me to my feet. He rammed me back against the wall, holding me there, the knife pricking my collarbone. "What's all this? What are you doing bolting out of the palace like a rat with the dogs after it? A thief? Come on, you little rat, before I choke you."

He shook me as if I were indeed a rat. I managed to gasp: "Nothing. I was doing no harm! Let me go!"

The other man said softly, out of the darkness: "Here's what he threw over the wall. A bag full of stuff."

"What's in it?" demanded my captor. And to me, "Keep quiet, you."

He had no need to warn me. I thought I could smell smoke now, and see the first flicker of light as my fire took hold of the roof beams. I flattened myself back even further into the black shadow under the wall.

The other man was examining my bundle. "Clothes ... sandals ... some jewelry by the feel of it ..."

He had moved out on to the towpath, and, with my eyes

now used to the darkness, I could make him out. A little weasel of a man, with bent shoulders, and a narrow, pointed face under a straggle of hair. No one I had ever seen.

I gave a gasp of relief. "You're not the King's men! Who are you, then? What do you want here?"

The weaselly man stopped rooting in my bag, and stared.

"That's no concern of yours," said the big man who held me. "We'll ask the questions. Why should you be so scared of the King's men? You know them all, eh?"

"Of course I do. I live in the palace. I'm—a slave there."

"Marric"—it was the Weasel, sharply—"look over there, there's a fire started. They're buzzing like a wasp's nest. No point in wasting time here over a runaway slave-brat. Slit his throat and let's run for it while we can."

"A moment," said the big man. "He may know something. Look now, you—"

"If you're going to slit my throat anyway," I said, "why should I tell you anything? *Who are you?*"

He ducked his head forward suddenly, peering at me. "Crowing mighty fine all of a sudden aren't you? Never mind who *we* are. A slave, eh? Running away?"

"Yes."

"Been stealing?"

"No."

"No? The jewelry in the bundle? And this—this isn't a slave's cloak." He tightened his grip on the stuff at my throat till I squirmed. "And that pony? Come on, the truth."

"All right." I hoped I sounded sullen and cowed enough for a slave now. "I did take a few things. It's the prince's pony, Myrddin's ... I—I found it straying. Truly, sir. He went out today and he's not back yet. He'll have been thrown, he's a rotten horseman. I—it was a bit of luck—they won't miss it till I'm well away." I plucked at his clothes beseechingly. "Please, sir, let me go. Please! What harm could I do—?"

"Marric, for pity's sake, there's no time." The flames had taken hold now, and were leaping. There was shouting from the palace, and the Weasel pulled at my captor's arm. "The tide's going out fast, and the gods only know if she's there at all, this weather. Listen to the noise—they'll be coming this way any minute."

"They won't," I said. "They'll be too busy putting the fire out to think of anything else. It was well away when I left it."

"When you left it?" Marric hadn't budged; he was staring down at me, and his grip was less fierce. "Did *you* start that fire?"

"Yes."

I had their full attention now, even Weasel's.

"Why?"

"I did it because I hate them. They killed my friend."

"Who did?"

"Camlach and his people. The new King."

There was a short silence. I could see Marric better now. He was a big, burly man, with a bush of black hair, and black eyes that glinted in the fire.

"And," I added, "if I'd stayed, they'd have killed me, too. So I burned the place and ran away. Please let me go now."

"Why should they want to kill you? They'll want to now, of course, with the place going up like a torch—but why, before that? What had you done?"

"Nothing. But I was the old King's slave, and . . . I suppose I heard things. Slaves hear everything. Camlach thinks I might be dangerous . . . He has plans . . . I knew about them. Believe me, sir," I said earnestly, "I'd have served him as well as I did the old King, but then he killed my friend."

"What friend? And why?"

"Another slave, a Saxon, his name was Cerdic. He spilled oil on the steps, and the old King fell. It was an accident, but they cut his throat."

Marric turned his head to the other. "Hear that, Hanno? That's true enough. I heard it in the town." Then back to me: "All right. Now you can tell us a bit more. You say you know Camlach's plans?"

But Hanno interrupted again, this time desperately. "Marric, for pity's sake! If you think he's got something to tell us, bring him along. He can talk in the boat, can't he? I tell you, if we wait much longer we'll lose the tide, and she'll be gone. There's dirty weather coming by the feel of it, and it's my guess that they won't wait." And then in Breton: "We can as easy ditch him later as now."

"Boat?" I said. "You're going on the river?"

"Where else? Do you think we can go by road? Look at the bridge." Marric jerked his head sideways. "All right, Hanno. Get in. We'll go."

He began to drag me across the towpath. I hung back. "Where are you taking me?"

"That's our affair. Can you swim?"

"No."

He laughed under his breath. It was not a reassuring sound. "Then it won't matter to you which way we go, will it? Come along." And he clapped his hand once more over my mouth, swung me up as if I had been no heavier than my own bundle, and strode across the path to the oily dark glimmer that was the river.

The boat was a coracle, half hidden under the hanging bank. Hanno was already casting off. Marric went down the bank with a bump and a slither, dumped me in the lurching vessel, and clambered after me. As the coracle rocked out from under the bank he let me feel the knife again against the back of my neck. "There. Feel it? Now hold your tongue till we're clear of the bridge."

Hanno thrust off, and guided us out with the paddle into the current. A few feet from the bank I felt the river take hold of the boat, and we gathered speed. Hanno bent to the paddle and held her straight for the southern arch of the bridge.

Held in Marric's grip, I sat facing astern. Just as the current took us to sweep us southwards I heard Aster's high, frightened whinny as he smelt the smoke, and in the light of the now roaring fire I saw him, trailing a broken rein, burst from the wall's shadow and scud like a ghost along the towpath. Fire or no fire, he would make for the gate and his stable, and they would find him. I wondered what they would think, where they would look for me. Cerdic would be gone now, and my room with the painted chest, and the coverlet fit for a prince. Would they think I had found Cerdic's body, and in my fear and shock had dropped the lamp? That my own body was there, charred to nothing, in the remains of the servants' wing? Well, whatever they thought, it didn't matter. Cerdic had gone to his gods, and I, it seemed, was going to mine.

12

The black arch of the bridge swooped across the boat, and was gone. We fled downstream. The tide was almost on the turn, but the last of the ebb took us fast. The air freshened, and the boat began to rock.

The knife withdrew from my flesh. Across me Marric said:

"Well, so far so good. The brat did us a good turn with his fire. No one was watching the river to see a boat slip under the bridge. Now, boy, let's hear what you have to tell us. What's your name?"

"Myrddin Emrys."

"And you say you were—hey, wait a minute! Did you say Myrddin? Not the bastard?"

"Yes."

He let out a long whistling breath, and Hanno's paddle checked, to dip again hurriedly as the coracle swung and rocked across the current. "You heard that, Hanno? It's the bastard. Then why in the name of the spirits of lower earth did you tell us you were a slave?"

"I didn't know who you were. You hadn't recognized me, so I thought if you were thieves yourselves, or Vortigern's men, you'd let me go."

"Bag, pony, and all . . . So it was true you were running away? Well," he added thoughtfully, "if all tales be true, you're not much to be blamed for that. But why set the place on fire?"

"That was true, too. I told you. Camlach killed a friend of mine, Cerdic the Saxon, though he had done nothing to deserve it. I think they only killed him because he was mine and they meant to use his death against me. They put his body in my room for me to find. So I burnt the room. His people like to go to their gods like that."

"And the devil take anyone else in the palace?"

I said indifferently: "The servants' wing was empty. They were all at supper, or out looking for me, or serving Camlach. It's surprising—or perhaps it isn't—how quickly people can switch over. I expect they'll put the fire out before it reaches the King's apartments."

He regarded me in silence for a minute. We were still racing with the turning tide, well out in the estuary now. Hanno gave no sign of steering to the further bank. I pulled my cloak closer round me and shivered.

"Who were you running to?" asked Marric.

"Nobody."

"Look, boy, I want the truth, or bastard prince or not, you'll go over the side now. Hear me? You'd not last a week if you hadn't someone to go to, to take service with. Who did you have in mind? Vortigern?"

"It would be sensible, wouldn't it? Camlach's going with Vortimer."

"He's what?" His voice sharpened. "Are you sure?"

"Quite sure. He was playing with the idea before, and he quarrelled with the old King about it. He and his lot would have gone anyway, I think. Now, of course, he can take the whole kingdom with him, and shut it against Vortigern."

"And open it for who else?"

"I didn't hear that. Who is there? You can imagine, he wasn't being very open about it until tonight, when his father the King lay dead."

"Hm." He thought for a minute. "The old King leaves another son. If the nobles don't want this alliance—"

"A baby? Aren't you being a bit simple? Camlach's had a good example in front of him; Vortimer wouldn't be where he is if his father hadn't done just what Camlach will do."

"And that is?"

"You know as well as I do. Look, why should I say any more till I know who you are? Isn't it time you told me?"

He ignored that. He sounded thoughtful. "You seem to know a lot about it. How old are you?"

"Twelve. I'll be thirteen in September. But I don't need to be clever to know about Camlach and Vortimer. I heard him say so himself."

"Did you, by the Bull? And what else did you hear?"

"Quite a lot. I was always underfoot. Nobody took any notice of me. But my mother's going into retirement now at St. Peter's, and I wouldn't give you a fig for my chances, so I cleared out."

"To Vortigern?"

I said, honestly: "I've no idea. I—I have no plans. It might have to be Vortigern in the end. What choice is there but him, and the Saxon wolves hanging at our throats for all time till they've torn Britain piecemeal and swallowed her? Who else is there?"

"Well," said Marric, "Ambrosius."

I laughed. "Oh, yes, Ambrosius. I thought you were serious. I know you're from Less Britain, I can tell by your voices, but—"

"You asked who we were. We are Ambrosius' men."

There was a silence. I realized that the river banks had disappeared. Far off in the darkness to the north a light showed; the lighthouse. Some time back the rain had slackened and stopped. Now it was cold, with the wind off shore, and the water was choppy. The boat pitched and swung, and I felt the first qualm of sickness. I clutched my hands hard against my belly, against the cold as much as the sickness, and said sharply: "Ambrosius' men? Then you're spies? His spies?"

"Call us loyal men."

"Then it's true? It's true he's waiting in Less Britain?"

"Aye, it's true."

I said, aghast: "Then that's where you're going? You can't imagine you can get there in this horrible boat?"

Marric laughed, and Hanno said sourly, "We might have to, at that, if the ship's not there."

"What ship would be there in winter?" I demanded. "It's not sailing weather."

"It's sailing weather if you pay enough," said Marric dryly. "Ambrosius pays. The ship will be there." His big hand dropped on my shoulder, not ungently. "Never mind that, there's still things I want to know."

I curled up, hugging my belly, trying to take big breaths of the cold clear air. "Oh, yes, there's a lot I could tell you. But if you're going to drop me overboard anyway, I've nothing to lose, have I? I might as well keep the rest of my information to myself—or see if Ambrosius will pay for it. And there's your ship. Look; if you can't see it yet, you must be blind. Now don't talk to me any more, I feel sick."

I heard him laugh again under his breath. "You're a cool one, and no mistake. Aye, there's the ship, I can see her clearly enough now. Well, seeing who you are, we'll take you aboard. And I'll tell you the other reason; I liked what you said about your friend. That sounded true enough. So you can be loyal, eh? And you've no call to be loyal to Camlach, by all accounts, or to Vortigern. Could you be loyal to Ambrosius?"

"I'll know when I see him."

His fist sent me sprawling to the bottom of the boat. "Princeling or not, keep a civil tongue in your head when you speak of him. There's many a hundred men think of him as their King, rightwise born."

I picked myself up, retching. A low hail came from near at hand, and in a moment we were rocking in the deeper shadow of the ship.

"If he's a man, that'll be enough," I said.

The ship was small, compact and low in the water. She lay there, unlighted, a shadow on the dark sea. I could just see the rake of her mast swaying—sickeningly, it seemed to me—against the scudding cloud that was only a little lighter than the black sky above. She was rigged like the merchantmen who traded in and out of Maridunum in the sailing weather, but I thought she looked cleaner built, and faster.

Marric answered the hail, then a rope snaked down overside, and Hanno caught it and made it fast.

"Come on, you, get moving. You can climb, can't you?"

Somehow, I got to my feet in the swinging coracle. The rope was wet, and jerked in my hands. From above an urgent voice came: "Hurry, will you? We'll be lucky if we get back at all, with the weather that's coming up."

"Get aloft, blast you," said Marric, roughly, giving me a shove. It was all it needed. My hands slipped, nerveless, from the rope, and I fell back into the coracle, landing half across the side, where I hung, gasping and retching, and beyond caring what fate overtook me or even a dozen kingdoms. If I had been stabbed or thrown into the sea at that point I doubt if I would even have noticed, except to welcome death as a relief. I simply hung there over the boat's side like a lump of sodden rags, vomiting.

I have very little recollection of what happened then. There was a good deal of cursing, and I think I remember Hanno urgently recommending Marric to cut his losses and throw me overboard; but I was picked up bodily and, somehow, slung up and into the waiting hands above. Then someone half-carried, half-dragged me below, and dropped me on a pile of bedding with a bucket to hand and the air from an open port blowing on my sweating face.

I believe the journey took four days. Rough weather there certainly was, but at least it was behind us, and we made spanking speed. I stayed below the whole time, huddled thankfully in the blankets under the port-hole, hardly venturing to lift my head. The worst of the sickness abated after a time, but I doubt if I could have moved, and mercifully no one tried to make me.

Marric came down once. I remember it vaguely, as if it were a dream. He picked his way in over a pile of old anchor chain to where I lay, and stood, his big form stooping, peering down at me. Then he shook his head. "And to think I thought we'd done ourselves a good turn, picking you up. We should have thrown you over the side in the first place, and saved a lot of trouble. I reckon you haven't very much more to tell us, anyway?"

I made no reply.

He gave a queer little grunt that sounded like a laugh, and went out. I went to sleep, exhausted.

When I woke, I found that my wet cloak, sandals and tunic had been removed, and that, dry and naked, I was cocooned deep in blankets. Near my head was a water jar, its mouth stoppered with a twist of rag, and a hunk of barley bread.

I couldn't have touched either, but I got the message. I slept.

Then one day shortly before dusk, we came in sight of the Wild Coast, and dropped anchor in the calm waters of Morbihan that men call the Small Sea.

BOOK II

THE FALCON

1

The first I knew of our coming to shore was being roused, still heavy with that exhausted sleep, by voices talking over me.

"Well, all right, if you believe him, but do you really think even a bastard prince would be abroad in those clothes? Everything soaking, not even a gilt clasp to his belt, and look at his sandals. I grant you it's a good cloak, but it's torn. More likely the first story was true, and he's a slave running away with his master's things."

It was, of course, Hanno's voice, and he was talking in Breton. Luckily I had my back to them, curled up in the welter of blankets. It was easy to pretend to be asleep. I lay still, and tried to keep my breathing even.

"No, it's the bastard all right; I've seen him in the town. I'd have known him sooner if we'd been able to show a light." The deeper voice was Marric's. "In any case it would hardly matter who he was; slave or royal bastard, he's been privy to a lot in that palace that Ambrosius will want to listen to. And he's a bright lad; oh, yes, he's what he says he is. You don't learn those cool ways and that kind of talking in the kitchens."

"Well, but . . ." The change in Hanno's voice made my skin shift on my bones. I kept very still.

"Well but what?"

The Weasel dropped his voice still further. "Maybe if we made him talk to us first . . . I mean, look at it this way. All that stuff he told us, hearing what King Camlach meant to do and all that. . . . If we'd got that information for ourselves and got away to report it, there'd be a fat purse for us, wouldn't there?"

Marric grunted. "And then when he gets ashore and tells someone where he comes from? Ambrosius would hear. He hears everything."

"Are you trying to be simple?" The question was waspish.

It was all I could do to keep still. There was a space

between my shoulder-blades where the skin tightened cold over the flesh as if it already felt the knife.

"Oh, I'm not as simple as that. I get you. But I don't see that it—"

"Nobody in Maridunum knows where he went." Hanno's whisper was hurried and eager. "As for the men who saw him come on board, they'll think we've taken him off with us now. In fact, that's what we'll do, take him with us now, and there are plenty of places between here and the town..." I heard him swallow. "I told you before we put out, it's senseless to have spent the money on his passage—"

"If we were going to get rid of him," said Marric bluntly, "we'd have done better not to have paid his passage at all. Have a bit of sense, we'll get the money back now in any case, and maybe a good bit over."

"How do you make that out?"

"Well, if the boy has got information, Ambrosius'll pay the passage, you can be sure of that. Then if it turns out he is the bastard—and I'm certain he is—there might be extra in it for us. Kings' sons—or grandsons—come in useful, as who should know better than Ambrosius?"

"Ambrosius must know the boy's useless as a hostage." Hanno sounded sullen.

"Who's to tell? And if he's no use either way to Ambrosius, then we keep the boy and sell him and split the proceeds. So leave it be, I tell you. Alive, he might be worth something; dead, he's worth nothing at all, and we might find ourselves out of pocket over his passage."

I felt Hanno's toe prodding me, not gently. "Doesn't look worth much either way at the moment. Ever know anyone so sick? He must have a stomach like a girl. Do you even suppose he can walk?"

"We can find out," said Marric, and shook me. "Here, boy, get up."

I groaned, rolled over slowly, and showed them what I hoped was a wretchedly pale face. "What is it? Are we there?" I asked it in Welsh.

"Yes, we're there. Come on now, get to your feet, we're going ashore."

I groaned again, more dismally than before, and clutched my belly. "Oh, God, no, leave me alone."

"A bucket of sea water," suggested Hanno.

Marric straightened. "There's hardly time." He spoke in Breton again. "He looks as if we'd have to carry him. No, we'll have to leave him; we've got to get straight to the Count. It's the night of the meeting, remember? He'll already know the ship's docked, and he'll be expecting to see us before he has to leave. We'd better get the report straight to him, or there'll be trouble. We'll leave the boy here for the time being. We can lock him up and tell the watch to keep an eye on him. We can be back well before midnight."

"You can, you mean," said Hanno sourly. "I've got something that won't wait."

"Ambrosius won't wait, either, so if you want the money for that, you'd better come. They've half finished unloading already. Who's on watch?"

Hanno said something, but the creak of the heavy door as they pulled it shut behind them, and then the thudding of the bars dropping into their sockets drowned the reply. I heard the wedges go in, then lost the sound of their voices and footsteps in the noises of the off-loading operation that was shaking the ship—the creak of winches, the shouts of men above me and a few yards away on shore, the hiss and squeak of running hawsers, and the thud of loads being lifted and swung overside on to the wharf.

I threw the blankets off and sat up. With the ceasing of the dreadful motion of the ship I felt steady again—even well, with a sort of light and purged emptiness that gave me a strange feeling of well-being, a floating, slightly unreal sensation, like the power one has in dreams. I knelt up on the bedding and looked about me.

They had lanterns on the wharf to work by, and light from these fell through the small square port-hole. It showed me the wide-mouthed jar, still in place, and a new hunk of barley bread. I unstoppered the jar and tasted the water cautiously. It was musty, tasting of the rag, but good enough, and it cleared the metallic sickness from my mouth. The bread was iron-hard, but I soused it in water until I could break off a piece to chew. Then I got up, and levered myself up to look out of the port-hole.

To do this I had to reach for the sill and pull myself up by my hands, finding a hold for my toes on one of the struts that lined the bulkhead. I had guessed by the shape of my prison that the hold was in the bows, and I now saw that this was correct. The ship lay alongside a stone-built wharf where a couple of lanterns hung on posts, and by their light some twenty men—soldiers—were working to bring the bales and loaded crates off the ship. To the back of the wharf was a row of solid-looking buildings, presumably for storage, but tonight it looked as if the merchandise were bound elsewhere. Carts waited beyond the lamp posts, the hitched mules patient. The men with the carts were in uniform, and armed, and there was an officer superintending the unloading.

The ship was moored close to the wharf amidships, where the gang-plank was. Her forward hawser ran from the rail above my head to the wharf, and this had allowed the bow to swing out from land, so that between me and the shore lay about fifteen feet of water. There were no lights at this end of the ship; the rope ran down into a comfortable pool of darkness, and beyond that was the deeper darkness of the buildings. But I would have to wait, I decided, till the unloading was finished, and the carts—and presumably the soldiers with them—moved off. There would be time later to escape, with only the watch on board, and perhaps even the lanterns gone from the wharf.

For of course I must escape. If I stayed where I was, my only hope of safety lay in Marric's goodwill, and this in its turn depended on the outcome of his interview with Ambrosius. And if for some reason Marric could not come back, and Hanno came instead . . .

Besides, I was hungry. The water and the hideous snack of soaked bread had set the juices churning in a ferociously empty belly, and the prospect of waiting two or three hours before anyone came back for me was intolerable, even without the fear of what that return might bring. And even if the best should happen, and Ambrosius send for me, I could not be too sure of my fate at his hands once he had all the information I could give him. Despite the bluff which had saved my life from the spies, this information was scanty enough, and Hanno had been right in guessing—and Ambrosius would know it—that I was useless as a hostage. My semi-royal status might impress Marric and Hanno, but neither being grandson to Vortigern's ally, nor nephew to Vortimer's, would be much of a recommendation to Ambrosius' kindness. It looked as if, royal or not, my lot would with luck be slavery, and without it, an unsung death.

And this I had no intention of waiting for. Not while the port-hole stood open, and the hawser ran, sagging only slightly, from just above me to the bollard on the wharf. The two spies, I supposed, were so little accustomed to dealing with prisoners of my size that they had not even given a thought

to the port-hole. No man, not even the weaselly Hanno,
could have attempted escape that way, but a slim boy could.
Even if they had thought of it, they knew I could not swim,
and they had not reckoned with the rope. But, eyeing it
carefully as I hung there in the port-hole, I thought I could
manage it. If the rats could go along it—I could see one
now, a huge fat fellow, sleek with scraps, creeping down
towards the shore—then so could I.

But I would have to wait. Meanwhile, it was cold, and I
was naked. I dropped lightly back into the hold, and turned
to hunt for my clothes.

The light from the shore was dim but sufficient. It showed
me the small cage of my prison with the blankets tumbled on
the pile of old sacks that had been my bed; a warped and
splitting sea-chest against a bulkhead; a pile of rusty chain
too heavy for me to shift; the water jar, and in the far
corner—"far" meaning two paces away—the vile bucket still
half-full of vomit. It showed me nothing else. It may have
been a kindly impulse which had made Marric strip me of
my sodden clothes, but either he had forgotten to return
them, or they had been kept back to prevent me from doing
this very thing.

Five seconds showed me that the chest contained nothing
but some writing tablets, a bronze cup, and some leather
sandal-thongs. At least, I thought, letting the lid down gently
on this unpromising collection, they had left me my sandals.
Not that I wasn't used to going barefoot, but not in winter,
not on the roads. ... For, naked or not, I had still to escape.
Marric's very precautions made me more than ever anxious
to get away.

What I would do, where I would go, I had no idea, but the
god had sent me safely out of Camlach's hands and across
the Narrow Sea, and I trusted my fate. As far as I had a
plan I intended to get near enough to Ambrosius to judge
what kind of man this was, then, if I thought there was
patronage there, or even only mercy, I could approach him
and offer him my story and my services. It never entered my
head that there might be anything absurd about asking a
prince to employ a twelve-year-old. I suppose that to this
extent at least, I was royal. Failing Ambrosius' service, I
believe I had some hazy idea of making my way to the
village north of Kerrec where Moravik came from, and
asking for her people.

The sacks I had been lying on were oldish, and beginning

to rot. It was easy enough to tear one of them open at the seams for my head and arms to go through. It made a dreadful garment, but it covered me after a fashion. I ripped a second one, and pulled that over my head as well, for warmth. A third would be too bulky. I fingered the blankets longingly, but they were good ones, too thick to tear, and would have been impossibly hampering on my climb out of the ship. Reluctantly, I let them lie. A couple of the leather thongs, knotted together, made a girdle. I stuffed the remaining lump of barley bread into the front of my sack, swilled my face, hands, and hair with the rest of the water, then went again to the port-hole and pulled myself up to look out.

While I was dressing I heard shouts and the tramp of feet, as if the men had been formed up ready to march. I now saw that this had indeed happened. Men and carts were moving off. The last of the carts, heavily loaded, was just creaking away past the buildings with the whip cracking over the straining mules. With them went the tramp of marching feet. I wondered what the cargo was; hardly grain at that time of year; more likely, I thought, metal or ore, to be unloaded by troops and sent to the town under guard. The sounds receded. I looked carefully round. The lanterns still hung from the posts, but as far as I could see the wharf was deserted. It was time to go, before the watch decided to come forward to check on the prisoner.

For an active boy, it was easy. I was soon sitting astride the sill of the port-hole, with my body outside and my legs gripping the bulkhead while I reached up for the rope. There was a bad moment when I found I could not reach it, and would have to stand, holding myself somehow against the hull of the ship, above the black depths between ship and wharf where the oily water lapped and sucked, rustling its drifts of refuse against the dripping walls. But I managed it, clawing up the ship's side as if I had been another of the shoregoing rats, till at last I could stretch upright and grasp the hawser. This was taut and dry, and went down at a gentle angle towards the bollard on the wharf. I gripped it with both hands, twisted to face outwards, then swung my legs free of the ship and up over the rope.

I had meant to let myself down gently, hand over hand, to land in the shadows, but what I hadn't reckoned on, being no seaman, was the waterborne lightness of a small ship. Even my slender weight, as I hitched myself down the rope, made her curtsy, sharply and disconcertingly, and then, tilting, swing her bow suddenly in towards the wharf. The hawser sagged, slackened, drooped under my weight as the strain was loosed, then went down into a loop. Where I swung, clinging like a monkey, it suddenly hung vertical. My feet lost their grip and slid away from me; my hands could not hold my weight. I went down the ship's side on that hawser like a bead on a string.

If the ship had swung more slowly I would have been crushed as she ground against the wharf-side, or drowned as I reached the bottom of the loop, but she went like a horse shying. As she jarred the edge of the wharf I was just above it, and the jerk loosened what was left of my grip and flung me clear. I missed the bollard by inches, and landed sprawling on the frost-hard ground in the shadow of a wall.

2

There was no time to wonder whether I was hurt. I could hear the slap of bare feet on the deck above me as the watch raced along to see what had happened. I bunched, rolled, and was on my feet and running before his bobbing lantern reached the side. I heard him shout something, but I had already dodged round the corner of the buildings, and was sure he had not seen me. Even if he had, I thought I was safe enough. He would check my prison first, and even then I doubted if he would dare leave the ship. I leaned for a moment or two against the wall, hugging the rope burns on my hands, and trying to adjust my eyes to the night.

Since I had come from near-darkness in my prison, this took no more than a few seconds, and I looked quickly about me to get my bearings.

The shed that hid me was the end one of the row, and behind it—on the side away from the wharf—was the road, a straight ribbon of gravel, making for a cluster of lights some distance away. This no doubt was the town. Nearer, just where the road was swallowed by darkness, was a dim and shifting gleam, which must be the tail light of the last wagon. Nothing else moved.

It was a fairly safe guess that any wagons so guarded were bound for Ambrosius' headquarters. I had no idea whether I could get to him, or even into any town or village, but all I wanted at this stage was to find something to eat, and somewhere warm where I could hide and eat it, and wait for daylight. Once I got my bearings, no doubt the god would lead me still.

He would also have to feed me. I had originally meant to sell one of my brooches for food, but now, I thought, as I jogged in the wake of the wagons, I would have to steal something. At the very worst, I still had a hunk of barley bread. Then somewhere to hide until daylight. . . . If Ambrosius was at "a meeting," as Marric had said, it would be worse than useless to go to his headquarters and ask to see him now. Whatever my sense of my own importance, it did not stretch to privileged treatment by Ambrosius' soldiers if I turned up dressed like this in his absence. Come daylight, we should see.

It was cold. My breath puffed, grey on the black and icy air. There was no moon, but the stars were out like wolves' eyes, glaring. Frost glittered on the stones of the road, and rang under the hoofs and wheels ahead of me. Mercifully there was no wind, and my blood warmed with running, but I dared not catch up with the convoy, which went slowly, so that from time to time I had to check and hang back, while the freezing air bit through the ragged sacks and I flailed my arms against my body for warmth.

Fortunately there was plenty of cover; bushes, sometimes in crouching clusters, sometimes singly, hunched as they had frozen in the path of the prevailing wind, still reaching after it with stiff fingers. Among them great stones stood, rearing sharp against the stars. I took the first of these for a huge milestone, but then saw others, in ranks, thrusting from the turf like storm-blasted avenues of trees. Or like colonnades where gods walked—but not gods that I knew. The starlight struck the face of the stone where I had paused to wait, and something caught my eye, a shape rudely carved in the granite, and etched by the cold light like lampblack. An axe, two-headed. The standing stones stretched away from me into darkness like a march of giants. A dry thistle, broken down to the stalk, stabbed my bare leg. As I turned away I glanced at the axe again. It had vanished.

I ran back to the road, clamping my teeth against the shivering. It was the cold, of course, that made me shiver; what else? The wagons had drawn ahead again, and I ran after, keeping to the turf at the road's edge, though this in fact seemed as hard as the gravel. The frost broke and squeaked under my sandals. Behind me the silent army of stones marched dwindling into the dark, and before me now were the lights of a town and the warmth of its houses reaching out to meet me. I think it was the first time that I, Merlin, had run towards light and company, run from solitude as if it were a ring of wolves' eyes driving one nearer the fire.

It was a walled town. I should have guessed it, so near the sea. There was a high earthwork and above that a palisade, and the ditch outside the earthwork was wide and white with ice. They had smashed the ice at intervals, so that it would not bear; I could see the black stars and the crisscross map of cracks just skinning over with grey glass as the new ice formed. There was a wooden bridge across to the gate, and here the wagons halted, while the officer rode forward to speak to the guards, and the men stood like rocks while the mules stamped and blew and jingled their harness, eager for the warmth of the stable.

If I had had any idea of jumping on the back of a wagon and being carried in that way, I had had to abandon it. All the way to the town the soldiers had been strung out in a file to either side of the convoy, with the officer riding out to one side where he could scan the whole. Now, as he gave the order to advance and break step for the bridge, he wheeled his horse and rode back himself to the tail of the column, to see the last cart in. I caught a glimpse of his face, middle-aged, bad-tempered and catarrhal with cold. Not the man to listen patiently, or even to listen at all. I was safer outside with the stars and the marching giants.

The gate thudded shut behind the convoy, and I heard the locks drive home.

There was a path, faintly discernible, leading off eastward along the edge of the ditch. When I looked that way I saw that, some way off, so far that they must mark some kind of settlement or farm well beyond the limits of the town, more lights showed.

I turned along the path at a trot, chewing at my chunk of barley bread as I went.

The lights turned out to belong to a fair-sized house whose buildings enclosed a courtyard. The house itself, two storeys high, made one wall of the yard, which was bounded on the other three sides by single-storey buildings—baths, servants' quarters, stables, bakehouse—the whole enclosure high-walled and showing only a few slit windows well beyond my reach. There was an arched gateway, and beside this in an iron bracket set at the height of a man's reach, a torch spluttered, sulky with damp pitch. There were more lights inside the yard, but I could hear no movement or voices. The gate, of course, was shut fast.

Not that I would have dared go in that way, to meet some summary fate at the porter's hands. I skirted the wall, looking hopefully for a way to climb in. The third window was the bakehouse; the smells were hours old, and cold, but still would have sent me swarming up the wall, save that the window was a bare slit which would not have admitted even me.

The next was a stable, and the next also. . . . I could smell the horse-smells and beast-smells mingling, and the sweetness of dried grass. Then the house, with no windows at all facing outwards. The bathhouse, the same. And back to the gate.

A chain clanged suddenly, and within a few feet of me, just inside the gate, a big dog gave tongue like a bell. I believe I jumped back a full pace, then flattened myself against the wall as I heard a door open somewhere close. There was a pause, while the dog growled and someone listened, then a man's voice said something curt, and the door shut. The dog grumbled to itself for a bit, snuffling at the foot of the gate, then dragged its chain back to the kennel, and I heard it settling again into its straw.

There was obviously no way in to find shelter. I stood for a while, trying to think, with my back pressed to the cold wall that still seemed warmer than the icy air. I was shaking so violently now with the cold that I felt as if my very bones were chattering. I was sure I had been right to leave the ship, and not to trust myself to the troops' mercy, but now I began to wonder if I dared knock at the gate and beg for shelter. I would get rough shrift as a beggar, I knew, but if I stayed out here I might well die of cold before morning.

Then I saw, just beyond the torchlight's reach, the low black shape of a building that must be a cattle shed or shippon, some twenty paces away and at the corner of a field surrounded by low banks crowned with thorn bushes. I could hear cattle moving there. At least there would be their warmth to share, and if I could force my chattering teeth through it, I still had a heel of barley bread.

I had taken a pace away from the wall, moving, I could have sworn, without a sound, when the dog came out of his kennel with a rush and a rattle, and set up his infernal baying again. This time the house door opened immediately, and I heard a man's step in the yard. He was coming towards the gate. I heard the rasp of metal as he drew some weapon. I was just turning to run when I heard, clear and sharp on the frosty air, what the dog had heard. The sound of hoofs, full gallop, coming this way.

Quick as a shadow, I ran across the open ground towards the shed. Beside it a gap in the bank made a gateway, which had been blocked with a dead thorn-tree. I shoved through this, then crept—as quietly as I could, not to disturb the beasts—to crouch in the shed doorway, out of sight of the house gate.

The shed was only a small, roughly built shelter, with walls not much more than man-height, thatched over, and crowded with beasts. These seemed to be young bullocks for the most part, too thronged to lie down, but seemingly content enough with each other's warmth, and some dry fodder to chew over. A rough plank across the doorway made a barrier to keep them in. Outside, the field stretched empty in the starlight, grey with frost, and bounded with its low banks ridged with those hunched and crippled bushes. In the center of the field was one of the standing stones.

Inside the gateway, I heard the man speak to silence the dog. The sound of hoofs swelled, hammering up the iron track, then suddenly the rider was on us, sweeping out of the dark and pulling his horse up with a scream of metal on stone and a flurry of gravel and frozen turf, and the thud of the beast's hoofs right up against the wood of the gate. The man inside shouted something, a question, and the rider answered him even in the act of flinging himself down from the saddle.

"Of course it is. Open up, will you?"

I heard the door grate as it was dragged open, then the two men talking, but apart from a word here and there, could not distinguish what they said. It seemed, from the movement of the light, that the porter (or whoever had come to the gate) had lifted the torch down from its socket. Moreover, the light was moving this way, and both men with it, leading the horse.

I heard the rider say, impatiently: "Oh, yes, it'll be well enough here. If it comes to that, it will suit me to have a quick getaway. There's fodder there?"

"Aye, sir. I put the young beasts out here to make room for the horses."

"There's a crowd, then?" The voice was young, clear, a little harsh, but that might only be cold and arrogance combined. A patrician voice, careless as the horsemanship that had all but brought the horse down on its haunches in front of the gate.

"A fair number," said the porter. "Mind now, sir, it's through this gap. If you'll let me go first with the light . . ."

"I can see," said the young man irritably, "if you don't shove the torch right in my face. Hold up, you." This to the horse as it pecked at a stone.

"You'd best let me go first, sir. There's a thorn bush across the gap to keep them in. If you'll stand clear a minute, I'll shift it."

I had already melted out of the shed doorway and round the corner, where the rough wall met the field embankment. There were turfs stacked here, and a pile of brushwood and dried bracken that I supposed were winter bedding. I crouched down behind the stack.

I heard the thorn-tree being lifted and flung aside. "There, sir, bring him through. There's not much room, but if you're sure you'd as soon leave him out here—"

"I said it would do. Shift the plank and get him in. Hurry, man, I'm late."

"If you leave him with me now, sir, I'll unsaddle for you."

"No need. He'll be well enough for an hour or two. Just loosen the girth. I suppose I'd better throw my cloak over him. Gods, it's cold . . . Get the bridle off, will you? I'm getting in out of this . . ."

I heard him stride away, spurs clinking. The plank went back into place, and then the thorn-tree. As the porter hurried after him I caught something that sounded like, "And let me in at the back, where the father won't see me."

The big gate shut behind them. The chain rattled, but the dog stayed silent. I heard the men's steps crossing the yard, then the house door shut on them.

3

Even if I had dared to risk the torchlight and the dog, to scramble over the bank behind me and run the twenty paces to the gate, there would have been no need. The god had done his part; he had sent me warmth and, I discovered, food.

No sooner had the gate shut than I was back inside the shippon, whispering reassurance to the horse as I reached to rob him of the cloak. He was not sweating much; he must have galloped only the mile or so from the town, and in that shed among the crowded beasts he could take no harm from cold; in any case, my need came before his, and I had to have that cloak. It was an officer's cloak, thick, soft, and good. As I laid hold of it I found, to my excitement, that my lord had left me not only his cloak, but a full saddle-bag as well. I stretched up, tiptoe, and felt inside.

A leather flask, which I shook. It was almost full. Wine, certainly; that young man would never carry water. A napkin with biscuits in it, and raisins, and some strips of dried meat.

The beasts jostled, dribbling, and puffed their warm breath at me. The long cloak had slipped to trail a corner in the dirt under their hoofs. I snatched it up, clutched the flask and food to me, and slipped out under the barrier. The pile of brushwood in the corner outside was clean, but I would hardly have cared if it had been a dung-heap. I burrowed into it, wrapped myself warmly in the soft woollen folds, and steadily ate and drank my way through everything the god had sent me.

Whatever happened, I must not sleep. Unfortunately it seemed that the young man would not be here for more than an hour or two; but this with the bonus of food should be time enough to warm me so that I might bed down in comfort till daylight. I would hear movement from the house in time to slip back to the shed and throw the cloak into place. My lord would hardly be likely to notice that his marching rations had gone from his saddle-bag.

I drank some more wine. It was amazing how even the stale ends of the barley bread tasted the better for it. It was good stuff, potent and sweet, and tasting of raisins. It ran warm into my body, till the rigid joints loosened and melted and stopped their shaking, and I could curl up warm and relaxed in my dark nest, with the bracken pulled right up over me to shut out the cold.

I must have slept a little. What woke me I have no idea; there was no sound. Even the beasts in the shed were still.

It seemed darker, so that I wondered if it were almost

dawn, when the stars fade. But when I parted the bracken and peered out I saw they were still there, burning white in the black sky.

The strange thing was, it was warmer. Some wind had risen, and had brought cloud with it, scudding drifts that raced high overhead, then scattered and wisped away so that shadow and starlight broke one after the other like waves across the frost-grey fields and still landscape, where the thistles and stiff winter grasses seemed to flow like water, or like a cornfield under the wind. There was no sound of the wind blowing.

Above the flying veils of cloud the stars were brilliant, studding a black dome. The warmth and my curled posture in the dark must (I thought) have made me dream of security, of Galapas and the crystal globe where I had lain curled, and watched the light. Now the brilliant arch of stars above me was like the curved roof of the cave with the light flashing off the crystals, and the passing shadows flying, chased by the fire. You could see points of red and sapphire, and one star steady, beaming gold. Then the silent wind blew another shadow across the sky with light behind it, and the thorn-trees shivered, and the shadow of the standing stone.

I must be buried too deep and snug in my bed to hear the rustle of the wind through grass and thorn. Nor did I hear the young man pushing his way through the barrier that the porter had replaced across the gap in the bank. For, suddenly, with no warning, he was there, a tall figure, striding across the field, as shadowy and quiet as the wind.

I shrank, like a snail into its shell. Too late now to run and replace the cloak. All I could hope was that he would assume the thief had fled, and not search too near. But he did not approach the shed. He was making straight across the field, away from me. Then I saw, half in, half out of the shadow of the standing stone, the white animal grazing. His horse must have broken loose. The gods alone knew what it found to eat in that winter field, but I could see it, ghostly in the distance, the white beast grazing beside the standing stone. And it must have rubbed the girth till it snapped; its saddle, too, was gone.

At least in the time he would take to catch it, I should be able to get away ... or better still, drop the cloak near the shed, where he would think it had slid from the horse's back, and then get back to my warm nest till he had gone. He could only blame the porter for the animal's escape; and justly; I had not touched the bar across the doorway. I raised myself cautiously, watching my chance.

The grazing animal had lifted its head to watch the man's approach. A cloud swept across the stars, blackening the field. Light ran after the shadow across the frost. It struck the standing stone. I saw that I had been wrong; it was not the horse. Nor—my next thought—could it be one of the young beasts from the shed. This was a bull, a massive white bull, full-grown, with a royal spread of horns and a neck like a thunder-cloud. It lowered its head till the dewlap brushed the ground, and pawed once, twice.

The young man paused. I saw him now, clearly, as the shadow lifted. He was tall and strongly built, and his hair looked bleached in the starlight. He wore some sort of foreign dress—trousers cross-bound with thongs below a tunic girded low on the hips, and a high loose cap. Under this the fair hair blew round his face like rays. There was a rope in his hand, held loosely, its coils brushing the frost. His cloak flew in the wind; a short cloak, of some dark colour I could not make out.

His cloak? Then it could not be my young lord. And after all, why should that arrogant young man come with a rope to catch a bull that had strayed in the night?

Without warning, and without a sound, the white bull charged. Shadow and light rushed with it, flickering, blurring the scene. The rope whirled, snaked into a loop, settled. The man leapt to one side as the great beast tore past him and came to a sliding stop with the rope snapping taut and the frost smoking up in clouds from the side-slipping hoofs.

The bull whirled, and charged again. The man waited without moving, his feet planted slightly apart, his posture casual, almost disdainful. As the bull reached him he seemed to sway aside, lightly, like a dancer. The bull went by him so close that I saw a horn shear the swirling cloak, and the beast's shoulder passed the man's thigh like a lover seeking a caress. The man's hands moved. The rope whipped up into a ring, and another loop settled round the royal horns. The man leaned against it, and as the beast came up short once more, turning sharp in its own smoke, the man jumped.

Not away. Towards the bull, clean on to the thick neck, with knees digging into the dewlap, and fierce hands using the rope like reins.

The bull stopped dead, his feet four-square, his head thrust downwards with his whole weight and strength against the rope. There was still no sound that I could hear, no sound of hoof or crack of rope or bellow of breath. I was half out of the brushwood now, rigid and staring, heedless of anything save the fight between man and bull.

A cloud stamped the field again with darkness. I got to my feet. I believe I meant to seize the plank from the shed and rush with it across the field to give what futile help I could. But before I could move the cloud had fled, to show me the bull standing as before, the man still on its neck. But now the beast's head was coming up. The man had dropped the rope, and his two hands were on the bull's horns, dragging them back ... back ... up. ... Slowly, almost as if in a ritual of surrender, the bull's head lifted, the powerful neck stretched up, exposed.

There was a gleam in the man's right hand. He leaned forward, then drove the knife down and across.

Still in silence, slowly, the bull sank to its knees. Black flowed over the white hide, the white ground, the white base of the stone.

I broke from my hiding place and ran, shouting something —I have no idea what—across the field towards them.

I don't know what I meant to do. The man saw me coming, and turned his head, and I saw that nothing was needed. He was smiling, but his face in the starlight seemed curiously smooth and unhuman in its lack of expression. I could see no sign of stress or effort. His eyes were expressionless too, cold and dark, with no smile there.

I stumbled, tried to stop, caught my feet in the trailing cloak, and fell, rolling in a ridiculous and helpless bundle towards him, just as the white bull, slowly heeling over, collapsed. Something struck me on the side of the head. I heard a sharp childish sound which was myself crying out, then it was dark.

4

Someone kicked me again, hard, in the ribs. I grunted and rolled, trying to get out of range, but the cloak hampered me. A torch, stinking with black smoke, was thrust down, almost into my face. The familiar young voice said, angrily: "My cloak, by God! Grab hold of him, you, quick. I'm damned if I touch him, he's filthy."

They were all round me, feet scuffling the frost, torches flaring, men's voices curious, or angry, or indifferently amused. Some were mounted, and their horses skirmished on the edge of the group, stamping and fidgeting with cold.

I crouched, blinking upwards. My head ached, and the flickering scene above me swam unreal, in snatches, as if reality and dream were breaking and dovetailing one across the other to split the senses. Fire, voices, the rocking of a ship, the white bull falling . . .

A hand tore the cloak off me. Some of the rotten sacking went with it, leaving me with a shoulder and side bare to the waist. Someone grabbed my wrist and yanked me to my feet and held me. His other hand took me roughly by the hair, and pulled my head up to face the man who stood over me. He was tall, young, with light brown hair showing reddish in the torchlight, and an elegant beard fringing his chin. His eyes were blue, and looked angry. He was cloakless in the cold. He had a whip in his left hand.

He eyed me, making a sound of disgust. "A beggar's brat, and stinking, at that. I'll have to burn the thing, I suppose. I'll have your hide for this, you bloody little vermin. I suppose you were going to steal my horse as well?"

"No, sir. I swear it was only the cloak. I would have put it back, I promise you."

"And the brooch as well?"

"Brooch?"

The man holding me said: "Your brooch is still in the cloak, my lord."

I said quickly: "I only borrowed it, for warmth—it was so cold, so I—"

"So you just stripped my horse and left him to catch cold? Is that it?"

"I didn't think it would harm him, sir. It was warm in the shed. I would have put it back, really I would."

"For me to wear after you, you stinking little rat? I ought to slit your throat for this."

Someone—one of the mounted men—said: "Oh, leave it. There's no harm done except that your cloak will have to go to the fuller tomorrow. The wretched boy's half naked, and it's cold enough to freeze a salamander. Let him go."

"At least," said the young officer between his teeth, "it will warm me up to thrash him. Ah, no, you don't—hold him fast, Cadal."

The whip whistled back. The man who held me tightened

his grip as I fought to tear free, but before the whip could fall a shadow moved in front of the torchlight and a hand came lightly down, no more than a touch, on the young man's wrist.

Someone said: "What's this?"

The men fell silent, as if at an order. The young man dropped the whip to his side, and turned.

My captor's grip had slackened as the newcomer spoke, and I twisted free. I might possibly have doubled away between the men and horses and run for it, though I suppose a mounted man could have run me down in seconds. But I made no attempt to get away. I was staring.

The newcomer was tall, taller than my cloakless young officer by half a head. He was between me and the torches, and I could not see him well against the flame. The flares swam still, blurred and dazzling; my head hurt, and the cold had sprung back at me like a toothed beast. All I saw was the tall shadowy figure watching me, dark eyes in an expressionless face.

I took a breath like a gasp. "It was you! You saw me, didn't you? I was coming to help you, only I tripped and fell. I wasn't running away—tell him that, please, my lord. I did mean to put the cloak back before he came for it. Please tell him what happened!"

"What are you talking about? Tell him what?"

I blinked against the glare of the torches. "About what happened just now. It was—it was you who killed the bull?"

"Who *what*?"

It had been quiet before, but now there was silence, complete except for the men's breathing as they crowded round, and the fidgeting of the horses.

The young officer said sharply: "What bull?"

"The white bull," I said. "He cut its throat, and the blood splashed out like a spring. That was how I got your cloak dirty. I was trying—"

"How the hell did you know about the bull? Where were you? Who's been talking?"

"Nobody," I said, surprised. "I saw it all. Is it so secret? I thought I must be dreaming at first, I was sleepy after the bread and wine—"

"By the Light!" It was the young officer still, but now the others were exclaiming with him, their anger breaking round me. "Kill him, and have done" . . . "He's lying" . . . "Lying to save his wretched skin" . . . "He must have been spying" . . .

The tall man had not spoken. Nor had he taken his eyes off me. From somewhere, anger poured into me, and I said hotly, straight to him: "I'm not a spy, or a thief! I'm tired of this! What was I to do, freeze to death to save the life of a horse?" The man behind me laid a hand on my arm, but I shook him off with a gesture that my grandfather himself might have used. "Nor am I a beggar, my lord. I'm a free man come to take service with Ambrosius, if he'll have me. That's what I came here for, from my own country, and it was . . . it was an accident that I lost my clothes. I—I may be young, but I have certain knowledge that is valuable, and I speak five languages . . ." My voice faltered. Someone had made a stifled sound like a laugh. I set my chattering teeth and added, royally: "I beg you merely to give me shelter now, my lord, and tell me where I may seek him out in the morning."

This time the silence was so thick you could have cut it. I heard the young officer take breath to speak, but the other put out a hand. He must, by the way they waited for him, be their commander. "Wait. He's not being insolent. Look at him. Hold the torch higher, Lucius. Now, what's your name?"

"Myrddin, sir."

"Well, Myrddin, I'll listen to you, but make it plain and make it quick. I want to hear this about the bull. Start at the beginning. You saw my brother stable his horse in the shed yonder, and you took the cloak off its back for warmth. Go on from there."

"Yes, my lord," I said. "I took the food from the saddle-bag, too, and the wine—"

"You were talking about *my* bread and wine?" demanded the young officer.

"Yes, sir. I'm sorry, but I'd hardly eaten for four days—"

"Never mind that," said the commander curtly. "Go on."

"I hid in the brushwood stack at the corner of the shed, and I think I went to sleep. When I woke I saw the bull, over by the standing stone. He was grazing there, quite quiet. Then you came, with the rope. The bull charged, and you roped it, and then jumped on its back and pulled its head up and killed it with a knife. There was blood everywhere. I was running to help. I don't know what I could have done, but I ran, all the same. Then I tripped over the cloak, and fell. That's all."

I stopped. A horse stamped, and a man cleared his throat.

Nobody spoke. I thought that Cadal, the servant who had held me, moved a little further away.

The commander said, very quietly: "Beside the standing stone?"

"Yes, sir."

He turned his head. The group of men and horses was very near the stone. I could see it behind the horsemen's shoulders, thrusting up torchlit against the night sky.

"Stand aside and let him see," said the tall man, and some of them moved.

The stone was about thirty feet away. Near its base the frosty grass showed scuffled by boots and hoofprints, but no more. Where I had seen the white bull fall, with the black blood gushing from its throat, there was nothing but the scuffled frost, and the shadow of the stone.

The torch-bearer had shifted the torch to throw light towards the stone. Light fell now straight on my questioner, and for the first time I saw him plainly. He was not as young as I had thought; there were lines in his face, and his brows were down, frowning. His eyes were dark, not blue like his brother's, and he was more heavily built than I had supposed. There was a flash of gold at his wrists and collar, and a heavy cloak dropped in a long line from shoulder to heel.

I said, stammering: "It wasn't you. I'm sorry, it—I see now, I must have dreamed it. No one would come with a rope, and a short knife, alone against a bull ... and no man could drag a bull's head up and slit its throat ... it was one of my—it was a dream. And it wasn't you, I can see that now. I—I thought you were the man in the cap. I'm sorry."

The men were muttering now, but no longer with threats. The young officer said, in quite a different tone from any he had used before: "What was he like, this 'man in the cap'?"

His brother said quickly: "Never mind. Not now." He put out a hand, took me by the chin, and lifted my face. "You say your name is Myrddin. Where are you from?"

"From Wales, sir."

"Ah. So you're the boy they brought from Maridunum?"

"Yes. You knew about me? Oh!" Made stupid by the cold and by bewilderment, I made the discovery I should have made long ago. My flesh shivered like a nervous pony's with cold, and a curious sensation, part excitement, part fear. "You must be the Count. You must be Ambrosius himself."

He did not trouble to answer. "How old are you?"

"Twelve, sir."

"And who are you, Myrddin, to talk of offering me service? What can you offer me, that I should not cut you down here and now, and let these gentlemen get in out of the cold?"

"Who I am makes no difference, sir. I am the grandson of the King of South Wales, but he is dead. My uncle Camlach is King now, but that's no help to me either; he wants me dead. So I'd not serve your turn even as a hostage. It's not who I am, but what I am that matters. I have something to offer you, my lord. You will see, if you let me live till morning."

"Ah, yes, valuable information, and five languages. And dreams, too, it seems." The words were mocking, but he was not smiling. "The old King's grandson, you say? And Camlach not your father? Nor Dyved, either, surely? I never knew the old man had a grandson, barring Camlach's baby. From what my spies told me I took you to be his bastard."

"He used sometimes to pass me off as his own bastard—to save my mother's shame, he said, but she never saw it as shame, and she should know. My mother was Niniane, the old King's daughter."

"Ah." A pause. "Was?"

I said: "She's still alive, but by now she's in St. Peter's nunnery. You might say she joined them years ago, but she's only been allowed to leave the palace since the old King died."

"And your father?"

"She never spoke of him, to me or any man. They say he was the Prince of Darkness."

I expected the usual reaction to that, the crossed fingers or the quick look over the shoulder. He did neither. He laughed.

"Then no wonder you talk of helping kings to their kingdoms, and dream of gods under the stars." He turned aside then, with a swirl of the big cloak. "Bring him along, one of you. Uther, you may as well give him your cloak again before he dies in front of our eyes."

"Do you think I'd touch it after him, even if he were the Prince of Darkness in person?" asked Uther.

Ambrosius laughed. "If you ride that poor beast of yours in your usual fashion you'll be warm enough without. And if your cloak is dabbled with the blood of the Bull, then it's not for you, tonight, is it?"

"Are you blaspheming?"

"I?" said Ambrosius, with a sort of cold blankness.

His brother opened his mouth, thought better of it, shrugged, and vaulted into his grey's saddle. Someone flung the cloak to me, and—as I struggled with shaking hands to wrap it round me again—seized me, bundled me up in it anyhow, and threw me up like a parcel to some rider on a wheeling horse. Ambrosius swung to the saddle of a big black.

"Come, gentlemen."

The black stallion jumped forward, and Ambrosius' cloak flew out. The grey pounded after him. The rest of the cavalcade strung out at a hand-gallop along the track back to the town.

5

Ambrosius' headquarters was in the town. I learned later that the town had, in fact, grown up round the camp where Ambrosius and his brother had, during the last couple of years, begun to gather and train the army that had for so long been a mythical threat to Vortigern, and now, with the help of King Budec, and troops from half the countries of Gaul, was growing into a fact. Budec was King of Less Britain, and cousin of Ambrosius and Uther. He it was who had taken the brothers in twenty years ago when they— Ambrosius then ten years old, and Uther still at his nurse's breast—were carried overseas into safety after Vortigern had murdered their elder brother the King. Budec's own castle was barely a stone's throw from the camp that Ambrosius had built, and round the two strongpoints the town had grown up, a mixed collection of houses, shops and huts, with the wall and ditch thrown round for protection. Budec was an old man now, and had made Ambrosius his heir, as well as Comes or Count of his forces. It had been supposed in the past that the brothers would be content to stay in Less Britain and rule it after Budec's death; but now that Vortigern's grip on Greater Britain was slackening, the money and the men were pouring in, and it was an open secret that Ambrosius had his eye on South and West Britain for himself, while Uther—even at twenty a brilliant soldier—would, it was hoped, hold Less Britain, and so for another generation at least provide between the two kingdoms a Romano-Celtic rampart against the barbarians from the north.

I soon found that in one respect Ambrosius was pure Roman. The first thing that happened to me after I was dumped, cloak and all, between the door-posts of his outer hall, was that I was seized, unwrapped, and—exhausted by now beyond protest or question—deposited in a bath. The heating system certainly worked here; the water was steaming hot, and thawed my frozen body in three painful and ecstatic minutes. The man who had carried me home—it was Cadal, who turned out to be one of the Count's personal servants—bathed me himself. Under Ambrosius' own orders, he told me curtly, as he scrubbed and oiled and dried me, and then stood over me as I put on a clean tunic of white wool only two sizes too big.

"Just to make sure you don't bolt again. He wants to talk to you, don't ask me why. You can't wear those sandals in this house, Dia knows where you've been with them. Leastways, it's obvious where you've been with them; cows, was it? You can go barefoot, the floors are warm. Well, at least you're clean now. Hungry?"

"Are you joking?"

"Come along, then. Kitchen's this way. Unless, being a king's grand-bastard, or whatever it was you told him, you're too proud to eat in the kitchen?"

"Just this once," I said, "I'll put up with it."

He shot me a look, scowled, and then grinned. "You've got guts, I'll give you that. You stood up to them a fair treat. Beats me how you thought of all that stuff quick enough. Rocked 'em proper. I wouldn't have given two pins for your chances once Uther laid hands on you. You got yourself a hearing, anyway."

"It was true."

"Oh, sure, sure. Well, you can tell him all over again in a minute, and see you make it good, because he don't like them that wastes his time, see?"

"Tonight?"

"Certainly. You'll find that out if you live till morning; he doesn't waste much time sleeping. Nor does Prince Uther, come to that, but then he's not working, exactly. Not at his papers, that is, though they reckon he puts in a bit of uncommon hard labour in other directions. Come along."

Yards before we reached the kitchen door the smell of hot food came out to meet me, and with it the sound of frying.

The kitchen was a big room, and seemed, to my eye, about as grand as the dining-room at home. The floor was of smooth red tiles, there was a raised hearth at each end of the room, and along the walls the chopping-slabs with store-jars of oil and wine below them and shelves of dishes above. At one of the hearths a sleepy-eyed boy was heating the oil in a skillet; he had kindled fresh charcoal in the burners, and on one of these a pot of soup simmered, while sausages spat and crackled over a grill, and I could smell chicken frying. I noticed that—in spite of Cadal's implied disbelief in my story—I was given a platter of Samian ware so fine that it must be the same used at the Count's own table, and the wine came in a glass goblet and was poured from a glazed red jar with a carved seal and the label "Reserve." There was even a fine white napkin.

The cook-boy—he must have been roused from his bed to make the meal for me—hardly bothered to look who he was working for; after he had dished up the meal he scraped the burners hurriedly clean for morning, did an even sketchier job of scouring his pans, then with a glance at Cadal for permission, went yawning back to bed. Cadal served me himself, and even fetched fresh bread hot from the bake-house, where the first batch had just come out for morning. The soup was some savoury concoction of shellfish, which they eat almost daily in Less Britain. It was smoking hot and delicious, and I thought I had never eaten anything so good, until I tried the chicken, crisp-fried in oil, and the grilled sausages, brown and bursting with spiced meat and onions. I mopped the platter dry with the new bread, and shook my head when Cadal handed a dish of dried dates and cheese and honey cakes.

"No, thank you."

"Enough?"

"Oh, yes." I pushed the platter away. "That was the best meal I ever ate in my life. Thank you."

"Well," he said, "hunger's the best sauce, they say. Though I'll allow the food's good here." He brought fresh water and a towel and waited while I rinsed my hands and dried them. "Well, I might even credit the rest of your story now."

I looked up. "What d'you mean?"

"You didn't learn your manners in a kitchen, that's for sure. Ready? Come along then; he said to interrupt him even if he was working."

Ambrosius, however, was not working when we got to his room. His table—a vast affair of marble from Italy—was indeed littered with rolls and maps and writing materials, and the Count was in his big chair behind it, but he sat half sideways, chin on fist, staring into the brazier which filled the room with warmth and the faint scent of apple-wood.

He did not look up as Cadal spoke to the sentry, and with a clash of arms the latter let me by.

"The boy, sir." This was not the voice Cadal had used to me.

"Thank you. You can go to bed, Cadal."

"Sir."

He went. The leather curtains fell to behind him. Ambrosius turned his head then. He looked me up and down for some minutes in silence. Then he nodded towards a stool.

"Sit down."

I obeyed him.

"I see they found something for you to wear. Have you been fed?"

"Yes, thank you, sir."

"And you're warm enough now? Pull the stool nearer the fire if you want to."

He turned straight in the chair, and leaned back, his hands resting on the carved lions' heads of the arms. There was a lamp on the table between us, and in its bright steady light any resemblance between the Count Ambrosius and the strange man of my dream had vanished completely.

It is difficult now, looking back from this distance in time, to remember my first real impression of Ambrosius. He would be at that time not much more than thirty years old, but I was only twelve, and to me, of course, he already seemed venerable. But I think that in fact he did seem older than his years; this was a natural result of the life he had led, and the heavy responsibility he had borne since he was a little younger than myself. There were lines round his eyes, and two heavy furrows between his brows which spoke of decision and perhaps temper, and his mouth was hard and straight, and usually unsmiling. His brows were dark like his hair, and could bar his eyes formidably with shadow. There was the faint white line of a scar running from his left ear half over his cheekbone. His nose looked Roman, high-bridged and prominent, but his skin was tanned rather than olive, and there was something about his eyes which spoke of black Celt rather than Roman. It was a bleak face, a face (as I would find) that could cloud with frustration or anger, or even with the hard control that he exerted over these, but it was a face to trust. He was not a man one could love easily, certainly not a man to like, but a man either to hate or to worship. You either fought him, or followed him. But it had to be one or the other; once you came within reach of him, you had no peace.

All this I had to learn. I remember little now of what I thought of him, except for the deep eyes watching me past the lamp, and his hands clasped on the lions' heads. But I remember every word that was said.

He looked me up and down. "Myrddin, son of Niniane, daughter of the King of South Wales . . . and privy, they tell me, to the secrets of the palace at Maridunum?"

"I—did I say that? I told them I lived there, and heard things sometimes."

"My men brought you across the Narrow Sea because you said you had secrets which would be useful to me. Was that not true?"

"Sir," I said a little desperately, "I don't know what might be useful to you. To them I spoke the language I thought they would understand. I thought they were going to kill me. I was saving my life."

"I see. Well, now you are here, and safely. Why did you leave your home?"

"Because once my grandfather had died, it was not safe for me there. My mother was going into a nunnery, and Camlach my uncle had already tried to kill me, and his servants killed my friend."

"Your friend?"

"My servant. His name was Cerdic. He was a slave."

"Ah, yes. They told me about that. They said you set fire to the palace. You were perhaps a little—drastic?"

"I suppose so. But someone had to do him honour. He was mine."

His brows went up. "Do you give that as a reason, or as an obligation?"

"Sir?" I puzzled it out, then said, slowly: "Both, I think."

He looked down at his hands. He had moved them from the chair arms, and they were clasped on the table in front of him. "Your mother, the princess." He said it as if the thought sprang straight from what we had been saying. "Did they harm her, too?"

"Of course not!"

He looked up at my tone. I explained quickly. "I'm sorry, my lord, I only meant, if they'd been going to harm her, how could I have left? No, Camlach would never harm her. I told you, she'd spoken for years of wanting to go into St. Peter's nunnery. I can't even remember a time when she didn't receive any Christian priest who visited Maridunum, and the Bishop himself, when he came from Caerleon, used to lodge in the palace. But my grandfather would never let her go. He and the Bishop used to quarrel over her—and over me. ... The Bishop wanted me baptized, you see, and my grandfather wouldn't hear of it. I—I think perhaps he kept it as a bribe to my mother, if she'd tell him who my father was, or perhaps if she'd consent to marry where he chose for her, but she never consented, or told him anything." I paused, wondering if I was saying too much, but he was watching me steadily, and it seemed attentively. "My grandfather swore she should never go into the Church," I added, "but as soon as he died she asked Camlach, and he allowed it. He would have shut me up, too, so I ran away."

He nodded. "Where did you intend to go?"

"I didn't know. It was true, what Marric said to me in the boat, that I'd have to go to someone. I'm only twelve, and because I can't be my own master, I must find a master. I didn't want Vortigern, or Vortimer, and I didn't know where else to go."

"So you persuaded Marric and Hanno to keep you alive and bring you to me?'

"Not really," I said honestly. "I didn't know at first where they were going, I just said anything I could think of to save myself. I had put myself into the god's hand, and he had sent me into their path, and then the ship was there. So I made them bring me across."

"To me?"

I nodded. The brazier flickered, and the shadows danced. A shadow moved on his cheek, as if he was smiling. "Then why not wait till they did so? Why jump ship and risk freezing to death in an icy field?"

"Because I was afraid they didn't mean to bring me to you after all. I thought that they might have realized how—how little use I would be to you."

"So you came ashore on your own in the middle of a winter's night, and in a strange country, and the god threw you straight at my feet. You and your god between you, Myrddin, make a pretty powerful combination. I can see I have no choice."

"My lord?"

"Perhaps you are right, and there are ways in which you

can serve me." He looked down at the table again, picked up a pen, and turned it over in his hand, as if he examined it. "But tell me first, why are you called Myrddin? You say your mother never told you who your father was? Never even hinted? Might she have called you after him?"

"Not by calling me Myrddin, sir. That's one of the old gods—there's a shrine just near St. Peter's gate. He was the god of the hill nearby, and some say of other parts beyond South Wales. But I have another name." I hesitated. "I've never told anyone this before, but I'm certain it was my father's name."

"And that is?"

"Emrys. I heard her talking to him once, at night, years ago when I was very small. I never forgot. There was something about her voice. You can tell."

The pen became still. He looked at me under his brows. "Talking to him? Then it was someone in the palace?"

"Oh, no, not like that. It wasn't real."

"You mean it was a dream? A vision? Like this tonight of the bull?"

"No, sir. And I wouldn't have called that a dream, either—it was real, too, in a different way. I have those sometimes. But the time I heard my mother. ... There was an old hypocaust in the palace that had been out of use for years; they filled it in later, but when I was young—when I was little—I used to crawl in there to get away from people. I kept things there ... the sort of things you keep when you're small, and if they find them, they throw them away."

"I know. Go on."

"Do you? I—well, I used to crawl through the hypocaust, and one night I was under her chamber, and heard her talking to herself, out loud, as you do when you pray sometimes. I heard her say 'Emrys,' but I don't remember what else." I looked at him. "You know how one catches one's own name, even if one can't hear much else? I thought she must be praying for me, but when I was older and remembered it, it came to me that the 'Emrys' must be my father. There was something about her voice ... and anyway, she never called me that; she called me Merlin."

"Why?"

"After a falcon. It's a name for the *corwalch*."

"Then I shall call you Merlin, too. You have courage, and it seems as if you have eyes that can see a long way. I might need your eyes, some day. But tonight you can start with simpler things. You shall tell me about your home. Well, what is it?"

"If I'm to serve you ... of course I will tell you anything I can. ... But—" I hesitated, and he took the words from me:

"But you must have my promise that when I invade Britain no harm will come to your mother? You have it. She shall be safe, and so shall any other man or woman you may ask me to spare for their kindness to you."

I must have been staring. "You are—very generous."

"If I take Britain, I can afford to be. I should perhaps have made some reservations." He smiled. "It might be difficult if you wanted an amnesty for your uncle Camlach?"

"It won't arise," I said. "When you take Britain, he'll be dead."

A silence. His lips parted to say something, but I think he changed his mind. "I said I might use those eyes of yours some day. Now, you have my promise, so let us talk. Never mind if things don't seem important enough to tell. Let me be the judge of that."

So I talked to him. It did not strike me as strange then that he should talk to me as if I were his equal, nor that he should spend half the night with me asking questions which in part his spies could have answered. I believe that twice, while we talked, a slave came in silently and replenished the brazier, and once I heard the clash and command of the guard changing outside the door. Ambrosius questioned, prompted, listened, sometimes writing on a tablet in front of him, sometimes staring, chin on fist, at the table-top, but more usually watching me with that steady, shadowed stare. When I hesitated, or strayed into some irrelevancy, or faltered through sheer fatigue, he would prod me back with his questions towards some unseen goal, as a muleteer goads his mule.

"This fortress on the River Seint, where your grandfather met Vortigern. How far north of Caerleon? By which road? Tell me about the road. ... How is the fortress reached from the sea?"

And: "The tower where the High King lodged, Maximus' Tower—Macsen's, you call it. ... Tell me about this. How many men were housed there. What road there is to the harbour ..."

Or: "You say the King's party halted in a valley pass, south of the Snow Hill, and the kings went aside together. Your man Cerdic said they were looking at an old stronghold

on the crag. Describe the place ... the height of the crag.
How far one should see from the top, to the north ... the
south ... the east."

Or: "Now think of your grandfather's nobles. How many
will be loyal to Camlach? Their names? How many men?
And of his allies, who? Their numbers ... their fighting
power. . . ?"

And then, suddenly: "Now tell me this. How did you know
Camlach was going to Vortimer?"

"He said so to my mother," I told him, "by my grandfather's bier. I heard him. There had been rumours that this
would happen, and I knew he had quarrelled with my grandfather, but nobody knew anything for certain. Even my
mother only suspected what he meant to do. But as soon as
the King was dead, he told her."

"He announced this straight away? Then how was it that
Marric and Hanno heard nothing, apart from the rumours of
the quarrel?"

Fatigue, and the long relentless questioning had made me
incautious. I said, before I thought: "He didn't announce it.
He told only her. He was alone with her."

"Except for you?" His voice changed, so that I jumped on
my stool. He watched me under his brows. "I thought you
told me the hypocaust had been filled in?"

I merely sat and looked at him. I could think of nothing to
say.

"It seems strange, does it not," he said levelly, "that he
should tell your mother this in front of you, when he must
have known you were his enemy? When his men had just
killed your servant? And then, after he had told you of his
secret plans, how did you get out of the palace and into the
hands of my men, to 'make' them bring you with them to
me?"

"I—" I stammered. "My lord, you cannot think that I—
my lord, I told you I was no spy. I—all I have told you is
true. He did say it, I swear it."

"Be careful. It matters whether this is true. Your mother
told you?"

"No."

"Slaves' talk, then? That's all?"

I said desperately: "I heard him myself."

"Then where were you?"

I met his eyes. Without quite realizing why, I told the

simple truth. "My lord, I was asleep in the hills, six miles off."

There was a silence, the longest yet. I could hear the embers settling in the brazier, and some distance off, outside, a dog barking. I sat waiting for his anger.

"Merlin."

I looked up.

"Where do you get the Sight from? Your mother?"

Against all expectation, he believed me. I said eagerly: "Yes, but it is different. She saw only women's things, to do with love. Then she began to fear the power, and let it be."

"Do you fear it?"

"I shall be a man."

"And a man takes power where it is offered. Yes. Did you understand what you saw tonight?"

"The bull? No, my lord, only that it was something secret."

"Well, you will know some day, but not now. Listen."

Somewhere, outside, a cock crowed, shrill and silver like a trumpet. He said: "That, at any rate, puts paid to your phantoms. It's high time you were asleep. You look half dead for lack of it." He got to his feet. I slid softly from the stool and he stood for a moment looking down at me. "I was ten when I sailed for Less Britain, and I was sick all the way."

"So was I," I said.

He laughed. "Then you will be as exhausted as I was. When you have slept, we'll decide what to do with you." He touched a bell, and a slave opened the door and stood aside, waiting. "You'll sleep in my room tonight. This way."

The bedchamber was Roman, too. I was to find that by comparison with, say, Uther's, it was austere enough, but to the eyes of a boy used to the provincial and often makeshift standards of a small outlying country, it seemed luxurious, with the big bed spread with scarlet wool blankets and a fur rug, the sheepskins on the floor, and the bronze tripod as high as a man, where the triple lamps, shaped like small dragons, mouthed tongues of flame. Thick brown curtains kept out the icy night, and it was very quiet.

As I followed Ambrosius and the slave past the guards— there were two on the door, rigid and unmoving except for their eyes which slid, carefully empty of speculation, from Ambrosius to me—it occurred to me for the first time to wonder whether he might be, perhaps, Roman in other ways. But he only pointed to an archway where another of the brown curtains half hid a recess with a bed in it. I suppose a slave slept there sometimes, within call.

The servant pulled the curtain aside and showed me the blankets folded across the mattress, and the good pillows stuffed with fleece, then left me and went to attend Ambrosius.

I took off my borrowed tunic and folded it carefully. The blankets were thick, new wool, and smelt of cedarwood. Ambrosius and the slave were talking, but softly, and their voices came like echoes from the far end of a deep, quiet cave. It was bliss only to be in a real bed again, to lie, warm and fed, in a place that was beyond even the sound of the sea. And safe.

I think he said "Good night," but I was already submerged in sleep, and could not drag myself to the surface to answer. The last thing I remember is the slave moving softly to put out the lamps.

6

When I awoke next morning it was late. The curtains had been drawn back, letting in a grey and wintry day, and Ambrosius' bed was empty. Outside the windows I could see a small courtyard where a colonnade framed a square of garden, at the center of which a fountain played—in silence, I thought, till I saw that the cascade was solid ice.

The tiles of the floor were warm to my bare feet. I reached for the white tunic which I had left folded on a stool by the bed, but instead I saw that someone had put there a new one of dark green, the colour of yew trees, which fitted. There was a good leather belt to go with it, and a pair of new sandals replacing my old ones. There was even a cloak, this time of a light beech-green, with a copper brooch to fasten it. There was something embossed on the brooch; a dragon, enamelled in scarlet, the same device I had seen last night on the seal-ring he wore.

It was the first time that I remember feeling as if I looked like a prince, and I found it strange that this should happen at the moment when you would have thought I had reached the bottom of my fortunes. Here in Less Britain I had nothing, not even a bastard name to protect myself with, no kin, not even a rag of property. I had hardly spoken with any man except Ambrosius, and to him I was a servant, a dependent, something to be used, and only alive by his sufferance.

Cadal brought me my breakfast, brown bread and honeycomb and dried figs. I asked where Ambrosius was.

"Out with the men, drilling. Or rather, watching the exercises. He's there every day."

"What do you suppose he wants me to do?"

"All he said was, you could stay around here till you were rested, and to make yourself at home. I've to send someone to the ship, so if you'll tell me what your traps were that you lost, I'll have them brought."

"There was nothing much, I didn't have time. A couple of tunics and a pair of sandals wrapped in a blue cloak, and some little things—a brooch, and a clasp my mother gave me, things like that." I touched the expensive folds of the tunic I wore. "Nothing as good as this. Cadal, I hope I can serve him. Did he say what he wanted of me?"

"Not a word. You don't think he tells me his secret thoughts, do you? Now you just do as he says, make yourself at home, keep your mouth shut, and see you don't get into trouble. I don't suppose you'll be seeing much of him."

"I didn't suppose I would," I said. "Where am I to live?"

"Here."

"In this room?"

"Not likely. I meant, in the house."

I pushed my plate aside. "Cadal, does my lord Uther have a house of his own?"

Cadal's eyes twinkled. He was a short stocky man, with a square, reddish face, a black shag of hair, and small black eyes no bigger than olives. The gleam in them now showed me that he knew exactly what I was thinking, and moreover that everyone in the house must know exactly what had passed between me and the prince last night.

"No, he hasn't. He lives here, too. Cheek by jowl, you might say."

"Oh."

"Don't worry; you won't be seeing much of him, either. He's going north in a week or two. Should cool him off quickly, this weather . . . He's probably forgotten all about you by now, anyway." He grinned and went out.

He was right; during the next couple of weeks I saw very little of Uther, then he left with troops for the north, on some expedition designed half as an exercise for his compa-

ny, half as a foray in search of supplies. Cadal had guessed
right about the relief this would bring me; I was not sorry to
be out of Uther's range. I had the idea that he had not
welcomed my presence in his brother's house, and indeed
that Ambrosius' continued kindness had annoyed him quite a
lot.

I had expected to see very little of the Count after that
first night when I had told him all I knew, but thereafter he
sent for me on most evenings when he was free, sometimes
to question me and to listen to what I could tell him of
home, sometimes—when he was tired—to have me play to
him, or, on several occasions, to take a hand at chess. Here,
to my surprise, we were about even, and I do not think he let
me beat him. He was out of practice, he told me; the usual
game was dice, and he was not risking that against an infant
soothsayer. Chess, being a matter of mathematics rather than
magic, was less susceptible to the black arts.

He kept his promise, and told me what I had seen that first
night by the standing stone. I believe, had he told me to, I
would even have dismissed it as a dream. As time went on,
the memory had grown blurred and fainter, until I had begun
to think it might have been a dream fostered by cold and
hunger and some dim recollection of the faded picture on the
Roman chest in my room at Maridunum, the kneeling bull
and the man with a knife under an arch studded with stars.
But when Ambrosius talked about it, I knew I had seen more
than was in the painting. I had seen the soldiers' god, the
Word, the Light, the Good Shepherd, the mediator between
the one God and man. I had seen Mithras, who had come
out of Asia a thousand years ago. He had been born, Ambrosius told me, in a cave at mid-winter, while shepherds watched
and a star shone; he was born of earth and light, and
sprang from the rock with a torch in his left hand and a
knife in his right. He killed the bull to bring life and fertility
to the earth with its shed blood, and then, after his last meal
of bread and wine, he was called up to heaven. He was the
god of strength and gentleness, of courage and self-restraint.
"The soldiers' god," said Ambrosius again, "and that is why
we have re-established his worship here—to make, as the
Roman armies did, some common meeting-ground for the
chiefs and petty kings of all tongues and persuasions who
fight with us. About his worship I can't tell you, because it is
forbidden, but you will have gathered that on that first night
I and my officers had met for a ceremony of worship, and

your talk about bread and wine and bull-slaying sounded very much as if you had seen more of our ceremony than we are even allowed to speak about. You will know it all one day, perhaps. Till then, be warned, and if you are asked about your vision, remember that it was only a dream. You understand?"

I nodded, but with my mind filled, suddenly, with only one thing he had said. I thought of my mother and the Christian priests, of Galapas and the well of Myrddin, of things seen in the water and heard in the wind. "You want me to be an initiate of Mithras?"

"A man takes power where it is offered," he said again. "You have told me you don't know what god has his hand over you; perhaps Mithras was the god in whose path you put yourself, and who brought you to me. We shall see. Meanwhile, he is still the god of armies, and we shall need his help. ... Now bring the harp, if you will, and sing to me."

So he dealt with me, treating me more as a prince than I had ever been treated in my grandfather's house, where at least I had had some sort of claim to it.

Cadal was assigned to me as my own servant. I thought at first he might resent this, as a poor substitute for serving Ambrosius, but he did not seem to mind, in fact I got the impression that he was pleased. He was soon on easy terms with me, and, since there were no other boys of my age about the place, he was my constant companion. I was also given a horse. At first they gave me one of Ambrosius' own, but after a day on that I asked shamefacedly if I might have something more my size, and was given a small stolid grey which—in my only moment of nostalgia—I called Aster.

So the first days passed. I rode out with Cadal at my side to see the country; this was still in the grip of frost, and soon the frost turned to rain so that the fields were churned mud and the ways were slippery and foul, and a cold wind whistled day and night across the flats, whipping the Small Sea to white on iron-grey, and blackening the northern sides of the standing stones with wet. I looked one day for the stone with the mark of the axe, and failed to find it. But there was another where in a certain light you could see a dagger carved, and a thick stone, standing a little apart, where under the lichen and the bird droppings stared the shape of an open eye. By daylight the stones did not breathe so cold on one's nape, but there was still something there, watching, and it was not a way my pony cared to go.

Of course I explored the town. King Budec's castle was in the center, on a rocky outcrop which had been crowned with a high wall. A stone ramp led up to the gate, which was shut and guarded. I often saw Ambrosius, or his officers, riding up this ramp, but never went myself any nearer than the guard post at the foot of it. But I saw King Budec several times, riding out with his men. His hair and his long beard were almost white, but he sat his big brown gelding like a man thirty years younger, and I heard countless stories of his prowess at arms and how he had sworn to be avenged on Vortigern for the killing of his cousin Constantius, even though it would take a lifetime. This, in fact, it threatened to do, for it seemed an almost impossible task for so poor a country to raise the kind of army that might defeat Vortigern and the Saxons, and gain a footing in Greater Britain. But soon now, men said, soon . . .

Every day, whatever the weather, men drilled on the flat fields outside the town walls. Ambrosius had now, I learned, a standing army of about four thousand men. As far as Budec was concerned they earned their keep a dozen times over, since not much more than thirty miles away his borders ran with those of a young king whose eye was weather-lifted for plunder, and who was held back only by rumours of Ambrosius' growing power and the formidable reputation of his men. Budec and Ambrosius fostered the idea that the army was mainly defensive, and saw to it that Vortigern learned nothing for certain: news of preparations for invasion reached him as before only in the form of rumours, and Ambrosius' spies made sure that these sounded like rumours. What Vortigern actually believed was what Budec was at pains that he should believe, that Ambrosius and Uther had accepted their fate as exiles, had settled in Less Britain as Budec's heirs, and were concerned with keeping the borders that would one day be their own.

This impression was fostered by the fact that the army was used as a foraging party for the town. Nothing was too simple or too rough for Ambrosius' men to undertake. Work which even my grandfather's rough-trained troops would have despised, these seasoned soldiers did as a matter of course. They brought in and stored wood in the town's yards. They dug and stored peat, and burned charcoal. They built and worked the smithies, making not only weapons of war, but tools for tilling and harvesting and building—spades, ploughshares, axes, scythes. They could break horses, and herd and drive cattle as well as butcher them; they built carts; they could pitch and mount guard over a camp in two hours flat, and strike it in one hour less. There was a corps of engineers who had half a square mile of workshops, and could supply anything from a padlock to a troop-ship. They were fitting themselves, in short, for the task of landing blindfold in a strange country and maybe living off it and moving fast across it in all weathers. "For," said Ambrosius once to his officers in front of me, "it is only to fair-weather soldiers that war is a fair-weather game. I shall fight to win, and after I have won, to hold. And Britain is a big country; compared with her, this corner of Gaul is no more than a meadow. So, gentlemen, we fight through spring and summer, but we do not retire at the first October frost to rest and sharpen our swords again for spring. We fight on—in snow, if we have to, in storm and frost and the wet mud of winter. And in all that weather and through all that time, we must eat, and fifteen thousand men must eat—well."

Shortly after this, about a month after my arrival in Less Britain, my days of freedom ended. Ambrosius found me a tutor.

Belasius was very different from Galapas and from the gentle drunkard Demetrius, who had been my official tutor at home. He was a man in his prime who was one of the Count's "men of business" and seemed to be concerned with the estimating and accounting side of Ambrosius' affairs; he was by training a mathematician and astronomer. He was half Gallo-Roman, half Sicilian, a tallish olive-faced man with long-lidded black eyes, a melancholy expression and a cruel mouth. He had an acid tongue and a sudden, vicious temper, but he was never capricious. I soon learned that the way to dodge his sarcasms and his heavy hand was to do my work quickly and well, and since this came easily to me and I enjoyed it, we soon understood one another, and got along tolerably well.

One afternoon towards the end of March we were working in my room in Ambrosius' house. Belasius had lodgings in the town, which he had been careful never to speak of, so I assumed he lived with some drab and was ashamed to risk my seeing her; he worked mainly in headquarters, but the offices near the treasury were always crowded with clerks and paymasters, so we held our daily tutorials in my room.

This was not a large chamber, but to my eyes very well appointed, with a floor of red tiles locally made, carved fruitwood furniture, a bronze mirror, and a brazier and lamp that had come from Rome.

Today, the lamp was lit even in the afternoon, for the day was dark and overcast. Belasius was pleased with me; we were doing mathematics, and it had been one of the days when I could forget nothing, but walked through the problems he set me as if the field of knowledge were an open meadow with a pathway leading plain across it for all to see.

He drew the flat of his hand across the wax to erase my drawing, pushed the tablet aside, and stood up.

"You've done well today, which is just as well, because I have to leave early."

He reached out and struck the bell. The door opened so quickly that I knew his servant must have been waiting just outside. The boy came in with his master's cloak over his arm, and shook it out quickly to hold it for him. He did not even glance my way for permission, but watched Belasius, and I could see he was afraid of him. He was about my age, or younger, with brown hair cut close to his head in a curled cap, and grey eyes too big for his face.

Belasius neither spoke nor glanced at him, but turned his shoulders to the cloak, and the boy reached up to fasten the clasp. Across his head Belasius said to me: "I shall tell the Count of your progress. He will be pleased."

The expression on his face was as near a smile as he ever showed. Made bold by this, I turned on my stool. "Belasius—"

He stopped halfway to the door. "Well?"

"You must surely know ... Please tell me. What are his plans for me?"

"That you should work at your mathematics and your astronomy, and remember your languages."

His tone was smooth and mechanical, but there was amusement in his eyes, so I persisted. "To become what?"

"What do you wish to become?"

I did not answer. He nodded, just as if I had spoken. "If he wanted you to carry a sword for him, you would be out in the square now."

"But—to live here as I do, with you to teach me, and Cadal as my servant ... I don't understand it. I should be serving him somehow, not just learning ... and living like this, like a prince. I know very well that I am only alive by his grace."

He regarded me for a moment under those long lids. Then he smiled. "It's something to remember. I believe you told him once that it was what you were, not who you were, that would matter. Believe me, he will use you, as he uses every-one. So stop wondering about it, and let it be. Now I must go."

The boy opened the door for him to show Cadal just pausing outside, with a hand raised to knock.

"Oh, excuse me, sir. I came to see when you'd be done for the day. I've got the horses ready, Master Merlin."

"We've finished already," said Belasius. He paused in the doorway and looked back at me. "Where were you planning to go?"

"North, I think, the road through the forest. The cause-way's still good and the road will be dry."

He hesitated, then said, to Cadal rather than to me: "Then keep to the road, and be home before dark." He nodded, and went out, with the boy at his heels.

"Before dark?" said Cadal. "It's been dark all day, and it's raining now, besides. Look, Merlin"—when we were alone we were less formal—"why don't we just take a look along to the engineers' workshops? You always enjoy that, and Tre-morinus ought to have got that ram working by now. What do you say we stay in town?"

I shook my head. "I'm sorry, Cadal, but I must go, rain or no rain. I've got the fidgets, or something, and I must get out."

"Well, then, a mile or two down to the port should do you. Come on, here's your cloak. It'll be pitch black in the forest; have a bit of sense."

"The forest," I said obstinately, turning my head while he fastened the pin. "And don't argue with me, Cadal. If you ask me, Belasius has the right ideas. *His* servant doesn't even dare to speak, let alone argue. I ought to treat you the same way—in fact I'll start straight away.... What are you grin-ning at?"

"Nothing. All right, I know when to give in. The forest it is, and if we lose ourselves and never get back alive, at least I'll have died with you, and won't have to face the Count."

"I really can't see that he'd care overmuch."

"Oh, he wouldn't," said Cadal, holding the door for me to go through. "It was only a manner of speaking. I doubt if he'd even notice, myself."

7

Once outside, it was not as dark as it had seemed, and it was warm, one of those heavy, dull days fraught with mists, and a small rain that lay on the heavy wool of our cloaks like frost.

About a mile to the north of the town the flattish salt-bitten turf began to give way to woodland, thin at first, with trees sticking up here and there solitary, with veils of white mist haunting their lower boughs or lying over the turf like pools, which now and then broke and swirled as a deer fled through.

The road north was an old one, paved, and the men who had built it had cleared the trees and scrub back on either side for a hundred paces, but with time and neglect the open verge had grown thick with whin and heather and young trees, so that now the forest seemed to crowd round you as you rode, and the way was dark.

Near the town we had seen one or two peasants carrying home fuel on their donkeys, and once one of Ambrosius' messengers spurred past us, with a stare, and what looked like a half-salute to me. But in the forest we met no one. It was the silent time between the thin birdsong of a March day and the hunting of the owls.

When we got among the big trees the rain had stopped, and the mist was thinning. Presently we came to a crossroads where a track—unpaved this time—crossed our own at right angles. The track was one used for hauling timber out of the forest, and also by the carts of charcoal burners, and, though rough and deeply rutted, it was clear and straight, and if you kept your horse to the edge, there was a gallop.

"Let's turn down here, Cadal."

"You know he said keep to the road."

"Yes, I know he did, but I don't see why. The forest's perfectly safe."

This was true. It was another thing Ambrosius had done; men were no longer afraid to ride abroad in Less Britain, within striking distance of the town. The country was constantly patrolled by his companies, alert and spoiling for something to do. Indeed, the main danger was (as I had once heard him admit) that his troops would over-train and grow stale, and look rather too hard for trouble. Meanwhile, the outlaws and disaffected men stayed away, and ordinary folk went about their business in peace. Even women could travel without much of an escort.

"Besides," I added, "does it matter what he said? He's not my master. He's only in charge of teaching me, nothing else. We can't possibly lose our way if we keep to the tracks, and if we don't get a canter now, it'll be too dark to press the horses when we get back to the fields. You're always complaining that I don't ride well enough. How can I, when we're always trotting along the road? Please, Cadal."

"Look, I'm not your master either. All right, then, but not far. And watch your pony; it'll be darker under the trees. Best let me go first."

I put a hand on his rein. "No. I'd like to ride ahead, and would you hold back a little, please? The thing is, I—I have so little solitude, and it's been something I'm used to. This was one of the reasons I had to come out this way." I added carefully: "It's not that I haven't been glad of your company, but one sometimes wants time to—well, to think things out. If you'll just give me fifty paces?"

He reined back immediately. Then he cleared his throat. "I told you I'm not your master. Go ahead. But go careful."

I turned Aster into the ride, and kicked him to a canter. He had not been out of his stable for three days, and in spite of the distance behind us he was eager. He laid his ears back, and picked up speed down the grass verge of the ride. Luckily the mist had almost gone, but here and there it smoked across the track saddle-high, and the horses plunged through it, fording it like water.

Cadal was holding well back; I could hear the thud of the mare's hoofs like a heavy echo of my pony's canter. The small rain had stopped, and the air was fresh and cool and resinous with the scent of pines. A woodcock flighted overhead with a sweet whispering call, and a soft tassel of spruce flicked a fistful of drops across my mouth and down inside the neck of my tunic. I shook my head and laughed, and the pony quickened his pace, scattering a pool of mist like spray. I crouched over his neck as the track narrowed, and branches whipped at us in earnest. It was darker; the sky thickened to nightfall between the boughs, and the forest rolled by in a dark cloud, wild with scent and silent but for Aster's scudding gallop and the easy pacing of the mare.

Cadal called me to stop. As I made no immediate response, the thudding of the mare's hoofs quickened, and drew

closer. Aster's ears flicked, then flattened again, and he began
to race. I drew him in. It was easy, as the going was heavy,
and he was sweating. He slowed and then stood and waited
quietly for Cadal to come up. The brown mare stopped. The
only sound in the forest now was the breathing of the horses.

"Well," he said at length, "did you get what you wanted?"

"Yes, only you called too soon."

"We'll have to turn back if we're to be in time for supper.
Goes well, that pony. You want to ride ahead on the way
back?"

"If I may."

"I told you there's no question, you do as you like. I know
you don't get out on your own, but you're young yet, and it's
up to me to see you don't come to harm, that's all."

"What harm could I come to? I used to go everywhere
alone at home."

"This isn't home. You don't know the country yet. You
could lose yourself, or fall off your pony and lie in the forest
with a broken leg—"

"It's not very likely, is it? You were told to watch me, why
don't you admit it?"

"To look after you."

"It could come to the same thing. I've heard what they
call you. 'The watchdog.' "

He grunted. "You don't need to dress it up. 'Merlin's black
dog,' that's the way I heard it. Don't think I mind. I do as he
says and no questions asked, but I'm sorry if it frets you."

"It doesn't—oh, it doesn't. I didn't mean it like that. . . .
It's all right, it's only . . . Cadal—"

"Yes?"

"Am I a hostage, after all?"

"That I couldn't say," said Cadal woodenly. "Come along,
then, can you get by?"

Where our horses stood the way was narrow, the center of
the ride having sunk into deep mud where water faintly
reflected the night sky. Cadal reined his mare back into the
thicket that edged the ride, while I forced Aster—who would
not wet his feet unless compelled—past the mare. As the
brown's big quarters pressed back into the tangle of oak and
chestnut there was suddenly a crash just behind her, and a
breaking of twigs, and some animal burst from the under-
growth almost under the mare's belly, and hurtled across the
ride in front of my pony's nose.

Both animals reacted violently. The mare, with a snort of

fear, plunged forward hard against the rein. At the same moment Aster shied wildly, throwing me half out of the saddle. Then the plunging mare crashed into his shoulder, and the pony staggered, whirled, lashed out, and threw me.

I missed the water by inches, landing heavily on the soft stuff at the edge of the ride, right up against a broken stump of pine which could have hurt me badly if I had been thrown on it. As it was I escaped with scratches and a minor bruise or two, and a wrenched ankle that, when I rolled over and tried to put it to the ground, stabbed me with pain momentarily so acute as to make the black woods swim.

Even before the mare had stopped circling Cadal was off her back, had flung the reins over a bough, and was stooping over me.

"Merlin—Master Merlin—are you hurt?"

I unclamped my teeth from my lip, and started gingerly with both hands to straighten my leg. "No, only my ankle, a bit."

"Let me see . . . No, hold still. By the dog, Ambrosius will have my skin for this."

"What was it?"

"A boar, I think. Too small for a deer, too big for a fox."

"I thought it was a boar, I smelled it. My pony?"

"Halfway home by now, I expect. Of course you had to let the rein go, didn't you?"

"I'm sorry. Is it broken?"

His hands had been moving over my ankle, prodding, feeling. "I don't think so . . . No, I'm sure it's not. You're all right otherwise? Here, come on, try if you can stand on it. The mare'll take us both, and I want to get back, if I can, before that pony of yours goes in with an empty saddle. I'll be for the lampreys, for sure, if Ambrosius sees him."

"It wasn't your fault. Is he so unjust?"

"He'll reckon it was, and he wouldn't be far wrong. Come on now, try it."

"No, give me a moment. And don't worry about Ambrosius, the pony hasn't gone home, he's stopped a little way up the ride. You'd better go and get him."

He was kneeling over me, and I could see him faintly against the sky. He turned his head to peer along the ride. Beside us the mare stood quietly, except for her restless ears and the white edge to her eye. There was silence except for an owl starting up, and far away on the edge of sound another, like its echo.

"It's pitch dark twenty feet away," said Cadal. "I can't see a thing. Did you hear him stop?"

"Yes." It was a lie, but this was neither the time nor the place for the truth. "Go and get him, quickly. On foot. He hasn't gone far."

I saw him stare down at me for a moment, then he got to his feet without a word and started off up the ride. As well as if it had been daylight, I could see his puzzled look. I was reminded, sharply, of Cerdic that day at King's Fort. I leaned back against the stump. I could feel my bruises, and my ankle ached, but for all that there came flooding through me, like a drink of warm wine, the feeling of excitement and release that came with the power. I knew now that I had had to come this way; that this was to be another of the hours when not darkness, nor distance, nor time meant anything. The owl floated silently above me, across the ride. The mare cocked her ears at it, watching without fear. There was the thin sound of bats somewhere above. I thought of the crystal cave, and Galapas' eyes when I told him of my vision. He had not been puzzled, not even surprised. It came to me to wonder, suddenly, how Belasius would look. And I knew he would not be surprised, either.

Hoofs sounded softly in the deep turf. I saw Aster first, approaching ghostly grey, then Cadal like a shadow at his head.

"He was there all right," he said, "and for a good reason. He's dead lame. Must have strained something."

"Well, at least he won't get home before we do."

"There'll be trouble over this night's work, that's for sure, whatever time we get home. Come on, then, I'll put you up on Rufa."

With a hand from him I got cautiously to my feet. When I tried to put weight on the left foot, it still hurt me quite a lot, but I knew from the feel of it that it was nothing but a wrench and would soon be better. Cadal threw me up on the mare's back, unhooked the reins from the bough, and gave them into my hand. Then he clicked his tongue to Aster, and led him slowly ahead.

"What are you doing?" I asked. "Surely she can carry us both?"

"There's no point. You can see how lame he is. He'll have to be led. If I take him in front he can make the pace. The mare'll stay behind him. —You all right up there?"

"Perfectly, thanks."

The grey pony was indeed dead lame. He walked slowly beside Cadal with drooping head, moving in front of me like a smoke-beacon in the dusk. The mare followed quietly. It would take, I reckoned, a couple of hours to get home, even without what lay ahead.

Here again was a kind of solitude, no sounds but the soft plodding of the horses' hoofs, the creak of leather, the occasional small noises of the forest round us. Cadal was invisible, nothing but a shadow beside the moving wraith of mist that was Aster. Perched on the big mare at a comfortable walk, I was alone with the darkness and the trees.

We had gone perhaps half a mile when, burning through the boughs of a huge oak to my right, I saw a white star, steady.

"Cadal, isn't there a shorter way back? I remember a track off to the south just near that oak tree. The mist's cleared right away, and the stars are out. Look, there's the Bear."

His voice came back from the darkness. "We'd best head for the road." But in a pace or two he stopped the pony at the mouth of the southgoing track, and waited for the mare to come up.

"It looks good enough, doesn't it?" I asked. "It's straight, and a lot drier than this track we're on. All we have to do is keep the Bear at our backs, and in a mile or two we should be able to smell the sea. Don't you know your way about the forest?"

"Well enough. It's true this would be shorter, if we can see our way. Well . . ." I heard him loosen his short stabbing sword in its sheath. "Not that there's likely to be trouble, but best be prepared, so keep your voice down, will you, and have your knife ready. And let me tell you one thing, young Merlin, if anything should happen, then you'll ride for home and leave me to it. Got that?"

"Ambrosius' orders again?"

"You could say so."

"All right, if it makes you feel better, I promise I'll desert you at full speed. But there'll be no trouble."

He grunted. "Anyone would think you knew."

I laughed. "Oh, I do."

The starlight caught, momentarily, the whites of his eyes, and the quick gesture of his hand. Then he turned without speaking and led Aster into the track going south.

8

Though the path was wide enough to take two riders abreast, we went in single file, the brown mare adapting her long, comfortable stride to the pony's shorter and very lame step.

It was colder now; I pulled the folds of my cloak round me for warmth. The mist had vanished completely with the drop in temperature, the sky was clear, with some stars, and it was easier to see the way. Here the trees were huge; oaks mainly, the big ones massive and widely spaced, while between them saplings grew thickly and unchecked, and ivy twined with the bare strings of honeysuckle and thickets of thorn. Here and there pines showed fiercely black against the sky. I could hear the occasional patter as damp gathered and dripped from the leaves, and once the scream of some small creature dying under the claws of an owl. The air was full of the smell of damp and fungus and dead leaves and rich, rotting things.

Cadal trudged on in silence, his eyes on the path, which in places was tricky with fallen or rotting branches. Behind him, balancing on the big mare's saddle, I was still possessed by the same light, excited power. There was something ahead of us, to which I was being led, I knew, as surely as the merlin had led me to the cavern at King's Fort.

Rufa's ears pricked, and I heard her soft nostrils flicker. Her head went up. Cadal had not heard, and the grey pony, preoccupied with his lameness, gave no sign that he could smell the other horses. But even before Rufa, I had known they were there.

The path twisted and began to go gently downhill. To either side of us the trees had retreated a little, so that their branches no longer met overhead, and it was lighter. Now to each side of the path were banks, with outcrops of rock and broken ground where in summer there would be foxgloves and bracken, but where now only the dead and wiry brambles ran riot. Our horses' hoofs scraped and rang as they picked their way down the slopes.

Suddenly Rufa, without checking her stride, threw up her head and let out a long whinny. Cadal, with an exclamation, stopped dead, and the mare pushed up beside him, head high, ears pricked towards the forest on our right. Cadal snatched at her bridle, pulled her head down, and shrouded her nostrils in the crook of his arm. Aster had lifted his head, too, but he made no sound.

"Horses," I said softly. "Can't you smell them?"

I heard Cadal mutter something that sounded like, "Smell anything, it seems you can, you must have a nose like a bitch fox," then, hurriedly starting to drag the mare off the track: "It's too late to go back, they'll have heard this bloody mare. We'd best pull off into the forest."

I stopped him. "There's no need. There's no trouble there, I'm certain of it. Let's go on."

"You talk fine and sure, but how can you know—?"

"I do know. In any case, if they meant us harm, we'd have known of it by now. They've heard us coming long since, and they must know it's only two horses and one of them lame."

But he still hesitated, fingering his short sword. The prickles of excitement fretted my skin like burrs. I had seen where the mare's ears were pointing—at a big grove of pines, fifty paces ahead, and set back above the right of the path. They were black even against the blackness of the forest. Suddenly I could wait no longer. I said impatiently: "I'm going, anyway. You can follow or not, as you choose." I jerked Rufa's head up and away from him, and kicked her with my good foot, so that she plunged forward past the grey pony. I headed her straight up the bank and into the grove.

The horses were there. Through a gap in the thick roof of pines a cluster of stars burned, showing them clearly. There were only two, standing motionless, with their heads held low and their nostrils muffled against the breast of a slight figure heavily cloaked and hooded against the cold. The hood fell back as he turned to stare; the oval of his face showed pale in the gloom. There was no one else there.

For one startled moment I thought that the black horse nearest me was Ambrosius' big stallion, then as it pulled its head free of the cloak I saw the white blaze on its forehead, and knew in a flash like a falling star why I had been led here.

Behind me, with a scramble and a startled curse, Cadal pulled Aster into the grove. I saw the grey gleam of his sword as he lifted it. "Who's that?"

I said quietly, without turning: "Put it up. It's Belasius ... At least that's his horse. Another with it, and the boy. That's all."

He advanced. His sword was already sliding back into its

housing. "By the dog, you're right, I'd know that white flash anywhere. Hey, Ulfin, well met. Where's your master?"

Even at six paces I heard the boy gasp with relief. "Oh, it's you, Cadal ... My lord Merlin ... I heard your horse whinny— I wondered— Nobody comes this way."

I moved the mare forward, and looked down. His face was a pale blur upturned, the eyes enormous. He was still afraid.

"It seems Belasius does," I said. "Why?"

"He—he tells me nothing, my lord."

Cadal said roundly: "Don't give us that. There's not much you don't know about him, you're never more than arm's length from him, day or night, everybody knows that. Come on, out with it. Where's your master?"

"I—he won't be long."

"We can't wait for him," said Cadal. "We want a horse. Go and tell him we're here, and my lord Merlin's hurt, and the pony's lame, and we've got to get home quickly ... Well? Why don't you go? For pity's sake, what's the matter with you?"

"I can't. He said I must not. He forbade me to move from here."

"As he forbade us to leave the road, in case we came this way?" I said. "Yes. Now, your name's Ulfin, is it? Well, Ulfin, never mind the horse. I want to know where Belasius is."

"I—I don't know."

"You must at least have seen which way he went?"

"N-no, my lord."

"By the dog," exclaimed Cadal, "who cares where he is, as long as we get the horse? Look, boy, have some sense, we can't wait half the night for your master, we've got to get home. If you tell him the horse was for my lord Merlin, he won't eat you alive this time, will he?" Then, as the boy stammered something: "Well, all right, do you want us to go and find him ourselves, and get his leave?"

The boy moved then, jamming a fist to his mouth, like an idiot. "No . . . You must not . . . You must not . . . !"

"By Mithras," I said—it was an oath I cultivated at the time, having heard Ambrosius use it—"what's he doing? Murder?"

On the word, the shriek came.

Not a shriek of pain, but worse, the sound of a man in mortal fear. I thought the cry contained a word, as if the terror was shaped, but it was no word that I knew. The scream rose unbearably, as if it would burst him, then was chopped off sharply as if by a blow on the throat. In the dreadful silence that followed a faint echo came, in a breath from the boy Ulfin.

Cadal stood frozen as he had turned, one hand holding his sword, the other grasping Aster's bridle. I wrenched the mare's head round and lashed the reins down on her neck. She bounded forward, almost unseating me. She plunged under the pines towards the track. I lay flat on her neck as the boughs swept past us, hooked a hand in her neck-strap, and hung on like a tick. Neither Cadal nor the boy had moved or made a sound.

The mare went down the bank with a scramble and a slither, and as we reached the path I saw, so inevitably that I felt no surprise—nor indeed any thought at all—another path, narrow and overgrown, leading out of the track to the other side, just opposite the grove of pines.

I hauled on the mare's mouth, and when she jibbed, trying to head down the broader track for home, I lashed her again. She laid her ears flat and went into the path at a gallop.

The path twisted and turned, so that almost straight away our pace slackened, slowed, became a heavy canter. This was the direction from which that dreadful sound had come. It was apparent even in the starlight that someone had recently been this way. The path was so little used that winter grass and heather had almost choked it, but someone—something—had been thrusting a way through. The going was so soft that even a cantering horse made very little noise.

I strained my ears for the sound of Cadal coming after me, but could not hear him. It occurred to me only then that both he and the boy must have thought that, terrified by the shriek, I had run, as Cadal had bidden me, for home.

I pulled Rufa to a walk. She slowed willingly, her head up, her ears pricked forward. She was quivering; she, too, had heard the shriek. A gap in the forest showed three hundred paces ahead, so light that I thought it must mark the end of the trees. I watched carefully as we approached it, but nothing moved against the sky beyond.

Then, so softly that I had to strain my ears to make sure it was neither wind nor sea, I heard chanting.

My skin prickled. I knew now where Belasius was, and why Ulfin had been so afraid. And I knew why Belasius had said: "Keep to the road, and be home before dark."

I sat up straight. The heat ran over my skin in little waves, like catspaws of wind over water. My breathing came shallow and fast. For a moment I wondered if this was fear, then I knew it was still excitement. I halted the mare and slid silently from the saddle. I led her three paces into the forest, knotted the rein over a bough and left her there. My foot hurt when I put it to the ground, but the twinges were bearable, and I soon forgot them as I limped quickly towards the singing and the lighter sky.

9

I had been right in thinking that the sea was near. The forest ended in it, a stretch of sea so enclosed that at first I thought it was a big lake, until I smelled the salt and saw, on the narrow shingle, the dark slime of seaweeds. The forest finished abruptly, with a high bank where exposed roots showed through the clay which the tides had gnawed away year after year at the land's edge. The narrow strand was mainly of pebbles, but here and there bars of pale sand showed, and greyish, glimmering fans spreading fernlike between them, where shallow water ran seawards. The bay was very quiet, almost as if the frost of the past weeks had held it icebound, then, a pale line under the darkness, you could see the gap between the far headlands where the wide sea whitened. To the right—the south—the black forest climbed to a ridge, while to the north, where the land was gentler, the big trees gave shelter. A perfect harbour, you would have thought, till you saw how shallow it was, how at low tide the shapes of rock and boulder stuck black out of the water, shiny in the starlight with weed.

In the middle of the bay, so centered that at first I thought it must be man-made, was an island—what must, rather, be an island at high tide, but was now a peninsula, an oval of land joined to the shore by a rough causeway of stones, certainly man-made, which ran out like a navel cord to join it to the shingle. In the nearer of the shallow harbours made by the causeway and the shore a few small boats—coracles, I thought—lay beached like seals.

Here, low beside the bay, there was mist again, hanging here and there among the boughs like fishing nets hung out to dry. On the water's surface it floated in patches, spreading slowly till it curdled and thinned and then wisped away to nothing, only to thicken again elsewhere, and smoke slowly across the water. It lay round the base of the island so densely that this seemed to float on cloud, and the stars that hung above reflected a grey light from the mist that showed me the island clearly.

This was egg-shaped rather than oval, narrow at the causeway end, and widening towards the far end where a small hill, as regular in shape as a beehive, stood up out of the flat ground. Round the base of this hillock stood a circle of the standing stones, a circle broken only at the point facing me, where a wide gap made a gateway from which an avenue of the stones marched double, like a colonnade, straight down to the causeway.

There was neither sound nor movement. If it had not been for the dim shapes of the beached boats I would have thought that the shriek, the chanting, were figments of a dream. I stood just inside the edge of the forest, with my left arm round a young ash tree and the weight on my right foot, watching with eyes so completely adjusted to the dark of the forest that the mist-illuminated island seemed as light as day.

At the foot of the hill, directly at the end of the central avenue, a torch flared suddenly. It lit, momentarily, an opening low in the face of the hill, and clearly in front of this the torch-bearer, a figure in a white robe. I saw, then, that what I had taken to be banks of mist in the shadow of the cromlechs were groups of motionless figures also robed in white. As the torch lifted I heard the chanting begin again, very softly, and with a loose and wandering rhythm that was strange to me. Then the torch and its bearer slowly sank earthwards, and I realized that the doorway was a sunken one, and he was descending a flight of steps into the heart of the hill. The others crowded after him, groups clotting, coalescing round the doorway, then vanishing like smoke being sucked into an oven door.

The chanting still went on, but so faint and muffled that it sounded no more than the humming of bees in a winter hive. No tune came through, only the rhythm which sank to a mere throb in the air, a pulse of sound felt rather than heard, which little by little tightened and quickened till it beat fast and hard, and my blood with it . . .

Suddenly, it stopped. There was a pause of dead stillness, but a stillness so charged that I felt my throat knot and swell with tension. I found I had left the trees and stood clear on

the turf above the bank, my injury forgotten, my feet planted
apart, flat and squarely on the ground, as if my body were
rooted through them and straining to pull life from the earth
as a tree pulls sap. And like the shoot of a tree growing and
thrusting, the excitement in me grew and swelled, beating
through somehow from the depths of the island and along the
navel cord of the causeway, bursting up through flesh and
spirit so that when the cry came at length it was as if it had
burst from my own body.

A different cry this time, thin and edged, which might have
meant anything, triumph or surrender or pain. A death cry,
this time not from the victim, but from the killer.

And after it, silence. The night was fixed and still. The
island was a closed hive sealed over whatever crawled and
hummed within.

Then the leader—I assumed it was he, though this time the
torch was out—appeared suddenly like a ghost in the doorway
and mounted the steps. The rest came behind, moving not as
people move in a procession, but slowly and smoothly, in
groups breaking and forming, contained in pattern like a
dance, till once more they stood parted into two ranks beside
the cromlechs.

Again complete stillness. Then the leader raised his arms.
As if at a signal, white and shining like a knife-blade, the
edge of the moon showed over the hill.

The leader cried out, and this, the third cry, was unmistakably a call of triumphant greeting, and he stretched his arms
high above his head as if offering up what he held between
his hands.

The crowd answered him, chant and counterchant. Then as
the moon lifted clear of the hill, the priest lowered his arms
and turned. What he had offered to the goddess, he now
offered to the worshippers. The crowd closed in.

I had been so intent on the ceremony at the center of the
island that I had not watched the shore, or realized that the
mist, creeping higher, was now blurring the avenue itself. My
eyes, straining through the dark, saw the white shapes of the
people as part of the mist that clotted, strayed, and eddied
here and there in knots of white.

Presently I became aware that this, in fact, was what was
happening. The crowd was breaking apart, and the people, in
twos and threes, were passing silently down the avenue, in
and out of the barred shadows which the rising moon painted
between the stones. They were making for the boats.

I have no idea how long it had all taken, but as I came to myself I found that I was stiff, and where I had allowed my cloak to fall away I was soaked with the mist. I shook myself like a dog, backing again into the shelter of the trees. Excitement had spilled out of me, spirit as well as body, in a warm gush down my thighs, and I felt empty and ashamed. Dimly I knew that this was something different; this had not been the force I had learnt to receive and foster, nor was this spilled-out sensation the aftermath of power. That had left me light and free and keen as a cutting blade; now I felt empty as a licked pot still sticky and smelling with what it had held.

I bent, stiff-sinewed, to pull a swatch of wet and pallid grass, and cleaned myself, scrubbing my hands, and scooping mist drops off the turf to wash my face. The water smelt of leaves, and of the wet air itself, and made me think of Galapas and the holy well and the long cup of horn. I dried my hands on the inside of my cloak, drew it about me, and went back to my station by the ash tree.

The bay was dotted with the retreating coracles. The island had emptied, all but one tall white figure who came, now, straight down the center of the avenue. The mist cloaked, revealed, and cloaked him again. He was not making for a boat; he seemed to be heading straight for the causeway, but as he reached the end of the avenue he paused in the shadow of the final stone, and vanished.

I waited, feeling little except weariness and a longing for a drink of clear water and the familiarity of my warm and quiet room. There was no magic in the air; the night was as flat as old sour wine. In a moment, sure enough, I saw him emerge into the moonlight of the causeway. He was clad now in a dark robe. All he had done was drop his white robe off. He carried it over his arm.

The last of the boats was a speck dwindling in the darkness. The solitary man came quickly across the causeway. I stepped out from under the trees and down on to the shingle to meet him.

10

Belasius saw me even before I was clear of the trees' shadow. He made no sign except to turn aside as he stepped off the causeway. He came up, unhurried, and stood over me, looking down.

"Ah." It was the only greeting, said without surprise. "I might have known. How long have you been here?"

"I hardly know. Time passed so quickly. I was interested."

He was silent. The moonlight, bright now, fell slanting on his right cheek. I could not see the eyes veiled under the long dark lids, but there was something quiet, almost sleepy about his voice and bearing. I had felt the same after that releasing cry, there in the forest. The bolt had struck, and now the bow was unstrung.

He took no notice of my provocation, asking merely: "What brought you here?"

"I rode down when I heard the scream."

"Ah," he said again, then: "Down from where?"

"From the pine grove where you left your horse."

"Why did you come this way? I told you to keep to the road."

"I know, but I wanted a gallop, so we turned off into the main logging track, and I had an accident with Aster; he's wrenched a foreleg, so we had to lead him back. It was slow, and we were late, so we took a short cut."

"I see. And where is Cadal?"

"I think he thought I'd run for home, and he must have gone after me. At any rate he didn't follow me down here."

"That was sensible of him," said Belasius. His voice was still quiet, sleepy almost, but cat-sleepy, velvet sheathing a bright dagger-point. "But in spite of—what you heard—it did not in fact occur to you to run for home?"

"Of course not."

I saw his eyes glint for a moment under the long lids. " 'Of course not'?"

"I had to know what was going on."

"Ah. Did you know I would be here?"

"Not before I saw Ulfin and the horses, no. And not because you told me to keep to the road, either. But I—shall we say I knew something was abroad in the forest tonight, and that I had to find it?"

He regarded me for a moment longer. I had been right in thinking he would not look surprised. Then he jerked his head. "Come, it's cold, and I want my cloak." As I followed him up the grating shingle he added, over his shoulder: "I take it that Ulfin is still there?"

"I should think so. You have him pretty efficiently frightened."

"He has no need to be afraid, as long as he keeps away and sees nothing."

"Then it's true he doesn't know?"

"Whatever he knows or doesn't know," he said indifferently, "he has the sense to keep silent. I have promised him that if he obeys me in these things without question, then I shall free him in time to escape."

"Escape? From what?"

"Death when I die. It is normal to send the priests' servants with them."

We were walking side by side up the path. I glanced at him. He was wearing a dark robe, more elegant than anything I had seen at home, even the clothes Camlach wore; his belt was of beautifully worked leather, probably Italian, and there was a big round brooch at his shoulder where the moonlight caught a design of circles and knotted snakes in gold. He looked—even under the film which tonight's proceedings had drawn over him—Romanized, urbane, intelligent. I said: "Forgive me, Belasius, but didn't that kind of thing go out with the Egyptians? Even in Wales we would think it old-fashioned."

"Perhaps. But then you might say the Goddess herself is old-fashioned, and likes to be worshipped in the ways she knows. And our way is almost as old as she is, older than men can remember, even in songs or stones. Long before the bulls were killed in Persia, long before they came to Crete, long before even the sky-gods came out of Africa and these stones were raised to them, the Goddess was here in the sacred grove. Now the forest is closed to us, and we worship where we can, but wherever the Goddess is, be it stone or tree or cave, there is the grove called Nemet, and there we make the offering. —I see you understand me."

"Very well. I was taught these things in Wales. But it's a few hundred years since they made the kind of offering you made tonight."

His voice was smooth as oil. "He was killed for sacrilege. Did they not teach you—?" He stopped dead, and his hand dropped to his hip. His tone changed. "That's Cadal's horse." His head went round like a hunting dog's.

"I brought it," I said. "I told you my pony went lame. Cadal will have gone home. I suppose he took one of yours."

I unhitched the mare and brought her out into the moonlight of the open path. He was settling the dagger back in its sheath. We walked on, the mare following, her nose at my shoulder. My foot had almost ceased to hurt.

I said: "So, death for Cadal, too? This isn't just a question of sacrilege, then? Your ceremonies are so very secret? Is this a matter of a mystery, Belasius, or is what you do illegal?"

"It is both secret and illegal. We meet where we can. Tonight we had to use the island; it's safe enough—normally there's not a soul would come near it on the night of the equinox. But if word came to Budec there would be trouble. The man we killed tonight was a King's man; he's been held here for eight days now, and Budec's scouts have been searching for him. But he had to die."

"Will they find him now?"

"Oh, yes, a long way from here, in the forest. They will think a wild boar ripped him." Again that slanting glance. "You could say he died easily, in the end. In the old days he would have had his navel cut out, and would have been whipped round and round the sacred tree until his guts were wrapped round it like wool on a spindle."

"And does Ambrosius know?"

"Ambrosius is a King's man, too."

We walked for a few paces in silence. "Well, and what comes to me, Belasius?"

"Nothing."

"Isn't it sacrilege to spy on your secrets?"

"You're safe enough," he said dryly. "Ambrosius has a long arm. Why do you look like that?"

I shook my head. I could not have put it into words, even to myself. It was like suddenly having a shield put into your hand when you are naked in battle.

He said: "You weren't afraid?"

"No."

"By the Goddess, I think that's true. Ambrosius was right, you have courage."

"If I have, it's hardly the kind that you need admire. I thought once that I was better than other boys because there were so many of their fears I couldn't share or understand. I had others of my own, of course, but I learned to keep them to myself. I suppose that was a kind of pride. But now I am beginning to understand why, even when danger and death lie openly waiting in the path, I can walk straight by them."

He stopped. We were nearly at the grove. "Tell me why."

"Because they are not for me. I have feared for other

men, but never in that way for myself. Not yet. I think what
men fear is the unknown. They fear pain and death, because
these may be waiting round any corner. But there are times
when I know what is hidden, and waiting, or when—I told
you—I see it lying straight in the pathway. And I know
where pain and danger lie for me, and I know that death is
not yet to come; so I am not afraid. This isn't courage."

He said slowly: "Yes. I knew you had the Sight."

"It comes only sometimes, and at the god's will, not
mine." I had said too much already; he was not a man to
share one's gods with. I said quickly, to turn the subject:
"Belasius, you must listen to me. None of this is Ulfin's fault.
He refused to tell us anything, and would have stopped me if
he could."

"You mean that if there is any paying to be done, you're
offering to do it?"

"Well, it seems only fair, and after all, I can afford to." I
laughed at him, secure behind my invisible shield. "What's it
to be? An old-fashioned religion like yours must have a few
minor penalties held in reserve? Shall I die of the cramps in
my sleep tonight, or get ripped by a boar next time I ride in
the forest without my black dog?"

He smiled for the first time. "You needn't think you'll
escape quite freely. I've a use for you and this Sight of yours,
be sure of that. Ambrosius is not the only one who uses men
for what they are worth, and I intend to use you. You have
told me you were led here tonight; it was the Goddess herself
who led you, and to the Goddess you must go." He dropped
an arm round my shoulders. "You are going to pay for this
night's work, Merlin Emrys, in coin that will content her.
The Goddess is going to hunt you down, as she does all men
who spy on her mystery—but not to destroy you. Oh, no; not
Actaeon, my apt little scholar, but Endymion. She will take
you into her embrace. In other words, you are going to study
until I can take you with me to the sanctuary, and present
you there."

I would have liked to say, "Not if you wrapped my guts
round every tree in the forest," but I held my tongue. Take
power where it is offered, he had said, and—remembering
my vigil by the ash tree—there had been power there, of a
kind. We should see. I moved—but courteously—from under
the arm round my shoulders, and led the way up into the
grove.

If Ulfin had been frightened before, he was almost speechless with terror when he saw me with his master, and realized where I had been.

"My lord ... I thought he had gone home ... Indeed, my lord, Cadal said—"

"Hand me my cloak," said Belasius, "and put this thing in the saddle-bag."

He threw down the white robe which he had been carrying. It fell loosely, unfolding, near the tree Aster was tied to, and as it dropped near him, the pony shied and snorted. At first I thought this was just at the ghostly fall of white near his feet, but then I saw, black on the white, dimmed even as it was by the darkness of the grove, the stains and splashing, and I smelled, even from where I stood, the smoke and the fresh blood.

Ulfin held the cloak up mechanically. "My Lord"—he was breathless with fear and the effort of holding the restive horse at the same time—"Cadal took the pack horse. We thought my lord Merlin had gone back to the town. Indeed, sir, I was sure myself that he had gone that way. I told him nothing. I swear—"

"There's a saddle-bag on Cadal's mare. Put it there." Belasius pulled his cloak on and fastened it, then reached for the reins. "Hand me up."

The boy obeyed, trying, I could see, not only to excuse himself, but to gauge the strength of Belasius' anger. "My lord, please believe me, I said nothing. I'll swear it by any gods there are."

Belasius ignored him. He could be cruel, I knew; in fact, in all the time I knew him he never once spared a thought for another's anxiety or pain: more exactly, it never occurred to him that feeling could exist, even in a free man. Ulfin must have seemed at that moment less real to him than the horse he was controlling. He swung easily to the saddle, saying curtly, "Stand back." Then to me, "Can you manage the mare if we gallop? I want to get back before Cadal finds you're not home, and sets the place by the ears."

"I can try. What about Ulfin?"

"What about him? He'll walk your pony home, of course."

He swung his horse round, and rode out between the pine boughs. Ulfin had already run to bundle up the bloodstained robe and stuff it in the brown mare's saddle-bag. He hurried now to give me his shoulder, and somehow between us I scrambled into the saddle and settled myself. The boy stood back, silent, but I had felt how he was shaking. I suppose that for a slave it was normal to be so afraid. It came to me that he was even afraid to lead my pony home alone through the forest.

I hung on the rein for a moment and leaned down. "Ulfin, he's not angry with you; nothing will happen. I swear it. So don't be afraid."

"Did you . . . see anything, my lord?"

"Nothing at all." In the way that mattered this was the truth. I looked down at him soberly. "A blaze of darkness," I said, "and an innocent moon. But whatever I might have seen, Ulfin, it would not have mattered. I am to be initiated. So you see why he is not angry? That is all. Here, take this."

I slid my dagger from its sheath and flicked it to quiver point down in the pine needles.

"If it makes you easier," I said, "but you won't need it. You will be quite safe. Take it from me. I know. Lead my pony gently, won't you?"

I kicked the mare in the ribs and headed her after Belasius.

He was waiting for me—that is to say he was going at an easy canter, which quickened to a hand-gallop as I caught him up. The brown mare pounded behind him. I gripped the neck-strap and clung like a burr.

The track was open enough for us to see our way clearly in the moonlight. It sliced its way uphill through the forest to a crest from which, momentarily, one could see the glimmer of the town's lights. Then it plunged downhill again, and after a while we rode out of the forest onto the salt plains that fringed the sea.

Belasius neither slackened speed nor spoke. I hung on to the mare, watched the track over her shoulder, and wondered whether we would meet Cadal coming back for me with an escort, or if he would come alone.

We splashed through a stream, fetlock-deep, and then the track, beaten flat along the level turf, turned right in the direction of the main road. I knew where we were now; on our ride out I had noticed this track branching off just short of a bridge at the forest's edge. In a few minutes we would reach the bridge and the made road.

Belasius slackened his horse's pace and glanced over his shoulder. The mare thudded alongside, then he put up a hand and drew rein. The horses slowed to a walk.

"Listen."

Horses. A great many horses, coming at a fast trot along the paved road. They were making for the town.

A man's voice was briefly raised. Over the bridge came a flurry of tossing torches, and we saw them, a troop riding close. The standard in the torchlight showed a scarlet dragon.

Belasius' hand came hard down on my rein, and our horses stopped.

"Ambrosius' men," he said, at least that is what he began to say, when, clear as cock-crow, my mare whinnied, and a horse from the troop answered her.

Someone barked an order. The troop checked. Another order, and horses headed our way at the gallop. I heard Belasius curse under his breath as he let go my rein.

"This is where you leave me. Hang on now, and see you guard your tongue. Even Ambrosius' arm cannot protect you from a curse." He lashed my mare across the quarters, and she jumped forward, nearly unseating me. I was too busy to watch him go, but behind me there was a splash and a scramble as the black horse jumped the stream and was swallowed by the forest seconds before the soldiers met me and wheeled to either side to escort me back to their officer.

The grey stallion was fidgeting in the blaze of torches under the standard. One of my escorts had hold of the mare's bit, and led me forward.

He saluted. "Only the one, sir. He's not armed."

The officer pushed up his visor. Blue eyes widened, and Uther's too-well-remembered voice said: "It had to be you, of course. Well, Merlin the bastard, what are you doing here alone, and where have you been?"

11

I didn't answer straight away. I was wondering how much to say. To any other officer I might have told a quick and easy half-truth, but Uther was likely to ride me hard, and for anyone who had been at a meeting both "secret and illegal," Uther was not just any officer, he was dangerous. Not that there was any reason for me to protect Belasius, but I did not owe information—or explanation—to anyone but Ambrosius. In any case, to steer aside from Uther's anger came naturally.

So I met his eyes with what I hoped was an expression of

frankness. "My pony went lame, sir, so I left my servant to walk him home, and took my servant's horse to ride back myself." As he opened his mouth to speak, I hoisted the invisible shield that Belasius had put into my hand. "Usually your brother sends for me after supper, and I didn't wish to keep him waiting."

His brows snapped down at my mention of Ambrosius, but all he said was: "Why that way, at this hour? Why not by the road?"

"We'd gone some way into the forest when Aster hurt himself. We had turned east at the crossways into the logging track, and there was a path branching south from that which looked like a quicker way home, so we took it. The moonlight made it quite easy to see."

"Which path was this?"

"I don't know the forest, sir. It climbed the ridge and then down to a ford about a mile downstream."

He considered me for a moment, frowning. "Where did you leave your servant?"

"A little way along the second path. We wanted to be quite sure that it was the right way before he let me come on alone. He'll be about climbing the ridge now, I should think." I was praying, confusedly but sincerely, to whatever god might be listening, that Cadal was not at the moment riding back from town to find me.

Uther regarded me, sitting his fidgeting horse as if it did not exist. It was the first time I had realized how like his brother he was. And for the first time, too, I recognized something like power in him, and understood, young as I was, what Ambrosius had told me about his brilliance as a captain. He could judge men to a hairsbreadth. I knew he was looking straight through me, scenting a lie, not knowing where, or why, but wondering. And determined to find out
. . .

For once he spoke quite pleasantly, without heat, even gently. "You're lying, aren't you? Why?"

"Its quite true, my lord. If you look at my pony when he comes in—"

"Oh, yes, that was true. I've no doubt I'll find he's lame. And if I send men back up the path they'll find Cadal leading him home. But what I want to know—"

I said quickly: "Not Cadal, my lord; Ulfin. Cadal had other duties, and Belasius sent Ulfin with me."

"Two of a kind?" The words were contemptuous.

"My lord?"

His voice cracked suddenly with temper. "Don't bandy words with me, you little catamite. You're lying about something, and I want to know what. I can smell a lie a mile off." Then he looked past me, and his voice changed. "What's that in your saddle-bag?" A jerk of his head at one of the soldiers flanking me. A corner of Belasius' robe was showing. The man thrust his hand into the bag and pulled it out. On the soiled and crumpled white the stains showed dark and unmistakable. I could smell the blood even through the bubbling resin of the torches.

Behind Uther the horses snorted and tossed their heads, scenting it, and the men looked at one another. I saw the torch-bearers eyeing me askance, and the guard beside me muttered something under his breath.

Uther said, violently: "By all the gods below, so that was it! One of them, by Mithras! I should have known, I can smell the holy smoke on you from here! All right, bastard, you that's so mighty free with my brother's name, and so high in his favour, we'll see what he has to say to this. What have you to say for yourself now? There's not much point in denying it, is there?"

I lifted my head. Sitting the big mare, I could meet him almost eye to eye. "Deny? I'm denying that I've broken a law, or done anything the Count wouldn't like—and those are the only two things that matter, my lord Uther. I'll explain to him."

"By God you will! So Ulfin took you there?"

I said sharply: "Ulfin had nothing to do with it. I had already left him. In any case, he is a slave, and does as I bid him."

He spurred his horse suddenly, right up to the mare. He leaned forward, gripping the folds of my cloak at the neck, and tightening the grip till he half-lifted me from the saddle. His face was thrust close to mine, his armed knee hurting my leg as the horses stamped and sidled together. He spoke through his teeth. "And you do as I bid you, hear that. Whatever you may be to my brother, you obey me, too." He tightened the grip still further, shaking me. "Understand, Merlin Emrys?"

I nodded. He swore as my brooch-pin scratched him, and let me go. There was a streak of blood on his hand. I saw his eyes on the brooch. He flicked his fingers to the torch-bearer, and the man pushed nearer, holding the flame high. "He gave you that to wear? The red dragon?" Then he stopped short as his eyes came up to my face and fixed there, stared, widened. The intense blue seemed to blaze. The grey stallion sidled and he curbed it sharply, so that the foam sprang.

"Merlin Emrys . . ." He said it again, this time to himself, so softly that I hardly caught it. Then suddenly he let out a laugh, amused and gay and hard, not like anything I had heard from him before.

"Well, Merlin Emrys, you'll still have to answer to him for where you've been tonight!" He wheeled his horse, flinging over his shoulder to the men: "Bring him along, and see he doesn't fall off. It seems my brother treasures him."

The grey horse jumped under the spur, and the troop surged after him. My captors, still holding the brown mare's bridle, pounded after, with me between them.

The druid's robe lay trampled and filthy in the dirt, where the troop had ridden over it. I wondered if Belasius would see it and take warning.

Then I forgot him. I still had Ambrosius to face.

Cadal was in my room. I said with relief: "Well, thank the gods you didn't come back after me. I was picked up by Uther's lot, and he's blazing mad because he knows where I went."

"I know," said Cadal grimly. "I saw it."

"What do you mean?"

"I did ride back for you. I'd made sure you'd had the sense to run for home when you heard that . . . noise, so I went after you. When I saw no sign of you on the way I just thought you must have got a tidy turn of speed out of the mare—the ground was fair smoking under *me*, I can tell you! Then when—"

"You guessed what was happening? Where Belasius was?"

"Aye." He turned his head as if to spit on the floor, recollected himself, and made the sign against the evil eye. "Well, when I got back here, and no sign of you, I knew you must've gone straight down to see what was going on. High-handed little fool. Might have got yourself killed, meddling with that lot."

"So might you. But you went back."

"What else could I do? You should've heard what I was calling you, too. Proper little nuisance was the least of it. Well, I was about half a mile out of town when I saw them coming, and I pulled aside and waited for them to pass. You know that old posting station, the ruined one? I was there. I watched them go by, and you at the back under guard. So I guessed he knew. I followed them back to town as close as I dared, and cut home through the side streets. I've only just got in. He found out, then?"

I nodded, beginning to unfasten my cloak.

"Then there'll be the devil to pay, and no mistake," said Cadal. "How did he find out?"

"Belasius had put his robe in my saddle-bag, and they found it. They think it was mine." I grinned. "If they'd tried it for size they'd have had to think again. But that didn't occur to them. They just dropped it in the mud and rode over it."

"About right, too." He had gone down on one knee to unfasten my sandals. He paused, with one in his hand. "Are you telling me Belasius saw you? Had words with you?"

"Yes. I waited for him, and we walked back together to the horses. Ulfin's bringing Aster, by the way."

He ignored that. He was staring, and I thought he had lost colour.

"Uther didn't see Belasius," I said. "Belasius dodged in time. He knew they'd heard one horse, so he sent me forward to meet them, otherwise I suppose they'd have come after us both. He must have forgotten I had the robe, or else chanced their not finding it. Anybody but Uther wouldn't even have looked."

"You should never have gone near Belasius. It's worse than I thought. Here, let me do that. Your hands are cold." He pulled the dragon brooch off and took my cloak. "You want to watch it, you do. He's a nasty customer—they all are, come to that—and him most of all."

"Did you know about him?"

"Not to say know. I might have guessed. It's right up his street, if you ask me. But what I meant was, they're a nasty lot to tangle with."

"Well, he's the archdruid, or at least the head of this sect, so he'll carry some weight. Don't look so troubled, Cadal, I doubt if he'll harm me, or let anyone else harm me."

"Did he threaten you?"

I laughed. "Yes. With a curse."

"They say these things stick. They say the druids can send a knife after you that'll hunt you down for days, and all you know is the whistling noise in the air behind you just before it strikes."

"They say all sort of things. Cadal, have I another tunic

that's decent? Did my best one come back from the fuller? And I want a bath before I go to the Count."

He eyed me sideways as he reached in the clothes-chest for another tunic. "Uther will have gone straight to him. You know that?"

I laughed. "Of course. I warn you, I shall tell Ambrosius the truth."

"All of it?"

"All of it."

"Well, I suppose that's best," he said. "If anyone can protect you from them—"

"It's not that. It's simply that he ought to know. He has the right. Besides, what have I to hide from him?"

He said uneasily: "I was thinking about the curse ... Even Ambrosius might not be able to protect you from that."

"Oh, that to the curse." I made a gesture not commonly seen in noblemen's houses. "Forget it. Neither you nor I have done wrong, and I refuse to lie to Ambrosius."

"Some day I'll see you scared, Merlin."

"Probably."

"Weren't you even scared of Belasius?"

"Should I be?" I was interested. "He'll do me no harm." I unhooked the belt of my tunic, and threw it on the bed. I regarded Cadal. "Would you be afraid if you knew your own end, Cadal?"

"Yes, by the dog! Do you?"

"Sometimes, in snatches. Sometimes I see it. It fills me with fear."

He stood still, looking at me, and there was fear in his face. "What is it, then?"

"A cave. The crystal cave. Sometimes I think it is death, and at other times it is birth or a gate of vision, or a dark limbo of sleep ... I cannot tell. But some day I shall know. Till then, I suppose I am not afraid of much else. I shall come to the cave in the end, as you—" I broke off.

"As I what?" he said quickly. "What'll I come to?"

I smiled. "I was going to say 'As you will come to old age.'"

"That's a lie," he said roughly. "I saw your eyes. When you're seeing things, your eyes go queer; I've noticed it before. The black spreads and goes kind of blurred, dreaming-like—but not soft; no, your whole look goes cold, like cold iron, as if you neither saw nor cared about what's going on round you. And you talk as if you were just a voice and not a person ... Or as if you'd gone somewhere else and left your body for something else to speak through. Like a horn being blown through to make the sound carry. Oh, I know I've only seen it a couple of times, for a moment, but it's uncanny, and it frightens me."

"It frightens me, too, Cadal." I had let the green tunic slide from my body to the floor. He was holding out the grey wool robe I wore for a bedgown. I reached absently for it, and sat down on the bed's edge, with it trailing over my knees. I was talking to myself rather than Cadal. "It frightens me, too. You're right, that's how it feels, as if I were an empty shell with something working through me. I say things, see things, think things, till that moment I never knew of. But you're wrong in thinking I don't feel. It hurts me. I think this may be because I can't command whatever speaks through me ... I mean, I can't command it yet. But I shall. I know this, too. Some day I shall command this part of me that knows and sees, this god, and that really will be power. I shall know when what I foretell is human instinct, and when it is God's shadow."

"And when you spoke of my end, what was that?"

I looked up. Oddly enough it was less easy to lie to Cadal than it had been to Uther. "But I haven't seen your death, Cadal, no one's but my own. I was being tactless. I was going to say 'As you will come to a foreign grave somewhere ...'" I smiled. "I know this is worse than hell to a Breton. But I think it will happen to you ... That is, if you stay as my servant."

His look lightened, and he grinned. This was power, I thought, when a word of mine could frighten men like this. He said: "Oh, I'll do that all right. Even if he hadn't asked me to, I'd stay. You've an easy way with you that makes it a pleasure to look after you."

"Have I? I thought you found me a high-handed little fool, and a nuisance besides?"

"There you are, you see. I'd never have dared say that to anyone else your class, and all you do is laugh, and you twice royal."

"*Twice* royal? You can hardly count my grandfather as well as my—" I stopped. What stopped me was his face. He had spoken without thought, then, on a quick gasp, had tried to catch the words back into his mouth and unspeak them.

He said nothing, just stood there with the soiled tunic in his hand. I stood up slowly, the forgotten bedgown falling to the floor. There was no need for him to speak. I knew. I could not imagine how I had not known before, the moment I stood before Ambrosius in the frosty field and he stared down in the torchlight. He had known. And a hundred others must have guessed. I remembered now the sidelong looks of the men, the mutterings of the officers, the deference of servants which I had taken for respect for Ambrosius' commands, but which I saw now was deference to Ambrosius' son.

The room was still as a cave. The brazier flickered and its light broke and scattered in the bronze mirror against the wall. I looked that way. In the firelit bronze my naked body showed slight and shadowy, an unreal thing of firelight and darkness shifting as the flames moved. But the face was lit, and in its heavily defined planes of fire and shadow I saw his face as I had seen it in his room, when he sat over the brazier waiting for me to be brought to him. Waiting for me to come so that he could ask me about Niniane.

And here again the Sight had not helped me. Men that have god's-sight, I have found, are often human-blind.

I said to Cadal: "Everybody knows?"

He nodded. He didn't ask what I meant. "It's rumoured. You're very like him sometimes."

"I think Uther may have guessed. He didn't know before?"

"No. He left before the talk started to go round. That wasn't why he took against you."

"I'm glad to hear it," I said. "What was it, then? Just because I got across him over that business of the standing stone?"

"Oh, that, and other things."

"Such as?"

Cadal said, bluntly: "He thought you were the Count's catamite. Ambrosius doesn't go for women much. He doesn't go for boys either, come to that, but one thing Uther can't understand is a man who isn't in and out of bed with someone seven nights a week. When his brother bothered such a lot with you, had you in his house and set me to look after you and all that, Uther thought that's what must be going on, and he didn't half like it."

"I see. He did say something like that tonight, but I thought it was only because he'd lost his temper."

"If he'd bothered to look at you, or listen to what folks were saying, he'd have known fast enough."

"He knows now." I spoke with sudden, complete certainty.

"He saw it, back there on the road, when he saw the dragon brooch the Count gave me. I'd never thought about it, but of course he would realize the Count would hardly put the royal cipher on his catamite. He had the torch brought up, and took a good look at me. I think he saw it then." A thought struck me. "And I think Belasius knows."

"Oh, yes," said Cadal, "he knows. Why?"

"The way he talked ... As if he knew he daren't touch me. That would be why he tried to scare me with the threat of a curse. He's a pretty cool hand, isn't he? He must have been thinking very hard on the way up to the grove. He daren't put me quietly out of the way for sacrilege, but he had to stop me talking somehow. Hence the curse. And also—" I stopped.

"And also what?"

"Don't sound so startled. It was only another guarantee I'd hold my tongue."

"For the gods' sake, what?"

I shrugged, realized I was still naked, and reached for the bedgown again. "He said he would take me with him to the sanctuary. I think he would like to make a druid of me."

"He said that?" I was getting familiar with Cadal's sign to avert the evil eye. "What will you do?"

"I'll go with him ... once, at least. Don't look like that, Cadal. There isn't a cat's chance in a fire that I'll want to go more than once." I looked at him soberly. "But there's nothing in this world that I'm not ready to see and learn, and no god that I'm not ready to approach in his own fashion. I told you that truth was the shadow of God. If I am to use it, I must know who He is. Do you understand me?"

"How could I? What god are you talking about?"

"I think there is only one. Oh, there are gods everywhere, in the hollow hills, in the wind and the sea, in the very grass we walk on and the air we breathe, and in the bloodstained shadows where men like Belasius wait for them. But I believe there must be one who is God Himself, like the great sea, and all the rest of us, small gods and men and all, like rivers, we all come to Him in the end. —Is the bath ready?"

Twenty minutes later, in a dark blue tunic clipped at the shoulder by the dragon brooch, I went to see my father.

12

The secretary was in the anteroom, rather elaborately doing nothing. Beyond the curtain I heard Ambrosius' voice speaking quietly. The two guards at the door looked wooden.

Then the curtain was pulled aside and Uther came out. When he saw me he checked, hung on his heel as if to speak, then seemed to catch the secretary's interested look, and went by with a swish of the red cloak and a smell of horses. You could always tell where Uther had been; he seemed to soak up scents like a wash-cloth. He must have gone straight to his brother before he had even cleaned up after the ride home.

The secretary, whose name was Sollius, said to me: "You may as well go straight in, sir. He'll be expecting you."

I hardly even noticed the "sir." It seemed to be something I was already accustomed to. I went in.

He was standing with his back to the door, over by the table. This was strewn with tablets, and a stilus lay across one of them as if he had been interrupted while writing. On the secretary's desk near the window a half-unrolled book lay where it had been dropped.

The door shut behind me. I stopped just inside it, and the leather curtain fell closed with a ruffle and a flap. He turned.

Our eyes met in silence, it seemed for interminable seconds, then he cleared his throat and said: "Ah, Merlin," and then, with a slight movement of the hand, "Sit down."

I obeyed him, crossing to my usual stool near the brazier. He was silent for a moment, looking down at the table. He picked up the stilus, looked absently down at the wax, and added a word. I waited. He scowled down at what he had done, scored it out again, then threw the stilus down and said abruptly: "Uther has been to see me."

"Yes, sir."

He looked up under frowning brows. "I understand he came on you riding alone beyond the town."

I said quickly: "I didn't go out alone. Cadal was with me."

"Cadal?"

"Yes, sir."

"That's not what you told Uther."

"No, sir."

His look was keen now, arrested. "Well, go on."

"Cadal always attends me, my lord. He's—more than faithful. We went north as far as the logging track in the forest, and a short way along that my pony went lame, so Cadal gave me his mare, and we started to walk home." I took a breath. "We took a short cut, and came on Belasius and his servant. Belasius rode part of the way home with me, but it—it didn't suit him to meet Prince Uther, so he left me."

"I see." His voice gave nothing away, but I had the feeling that he saw quite a lot. His next question confirmed it. "Did you go to the druids' island?"

"You know about it?" I said, surprised. Then as he did not answer, waiting in cold silence for me to speak, I went on: "I told you Cadal and I took a short cut through the forest. If you know the island, you'll know the track we followed. Just where the path goes down to the sea there's a pine grove. We found Ulfin—that's Belasius' servant—there with the two horses. Cadal wanted to take Ulfin's horse and get me home quickly, but while we were talking to Ulfin we heard a cry—a scream, rather, from somewhere east of the grove. I went to see. I swear I had no idea the island was there, or what happened there. Nor had Cadal, and if he'd been mounted, as I was, he'd have stopped me. But by the time he'd taken Ulfin's horse and set off after me I was out of sight, and he thought I'd taken fright and gone home—which is what he'd told me to do—and it wasn't until he got right back here that he found I hadn't come this way. He went back for me, but by that time I'd come up with the troop." I thrust my hands down between my knees, clutching them tightly together. "I don't know what made me ride down to the island. At least, I do; it was the cry, so I went to see ... But it wasn't only because of the cry. I can't explain, not yet ..." I took a breath. "My lord—"

"Well?"

"I ought to tell you. A man was killed there tonight, on the island. I don't know who he was, but I heard that he was a King's man who has been missing for some days. His body will be found somewhere in the forest, as if a wild beast had killed him." I paused. There was nothing to be seen in his face. "I thought I should tell you."

"You went over to the island?"

"Oh, no! I doubt if I'd be alive now if I had. I found out later about the man who was killed. It was sacrilege, they

said. I didn't ask about it." I looked up at him. "I only went
down as far as the shore. I waited there in the trees, and
watched it—the dance and the offering. I could hear the
singing. I didn't know then that it was illegal . . . It's forbidden
at home, of course, but one knows it still goes on, and I
thought it might be different here. But when my lord Uther
knew where I'd been he was very angry. He seems to hate
the druids."

"The druids?" His voice was absent now. He still fidgeted
with the stilus on the table. "Ah, yes. Uther has no love for
them. He is one of Mithras' fanatics, and light is the enemy
of darkness, I suppose. Well, what is it?" This, sharply, to
Sollius, who came in with an apology, and waited just inside
the door.

"Forgive me, sir," said the secretary. "There's a messenger
from King Budec. I told him you were engaged, but he said
it was important. Shall I tell him to wait?"

"Bring him in," said Ambrosius. The man came in with a
scroll. He handed it to Ambrosius, who sat down in his great
chair and unrolled it. He read it, frowning. I watched him.
The flickering flames from the brazier spread, lighting the
planes of the face which already, it seemed, I knew as well as
I knew my own. The heart of the brazier glowed, and the
light spread and flashed. I felt it spreading across my eyes as
they blurred and widened . . .

"Merlin Emrys? Merlin?"
The echo died to an ordinary voice. The vision fled. I was
sitting on my stool in Ambrosius' room, looking down at my
hands clasping my knees. Ambrosius had risen and was standing over me, between me and the fire. The secretary had
gone, and we were alone.

At the repetition of my name I blinked and roused myself.
He was speaking. "What do you see, there in the fire?"

I answered without looking up. "A grove of whitethorn on a
hillside and a girl on a brown pony, and a young man with a
dragon brooch on his shoulder, and the mist knee-high."

I heard him draw a long breath, then his hand came down
and took me by the chin and lifted my face. His eyes were
intent and fierce.

"It's true, then, this Sight of yours. I have been so sure,
and now—now, beyond all doubt, it is true. I thought it was,
that first night by the standing stone, but that could have
been anything—a dream, a boy's story, a lucky guess to win

my interest. But this ... I was right about you." He took his hand from my face, and straightened. "Did you see the girl's face?"

I nodded.

"And the man's?"

I met his eyes then. "Yes, sir."

He turned sharply away and stood with his back to me, head bent. Once more he picked up the stilus from the table, turning it over and over with his fingers. After a while he said: "How long have you known?"

"Only since I rode in tonight. It was something Cadal said, then I remembered things, and how your brother stared tonight when he saw me wearing this." I touched the dragon brooch at my neck.

He glanced, then nodded. "Is this the first time you have had this—vision?"

"Yes. I had no idea. Now, it seems strange to me that I never even suspected—but I swear I did not."

He stood silent, one hand spread on the table, leaning on it. I don't know what I had expected, but I had never thought to see the great Aurelius Ambrosius at a loss for words. He took a turn across the room to the window, and back again, and spoke. "This is a strange meeting, Merlin. So much to say, and yet so little. Do you see now why I asked so many questions? Why I tried so hard to find what had brought you here?"

"The gods at work, my lord, they brought me here," I said. "Why did you leave her?"

I had not meant the question to come out so abruptly, but I suppose it had been pressing on me so long that now it burst out with the force of an accusation. I began to stammer something, but he cut me short with a gesture, and answered quietly.

"I was eighteen, Merlin, with a price on my head if I set foot in my own kingdom. You know the story—how my cousin Budec took me in when my brother the King was murdered, and how he never ceased to plan for vengeance on Vortigern, though for many years it seemed impossible. But all the time he sent scouts, took in reports, went on planning. And then when I was eighteen he sent me over myself, secretly, to Gorlois of Cornwall, who was my father's friend, and who has never loved Vortigern. Gorlois sent me north with a couple of men he could trust, to watch and listen and learn the lie of the land. Some day I'll tell you where we went, and what happened, but not now. What concerns you now is this ... We were riding south near the end of October, towards Cornwall to take ship for home, when we were set upon, and had to fight for it. They were Vortigern's men. I don't know yet whether they suspected us, or whether they were killing—as Saxons and foxes do—for wantonness and the sweet taste of blood. The latter, I think, or they would have made surer of killing me. They killed my two companions, but I was lucky; I got off with a flesh wound, and a knock on the head that struck me senseless, and they left me for dead. This was at dusk. When I moved and looked about me it was morning, and a brown pony was standing over me, with a girl on his back staring from me to the dead men and back again, with never a sound." The first glimmer of a smile, not at me, but at the memory. "I remember trying to speak, but I had lost a lot of blood, and the night in the open had brought on a fever. I was afraid she would take fright and gallop back to the town, and that would be the end of it. But she did not. She caught my horse and got my saddle-bag, and gave me a drink, then she cleaned the wound and tied it up and then—God knows how—got me across the horse and out of that valley. There was a place she knew of, she said, nearer the town, but remote and secret; no one ever went there. It was a cave, with a spring— What is it?"

"Nothing," I said. "I should have known. Go on. No one lived there then?"

"No one. By the time we got there I suppose I was delirious; I remember nothing. She hid me in the cave, and my horse too, out of sight. There had been food and wine in my saddle-bag, and I had my cloak and a blanket. It was late afternoon by then, and when she rode home she heard that the two dead men had already been found, with their horses straying nearby. The troop had been riding north; it wasn't likely that anyone in the town knew there should have been three corpses found. So I was safe. Next day she rode up to the cave again, with food and medicines ... And the next day, too." He paused. "And you know the end of the story."

"When did you tell her who you were?"

"When she told me why she could not leave Maridunum and go with me. I had thought till then that she was perhaps one of the Queen's ladies—from her ways and her talk I knew she had been bred in a king's house. Perhaps she saw the same in me. But it didn't matter. Nothing mattered, except that I was a man, and she a woman. From the first day, we both knew what would happen. You will understand how it was when you are older." Again the smile, this time touching mouth as well as eyes. "This is one kind of knowledge I think you will have to wait for, Merlin. The Sight won't help you much in matters of love."

"You asked her to go with you—to come back here?"

He nodded. "Even before I knew who she was. After I knew, I was afraid for her, and pressed her harder, but she would not come with me. From the way she had spoken I knew she hated and feared the Saxons, and feared what Vortigern was doing to the kingdoms, but still she would not come. It was one thing, she said, to do what she had done, but another to go across the seas with the man who, when he came back, must be her father's enemy. We must end it, she said, as the year was ending, and then forget."

He was silent for a minute, looking down at his hands.

I said: "And you never knew she had borne a child?"

"No. I wondered, of course. I sent a message the next spring, but got no answer. I left it then, knowing that if she wanted me, she knew—all the world knew—where to find me. Then I heard—it must have been nearly two years later—that she was betrothed. I know now that this was not true, but then it served to make me dismiss it from my mind." He looked at me. "Do you understand that?"

I nodded. "It may even have been true, though not in the way you'd understand it, my lord. She vowed herself to the Church when I should have no more need of her. The Christians call that a betrothal."

"So?" He considered for a moment. "Whatever it was, I sent no more messages. And when later on there was mention of a child, a bastard, it hardly crossed my mind that it could be mine. A fellow came here once, a travelling eye-doctor who had been through Wales, and I sent for him and questioned him, and he said yes, there was a bastard boy at the palace of such and such an age, red-haired, and the King's own."

"Dinias," I said. "He probably never saw me. I was kept out of the way ... And my grandfather did sometimes explain me away to strangers as his own. He had a few scattered around, here and there."

"So I gathered. So the next rumour of a boy—possibly the King's bastard, possibly his daughter's—I hardly listened to. It was all long past, and there were pressing things to do, and always there was the same thought—if she had borne a child to me, would she not have let me know? If she had wanted me, would she not have sent word?"

He fell silent then, back in his own thoughts. Whether I understood it all then, as he talked, I do not now recollect. But later, when the pieces shook together to make the mosaic, it was clear enough. The same pride which had forbidden her to go with her lover had forbidden her, once she discovered her pregnancy, to call him back. And it helped her through the months that followed. More than that; if—by flight or any other means—she had betrayed who her lover was, nothing would have stopped her brothers from travelling to Budec's court to kill him. There must—knowing my grandfather—have been angry oaths enough about what they would do to the man who had fathered her bastard. And then time moved on, and his coming grew remote, and then impossible, as if he were indeed a myth and a memory in the night. And then the other long love stepped in to supersede him, and the priests took over, and the winter tryst was forgotten. Except for the child, so like his father; but once her duty to him was done, she could go to the solitude and peace which—all those years ago—had sent her riding alone up the mountain valley, as later I was to ride out alone by the same path, and looking perhaps for the same things.

I jumped when he spoke again. "How hard a time of it did you have, as a no-man's-child?"

"Hard enough."

"You believe me when I say I didn't know?"

"I believe anything you tell me, my lord."

"Do you hate me for this, very much, Merlin?"

I said slowly, looking down at my hands: "There is one thing about being a bastard and a no-man's-child. You are free to imagine your father. You can picture for yourself the worst and the best; you can make your father for yourself, in the image of the moment. From the time I was big enough to understand what I was, I saw my father in every soldier and every prince and every priest. And I saw him, too, in every handsome slave in the kingdom of South Wales."

He spoke very gently, above me. "And now you see him in truth, Merlin Emrys. I asked you, do you hate me for the kind of life I gave you?"

I didn't look up. I answered, with my eyes on the flames: "Since I was a child I have had the world to choose from for a father. Out of them all, Aurelius Ambrosius, I would have chosen you."

Silence. The flames leapt like a heartbeat.

I added, trying to make it light: "After all, what boy would not choose the King of all Britain for his father?"

His hand came hard under my chin again, turning my head aside from the brazier and my eyes from the flames. His voice was sharp. "What did you say?"

"What did I say?" I blinked up at him. "I said I would have chosen you."

His fingers dug into my flesh. "You called me King of all Britain."

"Did I?"

"But this is—" he stopped. His eyes seemed to be burning into me. Then he let his hand drop, and straightened. "Let it go. If it matters, the god will speak again." He smiled down at me. "What matters now is what you said yourself. It isn't given to every man to hear this from his grown son. Who knows, it may be better this way, to meet as men, when we each have something to give the other. To a man whose children have been underfoot since infancy, it is not given, suddenly, to see himself stamped on a boy's face as I am stamped on yours."

"Am I so like?"

"They say so. And I see enough of Uther in you to know why everyone said you were mine."

"Apparently he didn't see it," I said. "Is he very angry about it, or is he only relieved to find I'm not your catamite after all?"

"You knew about that?" He looked amused. "If he'd think with his brains instead of his body sometimes he'd be the better for it. As it is, we deal together very well. He does one kind of work, as I another, and if I can make the way straight, he'll make a king after me, if I have no—"

He bit off the word. In the queer little silence that followed I looked at the floor.

"Forgive me." He spoke quietly, equal to equal. "I spoke without thought. For so long a time I have been used to the idea that I had no son."

I looked up. "It's still the truth, in the sense you mean. And it's certainly the truth as Uther will see it."

"Then if you see it the same way, my path is the smoother."

I laughed. "I don't see myself as a king. Half a king,

perhaps, or more likely a quarter—the little bit that sees and thinks, but can't do. Perhaps Uther and I between us might make one, if you go? He's larger than life already, wouldn't you say?"

But he didn't smile. His eyes had narrowed, with an arrested look. "This is how I have been thinking, or something like it. Did you guess?"

"No sir, how could I?" I sat up straight as it broke on me: "Is this how you thought you might use me? Of course I realize now why you kept me here, in your house, and treated me so royally, but I've wanted to believe you had plans for me—that I could be of use to you. Belasius told me you used every man according to his capacity, and that even if I were no use as a soldier, you would still use me somehow. This is true?"

"Quite true. I knew it straight away, before I even thought you might be my son, when I saw how you faced Uther that night in the field, with the visions still in your eyes, and the power all over you like a shining skin. No, Merlin, you will never make a king, or even a prince as the world sees it, but when you are grown I believe you will be such a man that, if a king had you beside him, he could rule the world. Now do you begin to understand why I sent you to Belasius?"

"He is a very learned man," I said cautiously.

"He is a corrupt man and dangerous," said Ambrosius directly. "But he is a sophisticated and clever man who has travelled a good deal and who has skills you will not have had the chance to master in Wales. Learn from him. I don't say follow him, because there are places where you must not follow him, but learn all you can."

I looked up, then nodded. "You know about him." It was a conclusion, not a question.

"I know he is a priest of the old religion. Yes."

"You don't mind this?"

"I cannot yet afford to throw aside valuable tools because I don't like their design," he said. "He is useful, so I use him. You will do the same, if you are wise."

"He wants to take me to the next meeting."

He raised his brows but said nothing.

"Will you forbid this?" I asked.

"No. Will you go?"

"Yes." I said slowly, and very seriously, searching for the words: "My lord, when you are looking for ... what I am looking for, you have to look in strange places. Men can never look at the sun, except downwards, at his reflection in things of earth. If he is reflected in a dirty puddle, he is still the sun. There is nowhere I will not look, to find him."

He was smiling. "You see? You need no guarding, except what Cadal can do." He leaned back against the edge of the table, half sitting, relaxed now and easy. "Emrys, she called you. Child of the light. Of the immortals. Divine. You knew that's what it meant?"

"Yes."

"Didn't you know it was the same as mine?"

"My name?" I asked, stupidly.

He nodded. "Emrys . . . Ambrosius; it's the same word. Merlinus Ambrosius—she called you after me."

I stared at him. "I—yes, of course. It never occurred to me." I laughed.

"Why do you laugh?"

"Because of our names. Ambrosius, prince of light . . . She told everyone that my father was the prince of darkness. I've even heard a song about it. We make songs of everything, in Wales."

"Some day you must sing it to me." Then he sobered suddenly. His voice deepened. "Merlinus Ambrosius, child of the light, look at the fire now, and tell me what you see." Then, as I looked up at him, startled, he said urgently: "Now, tonight, before the fire dies, while you are weary and there is sleep in your face. Look at the brazier, and talk to me. What will come to Britain? What will come to me, and to Uther? Look now, work for me, my son, and tell me."

It was no use; I was awake, and the flames were dying in the brazier; the power had gone, leaving only a room with rapidly cooling shadows, and a man and a boy talking. But because I loved him, I turned my eyes to the embers. There was utter silence, except for the hiss of ash settling, and the tick of the cooling metal.

I said: "I see nothing but the fire dying down in the brazier, and a burning cave of coal."

"Go on looking."

I could feel the sweat starting on my body, the drops trickling down beside my nose, under my arms, into my groin till my thighs stuck together. My hands worked on one another, tight between my knees till the bones hurt. My temples ached. I shook my head sharply to clear it, and looked up. "My lord, it's no use. I'm sorry, but it's no use. I don't command the god, he commands me. Some day it may be I shall see at will, or when you command me, but now it comes itself, or not at all." I spread my hands, trying to explain. "It's like waiting below a cover of cloud, then suddenly a wind shifts it and it breaks, and the light stabs down and catches me, sometimes full, sometimes only the flying edge of the pillars of sunlight. One day I shall be free of the whole temple. But not yet. I can see nothing." Exhaustion dragged at me. I could hear it in my voice. "I'm sorry, my lord. I'm no use to you. You haven't got your prophet yet."

"No," said Ambrosius. He put a hand down, and as I stood, drew me to him and kissed me. "Only a son, who has had no supper and who is tired out. Go to bed, Merlin, and sleep the rest of the night without dreaming. There is plenty of time for visions. Good night."

I had no more visions that night, but I did have a dream. I never told Ambrosius. I saw again the cave on the hillside, and the girl Niniane coming through the mist, and the man who waited for her beside the cave. But the face of Niniane was not the face of my mother, and the man by the cave was not the young Ambrosius. He was an old man, and his face was mine.

BOOK III

THE WOLF

1

I was five years with Ambrosius in Brittany. Looking back now, I see that much of what happened has been changed in my memory, like a smashed mosaic which is mended in later years by a man who has almost forgotten the first picture. Certain things come back to me plain, in all their colours and details; others—perhaps more important—come hazy, as if the picture had been dusted over by what has happened since, death, sorrow, changes of the heart. Places I always remember well, some of them so clearly that I feel even now as if I could walk into them, and that if I had the strength to concentrate, and the power that once fitted me like my robe, I might even now rebuild them here in the dark as I rebuilt the Giants' Dance for Ambrosius, all those years ago.

Places are clear, and ideas, which came to me so new and shining then, but not always the people: sometimes now as I search my memory I wonder if here and there I have confused them one with another, Belasius with Galapas, Cadal with Cerdic, the Breton officer whose name I forget now with my grandfather's captain in Maridunum who once tried to make me into the kind of swordsman that he thought even a bastard prince should want to be.

But as I write of Ambrosius, it is as if he were here with me now, lit against this darkness as the man with the cap was lit on that first frost-enchanted night in Brittany. Even without my robe of power I can conjure up against the darkness his eyes, steady under frowning brows, the heavy lines of his body, the face (which seems so young to me now) engraved into hardness by the devouring, goading will that had kept his eyes turned westward to his closed kingdom for the twenty-odd years it took him to grow from child to Comes and build, against all the odds of poverty and weakness, the striking force that grew with him, waiting for the time.

It is harder to write of Uther. Or rather it is hard to write of Uther as if he were in the past, part of a story that has been over these many years. Even more vividly than Ambrosius he is here with me; not here in the darkness—it is the part of me that was Myrddin that is here in the darkness. The part that was Uther is out there in the sunlight, keeping the coasts of Britain whole, following the design I made for him, the design that Galapas showed to me on a summer's day in Wales.

But there, of course, it is no longer Uther of whom I write. It is the man who was the sum of us, who was all of us—Ambrosius, who made me; Uther, who worked with me; myself, who used him, as I used every man who came to my hand, to make Arthur for Britain.

From time to time news came from Britain, and occasionally with it—through Gorlois of Cornwall—news of my home.

It seemed that after my grandfather's death, Camlach had not immediately deserted the old alliance with his kinsman Vortigern. He had to feel himself more secure before he would dare break away to support the "young men's party," as Vortimer's faction was called. Indeed, Vortimer himself had stopped short of open rebellion, but it seemed clear that this must come eventually. King Vortigern was back between the landslide and the flood; if he was to stay King of the British he must call on his Saxon wife's countrymen for help, and the Saxon mercenaries year by year increased their demands till the country was split and bleeding under what men openly called the Saxon Terror, and—in the West especially, where men were still free—rebellion only waited for a leader of leaders. And so desperate was Vortigern's situation becoming that he was forced against his better judgment to entrust the armed forces in the West more and more to Vortimer and his brothers, whose blood at least carried none of the Saxon taint.

Of my mother there was no news, except that she was safe in St. Peter's. Ambrosius sent her no message. If it came to her ears that a certain Merlinus Ambrosius was with the Count of Brittany, she would know what to think, but a letter or message direct from the King's enemy would endanger her unnecessarily. She would know, said Ambrosius, soon enough.

In fact it was five years before the break came, but the time went by like a tide-race. With the possibility of an opening developing in Wales and Cornwall, Ambrosius' preparations accelerated. If the men of the West wanted a leader he had every intention that it should be, not Vortimer, but himself. He would bide his time and let Vortimer be the wedge, but he and Uther would be the hammer that drove after it into the crack. Meanwhile hope in Less Britain ran high; offers of troops and alliances poured in, the countryside shook to the tramp of horses and marching feet, and the streets of the engineers and armourers rang far into the night as men redoubled their efforts to make two weapons in the time that before it had taken to make one. Now at last the break was coming, and when it came Ambrosius must be ready, and with no chance of failure. One does not wait half a lifetime gathering the material to make a killing spear, and then loose it at random in the dark. Not only men and materials, but time and spirit and the very wind of heaven must be right for him, and the gods themselves must open the gate. And for this, he said, they had sent me to him. It was my coming just at such a time with words of victory, and full of the vision of the unconquered god, which persuaded him (and even more important, the soldiers with him) that the time was at last approaching when he could strike with the certainty of victory. So—I found to my fear—he rated me.

Be sure I had never asked him again how he intended to use me. He made it clear enough, and between pride and fear and longing I fought to learn all that I could be taught, and to open myself for the power which was all I could give him. If he had wanted a prophet ready to hand he must have been disappointed; I saw nothing of importance during this time. Knowledge, I suppose, blocked the gates of vision. But this was the time for knowledge; I studied with Belasius till I outran him, learning, as he had never done, how to apply the calculations which to him were as much an art as songs were to me; even songs, indeed, I was to use. I spent long hours in the street of the engineers, and had frequently to be dragged by a grumbling Cadal from some oily piece of practical work which unfitted me, as he said, for any company but a bath-slave's. I wrote down, too, all I could remember of Galapas' medical teaching, and added practical experience by helping the army doctors whenever I could. I had the freedom of the camp and the town, and with Ambrosius' name to back me I took to this freedom like a hungry young wolf to his first full meal. I learned all the time, from every man or woman I met. I looked, as I had promised, in the light and the dark, at the sunshine and at the stale pool. I went with Ambrosius to the shrine of Mithras below the farmstead, and with Belasius to the gatherings in the forest. I was even allowed to sit silently at meetings between the Count and his captains, though nobody pretended that I would ever be much use in the field, "unless," said Uther once, half amused, half malicious, "he is to stand above us like Joshua holding the sun back, to give us more time to do the real work. Though joking apart, he might do worse ... the men seem to think of him as something halfway between a Courier of Mithras and a splinter of the True Cross—saving your presence, brother—and I'm damned certain he'd be more use stuck up on a hill like a lucky charm where they can see him, than down in the field where he wouldn't last five minutes." He had even more to say when, at the age of sixteen, I gave up the daily sword practice which gave a man the minimum training in self-defense; but my father merely laughed and said nothing. I think he knew, though as yet I did not, that I had my own kind of protection.

So I learned from everyone; the old women who gathered plants and cobwebs and seaweeds for healing; the travelling peddlers and quack healers; the horse doctors, the soothsayers, the priests. I listened to the soldiers' talk outside the taverns, and the officers' talk in my father's house, and the boys' talk in the streets. But there was one thing about which I learned nothing: by the time I left Brittany at seventeen, I was still ignorant of women. When I thought about them— which happened often enough—I told myself that I had no time, that there was a lifetime still ahead of me for such things, and that now I had work to do which mattered more. But I suppose the plain truth is that I was afraid of them. So I lost my desires in work, and indeed, I believe now that the fear came from the god.

So I waited, and minded my own business, which—as I saw it then—was to fit myself to serve my father.

One day I was in Tremorinus' workshop. Tremorinus, the master engineer, was a pleasant man who allowed me to learn all I could from him, gave me space in the workshops, and material to experiment with. This particular day I remember how when he came into the workshop and saw me busy over a model at my corner bench, he came over to have a look at it. When he saw what I was doing he laughed.

"I'd have thought there were plenty of those around without troubling to put up any more."

"I was interested in how they got them there." I tilted the scale model of the standing stone back into place.

He looked surprised. I knew why. He had lived in Less Britain all his life, and the landscape there is so seamed with the stones that men do not see them any more. One walks daily through a forest of stone, and to most men it seems dead stone ... But not to me. To me they still said something, and I had to find out what; but I did not tell Tremorinus this. I added, merely: "I was trying to work it out to scale."

"I can tell you something straight away: that's been tried, and it doesn't work." He was looking at the pulley I had rigged to lift the model. "That might do for the uprights, but only the lighter ones, and it doesn't work at all for the cap-stones."

"No. I'd found that out. But I'd had an idea ... I was going to tackle it another way."

"You're wasting your time. Let's see you getting down to something practical, something we need and can use. Now, that idea of yours for a light mobile crane might be worth developing ..."

A few minutes later he was called away. I dismantled the model, and sat down to my new calculations. I had not told Tremorinus about them; he had more important things to think about, and in any case he would have laughed if I had told him I had learned from a poet how to lift the standing stones.

It had happened this way.

One day about a week before this, as I walked by the water that guarded the town walls, I heard a man singing. The voice was old and wavering, and hoarse with over-use— the voice of a professional singer who has strained it above the noise of the crowd, and through singing with the winter cold in his throat. What caught my attention was neither the voice nor the tune, which could hardly be picked out, but the sound of my own name.

Merlin, Merlin, where art thou going?

He was sitting by the bridge, with a bowl for begging. I saw that he was blind, but the remnant of his voice was true, and he made no gesture with his bowl as he heard me stop near him, but sat as one sits at a harp, head bent, listening to what the strings say, with fingers stirring as if they felt the notes. He had sung, I would judge, in kings' halls.

Merlin, Merlin, where art thou going
So early in the day with thy black dog?

I have been searching for the egg,
The red egg of the sea-serpent,
Which lies by the shore in the hollow stone.
And I go to gather cresses in the meadow,
The green cress and the golden grasses,
The golden moss that gives sleep,
And the mistletoe high on the oak, the druids' bough
That grows deep in the woods by the running water.

Merlin, Merlin, come back from the wood and the foun-
    tain!
Leave the oak and the golden grasses
Leave the cress in the water-meadow,
And the red egg of the sea-serpent
In the foam by the hollow stone!

Merlin, Merlin, leave thy seeking!
There is no diviner but God.

Nowadays this song is as well known as the one of Mary
the Maiden, or the King and the Grey Seal, but it was the
first time I had heard it. When he knew who it was who had
stopped to listen, he seemed pleased that I should sit beside
him on the bank, and ask questions. I remember that on that
first morning we talked mostly of the song, then of himself; I
found he had been as a young man on Mona, the druids' isle,
and knew Caer'n-ar-Von and had walked on Snowdon. It was
in the druids' isle that he had lost his sight; he never told me
how, but when I told him that the sea-weeds and cresses that
I hunted along the shore were only plants for healing, not for
magic, he smiled and sang a verse I had heard my mother
sing, which, he said, would be a shield. Against what, he did
not say, nor did I ask him. I put money into his bowl, which
he accepted with dignity, but when I promised to find a harp
for him he went silent, staring with those empty eye-sockets,
and I could see he did not believe me. I brought the harp
next day; my father was generous, and I had no need even to
tell him what the money was for. When I put the harp into
the old singer's hands he wept, then took my hands and
kissed them.

After that, right up to the time I left Less Britain, I often

sought him out. He had travelled widely, in lands as far apart
as Ireland and Africa. He taught me songs from every
country, Italy and Gaul and the white North, and older songs
from the East—strange wandering tunes which had come
westward, he said, from the islands of the East with the men
of old who had raised the standing stones, and they spoke of
lores long forgotten except in song. I do not think he himself
thought of them as anything but songs of old magic, poets'
tales; but the more I thought about them, the more clearly
they spoke to me of men who had really lived, and work they
had really done, when they raised the great stones to mark
the sun and moon and build for their gods and the giant
kings of old.

I said something once about this to Tremorinus, who was
kindly as well as clever, and who usually managed to find
time for me; but he laughed and put it aside, and I said no
more. Ambrosius' technicians had more than enough to think
about in those days, without helping a boy to work out a set
of calculations of no practical use in the coming invasion. So
I let it be.

It was in the spring of my eighteenth year that the news
came finally from Britain. Through January and February,
winter had closed the seaways, and it was not till early
March, taking advantage of the cold still weather before the
gales began, that a small trading boat put into port, and
Ambrosius got news.

Stirring news it was—literally so, for within a few hours of
its coming, the Count's messengers were riding north and
east, to gather in his allies at last, and quickly, for the news
was late.

It appeared that Vortimer had finally, some time before,
broken with his father and the Saxon Queen. Tired of peti-
tioning the High King to break with his Saxon allies and
protect his own people from them, several of the British
leaders—among them the men of the West—had persuaded
Vortimer to take matters into his own hands at last, and had
risen with him. They had declared him King, and rallied to
his banner against the Saxons, whom they had succeeded in
driving back south and eastwards, till they took refuge with
their longships in the Isle of Thanet. Even there Vortimer
pursued them, and through the last days of autumn and the
beginning of winter had beleaguered them there until they

pleaded only to be allowed to depart in peace, packed up
their goods, and went back to Germany, leaving their women
and children behind them.

But Vortimer's victorious kingship did not last long. It was
not clear exactly what had happened, but the rumour was
that he had died of poison treacherously administered by a
familiar of the Queen. Whatever the truth of the matter, he
was dead, and Vortigern his father was once more in command. Almost his first act had been (and again the blame was
imputed to his wife) to send yet again for Hengist and his
Saxons to return to Britain. "With a small force," he had
said, "nothing but a mobile peace-keeping force to help him
impose order and pull together his divided kingdom." In fact,
the Saxons had promised three hundred thousand men. So
rumour said, and though it was to be supposed that rumour
lied, it was certain at any rate that Hengist planned to come
with a considerable force.

There was also a fragment of news from Maridunum. The
messenger was no spy of Ambrosius; the news we got was, as
it were, only the larger rumours. These were bad enough. It
seemed that my uncle Camlach, together with all his nobles—
my grandfather's men, the men that I knew—had risen with
Vortimer and fought beside him in the four pitched battles
against the Saxons. In the second, at Episford, Camlach had
been killed, along with Vortimer's brother Katigern. What
concerned me more was that after Vortimer's death reprisals
had been levelled at the men who had fought with him.
Vortigern had annexed Camlach's kingdom to join his own
lands of Guent, and, wanting hostages, had repeated his
action of twenty-five years earlier; he had taken Camlach's
children, one of them still an infant, and lodged them in the
care of Queen Rowena. We had no means of knowing if they
were still alive. Nor did we know if Olwen's son, who had
met the same fate, had survived. It seemed unlikely. Of my
mother there was no news.

Two days after the news came, the spring gales began, and
once more the seas were locked against us and against news.
But this hardly mattered; indeed, it worked both ways. If we
could get no news from Britain, they could have none of us,
and of the final accelerated preparations for the invasion of
Western Britain. For it was certain that the time had now
come. It was not only a case of marching to the relief of
Wales and Cornwall, but if there were to be any men left to

rally to the Red Dragon, the Red Dragon would have to fight for his crown this coming year.

"You'll go back with the first boat," said Ambrosius to me, but without looking up from the map which was spread on the table in front of him.

I was standing over by the window. Even with the shutters closed and curtains drawn I could hear the wind, and beside me the curtains stirred in the draught. I said: "Yes, sir," and crossed to the table. Then I saw his finger was pointing on the map. "I'm to go to Maridunum?"

He nodded. "You'll take the first westbound boat, and make your way home from wherever it docks. You are to go straight up to Galapas and get what news there is from him. I doubt if you would be recognized in the town, but take no risks. Galapas is safe. You can make him your base."

"There was no word from Cornwall, then?"

"Nothing, except a rumour that Gorlois was with Vortigern."

"With Vortigern?" I digested this for a moment. "Then he didn't rise with Vortimer?"

"As far as my information goes, no."

"He's trimming, then?"

"Perhaps. I find it hard to believe. It may mean nothing. I understand he has married a young wife, and it may only be that he kept within walls all winter to keep her warm. Or that he foresaw what would happen to Vortimer, and preferred to serve my cause by staying safe and apparently loyal to the High King. But until I know, I cannot send to him directly. He may be watched. So you are to go to Galapas, for the news from Wales. I'm told Vortigern's holed up there somewhere, while the length of Eastern Britain lies open to Hengist. I'll have to smoke the old wolf out first, then weld the West against the Saxons. But it will have to be fast. And I want Caerleon." He looked up then. "I'm sending your old friend with you—Marric. You can send word back by him. Let's hope you find all well. You'll want news yourself, I dare say."

"It can wait," I said.

He said nothing to that, but raised his brows at me, and then turned back to the map. "Well, sit down and I'll brief you myself. Let's hope you can get away soon."

I indicated the swaying curtains. "I shall be sick all the way."

He looked up from the map, and laughed. "By Mithras, I

hadn't thought of that. Do you suppose I shall be, too? A damned undignified way to go back to one's home."

"To one's kingdom," I said.

2

I crossed in early April, and on the same ship as before. But the crossing could not have been more different. This was not Myrddin, the runaway, but Merlinus, a well-dressed young Roman with money in his pocket, and servants in attendance. Where Myrddin had been locked naked in the hold, Merlinus had a comfortable cabin, and marked deference paid him by the captain. Cadal, of course, was one of my servants, and the other, to my own amusement though not his, was Marric. (Hanno was dead, having overreached himself, I gathered, in a little matter of blackmail.) Naturally I carried no outward sign of my connection with Ambrosius, but nothing would part me from the brooch he had given me; I wore this clipped inside the shoulder of my tunic. It was doubtful whether anyone would have recognized in me the runaway of five years ago, and certainly the captain gave no sign, but I held myself aloof, and was careful to speak nothing but Breton.

As luck would have it, the boat was going straight to the mouth of the Tywy and would anchor at Maridunum, but it had been arranged that Cadal and I were to be put off by boat as soon as the trader arrived in the estuary.

It was, in fact, my previous journey in reverse, but in the most important respect there was no difference. I was sick all the way. The fact that this time I had a comfortable bunk and Cadal to look after me, instead of sacks and a bucket in the hold, made not the slightest difference to me. As soon as the ship nosed out of the Small Sea, and met the windy April weather of the Bay, I left my brave stance in the bows and went below and lay down.

We had what they tell me was a fair wind, and we crept into the estuary and dropped anchor just before dawn, ten days before the Ides of April.

It was a still dawn, misty and cold. It was very quiet. The tide was just on the turn, beginning its flow up the estuary, and as our boat left the ship's side the only sound was the hiss and chuckle of water along her sides, and the soft splash of the paddles. Far away, faint and metallic, I could hear cocks crowing. Somewhere beyond the mist lambs were crying, answered by the deeper bleating of sheep. The air smelled soft, clear and salty, and in some curious way, of home.

We kept well out to the center of the stream, and the mist hid us from the banks. If we spoke at all, it was in whispers; once when a dog barked from the bank we heard a man speak to it almost as clearly as if he had been in the boat with us; this was sufficient warning, and we kept our voices down.

It was a strong spring tide, and took us fast. This was as well, for we had made anchor later than we should, and the light was growing. I saw the sailors who rowed us glance anxiously upwards and then lengthen their stroke. I leaned forward, straining my eyes for a glimpse of the bank I could recognize. Cadal said in my ear: "Glad to be back?"

"That depends on what we find. Mithras, but I'm hungry."

"That's not surprising," he said, with a sour chuckle. "What are you looking for?"

"There should be a bay—white sand with a stream coming down through trees—and a ridge behind it with a crest of pines. We'll put in there."

He nodded. The plan was that Cadal and I should be landed on the side of the estuary away from Maridunum, at a point I knew from which we could make our way unseen to join the road from the south. We would be travellers from Cornwall; I would do the talking, but Cadal's accent would pass with any but a native Cornishman. I had with me some pots of salve and a small chest of medicines, and if challenged could pass as a travelling doctor, a disguise that would serve as a pass to more or less anywhere I wanted to go.

Marric was still on board. He would go in with the trader, and disembark as usual at the wharf. He would try to find his old contacts in the town, and pick up what news he could. Cadal would go with me to the cave of Galapas, and act as connecting link with Marric to pass over what information I got. The ship was to lie for three days in the Tywy; when she sailed Marric would take the news back with her. Whether I and Cadal would be with him would depend on what we found; neither my father nor I forgot that after Camlach's part in the rebellion Vortigern must have been through Maridunum like a fox through a hen-run, and maybe his Saxons with him. My first duty was to get news of Vortigern, and send it back; my second to find my mother and see that she was safe.

It was good to be on land again; not dry land, for the grass at the head of the ridge was long and soaking, but I felt light and excited as the boat vanished under the mist and Cadal and I left the shore and made our way inland towards the road. I don't know what I expected to find in Maridunum; I don't even know that I cared overmuch; it was not the homecoming that made my spirits lift, but the fact that at last I had a job to do for Ambrosius. If I could not yet do a prophet's work for him, at least I could do a man's work, and then a son's. I believe that all the time I was half hoping that I would be asked to die for him. I was very young.

We reached the bridge without incident. Luck was with us there, for we fell in with a horse-trader who had a couple of nags in hand which he hoped to sell in the town. I bought one of them from him, haggling just enough to prevent suspicion; he was pleased enough with the price to throw in a rather worn saddle. By the time the transaction was finished it was full light and there were one or two people about, but no one gave us more than a cursory glance, except for one fellow who, apparently recognizing the horse, grinned, and said—to Cadal rather than to me—"Were you planning to go far, mate?"

I pretended not to hear, but from the corner of my eye saw Cadal spread his hands, shrug, and turn his eyes up in my direction. The look said, all too plainly, "I only follow where he goes, and he's crazy anyway."

Presently the towpath was empty. Cadal came alongside, and hooked a hand through the neck-strap. "He's right, you know. This old screw won't get you far. How far is it, anyway?"

"Probably not nearly as far as I remember. Six miles at the outside."

"Uphill most of the way, you said?"

"I can always walk." I smoothed a hand along the skinny neck. "He's not as much of a wreck as he looks, you know. There's not much wrong that a few good feeds won't put right."

"Then at least you won't have wasted your money. What are you looking at over that wall?"

"That's where I used to live."

We were passing my grandfather's house. It looked very

little changed. From the cob's back I could just see over the wall to the terrace where the quince tree grew, its brilliant flame-coloured blossoms opening to the morning sun. And there was the garden where Camlach had given me the poisoned apricot. And there the gate where I had run in tears.

The cob plodded on. Here was the orchard, the apple trees already swelling with buds, the grass springing rough and green round the little terrace where Moravik would sit and spin, while I played at her feet. And here, now, was the place I had jumped over the wall the night I ran away; here was the leaning apple tree where I had left Aster tethered. The wall was broken, and I could see in across the rough grass where I had run that night, from my room where Cerdic's body lay on its funeral pyre. I pulled the cob to a halt and craned to see further. I must have made a clean sweep that night: the buildings were all gone, my room, and along with it two sides of the outer court. The stables, I saw, were still the same; the fire had not reached them, then. The two sides of the colonnade that had been destroyed had been rebuilt in a modern style that seemed to bear no relation to the rest, big rough stones and crude building, square pillars holding up a timber roof, and square, deep windows. It was ugly, and looked comfortless; its only virtue would be that it was weatherproof. You might as well, I thought, settling back in the saddle and putting the cob in motion, live in a cave ...

"What are you grinning at?" asked Cadal.

"Only at how Roman I've become. It's funny, my home isn't here any more. And to be honest I don't think it's in Less Britain either."

"Where, then?"

"I don't know. Where the Count is, that's for sure. That will be this sort of place, I suppose, for some time to come." I nodded towards the walls of the old Roman barracks behind the palace. They were in ruins, and the place was deserted. So much the better, I thought; at least it didn't look as if Ambrosius would have to fight for it. Give Uther twenty-four hours, and the place would be as good as new. And here was St. Peter's, apparently untouched, showing no sign either of fire or spear. "You know something?" I said to Cadal, as we left the shadow of the nunnery wall and headed along the path towards the mill. "I suppose if I have anywhere I can call a home, it's the cave of Galapas."

"Doesn't sound all that Roman to me," said Cadal. "Give

me a good tavern any day and a decent bed and some mutton to eat, and you can keep all the caves there are."

Even with this sorry horse, the way seemed shorter than I remembered it. Soon we had reached the mill, and turned up across the road and into the valley. Time fell away. It seemed only yesterday that I had come up this same valley in the sunshine, with the wind stirring Aster's grey mane. Not even Aster's—for there under the same thorn-tree was surely the same half-wit boy watching the same sheep as on my very first ride. As we reached the fork in the path, I found myself watching for the ring-dove. But the hillside was still, except for the rabbits scuttering among the young bracken.

Whether the cob sensed the end of his journey, or whether he merely liked the feel of grass under his feet and a light weight on his back, he seemed to quicken his step. Ahead of me now I could see the shoulder of the hill beyond which lay the cave.

I drew rein by the hawthorn grove.

"Here we are. It's up there, above the cliff." I slipped out of the saddle and handed the reins to Cadal. "Stay here and wait for me. You can come up in an hour." I added, on an afterthought: "And don't be alarmed if you see what you think is smoke. It's the bats coming out of the cave."

I had almost forgotten Cadal's sign against the evil eye. He made it now, and I laughed and left him.

3

Before I had climbed round the little crag to the lawn in front of the cave, I knew.

Call it foresight; there was no sign. Silence, of course, but then there usually had been silence as I approached the cave. This silence was different. It was only after some moments that I realized what it was. I could no longer hear the trickle of the spring.

I mounted to the top of the path, came out on the sward, and saw. There was no need to go into the cave to know that he was not there, and never would be again.

On the flat grass in front of the cave-mouth was a scatter of debris. I went closer to look.

It had been done not so very long ago. There had been a fire here, a fire quenched by rain before everything could

properly be destroyed. There was a pile of sodden rubbish—
half-charred wood, rags, parchment gone again to pulp but
with the blackened edges still showing. I turned the nearest
piece of scorched wood over with my foot; from the carving
on it I knew what it was; the chest that had held his books.
And the parchment was all that remained of the books
themselves.

I suppose there was other stuff of his among the wreck of
rubbish. I didn't look further. If the books had gone, I knew
everything else would have gone too. And Galapas with
them.

I went slowly towards the mouth of the cave. I paused by
the spring. I could see why there had been no sound; someone had filled in the basin with stones and earth and more
wreckage thrown out of the cave. Through it all the water
welled still, sluggishly, oozing in silence over the stone lip and
down to make a muddy morass of the turf. I thought I could
see the skeleton of a bat, picked clean by the water.

Strangely enough, the torch was still on the ledge high
beside the mouth of the cave, and it was dry. There was no
flint or iron, but I made fire and, holding the torch before
me, went slowly inside.

I think my flesh was shivering, as if a cold wind blew out of
the cave and went by me. I knew already what I should find.

The place was stripped. Everything had been thrown out
to burn. Everything, that is, except the bronze mirror. This,
of course, would not burn, and I suppose it had been too
heavy to be looted. It had been wrenched from the wall and
stood propped against the side of the cave, tilted at a drunk-
en angle. Nothing else. Not even a stir and whisper from the
bats in the roof. The place echoed with emptiness.

I lifted the torch high and looked up towards the crystal
cave. It was not there.

I believe that for a couple of pulses of the torchlight I
thought he had managed to conceal the inner cave, and was
in hiding. Then I saw.

The gap into the crystal cave was still there, but chance,
call it what you will, had rendered it invisible except to
those who knew. The bronze mirror had fallen so that,
instead of directing light towards the gap, it directed
darkness. Its light was beamed and concentrated on a projec-
tion of rock which cast, clear across the mouth of the crystal
cave, a black wedge of shadow. To anyone intent only on the

pillage and destruction in the cave below, the gap would be hardly visible at all.

"Galapas?" I said, trying it out on the emptiness. "Galapas?"

There was the faintest of whispers from the crystal cave, a ghostly sweet humming like the music I had once listened for in the night. Nothing human; I had not expected it. But still I climbed up to the ledge, knelt down and peered in.

The torchlight caught the crystals, and threw the shadow of my harp, trembling, clear round the lighted globe. The harp stood, undamaged, in the center of the cave. Nothing else, except the whisper dying round the glittering walls. There must be visions there, in the flash and counterflash of light, but I knew I would not be open to them. I put a hand down to the rock and vaulted, torch streaming, back to the floor of the cave. As I passed the tilted mirror I caught a glimpse of a tall youth running in a swirl of flame and smoke. His face looked pale, the eyes black and enormous. I ran out on to the grass. I had forgotten the torch, which flamed and streamed behind me. I ran to the edge of the cliff, and cupped a hand to my mouth to call Cadal, but then a sound from behind me made me whip round and look upwards.

It was a very normal sound. A pair of ravens and a carrion crow had risen from the hill, and were scolding at me.

Slowly this time, I climbed the path that led up past the spring and out on the hillside above the cave. The ravens went higher, barking. Two more crows made off low across the young bracken. There was a couple still busy on something lying among the flowering blackthorn.

I whirled the torch and flung it streaming to scatter them. Then I ran forward.

There was no telling how long he had been dead. The bones were picked almost clean. But I knew him by the discoloured brown rags that flapped under the skeleton, and the one old broken sandal which lay flung nearby among the April daisies. One of the hands had fallen from the wrist, and the clean, brittle bones lay near my foot. I could see where the little finger had been broken, and had set again, crookedly. Already through the bare rib-cage the April grass was springing. The air blew clean and sunlit, smelling of flowering gorse.

The torch had been stubbed out in the fresh grass. I

stooped and picked it up. I should not have thrown it at them, I thought. His birds had given him a seemly waygoing.

A step behind me brought me round, but it was only Cadal.

"I saw the birds go up," he said. He was looking down at the thing under the blackthorn bushes. "Galapas?"

I nodded.

"I saw the mess down by the cave. I guessed."

"I hadn't realized I had been here so long."

"Leave this to me." He was stooping already. "I'll get him buried. Go you and wait down where we left the horse. I can maybe find some sort of tool down yonder, or I could come back—"

"No. Let him lie in peace under the thorn, We'll build the hill over him and let it take him in. We do this together, Cadal."

There were stones in plenty to pile over him for a barrow, and we cut sods with our daggers to turf it over. By the end of summer the bracken and foxgloves and young grasses would have grown right over and shrouded him. So we left him.

As we went downhill again past the cave I thought of the last time I had gone this way. I had been weeping then, I remembered, for Cerdic's death, for my mother's loss and Galapas', for who knew what foreknowledge of the future? *You will see me again,* he had said, *I promise you that.* Well, I had seen him. And some day, no doubt, his other promise would come true in its own fashion.

I shivered, caught Cadal's quick look, and spoke curtly. "I hope you had the sense to bring a flask with you. I need a drink."

4

Cadal had brought more than a flask with him, he had brought food—salt mutton and bread, and last season's olives in a bottle with their own oil. We sat in the lee of the wood and ate, while the cob grazed near us, and below in the distance the placid curves of the river glimmered through the April green of the fields and the young wooded hills. The mist had cleared, and it was a beautiful day.

"Well," said Cadal at length, "what's to do?"

"We go to see my mother. If she's still there, of course."
Then, with a savagery that broke through me so suddenly
that I had hardly known it was there: "By Mithras, I'd give a
lot to know who did that up yonder!"

"Why, who could it be except Vortigern?"

"Vortimer, Pascentius, anyone. When a man's wise and
gentle and good," I added bitterly, "it seems to me that any
man's, every man's hand is against him. Galapas could have
been murdered by an outlaw for food, or a herdsman for
shelter, or a passing soldier for a drink of water."

"That was no murder."

"What, then?"

"I meant, that was done by more than one. Men in a pack
are worse than lone ones. At a guess, it was Vortigern's men,
on their way up from the town."

"You're probably right. I shall find out."

"You think you'll get to see your mother?"

"I can try."

"Did he—have you any messages for her?" It was, I
suppose, the measure of my relationship with Cadal that he
dared to ask the question.

I answered him quite simply. "If you mean did Ambrosius
ask me to tell her anything, no. He left it to me. What I do
tell her depends entirely on what's happened since I left. I'll
talk to her first, and judge how much to tell her after that.
Don't forget, I haven't seen her for a long time, and people
change. I mean, their loyalties change. Look at mine. When I
last saw her I was only a child, and I have only a child's
memories—for all I know I misunderstood her utterly, the
way she thought and the things she wanted. Her loyalties
may lie elsewhere—not just the Church, but the way she feels
about Ambrosius. The gods know there'd be no blame to her
if she had changed. She owed Ambrosius nothing. She took
good care of that."

He said thoughtfully, his eyes on the green distance thread-
ed by the glinting river: "The nunnery hadn't been touched."

"Exactly. Whatever had happened to the rest of the town,
Vortigern had let St. Peter's be. So you see I've to find out
who is in which camp before I give any messages. What she
hasn't known about for all these years, it won't hurt her to
go on not knowing for as many more days. Whatever
happens, with Ambrosius coming so soon, I mustn't take the
risk of telling her too much."

He began to pack away the remains of the meal while I sat, chin on hand, thinking, my eyes on the bright distance.

I added, slowly: "It's simple enough to find out where Vortigern is now, and if Hengist's landed already, and with how many men. Marric will probably find out without too much trouble. But there were other soundings the Count wanted me to take—things they'll hardly know about in the nunnery—so now that Galapas is dead, I'll have to try elsewhere. We'll wait here till dusk, then go down to St. Peter's. My mother will be able to tell me who I can still go to in safety." I looked at him. "Whatever king she favours, she's not likely to give me away."

"That's true enough. Well, let's hope they'll let her see you."

"If she knows who's asking for her, I imagine it will take more than a word from the Abbess to stop her from seeing me. Don't forget she's still a king's daughter." I lay back on the warm grass, my hands behind my head. "Even if I'm not yet a king's son . . ."

But, king's son or no, there was no getting into the nunnery.

I had been right in thinking there had been no damage done here. The high walls loomed unbroken and unscarred, and the gates were new and solid, of oak hinged and bolted with iron. They were fast shut. Nor—mercifully—did any welcoming torch burn outside. The narrow street was empty and unlit in the early dusk. At our urgent summons a small square window in the gate opened, and an eye was applied to the grille.

"Travellers from Cornwall," I said softly. "I must have word with the Lady Niniane."

"The Lady who?" It was the flat, toneless voice of the deaf. Wondering irritably why a deaf portress should be put at the gate, I raised my voice a little, going closer to the grille.

"The Lady Niniane. I don't know what she calls herself now, but she was sister of the late King. Is she with you still?"

"Aye, but she'll see nobody. Is it a letter you have? She can read."

"No, I must have speech with her. Go and take word to her; tell her it's—one of her family."

"Her family?" I thought I saw a flicker of interest in the eyes. "They're most of them dead and gone. Do you not get news in Cornwall? Her brother the King died in battle last year, and the children have gone to Vortigern. Her own son's been dead these five years."

"I knew that. I'm not her brother's family. And I'm as loyal as she is to the High King. Go and tell her that. And look—take this for your . . . devotions."

A pouch passed through the grille and was grabbed in a quick monkey-snatch. "I'll take a message for you. Give me your name. I don't say she'll see you, mind, but I'll take her your name."

"My name's Emrys." I hesitated. "She knew me once. Tell her that. And hurry. We'll wait here."

It was barely ten minutes before I heard the steps coming back. For a moment I thought it might be my mother, but it was the same old eyes that peered at me through the grille, the same clawed hand laying hold of the bars. "She'll see you. Oh no, not now, young master. You can't come in. Nor she can't come out yet, not till prayers is over. Then she'll meet you on the river walk, she says; there's another gate in the wall there. But not to let anyone see you."

"Very well. We'll be careful."

I could see the whites of the eyes turning, as she tried to see me in the shadows. "Knew you, she did, straight away. Emrys, eh? Well, don't worry that I'll say aught. These be troubled times, and the least said the better, no matter what about."

"What time?"

"An hour after moonrise. You'll hear the bell."

"I'll be there," I said, but the grille was already shut.

There was a mist rising again from the river. This would help, I thought. We went quietly down the lane which skirted the nunnery walls. It led away from the streets, down towards the towpath.

"What now?" asked Cadal. "It's two hours yet till moonrise, and by the look of the night we'll be lucky if we ever see a moon at all. You'll not risk going into the town?"

"No. But there's no sense in waiting about in this drizzle. We'll find a place out of the wet where we can hear the bell. This way."

The stableyard gate was locked. I wasted no time on it, but led the way to the orchard wall. No lights showed in the palace. We scrambled over where the wall was broken, and walked up through the damp grass of the orchard and into my grandfather's garden. The air was heavy with the smell of damp earth and growing things, mint and sweetbriar and moss and young leaves heavy with wet. Last year's ungathered fruit squelched under our feet. Behind us the gate creaked, emptily.

The colonnades were empty, the doors shut, the shutters fastened close over the windows. The place was all darkness and echoes and the scuttle of rats. But there was no damage that I could see. I suppose that, when Vortigern took the town, he had meant to keep the house for himself, and had somehow persuaded or forced his Saxons to bypass it in their looting as—from fear of the bishops—he had forced them to bypass St. Peter's. So much the better for us. We should at least have a dry and comfortable wait. My time with Tremorinus had been wasted indeed if I could not have picked every lock in the place.

I was just saying as much to Cadal when suddenly, round the corner of the house, treading softly as a cat on the mossy flagstones, came a young man walking fast. He stopped dead at the sight of us, and I saw his hand flash down to his hip. But even while Cadal's weapon hissed free of its sheath in reply the young man peered, stared, and then exclaimed: "Myrddin, by the holy oak!"

For a moment I genuinely didn't recognize him, which was understandable, since he was not much older than myself, and had changed as much in five years. Then, unmistakably, I saw who it was; broad shoulders, thrusting jaw, hair that even in the twilight showed red. Dinias, who had been prince and king's son when I was a nameless bastard; Dinias, my "cousin," who would not even recognize that much of a tie with me, but who had claimed the title of Prince for himself, and been allowed to get away with it.

He would hardly now be taken for a prince. Even in that fading light I could see that he was dressed, not poorly, but in clothes that a merchant might have worn, and he had only one jewel, an arm-ring of copper. His belt was of plain leather, his sword-hilt plain also, and his cloak, though of good stuff, was stained and frayed at the edge. About his whole person was that indefinable air of seediness which comes from relentless calculation from day to day or perhaps even from meal to meal.

Since in spite of the considerable changes he was still indisputably my cousin Dinias, it was to be supposed that once he had recognized me, there was little point in pretending he was wrong. I smiled and held out my hand. "Welcome, Dinias. Yours is the first known face I've seen today."

"What in the name of the gods are you doing here? Everyone said you were dead, but I didn't believe it."

His big head thrust out, peering close as the quick eyes looked me up and down. "Wherever you were, you've done all right, seemingly. How long have you been back?"

"We came today."

"Then you've heard the news?"

"I knew Camlach was dead. I'm sorry about that ... if you were. As you'll know, he was no friend of mine, but that was hardly political ..." I paused, waiting. Let him make the moves. I saw from the corner of an eye that Cadal was tensed and watchful, a hand still to his hip. I moved my own hand, palm downwards in a slight flattening movement, and saw him relax.

Dinias lifted a shoulder. "Camlach? He was a fool. I told him which way the wolf would jump." But as he spoke I saw his eyes slide sideways towards the shadows. It seemed that men watched their tongues these days in Maridunum. His eyes came back to me, suspicious, wary. "What's your business here, anyway? Why did you come back?"

"To see my mother. I've been in Cornwall, and all we got there was rumours of fighting, and when I heard Camlach was dead, and Vortimer, I wondered what had happened at home."

"Well, she's alive, you'll have found that out? The High King"—rather loudly—"respects the Church. I doubt if you'll get to see her, though."

"You're probably right. I went up to the nunnery, and they wouldn't let me in. But I'll be here for a few days. I'll send a message in, and if she wants to see me, I imagine she'll find a way of doing so. But at least I know she's safe. It's a real stroke of luck, running into you like this. You'll be able to give me the rest of the news. I had no idea what I might find here, so as you see, I came in this morning quietly, alone with my servant."

"Quietly is right. I thought you were thieves. You're lucky I didn't cut you down and ask questions afterwards."

It was the old Dinias, the bullying note there again, an immediate response to my mild, excusing tone.

"Well, I wasn't taking any risks till I knew how the family stood. I went off to St. Peter's—I waited till dusk to do that—then I came to take a look round here. Is the place empty then?"

"I'm still living here. Where else?"

The arrogance rang as hollow as the empty colonnade, and for a moment I felt tempted to ask him for hospitality and see what he would say. As if the thought had struck him at the same moment he said quickly: "Cornwall, eh? What's the news from there? They say Ambrosius' messengers are scuttling across the Narrow Sea like waterflies."

I laughed. "I wouldn't know. I've been leading a sheltered life."

"You picked the right place." The contempt that I remembered so well was back in his voice. "They say old Gorlois spent the winter snugged down in bed with a girl barely turned twenty, and left the rest of the kings to play their own games out in the snow. They say she'd make Helen of Troy look like a market-woman. What's she like?"

"I never saw her. He's a jealous husband."

"Jealous of you?" He laughed, and followed it with a comment that made Cadal, behind me, suck in his breath. But the jibe had put my cousin back in humour, and off his guard. I was still the little bastard cousin, and of no account. He added: "Well, it would suit you. You had a peaceful winter, you with your goatish old Duke, while the rest of us tramped the country after the Saxons."

So he had fought with Camlach and Vortimer. It was what I had wanted to know. I said mildly: "I was hardly responsible for the Duke's policy. Nor am I now."

"Hah! It's as well for you. You knew he was in the north with Vortigern?"

"I knew he had left to join him—at Caer'n-ar-Von, was it? Are you going up there yourself?" I put the gentlest of queries into my voice, adding meekly: "I wasn't really in a position to hear much news that mattered."

A chill current of air eddied, loaded with damp, between the pillars. From some broken gutter above us water suddenly spilled over, to splash between us on the flagstones. I saw him gather his cloak round him. "Why are we standing here?" He spoke with a brusque heartiness that ran as false as the arrogance. "Come and exchange news over a flask of wine, eh?"

I hesitated, but only for a moment. It seemed obvious that Dinias had his own reasons for keeping out of the High King's eye; for one thing, if he had managed to live down his association with Camlach, he would surely be with Vortigern's army, not skulking here in this threadbare fashion in an empty palace. For another, now that he knew I was in Maridunum, I preferred to keep him under my eye than leave him now to go and talk to whom he would.

So I accepted with every appearance of flattered pleasure, only insisting that he must join me for supper, if he could tell me where a good meal was to be found, and a warm seat out of the wet . . . ?

Almost before the words were out he had me by the arm and was hurrying me across the atrium and out through the street door.

"Fine, fine. There's a place over on the west side, beyond the bridge. The food's good, and they get the kind of clients that mind their own business." He winked. "Not that you'll be wanting to bother with a girl, eh? Though you don't look as if they'd made a clerk of you after all . . . ? Well, no more for now, it doesn't do to look as though you've too much to talk about these days . . . You either fall foul of the Welsh or you fall foul of Vortigern—and the place is crawling with his spies just now. I don't know who it is they're looking for, but there's a story going about— No, take your trash away." This to a beggar who thrust a tray of rough-cut stones and leather laces in front of us. The man moved back without a word. I saw that he was blind in one eye from a cut; a hideous scar ran right up one cheek, and had flattened the bridge of the nose. It looked as if it had been a sword cut.

I dropped a coin on the tray as we passed, and Dinias shot me a look that was far from friendly. "Times have changed, eh? You must have struck it rich in Cornwall. Tell me, what happened that night? Did you mean to set the whole damned place on fire?"

"I'll tell you all about it over supper," I said, and would say no more till we reached the shelter of the tavern, and got a bench in the corner with our backs to the wall.

5

I had been right about Dinias' poverty. Even in the smoky murk of the tavern's crowded room I could see the threadbare state of his clothes, and sense the air half of resentment, half of eagerness, with which he watched while I ordered food and a jug of their best wine. While it was coming I excused myself and had a quick word aside with Cadal.

"I may get some of the facts we want from him. In any case I thought it better to stick to him—I'd rather he came under my eye for the moment. The odds are he'll be drunk enough by moonrise to be harmless, and I'll either get him bedded down safe with a girl, or if he's past it I'll see him home on my way to the nunnery. If I don't look like getting out of here by moonrise, get over yourself to the gate on the towpath to meet my mother. You know our story. Tell her I'm coming, but I fell in with my cousin Dinias and have to get rid of him first. She'll understand. Now get yourself some food."

"Watch your step, I would, Merlin. Your cousin, did you say? Proper daisy he is, and no mistake. He doesn't like you."

I laughed. "You think that's news? It's mutual."

"Oh. Well, as long as you watch it."

"I'll do that."

Dinias' manners were still good enough to make him wait till I had dismissed Cadal and sat down to pour the wine. He had been right about the food; the pie they brought us was stuffed full of beef and oysters in a thick, steaming gravy, and though the bread was made from barley meal it was fresh. The cheese was not, and was excellent. The tavern's other wares seemed to match the food; from time to time one got a glimpse of them as a girl peered giggling in through a curtained door, and some man put his cup down and hurried after her. From the way Dinias' eyes lingered on the curtain even while he ate, I thought I might have little difficulty in getting rid of him safely once I had the information I wanted.

I waited until he was halfway through his pie before I started asking questions. I hardly liked to wait longer for, from the way he reached for the wine-jug almost—in spite of his hunger—between every mouthful, I was afraid that if I left it too long he would not be clear-headed enough to tell me what I wanted.

Until I was quite sure how the land lay I was not prepared to venture on ground that might be tricky, but, my family being what it was, I could glean a good deal of the information Ambrosius wanted from simply asking questions about my relatives. These he answered readily enough.

To begin with, I had been presumed dead ever since the night of the fire. Cerdic's body had been destroyed, and the whole of that side of the courtyard along with it, and when

my pony had found its way home and there was no sign of
me, it could only be presumed that I had perished along with
Cerdic and vanished the same way. My mother and Camlach
had sent men out to search the countryside, but of course
found no trace of me. It appeared there had been no sugges-
tion of my having left by sea. The trading ship had not put in
to Maridunum, and no one had seen the coracle.

My disappearance—not remarkably—had made very little
stir. What my mother had thought about it no one knew, but
she had apparently retired into the seclusion of St. Peter's
very soon afterwards. Camlach had lost no time in declaring
himself King, and for form's sake offered Olwen his protection, but since his own wife had one son and was heavy with
another, it was an open secret that Queen Olwen would soon
be married off to some harmless and preferably distant
chieftain . . . And so on, and so on.

So much for news of the past, which was none of it news
to me or news for Ambrosius. As Dinias finished his meal
and leaned back against the wall loosening his belt, relaxed
by the food and wine and warmth, I thought it time to steer
near more immediate questions of the present. The tavern
had filled up now, and there was plenty of noise to cover
what we were saying. One or two of the girls had come out
from the inner rooms, and there was a good deal of laughter
and some horseplay. It was quite dark now outside, and
apparently wetter than ever; men came in shaking themselves
like dogs and shouting for mulled drinks. The atmosphere
was heavy with peat smoke and charcoal from the grills and
the smells of hot food and the reek of cheap oil-lamps. I had
no fear of recognition: anyone would have had to lean right
over our table and peer into my face to see me properly at
all.

"Shall I send for more meat?" I asked.

Dinias shook his head, belched, and grinned. "No thanks.
That was good. I'm in your debt. Now for your news. You've
heard mine. Where have you been these past years?" He
reached again for the jug of wine and up-ended it over his
empty cup. "Damned thing's empty. Send for more?"

I hesitated. It appeared he had a poor head for wine, and I
didn't want him drunk too soon.

He mistook my hesitation. "Come on, come on, you surely
don't grudge me another jug of wine, eh? It isn't every day a
rich young relative comes back from Cornwall. What took
you there, eh? And what have you been doing all this time?

Come on, young Myrddin, let's hear about it, shall we? But first, the wine."

"Well, of course," I said, and gave the order to the pot-boy. "But don't use my name here, if you don't mind. I'm calling myself Emrys now till I see which way the wind blows."

He accepted this so readily that I realized things were even trickier in Maridunum than I had thought. It seemed it was dangerous to declare oneself at all. Most of the men in the tavern looked Welsh; there were none I recognized, which was hardly surprising, considering the company I had kept five years ago. But there was a group near the door who, from their fair hair and beards, might have been Saxon. I supposed they were Vortigern's men. We said nothing until the pot-boy had dumped a fresh flask on the table in front of us. My cousin poured it, pushed his plate aside, leaned back and looked at me enquiringly.

"Well, come on, tell me about yourself. What happened that night you left? Who did you go with? You couldn't have been more than twelve or thirteen when you went, surely?"

"I fell in with a pair of traders going south," I told him. "I paid my way with one of the brooches that my gr—that the old King gave me. They took me with them as far as Glastonbury. Then I had a bit of luck—fell in with a merchant who was travelling west into Cornwall with glass goods from the Island, and he took me along." I looked down as if avoiding his eye, and twisted the cup between my fingers. "He wanted to set up as a gentleman, and thought it would do him credit to have a boy along who could sing and play the harp, and read and write as well."

"Hm. Very likely." I had known what he would think of my story, and indeed, his tone held satisfaction, as if his contempt of me had been justified. So much the better. It didn't matter to me what he thought. "Then?" he asked.

"Oh, I stayed with him for a few months, and he was pretty generous, he and his friends. I even made a fair amount on the side."

"Harping?" he asked, with a lift of the lip.

"Harping," I said blandly. "Also reading and writing—I did the man's accounts for him. When he came back north he wanted me to stay with him, but I didn't want to come back. Didn't dare," I added, disarmingly frank. "It wasn't hard to find a place in a religious house. Oh, no, I was too young to be anything but a layman. To tell you the truth, I quite enjoyed it; it's a very peaceful life. I've been busy helping them to write out copies of a history of the fall of Troy." His expression made me want to laugh, and I looked down at my cup again. It was good ware, Samian, with a high gloss, and the potter's mark was clear. A.M. *Ambrosius made me,* I thought suddenly, and smoothed the letters gently with my thumb as I finished for Dinias the account of the five harmless years spent by his bastard cousin. "I worked there until the rumours started coming in from home. I didn't pay much heed to them at first—rumours were always flying. But when we knew that it was true about Camlach's death, and then Vortimer's, I began to wonder what might have happened in Maridunum. I knew I had to see my mother again."

"You're going to stay here?"

"I doubt it. I like Cornwall, and I have a home there of a sort."

"Then you'll become a priest?"

I shrugged. "I hardly know yet. It's what they always meant me for, after all. Whatever the future is there, my place here is gone—if I ever had one. And I'm certainly no warrior."

He grinned at that. "Well, you never were, exactly, were you? And the war isn't over; it's hardly begun, let me tell you." He leaned across the table confidentially, but the movement knocked his cup so that it rocked, and the wine washed up to the rim. He grabbed and steadied it. "Nearly spilled that, and the wine's nearly out again. Not bad stuff, eh? What about another?"

"If you like. But you were saying—?"

"Cornwall, now. I've always thought I'd like to go there. What are they saying there about Ambrosius?"

The wine was already talking. He had forgotten to be confidential; his voice was loud, and I saw one or two heads turn in our direction.

He took no notice. "Yes, I imagine you'd hear down there, if there was any news to hear. They say that's where he'll land, eh?"

"Oh," I said easily, "there's talk all the time. There has been for years, you know how it is. He hasn't come yet, so your guess is as good as mine."

"Like a bet on it?" I saw he had reached into the pouch at his waist and brought out a pair of dice, which he tossed idly from hand to hand. "Come on, give you a game?"

"No, thanks. At any rate, not here. Look, Dinias, I'll tell

you what, we'll get another flask, or two if you like, and go home and drink them there?"

"Home?" He sneered, loose-lipped. "Where's that? An empty palace?"

He was still talking loudly, and from across the room I noticed someone watching us. Nobody I knew. Two men in dark clothes, one with fringe of black beard, the other thin-faced and red-headed, with a long nose like a fox. Welshmen, by the look of them. They had a flask on a stool in front of them, and cups in their hands, but the flask had been at the same level now for a good half hour. I glanced at Dinias. I judged he had reached the stage now of being disposed either to friendly confidences or a loud quarrel. To insist on leaving now might be to provoke that quarrel, and if we were being watched, and if the crowd near the door were indeed Vortigern's men, it would be better to stay here and talk quietly than to take my cousin out into the street, and perhaps be followed. What, after all, did a mention of Ambrosius' name matter? It would be on every man's lips, and if, as seemed likely, rumours had been flying more thickly than usual of late, everyone, Vortigern's friends and enemies alike, would be discussing them.

Dinias had dropped the dice on the table, and was pushing them here and there with a reasonably steady forefinger. At least they would give us an excuse for a heads-together session in our corner. And dice might take his attention off the wine flask.

I brought out a handful of small coins. "Look, if you really want a game. What can you put on the table?"

As we played I was conscious that Blackbeard and the foxy man were listening. The Saxons near the door seemed harmless enough; most of them were three parts drunk already, and talking too loudly among themselves to pay attention to anyone else. But Blackbeard seemed to be interested.

I threw the dice. Five and four. Too good; I wanted Dinias to win something. I could hardly offer him money to get him behind the curtain with a girl. Meanwhile, to put Blackbeard off the scent . . .

I said, not loudly, but very clearly: "Ambrosius, is it? Well, you know the rumours. I've heard nothing definite about him, only the usual stories that have been going the rounds these ten years. Oh, yes, men say he'll come to Cornwall, or Maridunum, or London, or Avon-mouth—you

can take your pick ... Your throw." Blackbeard's attention
had shifted. I leaned closer to watch Dinias' throw, and
lowered my voice. "And if he did come now, what would
happen? You'll know this better than I. Would what's left of
the West rise for him, or stand loyal to Vortigern?"

"The West would go up in flames. It's done that already,
God knows. Double or quits? Flames like the night you left.
God, how I laughed! Little bastard sets the place on fire and
goes. Why did you? That's mine, double five. Throw you
again."

"Right. Why did I go, you mean? I told you, I was afraid
of Camlach."

"I didn't mean that. I mean why did you set the place on
fire? Don't tell me it was an accident, because I don't believe
you."

"It was a funeral pyre. I lit it because they killed my
servant."

He stared, the dice for a moment still in his hands. "You
fired the King's palace for a *slave?*"

"Why not? I happened to like my servant better than I
liked Camlach."

He gave me a slightly fuddled look, and threw. A two and
a four. I scooped back a couple of coins.

"Damn you," said Dinias, "you've no right to win, you've
enough already. All right, again. Your servant, indeed!
You've a mighty high tone for a bastard playing at being a
scribe in a priest's cell."

I grinned. "You're a bastard, too, remember, dear cousin."

"Maybe, but at least I know who my father was."

"Keep your voice down, people are listening. All right,
throw you again."

A pause while the dice rattled. I watched them rather
anxiously. So far, they had tended to fall my way. How
useful it would be, I thought, if power could be brought to
bear on such small things; it would take no effort, and make
the way smoother. But I had begun to learn that in fact
power made nothing smoother; when it came it was like
having a wolf by the throat. Sometimes I had felt like that
boy in the old myth who harnessed the horses of the sun and
rode the world like a god until the power burned him to
death. I wondered if I would ever feel the flames again.

The dice fell from my very human fingers. A two and a
one. No need to have the power if you could have the luck.
Dinias gave a grunt of satisfaction and gathered them up,

while I slid some coins towards him. The game went on. I lost the next three throws, and the heap beside him grew respectably. He was relaxing. No one was paying us any attention; that had been imagination. It was time, perhaps, for a few more facts.

"Where's the King now?" I asked.

"Eh? Oh, aye, the King. He's been gone from here nearly a month. Moved north as soon as the weather slackened and the roads were open."

"To Caer'n-ar-Von, you said—Segontium?"

"Did I? Oh, well, I suppose he calls that his base, but who'd want to be caught in that corner between Y Wyddfa and the sea? No he's building himself a new stronghold, they say. Did you say you'd get another flask?"

"Here it comes. Help yourself. I've had enough. A stronghold, you said? Where?"

"What? Oh, yes. Good wine, this. I don't rightly know where he's building, somewhere in Snowdon. Told you. Dinas Brenin, they call it . . . Or would, if he could get it built."

"What's stopping him? Is there still trouble up there? Vortimer's faction still, or something new? They're saying in Cornwall that he's got thirty thousand Saxons at his back."

"At his back, on both sides—Saxons everywhere, our King has. But not with him. With Hengist—and Hengist and the King aren't seeing eye to eye. Oh, he's beset, is Vortigern, I can tell you!" Fortunately he was speaking quietly, his words lost in the rattle of dice and the uproar around us. I think he had half forgotten me. He scowled down at the table as he threw. "Look at that. The bloody things are ill-wished. Like King's Fort."

Somewhere the words touched a string of memory to a faint humming, as elusive and untraceable as a bee in the lime trees. I said casually, making my throw: "Ill-wished? How?"

"Hah, that's better. Should be able to beat that. Oh, well, you know these Northmen—if the wind blows colder one morning they say it's a dead spirit passing by. They don't use surveyors in that army, the soothsayers do it all. I heard he'd got the walls built four times to man height, and each time by next morning they'd cracked clear across. . . . How's that?"

"Not bad. I couldn't beat it, I'm afraid. Did he put guards on?"

"Of course. They saw nothing."

"Well, why should they?" It seemed that the luck was against us both; the dice were as ill-wished for Dinias as the walls for Vortigern. In spite of myself I threw a pair of doubles. Scowling, Dinias pushed half his pile towards me. I said: "It only sounds as if he picked a soft place. Why not move?"

"He picked the top of a crag, as pretty a place to defend as you'll find in all Wales. It guards the valley north and south, and stands over the road just where the cliffs narrow both sides, and the road is squeezed right up under the crag. And damn it, there's been a tower there before. The locals have called it King's Fort time out of mind."

King's Fort . . . Dinas Brenin . . . The humming swelled clear into a memory. Birches bone-white against a milk-blue sky. The scream of a falcon. Two kings walking together, and Cerdic's voice saying, *"Come down, and I'll cut you in on a dice game."*

Before I even knew, I had done it, as neatly as Cerdic himself. I flicked the still turning dice with a quick finger. Dinias, up-ending the empty flask over his cup, never noticed. The dice settled. A two and a one. I said ruefully: "You won't have much trouble beating that."

He did beat it, but only just. He pulled the coins towards him with a grunt of triumph, then sprawled half across the table, his elbow in a pool of spilled wine. Even if I did manage, I thought, to let this drunken idiot win enough money off me, I would be lucky if I could get him even as far as the curtain leading to the brothel rooms. My throw again. As I shook the box I saw Cadal in the doorway, waiting to catch my eye. It was time to be gone. I nodded, and he withdrew. As Dinias glanced to see whom I had signalled to I threw again, and flicked a settling six over with my sleeve. One and three. Dinias made a sound of satisfaction and reached for the box.

"Tell you what," I said, "one more throw and we'll go. Win or lose, I'll buy another flask and we'll take it with us and drink it in my lodgings. We'll be more comfortable than here." Once I got him outside, I reckoned, Cadal and I could deal with him."

"Lodgings? I could have given you lodgings. Plenty of room there, you needn't have sent your man to look for lodgings. Got to be careful these days, you know. There. A pair of fives. Beat that if you can, Merlin the bastard!" He tipped the last of the wine down his throat, swallowed, and leaned back, grinning

"I'll give you the game." I pushed the coins over to him, and made to stand up. As I looked round for the pot-boy to order the promised flask, Dinias slammed his hand down on the table with a crash. The dice jumped and rattled, and a cup went over, rolled, and smashed on the floor. Men stopped talking, staring.

"Oh, no, you don't! We'll play it out! Walk out just as the luck's turning again, would you? I'll not take that from you, or anyone else! Sit down and play, my bastard cousin—"

"Oh, for God's sake, Dinias—"

"All right, so I'm a bastard, too! All I can say is, better be the bastard of a king than a no-man's-child who never had a father at all!"

He finished with a hiccup, and someone laughed. I laughed too, and reached for the dice. "All right, we'll take them with us. I told you, win or lose, we'd take a flask home. We can finish the game there. It's time we drank one another into bed."

A hand fell on my shoulder, heavily. As I twisted to see who it was, someone came on my other side and gripped my arm. I saw Dinias stare upwards, gaping. Around us the drinkers were suddenly silent.

Blackbeard tightened his grip. "Quietly, young sir. We don't want a brawl, do we? Could we have a word with you outside?"

6

I got to my feet. There was no clue in the staring faces round me. Nobody spoke.

"What's all this about?"

"Outside, if you please," repeated Blackbeard. "We don't want a—"

"I don't in the least mind having a brawl," I said crisply. "You'll tell me who you are before I'll go a step with you. And to start with, take your hands off me. Landlord, who are these men?"

"King's men, sir. You'd best do as they say. If you've got nothing to hide—"

" 'You've got nothing to fear'?" I said. "I know that one,

and it's never true." I shoved Blackbeard's hand off my
shoulder and turned to face him. I saw Dinias staring with
his mouth slack. This, I supposed, was not the meek-voiced
cousin he knew. Well, the time for that was past. "I don't
mind these men hearing what you have to say. Tell me here.
Why do you want to talk to me?"

"We were interested in what your friend here was saying."

"Then why not talk to him?"

Blackbeard said stolidly: "All in good time. If you'd tell
me who you are, and where you come from—?"

"My name is Emrys, and I was born here in Maridunum. I
went to Cornwall some years ago, when I was a child, and
now had a fancy to come home and hear the news. That's
all."

"And this young man? He called you 'cousin'."

"That was a form of speech. We are related, but not
nearly. You probably also heard him call me 'bastard'."

"Wait a minute." The new voice came from behind me,
among the crowd. An elderly man with thin grey hair,
nobody I recognized, pushed his way to the front. "I know
him. He's telling the truth. Why, that's Myrddin Emrys, sure
enough, that was the old King's grandson." Then to me,
"You won't remember me, sir. I was your grandfather's
steward, one of them. I tell you this"—he stretched his neck,
like a hen, peering up at Blackbeard—"King's men or no
King's men, you've no business to lay a hand on this young
gentleman. He's told you the truth. He left Maridunum five
years ago—that's right, five, it was the night the old King
died—and nobody heard tell where he'd gone. But I'll take
any oath you like he would never raise a hand against King
Vortigern. Why, he was training to be a priest, and never
took arms in his life. And if he wants a quiet drink with
Prince Dinias, why, they're related, as he told you, and who
else would he drink with, to get the news of home?" He
nodded at me, kindly. "Yes, indeed, that's Myrddin Emrys,
that's a grown man now instead of a little boy, but I'd know
him anywhere. And let me tell you, sir, I'm mightily glad to
see you safe. It was feared you'd died in the fire."

Blackbeard hadn't even glanced at him. He was directly
between me and the door. He never took his eyes off me.
"Myrddin Emrys. The old King's grandson." He said it slowly. "And a bastard? Whose son, then?"

There was no point in denying it. I had recognized the

steward now. He was nodding at me, pleased with himself. I said: "My mother was the King's daughter, Niniane."

The black eyes narrowed. "Is this true?"

"Quite true, quite true." It was the steward, his goodwill to me patent in his pale stupid eyes.

Blackbeard turned to me again. I saw the next question forming on his lips. My heart was thumping, and I could feel the blood stealing up into my face. I tried to will it down.

"And your father?"

"I do not know." Perhaps he would only think that the blood in my face was shame.

"Speak carefully, now," said Blackbeard. "You must know. Who got you?"

"I do not know."

He regarded me. "Your mother, the King's daughter. You remember her?"

"I remember her well."

"And she never told you? You expect us to believe this?"

I said irritably: "I don't care what you believe or what you don't believe. I'm tired of this. All my life people have asked me this question, and all my life people have disbelieved me. It's true, she never told me. I doubt if she told anyone. As far as I know, she may have been telling the truth when she said I was begotten of a devil." I made a gesture of impatience. "Why do you ask?"

"We heard what the other young gentleman said." His tone and look were stolid. " 'Better to be a bastard and have a king for a father, than a no-man's-child who never had a father at all!' "

"If I take no offense why should you? You can see he's in his cups."

"We wanted to make sure, that's all. And now we've made sure. The King wants you."

"The King?" I must have sounded blank.

He nodded. "Vortigern. We've been looking for you for three weeks past. You're to go to him."

"I don't understand." I must have looked bewildered rather than frightened. I could see my mission falling round me in ruins, but with this was a mixture of confusion and relief. If they had been looking for me for three weeks, this surely could have nothing to do with Ambrosius.

Dinias had been sitting quietly enough in his corner. I thought that most of what was said had not gone through to him, but now he leaned forward, his hands flat on the wine-splashed table. "What does he want him for? Tell me that."

"You've no call to worry." Blackbeard threw it at him almost disdainfully "It's not you he wants. But I'll tell you what, since it was you led us to him, it's you who should get the reward."

"Reward?" I asked. "What talk is this?"

Dinias was suddenly stone sober. "I said nothing. What do you mean?"

Blackbeard nodded. "It was what you said that led us to him."

"He was only asking questions about the family—he's been away," said my cousin. "You were listening. Anybody could have listened, we weren't keeping our voices down. By the gods, if we wanted to talk treason would we have talked it here?"

"Nobody mentioned treason. I'm just doing my duty. The King wants to see him, and he's to come with me."

The old steward said, looking troubled now: "You can't harm him. He's who he says he is, Niniane's son. You can ask her yourself."

That brought Blackbeard round to face him quickly. "She's still alive?"

"Oh, yes, she's that all right. She's barely a stone's throw off, at the nunnery of St. Peter's, beyond the old oak at the crossways."

"Leave her alone," I said, really frightened now. I wondered what she might tell them. "Don't forget who she is. Even Vortigern won't dare to touch her. Besides, you've no authority. Either over me or her."

"You think not?"

"Well, what authority have you?"

"This." The short sword flashed in his hand. It was sharpened to a dazzle.

I said: "Vortigern's law, is it? Well, it's not a bad argument. I'll go with you, but it won't do you much good with my mother. Leave her alone, I tell you. She won't tell you any more than I."

"But at least we don't have to believe her when she says she doesn't know."

"But it's true." It was the steward, still chattering. "I tell you, I served in the palace all my life, and I remember it all. It used to be said she'd borne a child to the devil, to the prince of darkness."

Hands fluttered as people made the sign. The old man said, peering up at me: "Go with them, son, they'll not hurt Niniane's child, or her either. There'll come a time when the King will need the people of the West, as who should know better than he?"

"It seems I'll have to go with them, with the King's warrant so sharp at my throat," I said. "It's all right, Dinias, it wasn't your fault. Tell my servant where I am. Very well, you, take me to Vortigern, but keep your hands off me."

I went between them to the door, the drinkers making way for us. I saw Dinias stumble to his feet and come after. As we reached the street Blackbeard turned. "I was forgetting. Here, it's yours."

The purse of money jingled as it hit the ground at my cousin's feet.

I didn't turn. But as I went I saw, even without looking, the expression on my cousin's face as, with a quick glance to right and left, he stooped for the purse and tucked it into his waistband.

7

Vortigern had changed. My impression that he had grown smaller, less impressive, was not only because I myself, instead of being a child, was now a tall youth. He had grown, as it were, into himself. It did not need the makeshift hall, the court which was less a court than a gathering of fighting chiefs and such women as they kept by them, to indicate that this was a man on the run. Or rather, a man in a corner. But a cornered wolf is more dangerous than a free one, and Vortigern was still a wolf.

And he had certainly chosen his corner well. King's Fort was as I remembered it, a crag commanding the river valley, its crest only approachable along a narrow saddleback like a bridge. This promontory jutted out from a circle of rocky hills which provided in their shelter a natural corrie where horses could graze and where beasts could be driven in and guarded. All round the valley itself the mountains towered, grey with scree and still not green with spring. All the April rain had done was to bring a long cascade spilling a thousand feet from the summit to the valley's foot. A wild, dark, impressive place. If once the wolf dug himself in at the top of that crag, even Ambrosius would be hard put to it to get him out.

The journey took six days. We started at first light, by the road which leads due north out of Maridunum, a worse road than the eastbound way but quicker, even slowed down as we were by bad weather and the pace set by the women's litters. The bridge was broken at Pennal and more or less washed away, and nearly half a day was spent fording the Afon Dyfi, before the party could struggle on to Tomen-y-mur, where the road was good. On the afternoon of the sixth day we turned up the riverside track for Dinas Brenin, where the King lay.

Blackbeard had had no difficulty at all in persuading St. Peter's to let my mother go with him to the King. If he had used the same tactics as with me, this was understandable enough, but I had no opportunity to ask her, or even to find out if she knew any more than I did why Vortigern wanted us. A closed litter had been provided for her, and two women from the religious house travelled with her. Since they were beside her day and night it was impossible for me to approach her for private speech, and in fact she showed no sign of wanting to see me alone. Sometimes I caught her watching me with an anxious, even perhaps a puzzled look, but when she spoke she was calm and withdrawn, with never so much as a hint that she knew anything that Vortigern himself might not overhear. Since I was not allowed to see her alone, I had judged it better to tell her the same story I had told Blackbeard; even the same (since for all I knew he had been questioned) that I had told Dinias. She would have to think what she could about it, and about my reasons for not getting in touch with her sooner. It was, of course, impossible to mention Brittany, or even friends from Brittany, without risking her guess about Ambrosius, and this I dared not do.

I found her much changed. She was pale and quiet, and had put on weight, and with it a kind of heaviness of the spirit that she had not had before. It was only after a day or two, jogging north with the escort through the hills, that it suddenly came to me what this was; she had lost what she had had of power. Whether time had taken this, or illness, or whether she had abnegated it for the power of the Christian symbol that she wore on her breast, I had no means of guessing. But it had gone.

On one score my mind was set at rest straight away. My mother was treated with courtesy, even with distinction as befitted a king's daughter. I received no such distinction, but I was given a good horse, housed well at night, and my escort were civil enough when I tried to talk to them. Beyond that, they made very little effort with me; they would give no answer to any of my questions, though it seemed to me they knew perfectly well why the King wanted me. I caught curious and furtive glances thrown at me, and once or twice a look of pity.

We were taken straight to the King. He had set up his headquarters on the flat land between the crag and the river, from where he had hoped to oversee the building of his stronghold. It was a very different camp even from the makeshift ones of Uther and Ambrosius. Most of the men were in tents and, except for high earthworks and a palisade on the side towards the road, they apparently trusted to the natural defenses of the place—the river and crag on one side, the rock of Dinas Brenin on the other, and the impenetrable and empty mountains behind them.

Vortigern himself was housed royally enough. He received us in a hall whose wooden pillars were hung with curtains of bright embroidery, and whose floor of the local greenish slate was thickly strewn with fresh rushes. The high chair on the dais was regally carved and gilded. Beside him, on a chair equally ornate and only slightly smaller, sat Rowena, his Saxon Queen. The place was crowded. A few men in courtiers' dress stood near, but most of those present were armed. There was a fair sprinkling of Saxons. Behind Vortigern's chair on the dais stood a group of priests and holy men.

As we were brought in, a hush fell. All eyes turned our way. Then the King rose and, stepping down from the dais, came to meet my mother, smiling, and with both hands outstretched.

"I bid you welcome, Princess," he said, and turned to present her with ceremonial courtesy to the Queen.

The hiss of whispers ran round the hall, and glances were exchanged. The King had made it clear by his greeting that he did not hold my mother accountable for Camlach's part in the recent rebellion. He glanced at me, briefly but I thought with keen interest, gave me a nod of greeting, then took my mother's hand on his arm and led her up on to the dais. At a nod of his head, someone hurried to set a chair for her on the step below him. He bade her be seated, and he and the Queen took their places once more. Walking forward with my guards at my back, I stood below the dais in front of the King.

Vortigern spread his hands on the arms of his chair and sat upright, smiling from my mother to me with an air of welcome and even satisfaction. The buzz of whispers had died down. There was a hush. People were staring, expectant.

But all the King said was, to my mother: "I ask your pardon, Madam, for forcing this journey on you at such a time of year. I trust you were made comfortable enough?" He followed this up with smooth trivial courtesies while the people stared and waited, and my mother bent her head and murmured her polite replies, as upright and unconcerned as he. The two nuns who had accompanied her stood behind her, like waiting-women. She held one hand at her breast, fingering the little cross which she wore there as a talisman; the other lay among the brown folds on her lap. Even in her plain brown habit she looked royal.

Vortigern said, smiling: "And now will you present your son?"

"My son's name is Merlin. He left Maridunum five years ago after the death of my father, your kinsman. Since then he had been in Cornwall, in a house of religion. I commend him to you."

The King turned to me. "Five years? You would be little more than a child then, Merlin. How old are you now?"

"I am seventeen, sir." I met his gaze squarely. "Why have you sent for my mother and myself? I had hardly set foot in Maridunum again, when your men took me, by force."

"For that I am sorry. You must forgive their zeal. They only knew that the matter was urgent, and they took the quickest means to do what I wished." He turned back to my mother. "Do I have to assure you, Lady Niniane, that no harm will come to you? I swear it. I know that you have been in the House of St. Peter now for five years, and that your brother's alliance with my sons was no concern of yours."

"Nor of my son's, my lord," she said calmly. "Merlin left Maridunum on the night of my father's death, and from that day until now I have heard nothing from him. But one thing is certain, he had no part in the rebellion; why, he was only a child when he left his home—and indeed, now that I know he fled south that night, to Cornwall, I can only assume he went from very fear of my brother Camlach, who was no friend to him. I assure you, my lord King, that whatever I myself may have guessed of my brother's intentions towards you, my son knew nothing of them. I am at a loss to know why you should want him here."

To my surprise Vortigern did not even seem interested in my sojourn in Cornwall, nor did he look at me again. He rested his chin on his fist and watched my mother from under his brows. His voice and look were alike grave and courteous, but there was something in the air that I did not like. Suddenly I realized what it was. Even while my mother and the King talked, watching one another, the priests behind the King's chair watched me. And when I stole a glance out of the corners of my eyes at the people in the hall I found that here, too, there were eyes on me. There was a stillness in the room now, and I thought, suddenly: *Now he will come to it.*

He said quietly, almost reflectively: "You never married."

"No." Her lids drooped, and I knew she had become suddenly wary.

"Your son's father, then, died before you could be wed? Killed in battle, perhaps?"

"No, my lord." Her voice was quiet, but perfectly clear. I saw her hands move and tighten a little.

"Then he still lives?"

She said nothing, but bowed her head, so that her hood fell forward and hid her face from the other people in the hall. But those on the dais could still see her. I saw the Queen staring with curiosity and contempt. She had light blue eyes, and big breasts which bulged milk-white above a tight blue bodice. Her mouth was small. Her hands were as white as her breasts, but the fingers thick and ugly, like a servant's. They were covered with rings of gold and enamel and copper.

The King's brows drew together at my mother's silence, but his voice was still pleasant. "Tell me one thing, Lady Niniane. Did you ever tell your son the name of his father?"

"No." The tone of her voice, full and definite, contrasted oddly with the posture of bowed head and veiled face. It was the pose of a woman who is ashamed, and I wondered if she meant to look like this to excuse her silence. I could not see her face myself, but I saw the hand that held the fold of her long skirt. I was sharply reminded of the Niniane who had defied her father and refused Gorlan, King of Lanascol. Across that memory came another, the memory of my father's face, looking at me across the table in the lamplight. I banished it. He was so vividly in front of me that it seemed to me a wonder that the whole hall full of men could not see him. Then it came to me, sharply and with terror, that Vortigern had seen him. Vortigern knew. This was why we were here. He had heard some rumour of my coming, and was making sure. It remained to be seen whether I would be treated as a spy, or as a hostage.

I must have made some movement in spite of myself. My mother looked up, and I saw her eyes under the hood. She no longer looked like a princess; she looked like a woman who is afraid. I smiled at her, and something came back into her face, and I saw then that her fear was only for me.

I held myself still, and waited. Let him make the moves. Time enough to counter them when he had shown me the ground to fight from.

He twisted the big ring on his finger. "This is what your son told my messengers. And I have heard it said that no one else in the kingdom ever knew the name of his father. From what men tell me, Lady Niniane, and from what I know of you, your child would never be fathered by anyone base. Why not, then, tell him? It is a thing a man should know."

I said angrily, forgetting my caution: "What is it to you?"

My mother flashed me a look that silenced me. Then to Vortigern, "Why do you ask me these questions?"

"Lady," said the King, "I sent for you today, and for your son, to ask you one thing only. The name of his father."

"I repeat, why do you ask?"

He smiled. It was a mere baring of the teeth. I took a step. "Mother, he has no right to ask you this. He will not dare—"

"Silence him," said Vortigern.

The man beside me slapped a hand across my mouth, and held me fast. There was the hiss of metal as the other drew his sword and pressed it against my side. I stood still.

My mother cried out. "Let him go! If you hurt him, Vortigern, king or no king, I will never tell you, even if you kill me. Do you think I held the truth from my own father and my brother and even from my son for all these years, just to tell you for the asking?"

"You will tell me for your son's sake," said Vortigern. At his nod the fellow took his hand from my mouth, and stood back. But his hand was still on my arm, and I could feel the other's sword sharp through my tunic.

My mother had thrown back her hood now, and was sitting upright in her chair, her hands gripping the arms. Pale and shaken as she was, and dressed in the humble brown robe, she made the Queen look like a servant. The silence in the hall now was deathly. Behind the King's chair the priests stood staring. I held tightly to my thoughts. If these men were priests and magicians, then no thought of Ambrosius, not even his name, must come into my mind. I felt the sweat start on my body, and my thoughts tried to reach my mother and hold her, without forming an image which these men could see. But the power had gone, and there was no help here from the god; I did not even know if I was man enough for what might happen after she told them. I dared not speak again; I was afraid that if they used force against me she would speak to save me. And once they knew, once they started to question me . . .

Something must have reached her, because she turned and looked at me again, moving her shoulders under the rough robe as if she felt a hand touch her. As her eyes met mine I knew that this was nothing to do with power. She was trying, as women will, to tell me something with her eyes. It was a message of love and reassurance, but on a human level, and I could not understand it.

She turned back to Vortigern. "You choose a strange place for your questions, King. Do you really expect me to speak of these things here, in your open hall, and in the hearing of all comers?"

He brooded for a moment, his brows down over his eyes. There was sweat on his face, and I saw his hands twitch on the arms of the chair. The man was humming like a harpstring. The tension ran right through the hall, almost visibly. I felt my skin prickle, and a cold wolfspaw of fear walked up my spine. Behind the King one of the priests leaned forward and whispered. Then the King nodded. "The people shall leave us. But the priests and the magicians must remain."

Reluctantly, and with a buzz of chatter, people began to leave the hall. The priests stayed, a dozen or so men in long robes standing behind the chairs of the King and Queen. One of them, the one who had spoken to the King, a tall man who stood stroking his grey beard with a dirty ringed hand, was smiling. From his dress he was the head of them. I searched his face for signs of power, but, though the men were dressed in priests' robes, I could see nothing there but death. It was in all their eyes. More than that I could not see. The wolfspaw of cold touched my bones again. I stood in the soldier's grip without resistance.

"Loose him," said Vortigern. "I have no wish to harm the Lady Niniane's son. But you, Merlin, if you move or speak again before I give you leave, you will be taken from the hall."

The sword withdrew from my side, but the man still held it ready. The guards stood back half a pace from me. I neither moved nor spoke. I had never since I was a child felt so helpless, so naked of either knowledge or power, so stripped of God. I knew, with bitter failure, that if I were in the crystal cave with fires blazing and my master's eyes on me, I should see nothing. I remembered, suddenly, that Galapas was dead. Perhaps, I thought, the power had only come from him, and perhaps it had gone with him.

The King had turned his sunken eyes back to my mother. He leaned forward, his look suddenly fierce and intent.

"And now, Madam, will you answer my question?"

"Willingly," she said. "Why not?"

8

She had spoken so calmly that I saw the King's look of surprise. She put up a hand to push the hood back from her face, and met his eyes levelly.

"Why not? I see no harm in it. I might have told you sooner, my lord, if you had asked me differently, and in a different place. There is no harm now in men knowing. I am no longer in the world, and do not have to meet the eyes of the world, or hear their tongues. And since I know now that my son, too, has retired from the world, then I know how little he will care what the world says about him. So I will tell you what you want to know. And when I tell you, you will see why I have never spoken of this before, not even to my own father or to my son himself."

There was no sign of fear now. She was even smiling. She had not looked at me again. I tried to keep from staring at her, to school my face into blankness. I had no idea what she planned to say, but I knew that here would be no betrayal. She was playing some game of her own, and was secure in her own mind that this would avert whatever danger threatened me. I knew, for certain, that she would say nothing of Ambrosius. But still, everywhere in the hall, was death. Outside it had begun to rain, and the afternoon was wearing

on towards twilight. A servant came in at the door bearing
torches, but Vortigern waved him back. To do him justice, I
believe he was thinking of my mother's shame, but I thought
to myself: *There can be no help even there, no light, no
fire . . .*

"Speak, then," said Vortigern. "Who fathered your son?"

"I never saw him." She spoke quite simply. "It was no man
that I ever knew. " She paused, then said, without looking at
me, her eyes still level on the King: "My son will forgive me
for what he is soon to hear, but you have forced me, and this
he will understand."

Vortigern flashed me a look. I met it stonily. I was certain
of her now.

She went on: "When I was only young, about sixteen, and
thinking, as girls do, of love, it happened one Martinmas
Eve, after I and my women had gone to bed. The girl who
slept in my room was asleep, and the others were in the outer
chamber, but I could not sleep. After a while I rose from my
bed and went to the window. It was a clear night, with a
moon. When I turned back to my bed-place I saw what I
took to be a young man standing there, full in the middle of
my bedchamber. He was handsome, and young, dressed in a
tunic and long mantle, with a short sword at his side. He wore
rich jewels. My first thought was that he had broken in
through the outer chamber while my women slept; my second was that I was in my shift, and barefoot, with my hair
loose. I thought he meant mischief, and was opening my
mouth to call out and wake the women, when the youth
smiled at me, with a gesture as if to tell me to be quiet, he
meant me no harm. Then he stepped aside into the shadow,
and when I stole after, to look, there was no one there."

She paused. No one spoke. I remembered how she would
tell me stories when I was a child. The hall was quite still,
but I felt the man beside me quiver, as if he would have liked
to move away. The Queen's red mouth hung open, half in
wonder, half (I thought) in envy.

My mother looked at the wall above the King's head. "I
thought it had been a dream, or a girl's fancy bred of
moonlight. I went to bed and told no one. But he came
again. Not always at night; not always when I was alone. So
I realized it was no dream, but a familiar spirit who desired
something from me. I prayed, but still he came. While I was
sitting with my girls, spinning, or when I walked on dry days
in my father's orchard, I would feel his touch on my arm,

and his voice in my ear. But at these times I did not see him, and nobody heard him but I."

She groped for the cross on her breast and held it. The gesture looked so unforced and natural that I was surprised, until I saw that it was indeed natural, that she did not hold the cross for protection, but for forgiveness. I thought to myself, it is not the Christian God she should fear when she lies; she should be afraid of lying like this about the things of power. The King's eyes, bent on her, were fierce and, I thought, exultant. The priests were watching her as if they would eat her spirit alive.

"So all through that winter he came to me. And he came at night. I was never alone in my chamber, but he came through doors and windows and walls, and lay with me. I never saw him again, but heard his voice and felt his body. Then, in the summer, when I was heavy with child, he left me." She paused. "They will tell you how my father beat me and shut me up, and how when the child was born he would not give him a name fit for a Christian prince, but, because he was born in September, named him for the sky-god, the wanderer, who has no house but the woven air. But I called him Merlin always, because on the day of his birth a wild falcon flew in through the window and perched above the bed, and looked at me with my lover's eyes."

Her glance crossed mine then, a brief flash. This, then, was true. And the Emrys, too, she had given me that in spite of them; she had kept that much of him for me after all.

She had looked away. "I think, my lord King, that what I have told you will not altogether surprise you. You must have heard the rumours that my son was not as ordinary boys—it is not possible always to be silent, and I know there have been whispers, but now I have told you the truth, openly; and so I pray you, my lord Vortigern, to let my son and me go back in peace to our respective houses of religion."

When she had finished there was silence. She bowed her head and pulled up her hood again to hide her face. I watched the King and the men behind him. I thought to see him angry, frowning with impatience, but to my surprise his brows smoothed out, and he smiled. He opened his mouth to answer my mother, but the Queen forestalled him. She leaned forward, licking her red lips, and spoke for the first time, to the priests.

"Maugan, is this possible?"

It was the tall man, the bearded high priest, who answered her. He spoke without hesitation, bland and surprisingly emphatic. "Madam, it is possible. Who has not heard of these creatures of air and darkness, who batten on mortal men and women? In my studies, and in many of the books I have read, I have found stories of children being born into the world in this fashion." He eyed me, fondling his beard, then turned to the King. "Indeed, my lord, we have the authority of the ancients themselves. They knew well that certain spirits, haunting the air at night between the moon and the earth, cohabit at their will with mortal women, in the shape of men. It is certainly possible that this royal lady—this virtuous royal lady—was the victim of such a creature. We know—and she has said herself—that this was rumoured for many years. I myself spoke with one of her waiting-women who said that the child could surely be begotten of none but the devil, and that no man had been near her. And of the son himself, when he was a child, I heard many strange things. Indeed, King Vortigern, this lady's story is true."

No one looked any longer at Niniane. Every eye in the place was on me. I could see in the King's face nothing that was not at once ferocious and innocent, a kind of eager satisfaction like a child's, or a wild beast's when it sees its prey loitering nearer. Puzzled, I held my tongue and waited. If the priests believed my mother, and Vortigern believed the priests, then I could not see where danger could come from. No faintest hint had turned men's thoughts towards Ambrosius. Maugan and the King seemed to hurry with eager satisfaction down the path that my mother had opened for them.

The King glanced at my guards. They had moved back from me, no doubt afraid to stand so near a demon's child. At his sign they closed in again. The man on my right still held his sword drawn, but down by his side and out of my mother's view. It was not quite steady. The man on my left surreptitiously loosened his own blade in its sheath. Both men were breathing heavily, and I could smell fear on them.

The priests were nodding sagely, and some of them, I noticed, held their hands in front of them in the sign to ward off enchantment. It seemed that they believed Maugan, they believed my mother, they saw me as the devil's child. All that had happened was that her story had confirmed their own belief, the old rumours. This, in fact, was what she had been brought here for. And now they watched me with satisfaction, but also with a kind of wary fear.

My own fear was leaving me. I thought I began to see what they wanted. Vortigern's superstition was legendary. I remembered what Dinias had told me about the stronghold that kept falling down, and the reports of the King's sooth-sayers that it was bewitched. It seemed possible that, be-cause of the rumours of my birth, and possibly because of the childish powers I had shown before I left home, to which Maugan had referred, they thought I could advise or help them. If this was so, and they had brought me here because of my reputed powers, there might be some way in which I could help Ambrosius right from the enemy's camp. Perhaps after all the god had brought me here for this, perhaps he was still driving me. *Put yourself in his path* ... Well, one could only use what was to hand. If I had no power to use, I had knowledge.

I cast my mind back to the day at King's Fort, and to the flooded mine in the core of the crag, to which the dream had led me. I would certainly be able to tell them why their foundations would not stand. It was an engineer's answer, not a magician's. But, I thought, meeting the oyster eyes of Maugan as he dry-washed those long dirty hands before him, if it was a magician's answer they wanted, they should have it. And Vortigern with them.

I lifted my head. I believe I was smiling. "King Vorti-gern!"

It was like dropping a stone into a pool, the room was so still, so centered on me. I said strongly: "My mother has told you what you asked her. No doubt you will tell me now in what way I can serve you, but first I must ask you to keep your royal promise and let her go."

"The Lady Niniane is our honoured guest." The King's reply seemed automatic. He glanced at the open arcade that faced the river, where the white lances of the rain hissed down across a dark grey sky. "You are both free to go whenever you choose, but this is no time to begin the long journey back to Maridunum. You will surely wish to lie the night here, Madam, and hope for a dry day tomorrow?" He rose, and the Queen with him. "Rooms have been prepared, and now the Queen will take you there to rest and make ready to sup with us. Our court here, and our rooms, are a poor makeshift, but such as they are, they are at your service. Tomorrow you will be escorted home."

My mother had stood when they did. "And my son? You still have not told us why you brought us here for this?"

"Your son can serve me. He has powers which I can use. Now, Madam, if you will go with the Queen, I will talk to your son and tell him what I want of him. Believe me, he is as free as you are. I constrained him only until you told me the truth I wished to hear. I must thank you now for confirming what I had guessed." He put out a hand. "I swear to you, Lady Niniane, by any god you like, that I do not hold his birth against him, now or ever."

She regarded him for a moment, then bowed her head and, ignoring his gesture, came down to me, holding out both her hands. I crossed to her and took them in my own. They felt small and cold. I was taller than she was. She looked up at me with the eyes that I remembered; there was anxiety in them, and the dregs of anger, and some message urgently spoken in silence.

"Merlin, I would not have had you know it this way. I would have spared you this." But this was not what her eyes were saying.

I smiled down at her, and said carefully: "Mother, you told me nothing today that shocked me. Indeed, there's nothing you could tell me about my birth that I do not already know. Set yourself at rest."

She caught her breath and her eyes widened, searching my face. I went on, slowly: "Whoever my father was, it will not be held against me. You heard what the King promised. That is all we need to know."

Whether she got this part of the message I could not guess. She was still taking in what I had said first. "You knew? You knew?"

"I knew. You surely don't imagine that in all the years I've been away from you, and with the kind of studies I've undertaken, I never found out what parentage I had? It's some years now since my father made himself known to me. I assure you, I've spoken with him, not once but many times. I find nothing in my birth of which I need to be ashamed."

For a moment longer she looked at me, then she nodded, and the lids drooped over her eyes. A faint colour had come up into her face. She had understood me.

She turned away, pulling her hood up again to hide her face, and put her hand on the King's arm. She went from the room, walking between him and the Queen, and her two women followed them. The priests remained, clucking and whispering and staring. I took no notice of them, but watched my mother go.

The King paused in the doorway, and I heard his voice bidding my mother goodbye. There was a crowd waiting in the outer porch. They made way for Rowena and my mother, and the half-dozen women who were there followed them. I heard the swish of their dresses and the light voices of the women fade into the sound of the rain. Vortigern stood still in the doorway, watching them go. Outside the rain fell with a noise like a running river. It was darkening fast.

The King swung round on his heel and came back into the hall, with his fighting men behind him.

9

They crowded round me, muttering noisily, but holding back in a circle, like hounds before they close in for the kill. Death was back in the hall; I could feel it, but could not believe or understand it. I made a movement as if to follow my mother, and the swords of my guards lifted and quivered. I stood still.

I said sharply, to the King: "What's this? You gave your word. Are you so quickly forsworn?"

"Not forsworn. I gave my word that you should serve me, that I would never hold your birth against you. This is true. It is because of what I know about you, because you are the child of no man, that I have had you brought to me today. You will serve me, Merlin, because of your birth."

"Well?"

He mounted the steps to the throne and sat down again. His movements were slow and deliberate. All the men of the court had crowded in with him, and with them the torch-bearers. The hall filled with smoky light and the rustle and creak of leather and the clank of mail. Outside the rain hissed down.

Vortigern leaned forward, chin on fist. "Merlin, we have learned today what in part we already suspected, that you are the child of no man, but of a devil. As such, you require mercy from no man. But because your mother is a king's daughter, and therefore something is due to you, I shall tell you why I brought you here. You know perhaps that I am building a stronghold here on the rock they call the Fortress?"

"Everyone knows it," I said, "and everyone knows that it

will not stand, but falls down whenever it reaches man height."

He nodded. "And my magicians and wise men here, my advisers, have told me why. The foundations have not been properly laid."

"Well," I said, "that sounds remarkably like sense to me."

There was a tall old man to the King's right, beside the priests. His eyes were a bright angry blue under jutting white brows. He was watching me fixedly, and I thought I saw pity in his look. As I spoke, he put a hand up to his beard as if to hide a smile.

The King seemed not to have heard me. "They tell me," he said, "that a king's stronghold should be built on blood."

"They are talking, of course, in metaphors?" I said politely.

Maugan suddenly struck his staff on the floor of the dais. "They are talking literally!" he shouted. "The mortar should be slaked with blood! Blood should be sprinkled on the foundations. In ancient times no king built a fortress without observing this rite. The blood of a strong man, a warrior, kept the walls standing."

There was a sharp pause. My heart had begun to beat in slow, hard strokes that made the blood tingle in my limbs. I said, coldly: "And what has this to do with me? I am no warrior."

"You are no man, either," said the King harshly. "This is the magic, Merlin, that they have revealed to me, that I should seek out a lad who never had a father, and slake the foundations with his blood."

I stared at him, then looked round the ring of faces. There was shifting and muttering, and few eyes met mine, but I could see it in all their faces, the death I had smelled ever since I entered the hall. I turned back to the King.

"What rubbish is this? When I left Wales, it was a country for civilized men and for poets, for artists and for scholars, for warriors and kings who killed for their country, cleanly and in daylight. Now you talk of blood and human sacrifice. Do you think to throw modern Wales back to the rites of ancient Babylon and Crete?"

"I do not speak of 'human' sacrifice," said Vortigern. "You are the son of no man. Remember this."

In the stillness the rain lashed into the bubbling puddles on the ground outside. Someone cleared his throat. I caught the fierce blue glance of the old warrior. I had been right; there was pity there. But even those who pitied me were not going to raise a hand against this stupidity.

It had all come clear at last, like lightning breaking. This had been nothing to do with Ambrosius, or with my mother. She was safe enough, having merely confirmed what they wanted confirmed. She would even be honoured, since she had provided what they desired. And Ambrosius had never even entered their thoughts. I was not here as his son, his spy, his messenger; all they wanted was the "devil's child" to kill for their crude and dirty magic.

And, ironically enough, what they had got was no devil's child, not even the boy who once had thought to have power in his hands. All they had got was a human youth with no power beyond his human wits. But by the god, I thought, those might yet be enough . . . I had learned enough, power or no power, to fight them with their own weapons.

I managed to smile, looking beyond Maugan at the other priests. They were still making the sign against me, and even Maugan hugged his staff against his breast as if it had the power to protect him. "And what makes you so sure that my father the devil will not come to my aid?"

"Those are only words, King. There's no time to listen." Maugan spoke quickly and loudly, and the other priests pressed forward with him round the King's chair. They all spoke at once. "Yes, kill him now. There's no time to waste. Take him up to the crag and kill him now. You shall see that the gods will be appeased and the walls stand steady. His mother will not know, and even if she does, what can she do?"

There was a general movement, like hounds closing in. I tried to think, but I was empty even of coherent thought. The air stank and darkened. I could smell blood already, and the sword blades, held openly now against me, flashed in the torchlight. I fixed my eyes on the fireshot metal, and tried to empty my mind, but all I could see was the picked skeleton of Galapas, high on the hill in the sunlight, with the wings of the birds over him . . .

I said, to the swords: "Tell me one thing. Who killed Galapas?"

"What did he say? What did the devil's son say?" The question buzzed through the hall. A harsh voice said, loudly: "Let him speak." It was the old grey-bearded warrior.

"Who killed Galapas, the magician who lived on Bryn Myrddin above Maridunum?"

I had almost shouted it. My voice sounded strange, even to me. They fell silent, eyeing one another sideways, not understanding. Vortigern said: "The old man? They said he was a spy."

"He was a magician, and my master," I said. "And he taught me, Vortigern."

"What did he teach you?"

I smiled. "Enough. Enough to know that these men are fools and charlatans. Very well, Vortigern. Take me up to the crag and bring your knives with you, you and your soothsayers. Show me this fortress, these cracking walls, and see if I cannot tell you, better than they, why your fort will not stand. 'No man's child'!" I said it with contempt. "These are the things they conjure up, these foolish old men, when they can think of nothing else. Does it not occur to you, King, that the son of a spirit of darkness might have a magic that outstrips the spells of these old fools? If what they say is true, and if my blood will make these stones stand, then why did they watch them fall not once, not twice, but four times, before they could tell you what to do? Let me but see the place once, and I will tell you. By the God of gods, Vortigern, if my dead blood could make your fortress stand, how much better could my living body serve you?"

"Sorcery! Sorcery! Don't listen to him! What does a lad like him know of such matters?" Maugan began to shout, and the priests to cluck and chatter. But the old warrior said gruffly and sharply: "Let him try. There's no harm in that. Help you must have, Vortigern, be it from god or devil. Let him try, I say." And round the hall I heard the echoes from the fighting men, who would have no cause to love the priests: "Let him try."

Vortigern frowned in indecision, glancing from Maugan to the warriors, then at the grey arches where the rain fell. "Now?"

"Better now," they said. "There is not much time."

"No," I said clearly, "there is not much time." Silence again, all eyes on me. "The rain is heavy, Vortigern. What kind of king is it whose fortress is knocked down by a shower of rain? You will find your walls fallen yet again. This comes of building in the dark, with blind men for counsellors. Now take me to the top of your crag, and I will tell you why your walls have fallen. And if you listen to me instead of to these priests of darkness, I will tell you how to rebuild your stronghold in the light."

As I spoke, like the turning off of a tap, the downpour stopped. In the sudden quiet, men's mouths gaped. Even Maugan was dumb. Then like the pulling aside of a dark curtain, the sun came out.

I laughed. "You see? Come, King, take me to the top of the crag, and I will show you in sunlight why your walls fell down. But tell them to bring the torches. We shall need them."

10

Before we had fairly reached the foot of the crag I was proved right. The workmen could be seen crowded to the edge of the rock above, waiting for the King, and some of them had come down to meet him. Their foreman came panting up, a big man with rough sacking held gripped round his shoulders like a cloak, still sluicing with wet. He seemed hardy to have realized that the rain had stopped. He was pale, his eyes red-rimmed as if he had lacked sleep for nights. He stopped three paces away, eyeing the King nervously, and dashing the wet back of a hand across his face.

"Again?" said Vortigern briefly.

"Aye, my lord, and there's no one can say that it's a fault of ours, that I'll swear, any more than last time, or the times before. You saw yesterday how we were laying it this time. You saw how we cleared the whole site, to start again, and got right down to solid rock. And it is solid rock, my lord, I'll swear it. But still the wall cracks." He licked his lips, and his glance met mine and slid away from it, so that I knew he was aware of what the King and his soothsayers planned. "You're going up now, my lord?"

"Yes. Clear the men off the site."

The man swallowed, turned and ran up the twisting track. I heard him shouting. A mule was brought and the King mounted. My wrist was tied roughly to the harness. Magician or no, the sacrifice was to be given no chance to escape until he had proved himself. My guards kept close to my side. The King's officers and courtiers crowded round us, talking in low voices among themselves, but the priests held back, aloof and wary. I could see that they were not much afraid of the outcome; they knew as well as I did how much their magic was the power of their gods and how much illusion working on faith. They were confident that I could do no more than they; that even if I were one of their own kind they could find a way to defeat me. All I had to put against their smooth-worn rites was, they thought, the kind of bluff they were familiar with, and the luck that had stopped the rain and brought the sun out when I spoke.

The sun gleamed on the soaked grasses of the crag's crest. Here we were high above the valley where the river wound like a bright snake between its green verges. Steam rose from the roofs of the King's camp. Round the wooden hall and buildings the small skin tents clustered like toadstools, and men were no bigger than wood-lice crawling between them. It was a magnificent place, a true eagle's eyrie. The King halted his mule in a grove of wind-bitten oaks and pointed forward under the bare boughs.

"Yesterday you could have seen the western wall from here."

Beyond the grove was a narrow ridge, a natural hogsback or causeway, along which the workmen and their beasts had beaten a wide track. King's Fort was a craggy tower of rock, approached on one side by the causeway, and with its other three sides falling steeply away in dizzy slopes and cliffs. Its top was a plateau perhaps a hundred by a hundred paces, and would once have been rough grass with outcropping rock and a few stunted trees and bushes. Now it was a morass of churned mud round the wreck of the ill-wished tower. On three sides the walls of this had risen almost to shoulder height; on the fourth side the wall, newly split, sagged out in a chaos of piled stones, some fallen and half buried in mud, others still precariously mortared to outcrops of the living rock. Heavy poles of pine wood had been driven in here and there and canvas laid across to shelter the work from the rain. Some of the poles had fallen flat, some were obviously newly splintered by the recent crack. On those which were whole the canvas hung flapping, or had stretched and split with the wet. Everything was sodden, and pools stood everywhere.

The workmen had left the site and were crowded to one side of the plateau, near the causeway. They were silent, with fear in their faces. I could see that the fear was not of the King's anger at what had happened to the work, but of the force which they believed in and did not understand. There were guards at the entrance to the causeway. I knew that

without them not one workman would have been left on the
site.

The guards had crossed their spears, but when they recognized the King they drew them back. I looked up. "Vortigern, I cannot escape from you here unless I leap off the
crag, and that would sprinkle my blood just where Maugan
wants it. But neither can I see what is wrong with your
foundations unless you loose me."

He jerked his head, and one of my guards freed me. I
walked forward. The mule followed, stepping delicately
through the thick mud. The others came after. Maugan had
pressed forward and was speaking urgently to the King. I
caught words here and there: "Trickery . . . escape . . . now
or never . . . blood . . ."

The King halted, and the crowd with him. Someone said,
"Here, boy," and I looked round to see the greybeard holding
out a staff. I shook my head, then turned my back on them
and walked forward alone.

Water stood everywhere, glinting in soggy pools between
the tussocks, or on the curled fingers of young bracken
thrusting through the pallid grass of winter. The grey rock
glittered with it. As I walked slowly forward I had to narrow
my eyes against the wet dazzle to see at all.

It was the western wall that had fallen. This had been built
very near the edge of the crag, and though most of the
collapse had been inwards, there was a pile of fallen stuff
lying right out to the cliff's edge, where a new landslip
showed raw and slimy with clay. There was a space in the
north wall where an entrance was to be built; I picked my
way through this between the piles of rubble and workmen's
gear, and into the center of the tower.

Here the floor was a thick mess of churned mud, with
standing puddles struck to blinding copper by the sun. This
was setting now, in the last blaze of light before dusk, and
glared full in my eyes as I examined the collapsed wall, the
cracks, the angle of fall, the tell-tale lie of the outcrops.

All the time I was conscious of the stir and mutter of the
crowd. From time to time the sun flashed on bared weapons.
Maugan's voice, high and harsh, battered at the King's
silence. Soon, if I did nothing and said nothing, the crowd
would listen to him.

From where he sat his mule the King could see me
through the gap of the north entrance, but most of the crowd
could not. I climbed—or rather, mounted, such was my

dignity—the fallen blocks of the west wall, till I stood clear of the building that remained, and they could all see me. This was not only to impress the King. I had to see, from this vantage point, the wooded slopes below through which we had just climbed, trying, now that I was clear of the crowd and the jostling, to recognize the way I had taken up to the adit, all those years ago.

The voices of the crowd, growing impatient, broke in on me, and I slowly lifted both arms towards the sun in a kind of ritual gesture, such as I had seen priests use in summoning spirits. If I at least made some show as a magician it might keep them at bay, the priests in doubt and the King in hope, till I had had time to remember. I could not afford to cast falteringly through the wood like a questing dog; I had to lead them straight and fast, as the merlin had once led me.

And my luck held. As I raised my arms the sun went in and stayed in, and the dusk began to thicken.

Moreover, with the dazzle out of my eyes, I could see. I looked back along the side of the causeway to the curve of the hill where I had climbed, all those years ago, to get away from the crowd round the two kings. The slopes were thickly wooded, more thickly than I remembered. Already, in the shelter of the corrie, some early leaves were out, and the woods were dark with thorn and holly. I could not recognize the way I had gone through the winter woods. I stared into the thickening dusk, casting back in memory to the child who had gone scrambling there . . .

We had ridden in from the open valley, along that stream, under the thick trees, over that low ridge and into the corrie. The kings, with Camlach and Dinias and the rest, had sat on that southern slope, below the knot of oaks. The cooking fires had been there, the horses there. It had been noon, and as I walked away—that way—I had trodden on my shadow. I had sat down to eat in the shelter of a rock . . .

I had it now. A grey rock, cleft by a young oak. And on the other side of the rock the kings had gone by, walking up towards King's Fort. A grey rock, cleft by a young oak beside the path. And straight from it, up through the steep wood, the flight-path of the merlin.

I lowered my arms, and turned. Twilight had fallen quickly in the wake of the grey clouds. Below me the wooded slopes swam thick with dusk. Behind Vortigern the mass of cloud was edged sharply with yellow, and a single shaft of misty light fell steeply on the distant black hills. The men were in dark silhouette, their cloaks whipping in the wet breeze. The torches streamed.

Slowly I descended from my viewpoint. When I reached the center of the tower floor I paused, full in the King's view, and stretched my hands out, palms down, as if I were feeling like a diviner for what lay below the earth. I heard the mutter go round, and the harsh sound of contempt from Maugan. Then I dropped my hands and approached them.

"Well?" The King's voice was hard and dry with challenge. He fidgeted in the saddle.

I ignored him, walking on past the mule and heading straight for the thickest part of the crowd as if it was not there. I kept my hands still by my sides, and my eyes on the ground; I saw their feet hesitate, shuffle, move aside as the crowd parted to let me through. I walked back across the causeway, trying to move smoothly and with dignity over the broken and sodden ground. The guards made no attempt to stop me. When I passed one of the torch-bearers I lifted a hand, and he fell in beside me without a word.

The track that the workmen and their beasts had beaten out of the hillside was a new one, but, as I had hoped, it followed the old deer-trod which the kings had taken. Halfway down, unmistakable, I found the rock. Young ferns were springing in the crevice among the roots of the oak, and the tree showed buds already breaking among last year's oak-galls. Without a moment's hesitation I turned off the track, and headed into the steep tangle of the woods.

It was far more thickly overgrown than I remembered, and certainly nobody had been this way in a long time, probably not since Cerdic and I had pushed our way through. But I remembered the way as clearly as if it had still been noon of that winter's day. I went fast, and even where the bushes grew more than shoulder height I tried to go smoothly, unregarding, wading through them as if they were a sea. Next day I paid for my wizard's dignity with cuts and scratches and ruined clothes, but I have no doubt that at the time it was impressive. I remember when my cloak caught and dragged on something how the torch-bearer jumped forward like a slave to loosen and hold it for me.

Here was the thicket, right up against the side of the dell. More rock had fallen from the slope above, piling between the stems of the thorn trees like froth among the reeds of a backwater. Over it the bushes crowded, bare elderberry, honeysuckle like trails of hair, brambles sharp and whippy, ivy glinting in the torchlight. I stopped.

The mule slipped and clattered to a halt at my shoulder. The King's voice said: "What's this? What's this? Where are you taking us? I tell you, Merlin, your time is running out. If you have nothing to show us—"

"I have plenty to show you." I raised my voice so that all of them, pushing behind him, could hear me. "I will show you, King Vortigern, or any man who has courage enough to follow me, the magic beast that lies beneath your stronghold and eats at your foundations. Give me the torch."

The man handed it to me. Without even turning my head to see who followed, I plunged into the darkness of the thicket and pulled the bushes aside from the mouth of the adit.

It was still open, safely shored and square, with the dry shaft leading level into the heart of the hill.

I had to bend my head now to get in under the lintel. I stooped and entered, with the torch held out in front of me.

I had remembered the cave as being huge, and had been prepared to find that this, like other childhood memories, was false. But it was bigger even then I remembered. Its dark emptiness was doubled in the great mirror of water that had spread till it covered all the floor save for a dry crescent of rock six paces deep, just inside the mouth of the adit. Into this great, still lake the jutting ribs of the cave walls ran like buttresses to meet the angle of their own reflections, then on down again into darkness. Somewhere deeper in the hill was the sound of water falling, but here nothing stirred the burnished surface. Where, before, trickles had run and dripped like leaking faucets, now every wall was curtained with a thin shining veil of damp which slid down imperceptibly to swell the pool.

I advanced to the edge, holding the torch high. The small light of the flame pushed the darkness back, a palpable darkness, deeper even than those dark nights where the black is thick as a wild beast's pelt, and presses on you like a stifling blanket. A thousand facets of light glittered and flashed as the flames caught the sliding water. The air was still and cold and echoing with sounds like birdsong in a deep wood.

I could hear them scrambing along the adit after me. I thought quickly.

I could tell them the truth, coldly. I could take the torch and clamber up into the dark workings and point out faults which were giving way under the weight of the building work above. But I doubted if they would listen. Besides, as they kept saying, there was no time. The enemy was at the gates, and what Vortigern needed now was not logic and an engineer; he wanted magic, and something—anything—that promised quick safety, and kept his followers loyal. He himself might believe the voice of reason, but he could not afford to listen to it. My guess was that he would kill me first, and attempt to shore up the workings afterwards, probably with me in them. He would lose his workmen else.

The men came pouring in at the dark mouth of the adit like bees through a hive door. More torches blazed, and the dark slunk back. The floor filled with coloured cloaks and the glint of weapons and the flash of jewels. Eyes showed liquid as they looked around them in awe. Their breath steamed on the cold air. There was a rustle and mutter as of folk in a holy place, but no one spoke aloud.

I lifted a hand to beckon the King, and he came forward and stood with me at the edge of the pool. I pointed downwards. Below the surface something—a rock, perhaps— glimmered faintly, shaped like a dragon. I began to speak slowly, as it were testing the air between us. My words fell clear and leaden, like drops of water on rock.

"This is the magic, King Vortigern, that lies beneath your tower. This is why your walls cracked as fast as they could build. Which of your soothsayers could have showed you what I show you now?"

His two torch-bearers had moved forward with him; the others still hung back. Light grew, wavering from the walls, as they advanced. The streams of sliding water caught the light and flowed down to meet their reflections, so that fire seemed to rise through the pool like bubbles in sparkling wine to burst at the surface. Everywhere, as the torches moved, water glittered and sparked, jets and splashes of light breaking and leaping and coalescing across the still surface till the lake was liquid fire, and down the walls the lightfalls ran and glittered like crystals; like the crystal cave come alive and moving and turning round me; like the starred globe of midnight whirling and flashing.

I took my breath in painfully, and spoke again. "If you could drain this pool, King Vortigern, to find what lay beneath it—"

I stopped. The light had changed. Nobody had moved, and the air was still, but the torchlight wavered as men's hands shook. I could no longer see the King: the flames ran between us. Shadows fled across the streams and staircases of fire, and the cave was full of eyes and wings and hammering hoofs and the scarlet rush of a great dragon stooping on his prey . . .

A voice was shouting, high and monotonous, gasping. I could not get my breath. Pain broke through me, spreading from groin and belly like blood bursting from a wound. I could see nothing. I felt my hands knotting and stretching. My head hurt, and the rock was hard and streaming wet under my cheekbone. I had fainted, and they had seized me as I lay and were killing me: this was my blood seeping from me to spread into the pool and shore up the foundations of their rotten tower. I choked on breath like bile. My hands tore in pain at the rock, and my eyes were open, but all I could see was the whirl of banners and wings and wolves' eyes and sick mouths gaping, and the tail of a comet like a brand, and stars shooting through a rain of blood.

Pain went through me again, a hot knife into the bowels. I screamed, and suddenly my hands were free. I threw them up between me and the flashing visions and I heard my own voice calling, but could not tell what I called. In front of me the visions whirled, fractured, broke open in intolerable light, then shut again into darkness and silence.

11

I woke in a room splendidly lined with embroidered hangings, where sunlight spilled through the window to lay bright oblongs on a boarded floor.

I moved cautiously, testing my limbs. I had not been hurt. There was not even a trace of headache. I was naked, softly and warmly bedded in furs, and my limbs moved without a hint of stiffness. I blinked wonderingly at the window, then turned my head to see Cadal standing beside the bed, relief spreading over his face like light after cloud.

"And about time," he said.

"Cadal! Mithras, but it's good to see you! What's happened? Where is this?"

"Vortigern's best guest chamber, that's where it is. You fixed him, young Merlin, you fixed him proper."

"Did I? I don't remember. I got the impression that they were fixing me. Do you mean they're not still planning to kill me?"

"Kill you? Stick you in a sacred cave, more like, and sacrifice virgins to you. Pity it'd be such a waste. I could use a bit of that myself."

"I'll hand them over to you. Oh, Cadal, but it is good to see you! How did you get here?"

"I'd just got back to the nunnery gate when they came for your mother. I heard them asking for her, and saying they'd got you, and were taking the pair of you off to Vortigern at cocklight next day. I spent half the night finding Marric, and the other half trying to get a decent horse—and I might as well have saved myself the pains, I had to settle for that screw you bought. Even the pace you went, I was near a day behind you by the time you'd got to Pennal. Not that I wanted to catch up till I saw which way the land lay ... Well, never mind, I got here in the end—at dusk yesterday— and found the place buzzing like a hive that's been trodden on." He gave a short bark of a laugh. "It was 'Merlin this', and 'Merlin that' ... they call you 'the King's prophet' already! When I said I was your servant, they couldn't shove me in here fast enough. Seems there isn't exactly a rush to look after sorcerers of your class. Can you eat something?"

"No—yes. Yes, I can. I'm hungry." I pushed myself up against the pillows. "Wait a minute, you say you got here *yesterday?* How long have I slept?"

"The night and the day. It's wearing on for sunset."

"The night and the day? Then it's—Cadal, what's happened to my mother? Do you know?"

"She's gone, safe away home. Don't fret yourself about her. Get your food now, while I tell you. Here."

He brought a tray on which was a bowl of steaming broth, and a dish of meat with bread and cheese and dried apricots. I could not touch the meat, but ate the rest while he talked.

"She doesn't know a thing about what they tried to do, or what happened. When she asked about you last night they told her you were here, 'royally housed, and high in the King's favour.' They told her you'd spat in the priests' eyes, in a manner of speaking, and prophesied fit to beat Solomon, and were sleeping it off, comfortable. She came to take a look at you this morning to make sure, and saw you sleeping like a baby, then she went off. I didn't get a chance to speak to her, but I saw her go. She was royally escort .d, I can tell you; she'd half a troop of horse with her, and her women had litters nearly as grand as herself."

"You say I 'prophesied'? 'Spat in the priests' eyes'?" I put a hand to my head. "I wish I could remember . . . We were in the cave under King's Fort—they've told you about that, I suppose?" I stared at him. "What happened, Cadal?"

"You mean to tell me you don't remember?"

I shook my head. "All I know is, they were going to kill me to stop their rotten tower from falling down, and I put up a bluff. I thought if I could discredit their priests I might save my own skin, but all I ever hoped to do was to make a bit of time so that maybe I could get away."

"Aye, I heard what they were going to do. Some people are dead ignorant, you'd wonder at it." But he was watching me with the look that I remembered. "It was a funny kind of bluff, wasn't it? How did you know where to find the tunnel?"

"Oh, that. That was easy. I've been in these parts before, as a boy. I came to this very place once, years ago, with Cerdic who was my servant then, and I was following a falcon through the wood when I found that old tunnel."

"I see. Some people might call that luck—if they didn't know you, that is. I suppose you'd been right in?"

"Yes. When I first heard about the west wall cracking above, I thought it must be something to do with the old mine workings." I told him then, quickly, all that I could remember of what had happened in the cave. "The lights," I said, "the water glittering . . . the shouting . . . It wasn't like the 'seeings' I've had before—the white bull and the other things that I've sometimes seen. This was different. For one thing, it hurt far more. That must be what death is like. I suppose I did faint in the end. I don't remember being brought here at all."

"I don't know about that. When I got in to see you, you was just asleep, very deep, but quite ordinary, it seemed to me. I make no bones about it, I took a good look at you, to see if they'd hurt you, but I couldn't find any sign of it, bar a lot of scratches and grazes they said you'd got in the woods. Your clothes looked like it, too, I can tell you . . . But from the way you were housed here, and the way they spoke of you, I didn't think they'd dare raise a finger to you—not now. Whatever it was, a faint, or a fit or a trance, more like, you've put the wind up them proper, that you have."

"Yes, but how, exactly? Did they tell you?"

"Oh aye, they told me, the ones that could speak of it. Berric—he's the one that gave you the torch—he told me. He told me they'd all been set to cut your throat, those dirty old priests, and it seems if the King hadn't been at his wits' end, and impressed by your mother and the way the pair of you didn't seem frightened of them, he never would have waited. Oh, I heard all about it, don't worry. Berric said he'd not have given two pennies for your life back there in the hall when your mother told her story." He shot me a look. "All that rigmarole about the devil in the dark. Letting you in for this. What possessed her?"

"She thought it would help. I suppose she thought that the King had found out who my father was, and had had us dragged here to see if we had news of his plans. That's what I thought myself." I spoke thoughtfully. "And there was something else ... When a place is full of superstition and fear, you get to feel it. I tell you, it was breathing goose-pimples all over me. She must have felt it, too. You might almost say she took the same line as I did, trying to face magic with magic. So she told the old tale about my being got by an incubus, with a few extra flourishes to carry it across." I grinned at him. "She did it well. I could have believed it myself if I hadn't known otherwise. But never mind, go on. I want to know what happened in the cavern. Do you mean I talked some kind of sense?"

"Well now, I didn't mean that, exactly. Couldn't make head or tail of what Berric told me. He swore he had it nearly word for word—it seems he has ambitions to be a singer or something ... Well, what he said, you just stood there staring at the water running down the walls and then you started to talk, quite ordinary to start with, to the King, as if you was explaining how the shaft had been driven into the hill and the veins mined, but then the old priest—Maugan, isn't it?—started to shout 'This is fools' talk,' or something, when suddenly you lets out a yell that fair froze the balls on them—Berric's expression, not mine, he's not used to gentlemen's service—and your eyes turned up white and you put your hands up as if you was pulling the stars out of their sockets—Berric again, he ought to be a poet—and started to prophesy."

"Yes?"

"That's what they all say. All wrapped up, it was, with eagles and wolves and lions and boars and as many other beasts as they've ever had in the arena and a few more besides, dragons and such—and going hundreds of years forward, which is safe enough, Dia knows, but Berric said it sounded, the lot of it, as true as a trumpet, and as if you'd have given odds on it with your last penny."

"I may have to," I said dryly, "if I said anything about Vortigern or my father."

"Which you did," said Cadal.

"Well, I'd better know; I'm going to have to stick by it."

"It was all dressed up, like poets' stuff, red dragons and white dragons fighting and laying the place waste, showers of blood, all that kind of thing. But it seems you gave them chapter and verse for everything that's going to happen; the white dragon of the Saxons and the red dragon of Ambrosius fighting it out, the red dragon looking not so clever to begin with, but winning in the end. Yes. Then a bear coming out of Cornwall to sweep the field clear."

"A bear? You mean the Boar, surely; that's Cornwall's badge. Hm. Then he may be still for my father after all . . ."

"Berric said a bear. *Artos* was the word . . . he took notice, because he wondered about it himself. But you were clear about it, he says. Artos, you called him, Arthur . . . some name like that. You mean to tell me you don't remember a word of it?"

"Not a word."

"Well look, now, I can't remember any more, but if they start coming at you about it, you could find some way of getting them to tell you everything you said. It's quite the thing, isn't it, for prophets not to know what they were talking about? Oracles and that?"

"I believe so."

"All I mean is, if you've finished eating, and if you really feel all right, perhaps you'd better get up and dress. They're all waiting for you out there."

"What for? For the god's sake, they don't want more advice? Are they moving the site of the tower?"

"No. They're doing what you told them to do."

"What's that?"

"Draining the pool by a conduit. They've been working all night and day getting pumps rigged up to get the water out through the adit."

"But why? That won't make the tower any safer. In fact it

might bring the whole top of the crag in. Yes, I'm finished, take it away." I pushed the tray into his hands, and threw back the bed-covers. "Cadal, are you trying to tell me I said this in my—delirium?"

"Aye. You told them to drain the pool, and at the bottom they'd find the beasts that were bringing the King's fort down. Dragons, you said, red and white."

I sat on the edge of the bed, my head in my hands. "I remember something now ... something I saw. Yes, that must be it ... I did see something under the water, probably just a rock, dragon-shaped ... And I remember starting to say something to the King about draining the pool ... But I didn't tell them to drain it, I was saying 'Even if you drained the pool, it wouldn't help you.' At least, that's what I started to say." I dropped my hands and looked up. "You mean they're actually draining the place, thinking some water-beast is there underneath, rocking the foundations?"

"That's what you told them, Berric says."

"Berric's a poet, he's dressing it up."

"Maybe. But they're out there at it now, and the pumps have been working full blast for hours. The King's there, waiting for you."

I sat silent. He threw me a doubtful look, then took the tray out, and came back with towels and a silver basin of steaming water. While I washed he busied himself over a chest at the far side of the room, lifting clothes from it and shaking out the folds, while he talked over his shoulder. "You don't look worried. If they do drain that pool to the bottom, and there's nothing there—"

"There will be something there. Don't ask me what, I don't know, but if I said so ... It's true, you know. The things I see this way are true. I have the Sight."

His brows shot up. "You think you're telling me news? Haven't you scared the toe-nails off me a score of times with what you say and the things you see that no one else can see?"

"You used to be scared of me, didn't you, Cadal?"

"In a way. But I'm not scared now, and I've no intention of being scared. Someone's got to look after the devil himself, as long as he wears clothes and needs food and drink. Now if you're done, young master, we'll see if these things fit you that the King sent for you."

"The King sent them?"

"Aye. Looks like the sort of stuff they think a magician ought to wear."

I went over to look. *"Not* long white robes with stars and moons on them, and a staff with curled snakes? Oh, really, Cadal—"

"Well, your own stuff's ruined, you've got to wear something. Come on, you'll look kind of fancy in these, and it seems to me you ought to try and impress them, the spot you're in."

I laughed. "You may be right. Let me see them. Hm, no, not the white, I'm not competing with Maugan's coven. Something dark, I think, and the black cloak. Yes, that'll do. And I'll wear the dragon brooch."

"I hope you do right to be so sure of yourself." Then he hesitated. "Look, I know it's all wine and worship now, but maybe we ought to make a break for it straight away, not wait to see which way the dice fall? I could steal a couple of horses—"

" 'Make a break for it'? Am I still a prisoner, then?"

"There's guards all round. Looking after you this time, not holding on to you, but by the dog, it comes to the same thing." He glanced at the window. "It'll be dusk before long. Look, I could spin some tale out there to keep them quiet, and maybe you could pretend to go to sleep again till dark—"

"No. I must stay. If I can get Vortigern to listen to me ... Let me think, Cadal. You saw Marric the night we were taken. That means the news is on its way to my father, and if I'm any judge, he will move straight away. So far, lucky; the sooner the better; if he can catch Vortigern here in the West before he gets a chance to join again with Hengist ..." I thought for a moment. "Now, the ship was due to sail three—no, four days ago—"

"It sailed before you left Maridunum," he said briefly.

"What?"

He smiled at my expression. "Well, what did you expect? The Count's own son and his lady hauled off like that— nobody knew for sure why, but there were stories going about, and even Marric saw the sense in getting straight back to Ambrosius with *that* tale. The ship sailed with the tide the same dawn; she'd be out of the estuary before you'd hardly ridden out of town."

I stood very still. I remember that he busied himself around me, draping the black cloak, surreptitiously pulling a fold to cover the dragon brooch that pinned it.

Then I drew a long breath. "That's all I needed to know. Now I know what to do. 'The King's prophet,' did you say? They speak truer than they know. What the King's prophet must do now is to take the heart out of these Saxon-loving vermin, and drive Vortigern out of this tight corner of Wales into some place where Ambrosius can smoke him out quickly and destroy him."

"You think you can do this?"

"I know I can."

"Then I hope you know how to get us both out of here before they find out whose side you're on!"

"Why not? As soon as I know where Vortigern is bound for, we'll take the news to my father ourselves." I settled the cloak to my shoulders, and grinned at him. "So steal those horses, Cadal, and have them waiting down by the stream. There's a tree fallen clear across the water; you can't miss the place; wait there where there's cover. I'll come. But first I must go and help Vortigern uncover the dragons."

I made for the door, but he got there ahead of me, and paused with his hand on the latch. His eyes were scared. "You really mean leave you on your own in the middle of that wolfpack?"

"I'm not on my own. Remember that; and if you can't trust me, trust what is in me. I have learned to. I've learned that the god comes when he will, and how he will, rending your flesh to get into you, and when he has done, tearing himself free as violently as he came. Afterwards—now—one feels light and hollow and like an angel flying . . . No, they can do nothing to me, Cadal. Don't be afraid. I have the power."

"They killed Galapas."

"Some day they may kill me," I said. "But not today. Open the door."

12

They were all gathered at the foot of the crag where the workmen's track met the marshy level of the corrie. I was still guarded, but this time—at least in appearance—it was a guard of honour. Four uniformed men, with their swords safely sheathed, escorted me to the King.

They had laid duckboards down on the marshy ground to make a platform, and set a chair for the King. Someone had rigged a windbreak of woven saplings and brushwood on three sides, roofed it, and draped the lot with worked rugs and dyed skins. Vortigern sat there, chin on fist, silent. There was no sign of his Queen, or indeed of any of the women. The priests stood near him, but they kept back and did not speak. His captains flanked his chair.

The sun was setting behind the improvised pavilion in a splash of scarlet. It must have rained again that day; the grass was sodden, every blade heavy with drops. The familiar slate-grey clouds furled and unfurled slowly across the sunset. As I was led forward, they were lighting the torches. These looked small and dull against the sunset, more smoke than flame, dragged and flattened by the gusty breeze.

I waited at the foot of the platform. The King's eyes looked me up and down, but he said nothing. He was still reserving judgement. And why not, I thought. The kind of thing I seemed to have produced must be fairly familiar to him. Now he waited for proof of at least some part of my prophecy. If it was not forthcoming, this was still the time and the place to spill my blood. I wondered how the wind blew from Less Britain. The stream was a full three hundred paces off, dark under its oaks and willows.

Vortigern signed to me to take my place on the platform beside him, and I mounted it to stand at his right, on the opposite side from the priests. One or two of the officers moved aside from me; their faces were wooden, and they did not look at me, but I saw the crossed fingers, and thought: Dragon or no dragon, I can manage these. Then I felt eyes on me, and looked round. It was the greybeard. He was gazing fixedly at the brooch on my shoulder where my cloak had blown back from it. As I turned, his eyes lifted to mine. I saw his widen, then his hand crept to his side, not to make the sign, but to loosen his sword in its scabbard. I looked away. No one spoke.

It was an uncomfortable vigil. As the sun sank lower the chilly spring wind freshened, fretting at the hangings. Where puddles lay in the reedy ground the water rippled and splashed under the wind. Cold draughts knifed up between the duckboards. I could hear a curlew whistling somewhere up in the darkening sky, then it slanted down, bubbling like a waterfall, into silence. Above us the King's banner fluttered and snapped in the wind. The shadow of the pavilion lengthened on the soaked field.

From where we waited, the only sign of activity was some

coming and going in the trees. The last rays of the sun, level and red, shone full on the west face of King's Fort, lighting up the head of the crag crowned with the wrecked wall. No workmen were visible there; they must all be in the cave and the adit. Relays of boys ran across and back with reports of progress. The pumps were working well and gaining on the water; the level had sunk two spans in the last half hour ... If my lord King would have patience, the pumps had jammed, but the engineers were working on them and meanwhile the men had rigged a windlass and were passing buckets ... All was well again, the pumps were going now and the level was dropping sharply ... You could see the bottom, they thought ...

It was two full hours of chill, numb waiting, and it was almost dark, before lights came down the track and with them the crowd of workmen. They came fast but deliberately, not like frightened men, and even before they came close enough to be clearly seen, I knew what they had found. Their leaders halted a yard from the platform, and as the others came crowding up I felt my guards move closer.

There were soldiers with the workmen. Their captain stepped forward, saluting.

"The pool is empty?" asked Vortigern.

"Yes, sir."

"And what lies beneath it?"

The officer paused. He should have been a bard. He need not have paused to gather eyes: they were all on him already.

A gust of wind, sudden and stronger than before, tore his cloak to one side with a crack like a whip, and rocked the frame of the pavilion. A bird fled overhead, tumbling along the wind. Not a merlin: not tonight. Only a rook, scudding late home.

"There is nothing beneath the pool, sir." His voice was neutral, carefully official, but I heard a mutter go through the crowd like another surge of wind. Maugan was craning forward, his eyes bright as a vulture's, but I could see he did not dare to speak until he saw which way the King's mind was bending. Vortigern leaned forward.

"You are certain of this? You drained it to the bottom?"

"Indeed, sir." He signed to the men beside him, and three or four of them stepped forward to tip a clutter of objects in front of the platform. A broken mattock, eaten with rust, some flint axe-heads older than any Roman working, a belt buckle, a knife with its blade eaten to nothing, a short length of chain, a metal whip-stock, some other objects impossible to identify, and a few shards of cooking pots.

The officer showed a hand, palm up. "When I said 'nothing,' sir, I meant only what you might expect. These. And we got as near to the bottom as made no difference; you could see down to the rock and the mud, but we dredged the last bucket up, for good measure. The foreman will bear me out."

The foreman stepped forward then, and I saw he had a full bucket in his hand, the water slopping over the brim.

"Sir, it's true, there's naught there. You could see for yourself if you came up, sir, right to the bottom. But better not try it, the tunnel's awash with mud now, and not fit. But I brought the last pailful out, for you to see yourself."

With the word, he tipped the full bucket out, deluging the already sodden ground, and the water sloshed down to fill the puddle round the base of the royal standard. With the mud that had lain in the bottom came a few broken fragments of stone, and a silver coin.

The King turned then to look at me. It must be a measure of what had happened in the cavern yesterday that the priests still kept silent, and the King was clearly waiting, not for an excuse, but an explanation.

God knows I had had plenty of time to think, all through that long, cold silent vigil, but I knew that thinking would not help me. If he was with me, he would come now. I looked down at the puddles where the last red light of sunset lay like blood. I looked up across the crag where stars could be seen already stabbing bright in the clear east. Another gust of wind was coming; I could hear it tearing the tops of the oaks where Cadal would be waiting.

"Well?" said Vortigern.

I took a step forward to the edge of the platform. I felt empty still, but somehow I would have to speak. As I moved, the gust struck the pavilion, sharp as a blow. There came a crack, a flurry of sound like hounds worrying a deer, and a cry from someone, bitten short. Above our heads the King's banner whipped streaming out, then, caught in its ropes, bellied like a sail holding the full weight of the wind. The shaft, jerked sharply to and fro in soft ground loosened further by the thrown bucketful of water, tore suddenly free of the grabbing hands, to whirl over and down. It slapped flat on the sodden field at the King's feet.

The wind fled past, and in its wake was a lull. The banner

lay flat, held heavy with water. The white dragon on a green field. As we watched, it sagged slowly into a pool, and the water washed over it. Some last faint ray from the sunset bloodied the water. Someone said fearfully, "An omen," and another voice, loudly, "Great Thor, the Dragon is down!" Others began to shout. The standard-bearer, his face ashen, was already stooping, but I jumped off the platform in front of them all and threw up my arms.

"Can any doubt the god has spoken? Look up from the ground, and see where he speaks again!"

Across the dark east, burning white hot with a trail like a young comet, went a shooting star, the star men call the firedrake or dragon of fire.

"There it runs!" I shouted. "There it runs! The Red Dragon of the West! I tell you, King Vortigern, waste no more time here with these ignorant fools who babble of blood sacrifice and build a wall of stone for you, a foot a day! What wall will keep out the Dragon? I, Merlin, tell you, send these priests away and gather your captains round you, and get you away from the hills of Wales to your own country. King's Fort is not for you. You have seen the Red Dragon come tonight, and the White Dragon lie beneath him. And by God, you have seen the truth! Take warning! Strike your tents now, and go to your own country, and watch your borders lest the Dragon follow you and burn you out! You brought me here to speak, and I have spoken. I tell you, the Dragon is here!"

The King was on his feet, and men were shouting. I pulled the black cloak round me, and without hurrying turned away through the crowd of workmen and soldiers that milled round the foot of the platform. They did not try to stop me. They would as soon, I suppose, have touched a poisonous snake. Behind me, through the hubbub, I heard Maugan's voice and thought for a moment they were coming after me, but then men crowded off the platform, and began thrusting their way through the mob of workmen, on their way back to the encampment. Torches tossed. Someone dragged the sodden standard up and I saw it rocking and dripping where presumably his captains were clearing a path for the King. I drew the black cloak closer and slipped into the shadows at the edge of the crowd. Presently, unseen, I was able to step round behind the pavilion.

The oaks were three hundred paces away across the dark field. Under them the stream ran loud over smooth stones.

Cadal's voice said, low and urgent: "This way." A hoof sparked on stone. "I got you a quiet one," he said, and put a hand under my foot to throw me into the saddle.

I laughed a little. "I could ride the firedrake itself tonight. You saw it?"

"Aye, my lord. And I saw you, and heard you, too."

"Cadal, you swore you'd never be afraid of me. It was only a shooting star."

"But it came when it came."

"Yes. And now we'd better go while we can go. Timing is all that matters, Cadal."

"You shouldn't laugh at it, master Merlin."

"By the god," I said, "I'm not laughing."

The horses pushed out from under the dripping trees and went at a swift canter across the ridge. To our right a wooded hill blocked out the west. Ahead was the narrow neck of valley between hill and river.

"Will they come after you?"

"I doubt it."

But as we kicked the beasts to a gallop between ridge and river a horseman loomed, and our horses swerved and shied.

Cadal's beast jumped forward under the spur. Iron rasped. A voice, vaguely familiar, said clearly: "Put up. Friend."

The horses stamped and blew. I saw Cadal's hand on the other's rein. He sat quietly.

"Whose friend?"

"Ambrosius'."

I said: "Wait, Cadal, it's the greybeard. Your name, sir? And your business with me?"

He cleared his throat harshly. "Gorlois is my name, of Cornwall."

I saw Cadal's movement of surprise, and heard the bits jingle. He still had hold of the other's rein, and the drawn dagger gleamed. The old warrior sat unmoving. There was no sound of following hoofs.

"I said slowly: "Then, sir, I should rather ask you what your business is with Vortigern?"

"The same as yours, Merlin Ambrosius." I saw his teeth gleam in his beard. "I came north to see for myself, and to send word back to him. The West has waited long enough, and the time will be ripe, come spring. But you came early. I could have saved myself the pains, it seems."

"You came alone?"

He gave a short, hard laugh, like a dog barking. "To

Vortigern? Hardly. My men will follow. But I had to catch you. I want news." Then, harshly: "God's grief, man, do you doubt me? I came alone to you."

"No, sir. Let him go, Cadal. My lord, if you want to talk to me, you'll have to do it on the move. We should go, and quickly."

"Willingly." We set the horses in motion. As they struck into a gallop I said over my shoulder: "You guessed when you saw the brooch?"

"Before that. You have a look of him, Merlin Ambrosius." I heard him laugh again, deep in his throat. "And by God, there are times when you have a look of your devil-sire as well! Steady now, we're nearly at the ford. It'll be deep. They say wizards can't cross water?"

I laughed. "I'm always sick at sea, but I can manage this." The horses plunged across the ford unhindered, and took the next slope at a gallop. Then we were on the paved road, plain to see in the flying starlight, which leads straight across the high ground to the south.

We rode all night, with no pursuit. Three days later, in the early morning, Ambrosius came to land.

BOOK IV

THE RED
DRAGON

1

The way the chronicles tell it, you would think it took Ambrosius two months to get himself crowned King and pacify Britain. In fact, it took more than two years.

The first part was quick enough. It was not for nothing that he had spent all those years in Less Britain, he and Uther, developing an expert striking force the like of which had not been seen in any part of Europe since the disbanding nearly a hundred years ago of the force commanded by the Count of the Saxon Shore. Ambrosius had, in fact, modelled his own army on the force of the Saxon Shore, a marvellously mobile fighting instrument which could live off the country and do everything at twice the speed of the normal force. Caesar-speed, they still called it when I was young.

He landed at Totnes in Devon, with a fair wind and a quiet sea, and he had hardly set up the Red Dragon when the whole West rose for him. He was King of Cornwall and Devon before he even left the shore, and everywhere, as he moved northwards, the chiefs and kings crowded to swell his army. Eldol of Gloucester, a ferocious old man who had fought with Constantine against Vortigern, with Vortigern against Hengist, with Vortimer against both, and would fight anywhere for the sheer hell of it, met him at Glastonbury and swore faith. With him came a host of lesser leaders, not least his own brother Eldad, a bishop whose devout Christianity made the pagan wolves look like lambs by comparison, and set me wondering where he spent the dark nights of the winter solstice. But he was powerful; I had heard my mother speak of him with reverence; and once he had declared for Ambrosius, all Christian Britain came with him, urgent to drive back the pagan hordes moving steadily inland from their landing-places in the south and east. Last came Gorlois of Tintagel in Cornwall, straight from Vortigern's side with news of Vortigern's hasty move out of the Welsh mountains, and ready to ratify the oath of loyalty which, should Ambrosius be successful, would add the whole kingdom of Cornwall for the first time to the High Kingdom of Britain.

Ambrosius' main trouble, indeed, was not lack of support but the nature of it. The native Britons, tired of Vortigern, were fighting-mad to clear the Saxons out of their country and get their homes and their own ways back, but a great majority of them knew only guerrilla warfare, or the kind of hit-and-ride-away tactics that do well enough to harass the enemy, but will not hold him back for long if he means business. Moreover, each troop came with its own leader, and it was as much as any commander's authority was worth to suggest that they might regroup and train under strangers. Since the last trained legion had withdrawn from Britain almost a century before, we had fought (as we had done before the Romans ever came) in tribes. And it was no use suggesting that, for instance, the men of Devet might fight beside the men of North Wales even with their own leaders; throats would have been cut on both sides before the first trumpet ever sounded.

Ambrosius here, as everywhere, showed himself master. As ever he used each man for what that man's strength was worth. He sowed his own officers broadcast among the British—for co-ordination, he said, no more—and through them quietly adapted the tactics of each force to suit his central plan, with his own body of picked troops taking the main brunt of attack.

All this I heard later, or could have guessed from what I knew of him. I could have guessed, also, what would happen the moment his forces assembled and declared him King. His British allies clamoured for him to go straight after Hengist and drive the Saxons back to their own country. They were not unduly concerned with Vortigern. Indeed, such power as Vortigern had had was largely gone already, and it would have been simple enough for Ambrosius to ignore him and concentrate on the Saxons.

But he refused to give way to pressure. The old wolf must be smoked out first, he said, and the field cleared for the main work of battle. Besides, he pointed out, Hengist and his Saxons were Northmen, and particularly amenable to rumours and fear; let Ambrosius once unite the British to destroy Vortigern, and the Saxons would begin to fear him as a force really to be reckoned with. It was his guess that, given the time, they would bring together one large force to face him, which might then be broken at one blow.

They had a council about it, at the fort near Gloucester where the first bridge crosses the Sefern river. I could picture it, Ambrosius listening and weighing and judging, and answering with that grave easy way of his, allowing each man his say for pride; then taking at the end the decision he had meant to take from the beginning, but giving way here and there on the small things, so that each man thought he had made a bargain and got, if not what he wanted, then something near it, in return for a concession by his commander.

The upshot was that they marched northwards within the week, and came on Vortigern at Doward.

Doward is in the valley of the Guoy, which the Saxons pronounce Way or Wye. This is a big river, which runs deep and placid-seeming through a gorge whose high slopes are hung with forests. Here and there the valley widens to green pastures, but the tide runs many miles up river, and these low meadows are often, in winter, awash under a roaring yellow flood, for the great Wye is not so placid as it seems, and even in summer there are deep pools where big fish lie and the currents are strong enough to overturn a coracle and drown a man.

Well north of the limit of the tidal floods, in a wide curve of the valley, stand the two hills called Doward. The one to the north is the greater, thick with forest and mined with caves inhabited, men say, by wild beasts and outlawed men. The hill called Lesser Doward is also forested, but more thinly, since it is rocky, and its steep summit, rising above the trees, makes a natural citadel so secure that it has been fortified time out of mind. Long before even the Romans came, some British king built himself a fortress on the summit which, with its commanding view, and the natural defenses of crag and river, made a formidable stronghold. The hill is wide-topped, and its sides steep and rough, and though siege engines could at one point be dragged up in dead ground, this ended in crags where the engines were useless. Everywhere except at this point there was a double rampart and ditch to get through before the outer wall of the fortress could be reached. The Romans themselves had marched against it once, and only managed to reduce it through treachery. This was in the time of Caratacus. Doward was the kind of place that, like Troy, must be taken from within.

This time also, it was taken from within. But not by treachery; by fire.

Everyone knows what happened there.

Vortigern's men were hardly settled after their headlong flight from Snowdon, when Ambrosius' army came up the valley of the Wye, and encamped due west of Doward Hill, at a place called Ganarew. I never heard what store of provisions Vortigern had; but the place had been kept prepared, and it was well known that there were two good springs within the fortress which had not yet been known to fail; so it might well have taken Ambrosius some time to reduce it by siege. But a siege was just what he could not afford, with Hengist gathering his forces, and the April seas opening between Britain and the Saxon shores. Besides, his British allies were restless, and would never have settled down for a prolonged siege. It had to be quick.

It was both quick and brutal. I have heard it said since that Ambrosius acted out of vengeance for his long-dead brother. I do not believe this to be true. Such long-standing bitterness was not in his nature, and besides, he was a general and a good fighting commander before he was even a man. He was driven only by necessity, and in the end, by Vortigern's own brutality.

Ambrosius besieged the place in the conventional way for about three days. Where he could, he drew up siege engines and tried to break the defenses. He did indeed breach the outer rampart in two places above what was still called Romans' Way, but when he found himself stopped by the inner rampart and his troops exposed to the defenders, he withdrew. When he saw how long the siege would take, and how, even in the three days, some of his British troops quietly left him and went off on their own, like hounds after the rumour of Saxon hares, he decided to make an end quickly. He sent a man to Vortigern with conditions for surrender. Vortigern, who must have seen the defection of some of the British troops, and who well understood Ambrosius' position, laughed, and sent back the messenger without a message, but with the man's own two hands severed, and bound in a bloody cloth to the belt at his waist.

He stumbled into Ambrosius' tent just after sundown of the third day, and managed to stay on his feet long enough to give the only message he was charged with.

"They say that you may stay here, my lord, until your

army melts away, and you are left handless as I. They have food in plenty, sir, I saw it, and water—"

Ambrosius only said: "He ordered this himself?"

"The Queen," said the man. "It was the Queen." He pitched forward on the word at Ambrosius' feet, and from the dripping cloth at his belt the hands fell, sprawling.

"Then we will burn out the wasps' nest, queen and all," said Ambrosius. "See to him."

That night, to the apparent pleasure of the garrison, the siege engines were withdrawn from Romans' Way and the breached places in the outer rampart. Instead, great piles of brushwood and hewn branches were stacked in the gaps, and the army tightened its ring round the crest of the hill, with a circle of archers waiting, and men ready to cut down any who should escape. In the quiet hour before daylight the order was given. From every quarter the arrows, pointed with flaming, oil-soaked rags, showered into the fortress. It did not take long. The place was largely built of wood, and crowded with the wagons, provisions, beasts and their fodder. It burned fiercely. And when it was alight the brushwood outside the walls was fired, so that anyone leaping from the walls met another wall of fire outside. And outside that, the iron ring of the army.

They say that throughout, Ambrosius sat his big white horse, watching, till the flames made the horse as red as the Red Dragon above his head. And high on the fortress tower the White Dragon, showing against a plume of smoke, turned blood red as the flames themselves, then blackened and fell.

2

While Ambrosius was attacking Doward I was still at Maridunum, having parted from Gorlois on the ride south, and seen him on his way to meet my father.

It happened this way. All through that first night we rode hard, but there was no sign of pursuit, so at sunup we drew off the road and rested, waiting for Gorlois' men to come up with us. This they did during the morning, having been able, in the near-panic at Dinas Brenin, to slip away unobserved. They confirmed what Gorlois had already suggested to me, that Vortigern would head, not for his own fortress of Caer-Guent, but for Doward. And he was moving, they said, by the east-bound road through Caer Gai towards Bravonium. Once past Tomen-y-mur, there was no danger that we would be overtaken.

So we rode on, a troop now about twenty strong, but going easily. My mother, with her escort of fighting men, was less than a day ahead of us, and her party, with the litters, would be much slower than we were. We had no wish to catch up with them and perhaps force a fight which might endanger the women; it was certain, said Gorlois to me, that the latter would be delivered safely to Maridunum, "but," he added in his sharp, gruff way, "we shall meet the escort on their way back. For come back they will; they cannot know the King is moving east. And every man less for Vortigern is another for your father. We'll get news at Bremia, and camp beyond it to wait for them."

Bremia was nothing but a cluster of stone huts smelling of peat smoke and dung, black doorways curtained from wind and rain with hides or sacking, round which peered scared eyes of women and children. No men appeared, even when we drew rein in the midst of the place, and curs ran yapping round the horses' heels. This puzzled us, till (knowing the dialect) I called out to the eyes behind the nearest curtain, to reassure the people and ask for news.

They came out then, women, children, and one or two old men, crowding eagerly round us and ready to talk.

The first piece of news was that my mother's party had been there the previous day and night, leaving only that morning, at the Princess's insistence. She had been taken ill, they told me, and had stayed for half the day and the night in the head-man's house, where she was cared for. Her women had tried to persuade her to turn aside for a monastic settlement in the hills nearby, where she might rest, but she had refused, and had seemed better in the morning, so the party had ridden on. It had been a chill, said the head-man's wife; the lady had been feverish, and coughing a little, but she had seemed so much better next morning, and Maridunum was not more than a day's ride; they had thought it better to let her do as she desired . . .

I eyed the squalid huts, thinking that, indeed, the danger of a few more hours in the litter might well be less than such miserable shelter in Bremia, so thanked the woman for her kindness, and asked where her man had gone. As to that, she told me, all the men had gone to join Ambrosius . . .

She mistook my look of surprise. "Did you not know?

There was a prophet at Dinas Brenin, who said the Red Dragon would come. The Princess told me herself, and you could see the soldiers were afraid. And now he has landed. He is here."

"How can you know?" I asked her. "We met no messenger."

She looked at me as if I were crazed, or stupid. Had I not seen the firedrake? The whole village knew this for the portent, after the prophet had spoken so. The men had armed themselves, and had gone that very day. If the soldiers came back, the women and children would take to the hills, but everyone knew that Ambrosius could move more swiftly than the wind, and they were not afraid . . .

I let her run on while I translated for Gorlois. Our eyes met with the same thought. We thanked the woman again, gave her what was due for her care of my mother, and rode after the men of Bremia.

South of the village the road divides, the main way turning south-east past the gold mine and then through the hills and deep valleys to the broad valley of the Wye whence it is easy riding to the Sefern crossing and the south-west. The other, minor road goes straight south, a day's ride to Maridunum. I had decided that in any case I would follow my mother south and talk to her before I rejoined Ambrosius; now the news of her illness made this imperative. Gorlois would ride straight to meet Ambrosius and give him the news of Vortigern's movements.

At the fork where our ways parted we came on the villagers. They had heard us coming and taken cover—the place was all rocks and bushes—but not soon enough; the gusty wind must have hidden our approach from them till we were almost on them. The men were out of sight, but one of their miserable pack-donkeys was not, and stones were still rolling on the scree.

It was Bremia over again. We halted, and I called out into the windy silence. This time I told them who I was, and in a moment, it seemed, the roadside was bristling with men. They came crowding round our horses, showing their teeth and brandishing a peculiar assortment of weapons ranging from a bent Roman sword to a stone spearhead bound on a hay-rake. They told the same story as their women; they had heard the prophecy, and they had seen the portent; they were marching south to join Ambrosius, and every man in the West would soon be with them. Their spirit was high, and their condition pitiful; it was lucky we had a chance to help them.

"Speak to them," said Gorlois to me. "Tell them that if they wait another day here with us, they shall have weapons and horses. They have picked the right place for an ambush, as who should know better than they?"

So I told them that this was the Duke of Cornwall, and a great leader, and that if they would wait a day with us, we would see they got weapons and horses. "For Vortigern's men will come back this way," I told them. "They are not to know that the High King is already fleeing eastwards: they will come back by this road, so we will wait for them here, and you will be wise to wait with us."

So we waited. The escort must have stayed rather longer than need be in Maridunum, and after that cold damp ride who could blame them? But towards dusk of the second day they came back, riding at ease, thinking maybe of a night's shelter at Bremia.

We took them nicely by surprise, and fought a bloody and very unpleasant little action. One roadside skirmish is very like another. This one differed only from the usual in being better generalled and more eccentrically equipped, but we had the advantages both of numbers and of surprise, and did what we had set out to do, robbed Vortigern of twenty men for the loss of only three of our own and a few cuts. I came out of it more creditably than I would have believed possible, killing the man I had picked out before the fighting swept over and past me and another knocked me off my horse and would possibly have killed me if Cadal had not parried the stroke and killed the fellow himself. It was quickly over. We buried our own dead and left the rest for the kites, after we had stripped them of their arms. We had taken care not to harm the horses, and when next morning Gorlois said farewell and led his new troops south-east, every man had a horse, and a good weapon of some kind. Cadal and I turned south for Maridunum, and reached it by early evening.

The first person I saw as we rode down the street towards St. Peter's was my cousin Dinias. We came on him suddenly at a corner, and he jumped a foot and went white. I suppose rumours had been running like wildfire through the town ever since the escort had brought my mother back without me.

"Merlin. I thought—I thought—"

"Well met, cousin, I was coming to look for you."

He said quickly: "Look, I swear I had no idea who those men were—"

"I know that. What happened wasn't your fault. That isn't why I was looking for you."

"—and I was drunk, you know that. But even if I had guessed who they were, how was I to know they'd take you up on a thing like that? I'd heard rumours of what they were looking for, I admit, but I swear it never entered my head—"

"I said it wasn't your fault. And I'm back here again safely, aren't I? All's well that ends well. Leave it, Dinias. That wasn't what I wanted to talk to you about."

But he persisted. "I took the money, didn't I? You saw."

"And if you did? You didn't give information for money, you took it afterwards. It's different, to my mind. If Vortigern likes to throw his money away, then by all means rob him of it. Forget it, I tell you. Have you news of my mother?"

"I've just come from there. She's ill, did you know?"

"I got news on my way south," I said. "What's the matter with her? How bad?"

"A chill, they told me, but they say she's on the mend. I thought myself she still looked poor enough, but she was fatigued with the journey, and anxious about you. What did Vortigern want you for, in the end?"

"To kill me," I said briefly.

He stared, then began to stutter. "I—in God's name, Merlin, I know you and I have never been ... that is, there've been times—" He stopped, and I heard him swallow. "I don't sell my kinsmen, you know."

"I told you I believed you. Forget it. It was nothing to do with you, some nonsense of his soothsayers'. But as I said, here I am safe and sound."

"Your mother said nothing about it."

"She didn't know. Do you think she'd have let him send her tamely home if she had known what he meant to do? The men who brought her home, they knew, you can be sure of that. So they didn't let it out to her?"

"It seems not," said Dinias. "But—"

"I'm glad of that. I'm hoping to get to see her soon, this time in daylight."

"Then you're in no danger now from Vortigern?"

"I would be, I suppose," I said, "if the place was still full of his men, but I was told at the gate that they've cleared out to join him?"

"That's so. Some rode north, and some east to Caer-Guent. You've heard the news, then?"

"What news?"

Though there was nobody else in the street, he looked over his shoulder in the old, furtive way. I slid down out of the saddle, and threw the reins to Cadal. "What news?" I repeated.

"Ambrosius," he said softly. "He's landed in the southwest, they say, and marching north. A ship brought the story yesterday, and Vortigern's men started moving out straight away. But—if you've just ridden in from the north, surely you'd meet them?"

"Two companies, this morning. But we saw them in good time, and got off the road. We met my mother's escort the day before, at the crossways."

" 'Met'?" He looked startled. "But if they knew Vortigern wanted you dead—"

"They'd have known I had no business riding south, and cut me down? Exactly. So we cut them down instead. Oh, don't look at me like that—it wasn't magician's work, only soldiers'. We fell in with some Welsh who were on their way to join Ambrosius, and we ambushed Vortigern's troop and cut them up."

"The Welsh knew already? The prophecy, was it?" I saw the whites of his eyes in the dusk. "I'd heard about that . . . the place is buzzing with it. The troops told us. They said you'd showed them some kind of great lake under the crag—it was that place we stopped at years ago, and I'll swear there was no sign of any lake then—but there was this lake of water with dragons lying in it under the foundations of the tower. Is it true?"

"That I showed them a lake, yes."

"But the dragons. What were they?"

I said, slowly: "Dragons. Something conjured out of nothing for them to see, since without seeing they would not listen, let alone believe."

There was a little silence. Then he said, with fear in his voice: "And was it magic that showed you Ambrosius was coming?"

"Yes and no." I smiled. "I knew he was coming, but not when. It was the magic that told me he was actually on his way."

He was staring again. "You knew he was coming? Then you did have tidings in Cornwall? You might have told me."

"Why?"

"I'd have joined him."

I looked at him for a moment, measuring. "You can still join him. You and your other friends who fought with Vortimer. What about Vortimer's brother, Pascentius? Do you know where he is? Is he still hot against Vortigern?"

"Yes, but they say he's gone to make his peace with Hengist. He'll never join Ambrosius, he wants Britain for himself."

"And you?" I asked. "What do you want?"

He answered quite simply, for once without any bluster or bravado. "Only a place I can call my own. This, if I can. It's mine now, after all. He killed the children, did you know?"

"I didn't, but you hardly surprise me. It's a habit of his, after all." I paused. "Look, Dinias, there's a lot to say, and I've a lot to tell you. But first I've a favour to ask of you."

"What's that?"

"Hospitality. There's nowhere else I know of that I care to go until I've got my own place ready, and I've a fancy to stay in my grandfather's house again."

He said, without pretense or evasion: "It's not what it was."

I laughed. "Is anything? As long as there's a roof against this hellish rain, and a fire to dry our clothes, and something to eat, no matter what. What do you say we send Cadal for provisions, and eat at home? I'll tell you the whole thing over a pie and a flask of wine. But I warn you, if you so much as show me a pair of dice I'll yell for Vortigern's men myself."

He grinned, relaxing suddenly. "No fear of that. Come along, then. There's a couple of rooms still habitable, and we'll find you a bed."

I was given Camlach's room. It was draughty, and full of dust, and Cadal refused to let me use the bedding until it had lain in front of a roaring fire for a full hour. Dinias had no servant, except one slut of a girl who looked after him apparently in return for the privilege of sharing his bed. Cadal set her to carrying fuel and heating water while he took a message to the nunnery for my mother, and then went to the tavern for wine and provisions.

We ate before the fire, with Cadal serving us. We talked late but here it is sufficient to record that I told Dinias my story—or such parts of it as he would understand. There might have been some personal satisfaction in telling him the facts of my parentage, but until I was sure of him, and the countryside was known to be clear of Vortigern's men, I thought it better to say nothing. So I told him merely how I had gone to Brittany, and that I had become Ambrosius' man. Dinias had heard enough already of my "prophecy" in the cavern at King's Fort to believe implicitly in Ambrosius' coming victory, so our talk ended with his promise to ride westwards in the morning with the news, and summon what support he could for Ambrosius from the fringes of Wales. He would, I knew, have been afraid in any case to do other than keep that promise; whatever the soldiers had said about the occasion there in King's Fort, it was enough to strike my simple cousin Dinias with the most profound awe of my powers. But even without that, I knew I could trust him in this. We talked till almost dawn, then I gave him money and said good night.

(He was gone before I woke next morning. He kept his word, and joined Ambrosius later, at York, with a few hundred men. He was honourably received and acquitted himself well, but soon afterwards, in some minor engagement, received wounds of which he later died. As for me, I never saw him again.)

Cadal shut the door behind him. "At least there's a good lock and a stout bar."

"Are you afraid of Dinias?" I asked.

"I'm afraid of everybody in this cursed town. I'll not be happy till we're quit of it and back with Ambrosius."

"I doubt if you need worry now. Vortigern's men have gone. You heard what Dinias said."

"Aye, and I heard what you said, too." He had stooped to pick up the blankets from beside the fire, and paused with his arms full of bedding, looking at me. "What did you mean, you're getting your own place here ready? You're never thinking of setting up house here?"

"Not a house, no."

"That cave?"

I smiled at his expression. "When Ambrosius has done with me, and the country is quiet, that is where I shall go. I told you, didn't I, that if you stayed with me you'd live far from home?"

"We were talking about dying, as far as I remember. You mean, live there?"

"I don't know," I said. "Perhaps not. But I think I shall need a place where I can be alone, away, aside from things happening. Thinking and planning is one side of life; doing is another. A man cannot be doing all the time."

"Tell that to Uther."

"I am not Uther."

"Well, it takes both sorts, as they say." He dumped the blankets on the bed. "What are you smiling at?"

"Was I? Never mind. Let's get to bed, we'll have to be early at the nunnery. Did you have to bribe the old woman again?"

"Old woman nothing." He straightened. "It was a girl this time. A looker, too, what I could see of her with that sack of a gown and a hood over her head. Whoever puts a girl like that in a nunnery deserves—" He began to explain what they deserved, but I cut him short.

"Did you find out how my mother was?"

"They said she was better. The fever's gone, but she'll not rest quiet till she's seen you. You'll tell her everything now?"

"Yes."

"And then?"

"We join Ambrosius."

"Ah," he said, and when he had dragged his mattress to lie across the door, he blew out the lamp and lay down without another word to sleep.

My bed was comfortable enough, and the room, derelict or no, was luxury itself after the journey. But I slept badly. In imagination I was out on the road with Ambrosius, heading for Doward. From what I had heard of Doward, reducing it would not be an easy job. I began to wonder if after all I had done my father a disservice in driving the High King out of his Snowdon fastness. I should have left him there, I thought, with his rotten tower, and Ambrosius would have driven him back to the sea.

It was with an effort almost of surprise that I recalled my own prophecy. What I had done at Dinas Brenin, I had not done of myself. It was not I who had decided to send Vortigern fleeing out of Wales. Out of the dark, out of the wild and whirling stars, I had been told. The Red Dragon would triumph, the White would fall. The voice that had said so, that said so now in the musty dark of Camlach's room, was not my own; it was the god's. One did not lie awake looking for reasons; one obeyed, and then slept.

3

It was the girl Cadal had spoken of who opened the nunnery gate to us. She must have been waiting to receive us, for almost as soon as Cadal's hand was lifted to the bell-pull the gate opened and she motioned us to come in. I got a swift impression of wide eyes under the brown hood, and a supple young body shrouded in the rough gown, as she latched the heavy gate and, drawing her hood closer over her face and hair, led us quickly across the courtyard. Her feet, bare in canvas sandals, looked cold, and were splashed with mud from the puddled yard, but they were slim and well-shaped, and her hands were pretty. She did not speak, but led us across the yard and through a narrow passage between two buildings, into a larger square beyond. Here against the walls stood fruit trees, and a few flowers grew, but these were mostly weeds and wild-flowers, and the doors of the cells that opened off the courtyard were unpainted and, where they stood open, gave on bare little rooms where simplicity had become ugliness and, too often, squalor.

Not so in my mother's cell. She was housed with adequate— if not royal—comfort. They had let her bring her own furniture, the room was limewashed and spotlessly clean, and with the change in the April weather the sun had come out and was shining straight in through the narrow window and across her bed. I remembered the furniture; it was her own bed from home, and the curtain at the window was one she had woven herself, the red cloth with the green pattern that she had been making the day my uncle Camlach came home. I remembered, too, the wolfskin on the floor; my grandfather had killed the beast with his bare hands and the haft of his broken dagger; its beady eyes and snarl had terrified me when I was small. The cross that hung on the bare wall at the foot of her bed was of dull silver, with a lovely pattern of locked but flowing lines, and studs of amethyst that caught the light.

The girl showed me the door in silence, and withdrew. Cadal sat down on a bench outside to wait.

My mother lay propped on pillows, in the shaft of sunshine. She looked pale and tired, and spoke not much above a whisper, but was, she told me, on the mend. When I questioned her about the illness, and laid a hand on her temples, she put me aside, smiling and saying she was well enough looked after. I did not insist: half of healing is in the patient's trust, and no woman ever thinks her own son is much more than a child. Besides, I could see that the fever had gone, and now that she was no longer anxious over me, she would sleep.

So I merely pulled up the room's single chair, sat down and began to tell her all she wanted to know, without waiting for her questions: about my escape from Maridunum and the flight like the arrow from the god's bow straight from Britain to Ambrosius' feet, and all that had happened since. She lay back against her pillows and watched me with astonishment and some slowly growing emotion which I identified as the emotion a cage-bird might feel if you set it to hatch a merlin's egg.

When I had finished she was tired, and grey stood under her eyes so sharply drawn that I got up to go. But she looked contented, and said, as if it was the sum and finish of the story, as I suppose it was, for her:

"He has acknowledged you."

"Yes. They call me Merlin Ambrosius."

She was silent a little, smiling to herself. I crossed to the window and leaned my elbows on the sill, looking out. The sun was warm. Cadal nodded on his bench, half asleep. From across the yard a movement caught my eye; in a shadowed doorway the girl was standing, watching my mother's door as if waiting for me to come out. She had put back her hood, and even in the shadows I could see the gold of her hair and a young face lovely as a flower. Then she saw me watching her. For perhaps two seconds our eyes met and held. I knew then why the ancients armed the cruellest god with arrows; I felt the shock of it right through my body. Then she had gone, shrinking close-hooded back into the shadow, and behind me my mother was saying:

"And now? What now?"

I turned my back on the sunlight. "I go to join him. But not until you are better. When I go I want to take news of you."

She looked anxious. "You must not stay here. Maridunum is not safe for you."

"I think it is. Since the news came in of the landing, the place has emptied itself of Vortigern's men. We had to take to the hill-tracks on our way south; the road was alive with men riding to join him."

"That's true, but—"

"And I shan't go about, I promise you. I was lucky last night, I ran into Dinias as soon as I set foot in town. He gave me a room at home."

"Dinias?"

I laughed at her astonishment. "Dinias feels he owes me something, never mind what, but we agreed well enough last night." I told her what mission I had sent him on, and she nodded.

"He"—and I knew she did not mean Dinias—"will need every man who can hold a sword." She knitted her brows. "They say Hengist has three hundred thousand men. Will he"—and again she was not referring to Hengist—"be able to withstand Vortigern, and after him Hengist and the Saxons?"

I suppose I was still thinking of last night's vigil. I said, without pausing to consider how it would sound: "I have said so, so it must be true."

A movement from the bed brought my eyes down to her. She was crossing herself, her eyes at once startled and severe, and through it all afraid. "Merlin—" but on the word a cough shook her, so that when she managed to speak again it was only a harsh whisper: "Beware of arrogance. Even if God has given you power—"

I laid a hand on her wrist, stopping her. "You mistake me, madam. I put it badly. I only meant that the god had said it through me, and because he had said it, it must be true. Ambrosius must win, it is in the stars."

She nodded, and I saw the relief wash through her and slacken her, body and mind, like an exhausted child.

I said gently: "Don't be afraid for me, Mother. Whatever god uses me, I am content to be his voice and instrument. I go where he sends me. And when he has finished with me, he will take me back."

"There is only one God," she whispered.

I smiled at her. "That is what I am beginning to think. Now, go to sleep. I will come back in the morning."

I went to see my mother again next morning. This time I went alone. I had sent Cadal to find provisions in the market, Dinias' slut having vanished when he did, leaving us to fend for ourselves in the deserted palace. I was rewarded, for the girl was again on duty at the gate, and again led me to my mother's room. But when I said something to her she merely pulled the hood closer without speaking, so that again I saw no more of her than the slender hands and feet. The cobbles were dry today, and the puddles gone. She had washed her feet, and in the grip of the coarse sandals they looked as fragile as blue-veined flowers in a peasant's basket. Or so I told myself, my mind working like a singer's, where it had no right to be working at all. The arrow still thrummed where it had struck me, and my whole body seemed to thrill and tighten at the sight of her.

She showed me the door again, as if I could have forgotten it, and withdrew to wait.

My mother seemed a little better, and had rested well, she told me. We talked for a while; she had questions about the details of my story, and I filled them in for her. When I got up to go I asked, as casually as I could:

"The girl who opened the gate; she is young, surely, to be here? Who is she?"

"Her mother worked in the palace. Keridwen. Do you remember her?"

I shook my head. "Should I?"

"No." But when I asked her why she smiled, she would say nothing, and in face of her amusement I dared not ask any more.

On the third day it was the old deaf portress; and I spent the whole interview with my mother wondering if she had (as women will) seen straight through my carefully casual air to what lay beneath, and passed the word that the girl must be kept out of my way. But on the fourth day she was there, and this time I knew before I got three steps inside the gate that she had been hearing the stories about Dinas Brenin. She was so eager to catch a glimpse of the magician that she let the hood fall back a little, and in my turn I saw the wide eyes, grey-blue, full of a sort of awed curiosity and wonder. When I smiled at her and said something in greeting she ducked back inside the hood again, but this time she answered. Her voice was light and small, a child's voice, and she called me "my lord" as if she meant it.

"What's your name?" I asked her.

"Keri, my lord."

I hung back, to detain her. "How is my mother today, Keri?"

But she would not answer, just took me straight to the inner court, and left me there.

That night I lay awake again, but no god spoke to me, not even to tell me she was not for me. The gods do not visit you to remind you what you know already.

By the last day of April my mother was so much better that when I went again to see her she was in the chair by the window, wearing a woollen robe over her shift, and sitting full in the sun. A quince tree, pinioned to the wall outside, was heavy with rosy cups where bees droned, and just beside her on the sill a pair of white doves strutted and crooned.

"You have news?" she asked, as soon as she saw my face.

"A messenger came in today. Vortigern is dead and the Queen with him. They say that Hengist is coming south with a vast force, including Vortimer's brother Pascentius and the remnant of his army. Ambrosius is already on his way to meet them."

She sat very straight, looking past me at the wall. There was a woman with her today, sitting on a stool on the other side of the bed; it was one of the nuns who had attended her at Dinas Brenin. I saw her make the sign of the cross on her breast, but Niniane sat still and straight looking past me at something, thinking.

"Tell me, then."

I told her all I had heard about the affair at Doward. The woman crossed herself again, but my mother never moved. When I had finished, her eyes came back to me.

"And you will go now?"

"Yes. Will you give me a message for him?"

"When I see him again," she said, "it will be time enough."

When I took leave of her she was still sitting staring past the winking amethysts on the wall to something distant in place and time.

Keri was not waiting, and I lingered for a while before I crossed the outer yard, slowly, towards the gate. Then I saw her waiting in the deep shadow of the gateway's arch, and quickened my step. I was turning over a host of things to say, all equally useless to prolong what could not be prolonged, but there was no need. She put out one of those pretty hands and touched my sleeves, beseechingly. "My lord—"

Her hood was half back, and I saw tears in her eyes. I said sharply: "What's the matter?" I believe that for a wild moment I thought she wept because I was going. "Keri, what is it?"

"I have a toothache."

I gaped at her. I must have looked as silly as if I had just been slapped across the face.

"Here," she said, and put a hand to her cheek. The hood fell right back. "It's been aching for days. Please, my lord—"

I said hoarsely: "I'm not a toothdrawer."

"But if you would just touch it—"

"Or a magician," I started to say, but she came close to me, and my voice strangled in my throat. She smelled of honeysuckle. Her hair was barley-gold and her eyes grey like bluebells before they open. Before I knew it she had taken my hand between both of her own and raised it to her cheek.

I stiffened fractionally, as if to snatch it back, then controlled myself, and opened the palm gently along her cheek. The wide greybell eyes were as innocent as the sky. As she leaned towards me the neck of her gown hung forward slackly and I could see her breasts. Her skin was smooth as water, and her breath sweet against my cheek.

I withdrew the hand gently enough, and stood back. "I can do nothing about it." I suppose my voice was rough. She lowered her eyelids and stood humbly with folded hands. Her lashes were short and thick and golden as her hair. There was a tiny mole at the corner of her mouth.

I said: "If it's no better by morning, have it drawn."

"It's better already, my lord. It stopped aching as soon as you touched it." Her voice was full of wonder, and her hand crept up to the cheek where mine had lain. The movement was like a caress, and I felt my blood jerk with a beat like pain. With a sudden movement she reached for my hand again and quickly, shyly, stooped forward and pressed her mouth to it.

Then the door swung open beside me and I was out in the empty street.

4

It seemed, from what the messenger had told me, that Ambrosius had been right in his decision to make an end of Vortigern before turning on the Saxons. His reduction of Doward, and the savagery with which he did it, had their effect. Those of the invading Saxons who had ventured furthest inland began to withdraw northwards towards the wild debatable lands which had always provided a beachhead for invasion. They halted north of the Humber to fortify themselves where they could, and wait for him. At first Hengist believed that Ambrosius had at his command little more than the Breton invading army—and he was ignorant of the nature of that deadly weapon of war. He thought (it was reported) that very few of the island British had joined Ambrosius; in any case the Saxons had defeated the British, in their small tribal forces, so often that they despised them as easy meat. But now as reports reached the Saxon leader of the thousands who had flocked to the Red Dragon, and of the success of Doward, he decided to remain no longer fortified north of the Humber, but to march swiftly south again to meet the British at a place of his own choosing, where he might surprise Ambrosius and destroy his army.

Once again, Ambrosius moved with Caesar-speed. This was necessary, because where the Saxons had withdrawn, they had laid the country waste.

The end came in the second week of May, a week hot with sunshine that seemed to come from June, and interrupted by showers left over from April—a borrowed week, and, for the Saxons, a debt called in by fate. Hengist, with his preparations half complete, was caught by Ambrosius at Maesbeli, near Conan's Fort, or Kaerconan, that men sometimes call Conisburgh. This is a hilly place, with the fort on a crag, and a deep ravine running by. Here the Saxons had tried to prepare an ambush for Ambrosius' force, but Ambrosius' scouts got news of it from a Briton they came across lurking in a hilltop cave, where he had fled to keep his woman and two small children from the axes of the Northmen. So Ambrosius, forewarned, increased the speed of his march and caught up with Hengist before the ambush could be fully laid, thus forcing him into open battle.

Hengist's attempt to lay an ambush had turned the luck against him; Ambrosius, where he halted and deployed his army, had the advantage of the land. His main force, Bretons, Gauls, and island British from the south and southwest, waited on a gentle hill, with a level field ahead over which they could attack unimpeded. Among these troops, medley-wise, were other native British who had joined him, with their leaders. Behind this main army the ground rose gently, broken only by brakes of thorn and yellow gorse, to a long ridge which curved to the west in a series of low rocky hills, and on the east was thickly forested with oak. The men

from Wales—mountainy men—were stationed mainly on the
wings, the North Welsh in the oak forest and, separated from
them by the full body of Ambrosius' army, the South Welsh
on the hills to the west. These forces, lightly armed, highly
mobile and with scores to settle, were to hold themselves in
readiness as reinforcements, the swift hammer-blows which
could be directed during battle at the weakest points of the
enemy's defense. They could also be relied upon to catch and
cut down any of Hengist's Saxons who broke and fled the
field.

The Saxons, caught in their own trap, with this immense
winged force in front of them, and behind them the rock of
Kaerconan and the narrow defile where the ambush had been
planned, fought like demons. But they were at a disadvan-
tage: they started afraid—afraid of Ambrosius' reputation of
his recent ferocious victory at Doward, and more than both—
so men told me—of my prophecy to Vortigern which had
spread from mouth to mouth as quickly as the fires in
Doward tower. And of course the omens worked the other
way for Ambrosius. Battle was joined shortly before noon,
and by sunset it was all over.

I saw it all. It was my first great battlefield, and I am not
ashamed that it was almost my last. My battles were not
fought with sword and spear. If it comes to that, I had
already had a hand in the winning of Kaerconan before I
ever reached it; and when I did reach it, was to find myself
playing the very part that Uther had once, in jest, assigned to
me.

I had ridden with Cadal as far as Caerleon, where we
found a small body of Ambrosius' troops in possession of the
fortress, and another on its way to invest and repair the fort
at Maridunum. Also, their officer told me confidentially, to
make sure that the Christian community—"all the community," he added gravely, with the ghost of a wink at me, "such
is the commander's piety"—remained safe. He had been
detailed, moreover, to send some of his men back with me,
to escort me to Ambrosius. My father had even thought to
send some of my clothes. So I sent Cadal back, to his disgust,
to do what he could about Galapas' cave, and await me
there, then myself rode north-east with the escort.

We came up with the army just outside Kaerconan. The
troops were already deployed for battle and there was no
question of seeing the commander, so we withdrew, as in-
structed, to the western hill where the men of the South

Welsh tribes eyed one another distrustfully over swords held
ready for the Saxons below. The men of my escort troop
eyed me in something the same manner: they had not in-
truded on my silence on the ride, and it was plain they held
me in some awe, not only as Ambrosius' acknowledged son,
but as "Vortigern's prophet"—a title which had already stuck
to me and which it took me some years to shed. When I
reported with them to the officer in charge, and asked him to
assign me a place in his troop, he was horrified, and begged
me quite seriously to stay out of the fight, but to find some
place where the men could see me, and know, as he put it,
"that the prophet was here with them." In the end I did as he
wished, and withdrew to the top of a small rocky crag hard
by where, wrapping my cloak about me, I prepared to watch
the battlefield spread out below like a moving map.

Ambrosius himself was in the center; I could see the white
stallion with the Red Dragon glimmering above it. Out to the
right Uther's blue cloak glinted as his horse cantered along
the lines. The leader of the left wing I did not immediately
recognize; a grey horse, a big, heavy-built figure striding it, a
standard bearing some device in white which I could not at
first distinguish. Then I saw what it was. A boar. The Boar of
Cornwall. Ambrosius' commander of the left was none other
than the greybearded Gorlois, lord of Tintagel.

Nothing could be read of the order in which the Saxons
had assembled. All my life I had heard of the ferocity of
these great blond giants, and all British children were
brought up from babyhood on stories of their terror. They
went mad in war, men said, and could fight bleeding from a
dozen wounds, with no apparent lessening of strength or
ferocity. And what they had in strength and cruelty they
lacked in discipline. This seemed, indeed, to be so. There was
no order that I could see in the vast surge of glinting metal
and tossing horsehair which was perpetually on the move,
like a flood waiting for the dam to break.

Even from that distance I could pick out Hengist and his
brother, giants with long moustaches sweeping to their
chests, and long hair flying as they spurred their shaggy,
tough little horses up and down the ranks. They were
shouting, and echoes of the shouts came clearly; prayers to
the gods, vows, exhortations, commands, which rose towards
a ferocious crescendo, till on the last wild shout of "Kill, kill,
kill!" the axeheads swung up, glinting in the May sunlight,

and the pack surged forward towards the ordered lines of Ambrosius' army.

The two hosts met with a shock that sent the jackdaws squalling up from Kaerconan, and seemed to splinter the very air. It was impossible, even from my point of vantage, to see which way the fight—or rather, the several different movements of the fight—was going. At one moment it seemed as if the Saxons with their axes and winged helms were boring a way into the British host; at the next, you would see a knot of Saxons cut off in a sea of British, and then, apparently engulfed, vanish. Ambrosius' center block met the main shock of the charge, then Uther's cavalry, with a swift flanking movement, came in from the east. The men of Cornwall under Gorlois held back at first, but as soon as the Saxons' front line began to waver, they came in like a hammer-blow from the left and smashed it apart. After that the field broke up into chaos. Everywhere men were fighting in small groups, or even singly and hand to hand. The noise, the clash and shouting, even the smell of sweat and blood mingled, seemed to come up to this high perch where I sat with my cloak about me, watching. Immediately below me I was conscious of the stirring and muttering of the Welshmen, then the sudden cheer as a troop of Saxons broke and galloped in our direction. In a moment the hilltop was empty save for me, only that the clamour seemed to have washed nearer, round the foot of the hill like the tide coming in fast. A robin lighted on a blackthorn at my elbow, and began to sing. The sound came high and sweet and uncaring through all the noise of battle. To this day, whenever I think of the battle for Kaerconan, it brings to mind a robin's song, mingled with the croaking of the ravens. For they were already circling, high overhead: men say they can hear the clash of swords ten miles off.

It was finished by sunset. Eldol, Duke of Gloucester, dragged Hengist from his horse under the very walls of Kaerconan to which he had turned to flee, and the rest of the Saxons broke and fled, some to escape, but many to be cut down in the hills, or the narrow defile at the foot of Kaerconan. At first dusk, torches were lit at the gate of the fortress, the gates were thrown open, and Ambrosius' white stallion paced across the bridge and into the stronghold, leaving the field to the ravens, the priests, and the burial parties.

I did not seek him out straight away. Let him bury his

dead and clear the fortress. There was work for me down there among the wounded, and besides, there was no hurry now to give him my mother's message. While I had sat there in the May sunlight between the robin's song and the crash of battle, I knew that she had sickened again, and was already dead.

5

I made my way downhill between the clumps of gorse and the thorn trees. The Welsh troops had vanished, long since, to a man, and isolated shouts and battle cries showed where small parties were still hunting down the fugitives in forest and hill.

Below, on the plain, the fighting was over. They were carrying the wounded into Kaerconan. Torches weaved everywhere, till the plain was all light and smoke. Men shouted to one another, and the cries and groans of the wounded came up clearly, with the occasional scream of a horse, the sharp commands from the officers, and the tramp of the stretcher-bearers' feet. Here and there, in the dark corners away from the torchlight, men scurried singly or in pairs among the heaped bodies. One saw them stoop, straighten, and scurry off. Sometimes where they paused there was a cry, a sudden moan, sometimes the brief flash of metal or the quick downstroke of a shortened blow. Looters, rummaging among the dead and dying, keeping a few steps ahead of the official salvage parties. The ravens were coming down; I saw the tilt and slide of their black wings hovering above the torches, and a pair perched, waiting, on a rock not far from me. With nightfall the rats would be there, too, running up from the damp roots of the castle walls to attack the dead bodies.

The work of salvaging the living was being done as fast and efficiently as everything else the Count's army undertook. Once they were all within, the gates would be shut. I would seek him out, I decided, after the first tasks were done. He would already have been told that I was safely here, and he would guess I had gone to work with the doctors. There would be time, later, to eat, and then it would be time enough to talk to him.

On the field, as I made my way across, the stretcher

parties still strove to separate friend from foe. The Saxon dead had been flung into a heap in the center of the field; I guessed they would be burned according to custom. Beside the growing hill of bodies a platoon stood guard over the glittering pile of arms and ornaments taken from the dead men. The British dead were being laid nearer the wall, in rows for identification. There were small parties of men, each with an officer, bending over them one by one. As I picked my way through trampled mud oily and stinking with blood and slime I passed, among the armed and staring dead, the bodies of half a dozen ragged men—peasants or outlaws by the look of them. These would be looters, cut down or speared by the soldiers. One of them still twitched like a pinned moth, hastily speared to the ground by a broken Saxon weapon which had been left in his body. I hesitated, then went and bent over him. He watched me—he was beyond speech—and I could see he still hoped. If he had been cleanly speared, I would have drawn the blade out and let him go with the blood, but as it was, there was a quicker way for him. I drew my dagger, pulled my cloak aside out of the way, and carefully, so that I would be out of the jet of blood, stuck my dagger in at the side of his throat. I wiped it on the dead man's rags, and straightened to find a cold pair of eyes watching me above the levelled short sword three paces away.

Mercifully, it was a man I knew. I saw him recognize me, then he laughed and lowered his sword.

"You're lucky. I nearly gave it to you in the back."

"I didn't think of that." I slid the dagger back into its sheath. "It would have been a pity to die for stealing from that. What did you think he had worth taking?"

"You'd be surprised what you catch them taking. Anything from a corn plaster to a broken sandal strap." He jerked his head towards the high walls of the fortress. "He's been asking where you were."

"I'm on my way."

"They say you foretold this, Merlin? And Doward, too?"

"I said the Red Dragon would overcome the White," I said. "But I think this is not the end yet. What happened to Hengist?"

"Yonder." He nodded again towards the citadel. "He made for the fort when the Saxon line broke, and was captured just by the gate."

"I saw that. He's inside, then? Still alive?"

"Yes."

"And Octa? His son?"

"Got away. He and the cousin—Eosa, isn't it?—galloped north."

"So it isn't the end. Has he sent after them?"

"Not yet. He says there's time enough." He eyed me. "Is there?"

"How would I know?" I was unhelpful. "How long does he plan to stay here? A few days?"

"Three, he says. Time to bury the dead."

"What will he do with Hengist?"

"What do you think?" He made a little chopping movement downwards with the edge of his hand. "And long overdue, if you ask me. They're talking about it in there, but you could hardly call it a trial. The Count's said nothing as yet, but Uther's roaring to have him killed, and the priests want a bit of cold blood to round the day off with. Well, I'll have to get back to work, see if I can catch more civilians looting." He added as he turned away: "We saw you up there on the hill during the fighting. People were saying it was an omen."

He went. A raven flapped down from behind me with a croak, and settled on the breast of the man I had killed. I called to a torch-bearer to light me the rest of the way, and made for the main gate of the fortress.

While I was still some way short of the bridge a blaze of tossing torches came out, and in the middle of them, bound and held, the big blond giant that I knew must be Hengist himself. Ambrosius' troops formed a hollow square, and into this space his captors dragged the Saxon leader, and there must have forced him to his knees, for the flaxen head vanished behind the close ranks of the British. I saw Ambrosius himself then, coming out over the bridge, followed closely on his left by Uther, and on his other side by a man I did not know, in the robe of a Christian bishop, still splashed with mud and blood. Others crowded behind them. The bishop was talking earnestly in Ambrosius' ear. Ambrosius' face was a mask, the cold, expressionless mask I knew so well. I heard him say what sounded like, "You will see, they will be satisfied," and then, shortly, something else that caused the bishop at last to fall silent.

Ambrosius took his place. I saw him nod to an officer. There was a word of command, followed by the whistle and thud of a blow. A sound—it could hardly be called a growl—

of satisfaction from the watching men. The bishop's voice, hoarse with triumph: "So perish all pagan enemies of the one true God! Let his body be thrown now to the wolves and kites!" And then Ambrosius' voice, cold and quiet: "He will go to his own gods with his army round him, in the manner of his people." Then to the officer: "Send me word when all is ready, and I will come."

The bishop started to shout again, but Ambrosius turned away unheeding and, with Uther and the other captains, strode back across the bridge and into the fortress. I followed. Spears flashed down to bar my way, then—the place was garrisoned by Ambrosius' Bretons—I was recognized, and the spears withdrawn.

Inside the fortress was a wide square courtyard, now full of a bustling, trampling confusion of men and horses. At the far side a shallow flight of steps led to the door of the main hall and tower. Ambrosius' party was mounting the steps, but I turned aside. There was no need to ask where the wounded had been taken. On the east side of the square a long double-storeyed building had been organized as a dressing station; the sounds coming from this guided me. I was hailed thankfully by the doctor in charge, a man called Gandar, who had taught me in Brittany, and who avowedly had no use for either priests or magicians, but who very much needed another pair of trained hands. He assigned me a couple of orderlies, found me some instruments and a box of salves and medicines, and thrust me—literally—into a long room that was little better than a roofed shed, but which now held some fifty wounded men. I stripped to the waist and started work.

Somewhere around midnight the worst was done and things were quieter. I was at the far end of my section when a slight stir near the entrance made me look round to see Ambrosius, with Gandar and two officers, come quietly in and walk down the row of wounded, stopping by each man to talk or, with those worst wounded, to question the doctor in an undertone.

I was stitching a thigh wound—it was clean, and would heal, but it was deep and jagged, and to everyone's relief the man had fainted—when the group reached me. I did not look up, and Ambrosius waited in silence until I had done and, reaching for dressings the orderly had prepared, bandaged the wound. I finished, and got to my feet as the orderly came back with a bowl of water. I plunged my hands into this, and

looked up to see Ambrosius smiling. He was still in his
hacked and spattered armour, but he looked fresh and alert,
and ready if necessary to start another battle. I could see the
wounded men watching him as if they would draw strength
just from the sight.

"My lord," I said.

He stooped over the unconscious man. "How is he?"

"A flesh wound. He'll recover, and live to be thankful it
wasn't a few inches to the left."

"You've done a good job, I see." Then as I finished drying
my hands and dismissed the orderly with a word of thanks,
Ambrosius put out his own hand. "And now, welcome. I
believe we owe you quite a lot, Merlin. I don't mean for this;
I mean for Doward, and for today as well. At any rate the
men think so, and if soldiers decide something is lucky, then
it is lucky. Well, I'm glad to see you safe. You have news for
me, I believe."

"Yes." I said it without expression, because of the men
with us, but I saw the smile fade from his eyes. He hesitated,
then said quietly: "Gentlemen, give us leave." They went. He
and I faced one another across the body of the unconscious
man. Nearby a soldier tossed and moaned, and another cried
out and bit the sound back. The place smelled vile, of blood
and drying sweat and sickness.

"What is this news?"

"It concerns my mother."

I think he already knew what I was going to tell him. He
spoke slowly, measuring the words, as if each one carried
with it some weight that he ought to feel. "The men who
rode here with you . . . they brought me news of her. She had
been ill, but was recovered, they said, and safely back in
Maridunum. Was this not true?"

"It was true when I left Maridunum. If I had known the
illness was mortal, I would not have left her."

" 'Was' mortal?"

"Yes, my lord."

He was silent, looking down, but without seeing him, at the
wounded man. The latter was beginning to stir; soon he
would be back with the pain and the stench and the fear of
mortality. I said: "Shall we go out into the air? I've finished
here. I'll send someone back to this man."

"Yes. And you must get your clothes. It's a cool night."
Then, still without moving: "When did she die?"

"At sunset today."

He looked up quickly at that, his eyes narrow and intent, then he nodded, accepting it. He turned to go out, gesturing me to walk with him. As we went he asked me: "Do you suppose she knew?"

"I think so, yes."

"She sent no message?"

"Not directly. She said, 'When we meet again, it will be soon enough.' She is a Christian, remember. They believe—"

"I know what they believe."

Some commotion outside made itself heard, a voice barking a couple of commands, feet tramping. Ambrosius paused, listening. Someone was coming our way, quickly.

"We'll talk later, Merlin. You have a lot to tell me. But first we must send Hengist's spirit to join his fathers. Come."

They had heaped the Saxon dead high on the great stack of wood, and poured oil and pitch over them. At the top of the pyramid, on a platform roughly nailed together of planks, lay Hengist. How Ambrosius had stopped them robbing him I shall never know, but he had not been robbed. His shield lay on his breast, and a sword by his right hand. They had hidden the severed neck with a broad leather collar of the kind some soldiers use for throat guards. It was studded with gold. A cloak covered his body from throat to feet, and its scarlet folds flowed down over the rough wood.

As soon as the torches were thrust in below, the flames caught greedily. It was a still night, and the smoke poured upwards in a thick black column laced with fire. The edges of Hengist's cloak caught, blackened, curled, and then he was lost to sight in the gush of smoke and flames. The fire cracked like whips, and as the logs burned and broke, men ran, sweating and blackened, to throw more in. Even from where we stood, well back, the heat was intense, and the smell of burnt pitch and roasting meat came in sickening gusts on the damp night air. Beyond the lighted ring of watching men torches moved still on the battlefield, and one could hear the steady thud of spades striking into the earth for the British dead. Beyond the brilliant pyre, beyond the dark slopes of the far hills, the May moon hung, faint through the smoke.

"What do you see?"

Ambrosius' voice made me start. I looked at him, surprised. "See?"

"In the fire, Merlin the prophet."

"Nothing but dead men roasting."

"Then look and see something for me, Merlin. Where has Octa gone?"

I laughed. "How should I know? I told you all I could see."

But he did not smile. "Look harder. Tell me where Octa has gone. And Eosa. Where they will dig themselves in to wait for me. And how soon."

"I told you. I don't look for things. If it is the god's will that they should come to me, they come out of the flames, or out of the black night, and they come silently like the arrow out of ambush. I do not go to find the bowman; all I can do is stand with my breast bare and wait for the arrow to hit me."

"Then do it now." He spoke strongly, stubbornly. I saw he was quite serious. "You saw for Vortigern."

"You call it 'for' him? To prophesy his death? When I did that, my lord, I did not even know what I was saying. I suppose Gorlois told you what happened—even now, I couldn't tell you myself. I neither know when it will come, nor when it will leave me."

"Only today you knew about Niniane, and without either fire or darkness."

"That's true. But I can't tell you how, any more than how I knew what I told Vortigern."

"The men call you 'Vortigern's prophet.' You prophesied victory for us, and we had it, here and at Doward. The men believe you and have faith in you. So have I. Is it not a better title now to be 'Ambrosius' prophet'?"

"My lord, you know I would take any title from you that you cared to bestow. But this comes from somewhere else. I cannot call it, but I know that if it matters it will come. And when it comes, be sure I will tell you. You know I am at your service. Now, about Octa and Eosa I know nothing. I can only guess—and guess as a man. They fight still under the White Dragon, do they?"

His eyes narrowed. "Yes."

"Then what Vortigern's prophet said must still hold good."

"I can tell the men this?"

"If they need it. When do you plan to march?"

"In three days."

"Aiming for where?"

"York."

I turned up a hand. "Then your guess as a commander is

probably as good as my guess as a magician. Will you take me?"

He smiled. "Will you be any use to me?"

"Probably not as a prophet. But do you need an engineer? Or an apprentice doctor? Or even a singer?"

He laughed. "A host in yourself, I know. As long as you don't turn priest on me, Merlin. I have enough of them."

"You needn't be afraid of that."

The flames were dying down. The officer in charge of the proceedings approached, saluted, and asked if the men might be dismissed. Ambrosius gave him leave, then looked at me. "Come with me to York, then. I shall have work for you there. Real work. They tell me the place is half ruined, and I'll need someone to help direct the engineers. Tremorinus is at Caerleon. Now, find Caius Valerius and tell him to look after you, and bring you to me in an hour's time." He added over his shoulder as he turned away: "And in the meantime if anything should come to you out of the dark like an arrow, you'll let me know?"

"Unless it really is an arrow."

He laughed, and went.

Uther was beside me suddenly. "Well, Merlin the bastard? They're saying you won the battle for us from the hilltop?" I noticed, with surprise, that there was no malice in his tone. His manner was relaxed, easy, almost gay, like that of a prisoner let loose. I supposed this was indeed how he felt after the long frustrations of the years in Brittany. Left to himself Uther would have charged across the Narrow Sea before he was fairly into manhood, and been valiantly smashed in pieces for his pains. Now, like a hawk being flown for the first time at the quarry, he was feeling his power. I could feel it, too: it clothed him like folded wings. I said something in greeting, but he interrupted me. "Did you see anything in the flames just now?"

"Oh, not you, too," I said warmly. "The Count seems to think all I have to do is look at a torch and tell the future. I've been trying to explain it doesn't work like that."

"You disappoint me. I was going to ask you to tell my fortune."

"Oh, Eros, that's easy enough. In about an hour's time, as soon as you've settled your men, you'll be bedded down with a girl."

"It's not as much of a certainty as all that. How the devil did you know I'd managed to find one? They're not very thick on the ground just here—there's only about one man in fifty managed to get one. I was lucky."

"That's what I mean," I said. "Given fifty men and only one woman amongst them, then Uther has the woman. That's what I call one of the certainties of life. Where will I find Caius Valerius?"

"I'll send someone to show you. I'd come myself, only I'm keeping out of his way."

"Why?"

"When we tossed for the girl, he lost," said Uther cheerfully. "He'll have plenty of time to look after you. In fact, all night. Come along."

6

We went into York three days before the end of May.

Ambrosius' scouts had confirmed his guess about York; there was a good road north from Kaerconan, and Octa had fled up this with Eosa his kinsman, and had taken refuge in the fortified city which the Romans called Eboracum, and the Saxons Eoforwick, or York. But the fortifications at York were in poor repair, and the inhabitants, when they heard of Ambrosius' resounding victory at Kaerconan, offered the fleeing Saxons cold comfort. For all Octa's speed, Ambrosius was barely two days behind him, and at the sight of our vast army, rested, and reinforced by fresh British allies encouraged by the Red Dragon's victories, the Saxons, doubting whether they could hold the city against him, decided to beg for mercy.

I saw it myself, being right up in the van with the siege engines, under the walls. In its way it was more unpleasant even than a battle. The Saxon leader was a big man, blond like his father, and young. He appeared before Ambrosius stripped to his trews, which were of coarse stuff bound with thongs. His wrists likewise were bound, this time with a chain, and his head and body were smeared with dust, a token of humiliation he hardly needed. His eyes were angry, and I could see he had been forced into this by the cowardice—or wisdom, as you care to call it—of the group of Saxon and British notables who crowded behind him out of the city gate, begging Ambrosius for mercy on themselves and their families.

This time he gave it. He demanded only that the remnants of the Saxon army should withdraw to the north, beyond the old Wall of Hadrian, which (he said) he would count the border of his realm. The lands beyond this, so men say, are wild and sullen, and scarcely habitable, but Octa took his liberty gladly enough, and after him, eager for the same mercy, came his cousin Eosa throwing himself on Ambrosius' bounty. He received it, and the city of York opened its gates to its new king.

Ambrosius' first occupation of a town was always to follow the same pattern. First of all the establishment of order: he would never allow the British auxiliaries into the town; his own troops from Less Britain, with no local loyalties, were the ones that established and held order. The streets were cleared, the fortifications temporarily repaired, and plans drawn up for the future work and put into the hands of a small group of skilled engineers who were to call on local labour. Then a meeting of the city's leaders, a discussion on future policy, an oath of loyalty to Ambrosius, and arrangements made for the garrisoning of the city when the army departed. Finally a religious ceremony of thanksgiving with a feast and a public holiday.

In York, the first great city invested by Ambrosius, the ceremony was held in the church, on a blazing day near the end of June, and in the presence of the whole army, and a vast crowd of people.

I had already attended a private ceremony elsewhere.

It was not to be expected that there was still a temple of Mithras in York. The worship was forbidden, and in any case would have vanished when the last legion left the Saxon Shore almost a century ago, but in the day of the legions the temple at York had been one of the finest in the country. Since there was no natural cave nearby, it had originally been built below the house of the Roman commander, in a large cellar, and because of this the Christians had not been able to desecrate and destroy it, as was their wont with the sacred places of other men. But time and damp had done their work, and the sanctuary had crumbled into disrepair. Once, under a Christian governor, there had been an attempt to turn the place into a chapel-crypt, but the next governor had been outspokenly, not to say violently, opposed to this. He was a Christian himself, but he saw no reason why the perfectly good cellar under his house should not be used for what (to him) was the real purpose of a cellar, namely, to

store wine. And a wine store it had remained, till the day
Uther sent a working party down to clean and repair it for
the meeting, which was to be held on the god's own feast
day, the sixteenth day of June. This time the meeting was
secret, not from fear, but from policy, since the official
thanksgiving would be Christian, and Ambrosius would be
there to offer thanks in the presence of the bishops and all
the people. I myself had not seen the sanctuary, having been
employed during my first days in York on the restoring of
the Christian church in time for the public ceremony. But on
the feast of Mithras I was to present myself at the underground temple with others of my own grade. Most of these
were men I did not know, or could not identify by the voice
behind the mask; but Uther was always recognizable, and my
father would of course be there, in his office as Courier of
the Sun.

The door of the temple was closed. We of the lowest grade
waited our turn in the antechamber.

This was a smallish, square room, lit only by the two
torches held in the hands of the statues one to either side of
the temple door. Above the doorway was the old stone mask
of a lion, worn and fretted, part of the wall. To either side,
as worn and chipped, and with noses and members broken
and hacked away, the two stone torch-bearers still looked
ancient and dignified. The anteroom was chill, in spite of the
torches, and smelled of smoke. I felt the cold at work on my
body; it struck up from the stone floor into my bare feet, and
under the long robe of white wool I was naked. But just as
the first shiver ran up my skin, the temple door opened, and
in an instant all was light and colour and fire.

Even now, after all these years, and knowing all that I
have learned in a lifetime, I cannot find it in me to break the
vow I made of silence and secrecy. Nor, so far as I know,
has any man done so. Men say that what you are taught
when young, can never be fully expunged from your mind,
and I know that I, myself, have never escaped the spell of
the secret god who led me to Brittany and threw me at my
father's feet. Indeed, whether because of the curb on the
spirit of which I have already written, or whether by inter-
vention of the god himself, I find that my memory of his
worship has gone into a blur, as if it was a dream. And a
dream it may be, not of this time alone, but made up of all

the other times, from the first vision of the midnight field, to this night's ceremony, which was the last.

A few things I remember. More torch-bearers of stone. The long benches to either side of the center aisle where men reclined in their bright robes, the masks turned to us, eyes watchful. The steps at the far end, and the great apse with the arch like a cave-mouth opening on the cave within, where, under the star-studded roof, was the old relief in stone of Mithras at the bull-slaying. It must have been somehow protected from the hammers of the god-breakers, for it was still strongly carved and dramatic. There he was, in the light of the torches, the young man of the standing stone, the fellow in the cap, kneeling on the fallen bull and, with his head turned away in sorrow, striking the sword into its throat. At the foot of the steps stood the fire-altars, one to each side. Beside one of them a man robed and masked as a Lion, with a rod in his hand. Beside the other the Heliodromos, the Courier of the Sun. And at the head of the steps, in the center of the apse, the Father waiting to receive us.

My Raven mask had poor eyeholes, and I could only see straight forward. It would not have been seemly to look from side to side with that pointed bird-mask, so I stood listening to the voices, and wondering how many friends were here, how many men I knew. The only one I could be sure of was the Courier, tall and quiet there by the altar fire, and one of the Lions, either him by the archway, or one of the grade who watched from somewhere along the makeshift benches.

This was the frame of the ceremony, and all that I can remember, except the end. The officiating Lion was not Uther, after all. He was a shorter man, of thick build, and seemingly older than Uther, and the blow he struck me was no more than the ritual tap, without the sting that Uther usually managed to put into it. Nor was Ambrosius the Courier. As the latter handed me the token meal of bread and wine, I saw the ring on the little finger of his left hand, made of gold, enclosing a stone of red jasper with a dragon crest carved small. But when he lifted the cup to my mouth, and the scarlet robe slipped back from his arm, I saw a familiar scar white on the brown flesh, and looked up to meet the blue eyes behind the mask, alight with a spark of amusement that quickened to laughter as I started, and spilled the wine. Uther had stepped up two grades, it seemed, in the time since I had last attended the mysteries. And since

there was no other Courier present, there was only one place
for Ambrosius ...

I turned from the Courier to kneel at the Father's feet.
But the hands which took my own between them for the vow
were the hands of an old man, and when I looked up, the
eyes behind the mask were the eyes of a stranger.

Eight days later was the official ceremony of thanksgiving.
Ambrosius was there, with all his officers, even Uther, "for,"
said my father to me afterwards when we were alone, "as
you will find, all gods who are born of the light are brothers,
and in this land, if Mithras who gives us victory is to bear the
face of Christ, why, then, we worship Christ."

We never spoke of it again.

The capitulation of York marked the end of the first stage
of Ambrosius' campaign. After York we went to London in
easy stages, and with no more fighting, unless you count a
few skirmishes by the way. What the King had to undertake
now was the enormous work of reconstruction and the con-
solidation of his kingdom. In every town and strongpoint he
left garrisons of tried men under trusted officers, and appointed his own engineers to help organize the work of
rebuilding and repairing towns, roads and fortresses. Everywhere the picture was the same; once-fine buildings ruined or
damaged almost beyond repair; roads half obliterated
through neglect; villages destroyed and people hiding fearfully in caves and forests; places of worship pulled down or
polluted. It was as if the stupidity and lawless greed of the
Saxon hordes had cast a blight over the whole land. Everything that had given light—art, song, learning, worship, the
ceremonial meetings of the people, the feasts at Easter or
Hallowmass or midwinter, even the arts of husbandry, all
these had vanished under the dark clouds on which rode the
northern gods of war and thunder. And they had been invited
here by Vortigern, a British king. This, now, was all the
people remembered. They forgot that Vortigern had reigned
well enough for ten years, and adequately for a few more,
before he found that the war-spirit he had unleashed on his
country had outgrown his control. They remembered only
that he had gained his throne by bloodshed and treachery
and the murder of a kinsman—and that the kinsman had
been the true king. So they came flocking now to Ambrosius,
calling on him the blessings of their different gods, hailing him

with joy as King, the first "King of all Britain," the first shining chance for the country to be one.

Other men have told the story of Ambrosius' crowning and his first work as King of Britain; it has even been written down, so here I will only say that I was with him for the first two years as I have told, but then, in the spring of my twentieth year, I left him. I had had enough of councils and marching, and long legal discussions where Ambrosius tried to reimpose the laws that had fallen into disuse, and the everlasting meetings with elders and bishops droning like bees, days and weeks for every drop of honey. I was even tired of building and designing; this was the only work I had done for him in all the long months I served with the army. I knew at last that I must leave him, get out of the press of affairs that surrounded him; the god does not speak to those who have no time to listen. The mind must seek out what it needs to feed on, and it came to me at last that what work I had to do, I must do among the quiet of my own hills. So in spring, when we came to Winchester, I sent a message to Cadal, then sought Ambrosius out to tell him I must go.

He listened half absently; cares pressed heavily on him these days, and the years which had sat lightly on him before now seemed to weigh him down. I have noticed that this is often the way with men who set their lives towards the distant glow of one high beacon; when the hilltop is reached and there is nowhere further to climb, and all that is left is to pile more on the flame and keep the beacon burning, why, then, they sit down beside it and grow old. Where their leaping blood warmed them before, now the beacon fire must do it from without. So it was with Ambrosius. The King who sat in his great chair at Winchester and listened to me was not the young commander whom I had faced across the map-strewn table in Less Britain, or even the Courier of Mithras who had ridden to me across the frostbound field.

"I cannot hold you," he said. "You are not an officer of mine, you are only my son. You will go where you wish."

"I serve you. You know that. But I know now how best I can serve you. You spoke the other day of sending a troop towards Caerleon. Who's going?"

He looked down at a paper. A year ago he would have known without looking. "Priscus, Valens. Probably Sidonius. They go in two days' time."

"Then I'll go with them."

He looked at me. Suddenly it was the old Ambrosius back again. "An arrow out of the dark?"

"You might say so. I know I must go."

"Then go safely. And some day, come back to me."

Someone interrupted us then. When I left him he was already going, word by word, through some laborious draft of the new statutes for the city.

7

The road from Winchester to Caerleon is a good one, and the weather was fine and dry, so we did not halt in Sarum, but held on northwards while the light lasted, straight across the Great Plain.

A short way beyond Sarum lies the place where Ambrosius was born. I cannot even call to mind now what name it had gone by in the past, but already it was being called by his name, Amberesburg, or Amesbury. I had never been that way, and had a mind to see it, so we pressed on, and arrived just before sunset. I, together with the officers, was given comfortable lodging with the head man of the town—it was little more than a village, but very conscious now of its standing as the King's birthplace. Not far away was the spot where, many years ago, some hundred or more British nobles had been treacherously massacred by the Saxons and buried in a common grave. This place lay some way west of Amesbury, beyond the stone circle that men call the Giants' Dance, or the Dance of the Hanging Stones.

I had long heard about the Dance and had been curious to see it, so when the troop reached Amesbury, and were preparing to settle in for the night, I made my excuses to my host, and rode out westwards alone over the open plain. Here, for mile on mile, the long plain stretches without hill or valley, unbroken save for clumps of thorn-trees and gorse, and here and there a solitary oak stripped by the winds. The sun sets late, and this evening as I rode my tired horse slowly westwards the sky ahead of me was still tinged with the last rays, while behind me in the east the clouds of evening piled slate-blue, and one early star came out.

I think I had been expecting the Dance to be much less impressive than the ranked armies of stones I had grown accustomed to in Brittany, something, perhaps, on the scale

of the circle on the druids' island. But these stones were
enormous, bigger than any I had ever seen; and their very
isolation, standing as they did in the center of that vast and
empty plain, struck the heart with awe.

I rode some of the way round, slowly, staring, then
dismounted and, leaving my horse to graze, walked forward
between two standing stones of the outer circle. My shadow,
thrown ahead of me between their shadows, was tiny, a
pygmy thing. I paused involuntarily, as if the giants had
linked hands to stop me.

Ambrosius had asked me if this had been "an arrow out of
the dark." I had told him yes, and this was true, but I had
yet to find out why I had been brought here. All I knew was
that, now I was here, I wished myself away. I had felt
something of the same thing in Brittany as I first passed
among the avenues of stone; a breathing on the back of the
neck as if something older than time were looking over one's
shoulder; but this was not quite the same. It was as if the
ground, the stones that I touched, though still warm from the
spring sunlight, were breathing cold from somewhere deep
below.

Half reluctantly, I walked forward. The light was going
rapidly, and to pick one's way into the center needed care.
Time and storm—and perhaps the gods of war—had done
their work, and many of the stones were cast down to lie
haphazard, but the pattern could still be discerned. It was a
circle, but like nothing I had seen in Brittany, like nothing I
had even imagined. There had been, originally, an outer
circle of the huge stones, and where a crescent of these still
stood I saw that the uprights were crowned with a continuous
lintel of stones as vast as themselves, a great linked curve of
stone, standing like a giants' fence across the sky. Here and
there others of the outer circle were still standing, but most
had fallen, or were leaning at drunken angles, with the lintel
stones beside them on the ground. Within the bigger circle
was a smaller one of uprights, and some of the outer giants
had fallen against these and brought them flat. Within these
again, marking the center, was a horse-shoe of enormous
stones, crowned in pairs. Three of these trilithons stood intact; the fourth had fallen, and brought its neighbour down
with it. Echoing this once again was an inner horse-shoe of
smaller stones, nearly all standing. The center was empty,
and crossed with shadows.

The sun had gone, and with its going the western sky drained of colour, leaving one bright star in a swimming sea of green. I stood still. It was very quiet, so quiet that I could hear the sound of my horse cropping the turf, and the thin jingle of his bit as he moved. The only other sound was the whispering chatter of nesting starlings among the great trilithons overhead. The starling is a bird sacred to druids, and I had heard that in past time the Dance had been used for worship by the druid priests. There are many stories about the Dance, how the stones were brought from Africa, and put up by giants of old, or how they were the giants themselves, caught and turned to stone by a curse as they danced in a ring. But it was not giants or curses that were breathing the cold now from the ground and from the stones; these stones had been put here by men, and their raising had been sung by poets, like the old blind man of Brittany. A lingering shred of light caught the stone near me; the huge knob of stone on one sandstone surface echoed the hole in the fallen lintel alongside it. These tenons and sockets had been fashioned by men, craftsmen such as I had watched almost daily for the last few years, in Less Britain, then in York, London, Winchester. And massive as they were, giants' building as they seemed to be, they had been raised by the hands of workmen, to the commands of engineers, and to the sound of music such as I had heard from the blind singer of Kerrec.

I walked slowly forward across the circle's center. The faint light in the western sky threw my shadow slanting ahead of me, and etched, momentarily in fleeting light, the shape of an axe, two-headed, on one of the stones. I hesitated, then turned to look. My shadow wavered and dipped. I trod in a shallow pit and fell, measuring my length.

It was only a depression in the ground, the kind that might have been made, years past, by the falling of one of the great stones. Or by a grave . . .

There was no stone nearby of such a size, no sign of digging, no one buried here. The turf was smooth, and grazed by sheep and cattle, and under my hands as I picked myself up slowly, were the scented, frilled stars of daisies. But as I lay I had felt the cold strike up from below, in a pang as sudden as an arrow striking, and I knew that this was why I had been brought here.

I caught my horse, mounted and rode the two miles back to my father's birthplace.

We reached Caerleon four days later to find the place completely changed. Ambrosius intended to use it as one of his three main stations along with London and York, and Tremorinus himself had been working there. The walls had been rebuilt, the bridge repaired, the river dredged and its banks strengthened, and the whole of the east barrack block rebuilt. In earlier times the military settlement at Caerleon, circled by low hills and guarded by a curve of the river, had been a vast place; there was no need for even half of it now, so Tremorinus had pulled down what remained of the western barrack blocks and used the material on the spot to build the new quarters, the baths, and some brand-new kitchens. The old ones had been in even worse condition than the bathhouse at Maridunum, and now, "You'll have every man in Britain asking to be posted here," I told Tremorinus, and he looked pleased.

"We'll not be ready a moment too soon," he said. "The rumour's going round of fresh trouble coming. Have you heard anything?"

"Nothing. But if it's recent news I wouldn't have had it. We've been on the move for nearly a week. What kind of trouble? Not Octa again, surely?"

"No, Pascentius." This was Vortimer's brother who had fought with him in the rebellion, and fled north after Vortimer's death. "You knew he took ship to Germany? They say he'll come back."

"Give him time," I said, "you may be sure he will. Well, you'll send me any news that comes?"

"Send you? You're not staying here?"

"No. I'm going on to Maridunum. It's my home, you know."

"I had forgotten. Well, perhaps we'll see something of you; I'll be here myself a bit longer—we've started work on the church now." He grinned. "The bishop's been at me like a gadfly: it seems I snould have been thinking of that before I spent so much time on the things of this earth. And there's talk, too, of putting up some kind of monument to the King's victories. A triumphal arch, some say, the old Roman style of thing. Of course they're saying here in Caerleon that we should build the church for that—the glory of God with Ambrosius thrown in. Though myself I think if any bishop should get the credit of God's glory and the King's combined it should be Gloucester—old Eldad laid about him with the best of them. Did you see him?"

"I heard him."

He laughed. "Well, in any case you'll stay tonight, I hope? Have supper with me."

"Thanks. I'd like to."

We talked late into the night, and he showed me some of his plans and designs, and seemed flatteringly anxious that I should come back from Maridunum to see the various stages of the building. I promised, and next day left Caerleon alone, parrying an equally flattering and urgent request from the camp commandant to let him give me an escort. But I refused, and in the late afternoon came, alone, at last in sight of my own hills. There were rain clouds massing in the west, but in front of them, like a bright curtain, the slanting sunlight. One could see on a day like this why the green hills of Wales had been called the Black Mountains, and the valleys running through them the Valley of Gold. Bars of sunlight lay along the trees of the golden valleys, and the hills stood slate-blue or black behind them, with their tops supporting the sky.

I took two days for the journey, going easily, and noticing by the way, how the land seemed already to have got back its bloom of peace. A farmer building a wall barely looked my way as I rode by, and a young girl minding a flock of sheep smiled at me. And when I got to the mill on the Tywy, it seemed to be working normally; there were grain sacks piled in the yard, and I could hear the clack-clack-clack of the turning wheel.

I passed the bottom of the path which led up to the cave, and held on straight for the town. I believe I told myself that my first duty and concern was to visit St. Peter's to ask about my mother's death, and to see where she was buried. But when I got from my horse at the nunnery gate and lifted a hand to the bell, I knew from the knocking of my heart that I had told myself a lie.

I could have spared myself the deception; it was the old portress who let me in, and who led me straight, without being asked, through the inner court and down to the green slope near the river where my mother was buried. It was a lovely place, a green plot near a wall where pear trees had been brought early into blossom by the warmth, and where, above their snow, the white doves she had loved were rounding their breasts to the sun. I could hear the ripple of the river beyond the wall, and down through the rustling trees the note of the chapel bell.

The Abbess received me kindly, but had nothing to add to the account which I had received soon after my mother's death, and had passed on to my father. I left money for prayers, and for a carved stone to be made, and when I left, it was with her silver and amethyst cross tucked into my saddle-bag. One question I dared not ask, even when a girl who was not Keri brought wine for my refreshment. And finally, with my question unasked, I was ushered to the gate and out into the street. Here I thought for a moment that my luck had changed, for as I was untying my horse's bridle from the ring beside the gate I saw the old portress peering at me through the grille—remembering, no doubt, the gold I had given her on my first visit. But when I produced money and beckoned her close to shout my question in her ear, and even, after three repetitions, got through to her, the only answer was a shrug and the one word, "Gone," which—even if she had understood me—was hardly helpful. In the end I gave it up. In any case, I told myself, this was something that had to be forgotten. So I rode out of town and back over the miles to my valley with the memory of her face burned into everything I saw, and the gold of her hair lying in every shaft of the slanting sunlight.

Cadal had rebuilt the pen which Galapas and I had made in the hawthorn brake. It had a good roof and a stout door, and could easily house a couple of big horses. One—Cadal's own, I supposed—was already there.

Cadal himself must have heard me riding up the valley, because, almost before I had dismounted, he came running down the path by the cliff, had the bridle out of my hand, and, lifting both my hands in his, kissed them.

"Why, what's this?" I asked, surprised. He need have had no fears for my safety; the messages I had sent him had been regular and reassuring. "Didn't you get the message I was coming?"

"Yes, I got it. It's been a long time. You're looking well."

"And you. Is all well here?"

"You'll find it so. If you must live in a place like this, there's ways and ways of making it fit. Now get away up, your supper's ready." He bent to unbuckle the horse's girths, leaving me to go up to the cave alone.

He had had a long time in which to do it, but even so it came with a shock like a miracle. It was as it had always been, a place of green grass and sunlight. Daisies and hearts-ease starred the turf between the green curls of young bracken, and young rabbits whisked out of sight under the flowering blackthorn. The spring ran crystal clear, and crystal clear through the water of the well could be seen the silver gravel at the bottom. Above it, in its ferny niche, stood the carved figure of the god; Cadal must have found it when he cleared the rubbish from the well. He had even found the cup of horn. It stood where it had always stood. I drank from it, sprinkled the drops for the god, and went into the cave.

My books had come from Less Britain; the great chest was backed against the wall of the cave, where Galapas' box had been. Where his table had stood there was another, which I recognized from my grandfather's house. The bronze mirror was back in place. The cave was clean, sweet-smelling and dry. Cadal had built a hearth of stone, and logs were laid ready across it to light. I half expected to see Galapas sitting beside the hearth, and, on the ledge near the entrance, the falcon which had perched there on the night a small boy left the cave in tears. Deep among the shadows above the ledge at the rear was the gash of deeper shadow which hid the crystal cave.

That night, lying on the bed of bracken with the rugs pulled around me, I lay listening, after the dying of the fire, to the rustle of leaves outside the cave, and, beyond that, the trickle of the spring. They were the only sounds in the world. I closed my eyes and slept as I had not slept since I was a child.

8

Like a drunkard who, as long as there is no wine to be had, thinks himself cured of his craving, I had thought myself cured of the thirst for silence and solitude. But from the first morning of waking on Bryn Myrddin, I knew that this was not merely a refuge, it was my place. April lengthened into May, and the cuckoos shouted from hill to hill, the bluebells unfurled in the young bracken, and evenings were full of the sound of lambs crying, and still I had never once gone nearer the town than the crest of a hill two miles north where I gathered leaves and cresses. Cadal went down daily for supplies and for what news was current, and twice a messenger rode up the valley, once with a bundle of sketches from

Tremorinus, once with news from Winchester and money from my father—no letter, but confirmation that Pascentius was indeed massing troops in Germany, and war must surely come before the end of summer.

For the rest I read, and walked on the hills, and gathered plants and made medicines. I also made music, and sang a number of songs which made Cadal look sideways at me over his tasks and shake his head. Some of them are still sung, but most are best forgotten. One of the latter was this, which I sang one night when May was in town with all her wild clouds of blossom, and greybell turned to bluebell along the brakes.

> The land is grey and bare, the trees naked as bone,
> Their summer stripped from them; the willow's hair,
> The beauty of blue water, the golden grasses,
> Even the bird's whistle has been stolen,
> Stolen by a girl, robbed by a girl lithe as willow.
>
> Blithe she is as the bird on the May bough,
> Sweet she is as the bell in the tower,
> She dances over the bending rushes
> And her steps shine on the grey grass.
>
> I would take a gift to her, queen of maidens,
> But what is left to offer from my bare valley?
> Voices of wind in the reeds, and jewel of rain,
> And fur of moss on the cold stone.
> What is there left to offer but moss on the stone?
> She closes her eyes and turns from me in sleep.

The next day I was walking in a wooded valley a mile from home looking for wild mint and bitterweed, when, as if I had called her, she came up the path through the bluebells and bracken. For all I know, I may have called her. An arrow is an arrow, whichever god looses it.

I stood still by a clump of birches, staring as if she would vanish; as if I had indeed conjured her up that moment from dream and desire, a ghost in sunlight. I could not move, though my whole body and spirit seemed to leap at once to meet her. She saw me, and laughter broke in her face, and she came to me, walking lightly. In the chequer of dancing light and shadow as the birch boughs moved she still seemed insubstantial, as if her step would hardly stir the grasses, but then she came closer and it was no vision, but Keri as I remembered her, in brown homespun and smelling of honeysuckle. But now she wore no hood; her hair was loose over her shoulders, and her feet were bare. The sun glanced through the moving leaves, making her hair sparkle like light on water. She had her hands full of bluebells.

"My lord!" The small, breathless voice was full of pleasure.

I stood still with all my dignity round me like a robe, and under it my body fretting like a horse that feels curb and spur at the same time. I wondered if she were going to kiss my hand again, and if so, what I would do. "Keri! What are you doing here?"

"Why, gathering bluebells." The wide innocence of her look robbed the words of pertness. She held them up, laughing at me across them. God knows what she could see in my face. No, she was not going to kiss my hand. "Didn't you know I'd left St. Peter's?"

"Yes, they told me. I thought you must have gone to some other nunnery."

"No, never that. I hated it. It was like being in a cage. Some of them liked it, it made them feel safe, but not me. I wasn't made for such a life."

"They tried to do the same thing to me, once," I said.

"Did you run away, too?"

"Oh, yes. But I ran before they shut me up. Where are you living now, Keri?"

She did not seem to have heard the question. "You weren't meant for it, either? Being in chains, I mean?"

"Not those chains."

I could see her puzzling over this, but I was not sure what I had meant myself, so held my tongue, watching her without thought, feeling only the strong happiness of the moment.

"I was sorry about your mother," she said.

"Thank you, Keri."

"She died just after you'd left. I suppose they told you all about it?"

"Yes. I went to the nunnery as soon as I came back to Maridunum."

She was silent for a moment, looking down. She pointed a bare toe in the grass, a little shy dancing movement which set the golden apples at her girdle jingling. "I knew you had come back. Everyone's talking about it."

"Are they?"

She nodded. "They told me in town that you were a prince as well as a great magician ..." She looked up then, her voice fading to doubt, as she eyed me. I was wearing my oldest clothes, a tunic with grass stains that not even Cadal could remove, and my mantle was burred and pulled by thorns and brambles. My sandals were of canvas like a slave's; it was useless to wear leather through the long wet grass. Compared even with the plainly dressed young man she had seen before, I must look like a beggar. She asked, with the directness of innocence: "Are you still a prince, now that your mother is gone?"

"Yes. My father is the High King."

Her lips parted. "Your father? The King? I didn't know. Nobody said that."

"Not many people know. But now that my mother is dead, it doesn't matter. Yes, I am his son."

"The son of the High King ..." She breathed it, with awe. "And a magician, too. I know that's true."

"Yes. That is true."

"You once told me you weren't."

I smiled. "I told you I couldn't cure your toothache."

"But you did cure it."

"So you said. I didn't believe you."

"Your touch would cure anything," she said, and came close to me.

The neck of her gown hung slack. Her throat was pale as honeysuckle. I could smell her scent and the scent of the bluebells, and the bittersweet juice of the flowers crushed between us. I put out a hand and pulled at the neck of the gown, and the drawstring snapped. Her breasts were round and full and softer than anything I had imagined. They rounded into my hands like the breasts of my mother's doves. I believe I had expected her to cry out and pull away from me, but she nestled towards me warmly, and laughed, and put her hands up behind my head and dug her fingers into my hair and bit me on the mouth. Then suddenly she let her whole weight hang against me so that, reaching to hold her, plunging clumsily into the kiss, I stumbled forward and fell to the ground with her under me and the flowers scattering round us as we fell.

It took me a long time to understand. At first it was laughter and snatched breathing and all that burns down into the imagination in the night, but still held down hard and steady because of her smallness and the soft sounds she made when I hurt her. She was slim as a reed and soft with it, and you would have thought it would make me feel like a duke of the world, but then suddenly she made a sound deep in her throat as if she was strangling, and twisted in my arms as I have seen a dying man twist in pain, and her mouth came up like something striking, and fastened on mine.

Suddenly it was I who was strangling; her arms dragged at me, her mouth sucked me down, her body drew me into that tight and final darkness, no air, no light, no breath, no whisper of waking spirit. A grave inside a grave. Fear burned down into my brain like a white hot blade laid across the eyes. I opened them and could see nothing but the spinning light and the shadow of a tree laid across me whose thorns tore like spikes. Some shape of terror clawed my face. The thorn-tree's shadow swelled and shook, the cave-mouth gaped and the walls breathed, crushing me. I struggled back, out, tore myself away and rolled over apart from her, sweating with fear and shame.

"What's the matter?" Even her voice sounded blind. Her hands still moved over the space of air where I had been.

"I'm sorry, Keri. I'm sorry."

"What do you mean? What's happened?" She turned her head in its fallen flurry of gold. Her eyes were narrow and cloudy. She reached for me. "Oh, if that's all, come here. It's all right. I'll show you, just come here."

"No." I tried to put her aside gently, but I was shaking. "No, Keri. Leave me. No."

"What's the matter?" Her eyes opened suddenly wide. She pushed herself up on her elbow. "Why, I do believe you've never done it before. Have you? Have you?"

I didn't speak.

She gave a laugh that seemed meant to sound gay, but came shrilly. She rolled over again and stretched out her hands. "Well, never mind, you can learn, can't you? You're a man, after all. At least, I thought you were ..." Then, suddenly in a fury of impatience: "Oh, for God's sake. Hurry, can't you? I tell you, it'll be all right."

I caught her wrists and held them. "Keri, I'm sorry. I can't explain, but this is ... I must not, that's all I know. No, listen, give me a minute."

"Let me go!"

I loosed her and she pulled away and sat up. Her eyes were angry. There were flowers caught in her hair.

I said: "This isn't because of you, Keri, don't think that. It has nothing to do with you—"

"Not good enough for you, is that it? Because my mother was a whore?"

"Was she? I didn't even know." I felt suddenly immensely tired. I said carefully: "I told you this was nothing to do with you. You are very beautiful, Keri, and the first moment I saw you I felt—you must know what I felt. But this is nothing to do with feeling. It is between me and—it is something to do with my—" I stopped. It was no use. Her eyes watched me, bright and blank, then she turned aside with a little flouncing movement and began to tidy her dress. Instead of "power," I finished: "—something to do with my magic."

"Magic." Her lip was thrust out like a hurt child's. She knotted her girdle tight with a sharp little tug, and began to gather up the fallen bluebells, repeating spitefully: "Magic. Do you think I believe in your silly magic? Did you really think I even had the toothache, that time?"

"I don't know," I said wearily. I got to my feet.

"Well, maybe you don't have to be a man to be a magician. You ought to have gone into that monastery after all."

"Perhaps." A flower was tangled in her hair and she put a hand up to pull it out. The fine floss glinted in the sun like gossamer. My eye caught the blue mark of a bruise on her wrist. "Are you all right? Did I hurt you?"

She neither answered nor looked up, and I turned away. "Well, goodbye, Keri."

I had gone perhaps six steps when her voice stopped me. "Prince—"

I turned.

"So you do answer to it?" she said. "I'm surprised. Son of the High King, you say you are, and you don't even leave me a piece of silver to pay for my gown?"

I must have stood staring like a sleepwalker. She tossed the gold hair back over her shoulder and laughed up at me. Like a blind man fumbling, I felt in the purse at my belt and came out with a coin. It was gold. I took a step back towards her to give it to her. She leaned forward, still laughing, her hands out, cupped like a beggar's. The torn gown hung loose from the lovely throat. I flung the coin down and ran away from her, up through the wood.

Her laughter followed me till I was over the ridge and

down in the next valley and had flung myself on my belly
beside the stream and drowned the feel and the scent of her
in the rush of the mountain water that smelled of snow.

9

In June Ambrosius came to Caerleon, and sent for me. I
rode up alone, arriving one evening well past supper-time,
when the lamps had been lit and the camp was quiet. The
King was still working; I saw the spill of light from headquarters, and the glimmer on the dragon standard outside.
While I was still some way off I heard the clash of a salute,
and a tall figure came out whom I recognized as Uther.

He crossed the way to a door opposite the King's, but with
his foot on the bottom step saw me, stopped, and came back.
"Merlin. So you got here. You took your time, didn't you?"

"The summons was hasty. If I am to go abroad, there are
things I have to do."

He stood still. "Who said you were to go abroad?"

"People talk of nothing else. It's Ireland, isn't it? They say
Pascentius has made some dangerous allies over there, and
that Ambrosius wants them destroyed quickly. But why me?"

"Because it's their central stronghold he wants destroyed.
Have you ever heard of Killare?"

"Who hasn't? They say it's a fortress that's never been
taken."

"Then they say the truth. There's a mountain in the center
of all Ireland, and they say that from the summit of it you
can see every coast. And on top of that hill there's a fortress,
not of earth and palisades, but of strong stones. That, my
dear Merlin, is why you."

"I see. You need engines."

"We need engines. We have to attack Killare. If we can
take it, you can reckon that there'll be no trouble there for a
few years to come. So I take Tremorinus, and Tremorinus
insists on taking you."

"I gather the King isn't going?"

"No. Now I'll say good night; I have business to attend to,
or I would ask you in to wait. He's got the camp commandant with him, but I don't imagine they'll be long."

On this, he said a pleasant enough good night, and ran up

the steps into his quarters, shouting for his servant before he was well through the door.

Almost immediately, from the King's doorway, came the clash of another salute, and the camp commandant came out. Not seeing me, he paused to speak to one of the sentries, and I stood waiting until he had done.

A movement caught my eye, a furtive stir of shadow where someone came softly down a narrow passage between the buildings opposite, where Uther was housed. The sentries, busy with the commandant, had seen nothing. I drew back out of the torchlight, watching. A slight figure, cloaked and hooded. A girl. She reached the lighted corner and paused there, looking about her. Then, with a gesture that was secret rather than afraid, she pulled the hood closer about her face. It was a gesture I recognized, as I recognized the drift of scent on the air, like honeysuckle, and from under the hood the lock of hair curling, gold in the torchlight.

I stood still. I wondered why she had followed me here, and what she hoped to gain. I do not think it was shame I felt, not now, but there was pain, and I believe there was still desire. I hesitated, then took a step forward and spoke.

"Keri?"

But she paid no attention. She slid out from the shadows and, quickly and lightly, ran up the steps to Uther's door. I heard the sentry challenge her, then a murmur, and a soft laugh from the man.

When I drew level with Uther's doorway it was shut. In the light of the torch I saw the smile on the sentry's face.

Ambrosius was still sitting at his table, his servant hovering behind him in the shadows.

He pushed his papers aside and greeted me. The servant brought wine and poured it, then withdrew and left us alone.

We talked for a while. He told me what news there was since I had left Winchester; the building that had gone forward, and his plans for the future. Then we spoke of Tremorinus' work at Caerleon, and so came to the talk of war. I asked him for the latest about Pascentius, "for," I said, "we have been waiting weekly to hear that he had landed in the north and was harrying the countryside."

"Not yet. In fact, if my plans come to anything, we may hear nothing more of Pascentius until the spring, and then we shall be more than prepared. If we allow him to come now, he may well prove more dangerous than any enemy I have yet fought."

"I've heard something about this. You mean the Irish news?"

"Yes. The news is bad from Ireland. You know they have a young king there, Gilloman? A young firedrake, they tell me, and eager for war. Well, you may have heard it, the news is that Pascentius is contracted to Gilloman's sister. You see what this could mean? Such an alliance as that might put the north and west of Britain both at risk together."

"Is Pascentius in Ireland? We heard he was in Germany, gathering support."

"That is so," he said. "I can't get accurate information about his numbers, but I'd say about twenty thousand men. Nor have I yet heard what he and Gilloman plan to do." He lifted an eyebrow at me, amused. "Relax, boy, I haven't called you here to ask for a prediction. You made yourself quite clear at Kaerconan; I'm content to wait, like you, on your god."

I laughed. "I know. You want me for what you call 'real work'."

"Indeed. This is it. I am not content to wait here in Britain while Ireland and Germany gather their forces and then come together on both our coasts like a summer storm, and meet in Britain to overwhelm the north. Britain lies between them now, and she can divide them before ever they combine to attack."

"And you'll take Ireland first?"

"Gilloman," he said, nodding. "He's young and inexperienced—and he is also nearer. Uther will sail for Ireland before the month's end." There was a map in front of him. He half turned it so that I could see. "Here. This is Gilloman's stronghold; you'll have heard of it, I don't doubt. It is a mountain fortress called Killare. I have not found a man who has seen it, but I am told it is strongly fortified, and can be defended against any assault. I am told, indeed, that it has never fallen. Now, we can't afford to have Uther sit down in front of it for months, while Pascentius comes in at the back door. Killare must be taken quickly, and it cannot—they tell me—be taken by fire."

"Yes?" I had already noticed that there were drawings of mine on the table among the maps and plans.

He said, as if at a tangent: "Tremorinus speaks very highly of you."

"That's good of him." Then, at my own tangent: "I met Uther outside. He told me what you wanted."

"Then will you go with him?"

"I'm at your service, of course. But sir"—I indicated the drawings—"I have made no new designs. Everything I have designed has already been built here. And if there is so much hurry—"

"Not that, no. I'm asking for nothing new. The machines we have are good—and must serve. What we have built is ready now for shipping. I want you for more than this." He paused. "Killare, Merlin, is more than a stronghold, it is a holy place, the holy place of the Kings of Ireland. They tell me the crest of the hill holds a Dance of stone, a circle such as you knew in Brittany. And on Killare, men say, is the heart of Ireland and the holy place of Gilloman's kingdom. I want you, Merlin, to throw down the holy place, and take the heart out of Ireland."

I was silent.

"I spoke of this to Tremorinus," he said, "and he told me I must send for you. Will you go?"

"I have said I will. Of course."

He smiled, and thanked me, not as if he were High King and I a subject obeying his wish, but as if I were an equal giving him a favour. He talked then for a little longer about Killare, what he had heard of it, and what preparations he thought we should make, and finally leaned back, saying with a smile: "One thing I regret. I'm going to Maridunum, and I should have liked your company, but now there is no time for that. You may charge me with any messages you care to."

"Thank you, but I have none. Even if I had been there, I would hardly have dared to offer you the hospitality of a cave."

"I should like to see it."

"Anyone will tell you the way. But it's hardly fit to receive a King."

I stopped. His face was lit with a laughter that all at once made him look twenty again. I set down my cup. "I am a fool. I had forgotten."

"That you were begotten there? I thought you had. I can find my way to it, never fear."

He spoke then about his own plans. He himself would stay in Caerleon, "for if Pascentius attacks," he told me, "my guess is that he will come down this way"—his finger traced a line on the map—"and I can catch him south of Carlisle. Which brings me to the next thing. There was something else I wanted to discuss with you. When you last came through Caerleon on your way to Maridunum in April, I believe you had a talk with Tremorinus?"

I waited.

"About this." He lifted a sheaf of drawings—not mine—and handed them across. They were not of the camp, or indeed of any buildings I had seen. There was a church, a great hall, a tower. I studied them for a few minutes in silence. For some reason I felt tired, as if my heart were too heavy for me. The lamp smoked and dimmed and sent shadows dancing over the papers. I pulled myself together, and looked up at my father. "I see. You must be talking about the memorial building?"

He smiled. "I'm Roman enough to want a visible monument."

I tapped the drawings. "And British enough to want it British? Yes, I heard that, too."

"What did Tremorinus tell you?"

"That it was thought some kind of monument to your victories should be erected, and to commemorate your kingship of a united kingdom. I agreed with Tremorinus that to build a triumphal arch here in Britain would be absurd. He did say that some churchmen wanted a big church built—the bishop of Caerleon, for instance, wanted one here. But surely, sir, this would hardly do? If you build at Caerleon you'll have London and Winchester, not to mention York, thinking it should have been there. Of them all, I suppose, Winchester would be the best. It is your capital."

"No. I've had a thought about this myself. When I travelled up from Winchester, I came through Amesbury ..." He leaned foward suddenly. "What's the matter, Merlin? Are you ill?"

"No. It's a hot night, that's all. A storm coming, I think. Go on. You came through Amesbury."

"You knew it was my birthplace? Well, it seemed to me that to put my monument in such a place could give no cause for complaint—and there is another reason why it's a good choice." He knitted his brows. "You're like a sheet, boy. Are you sure you're all right?"

"Perfectly. Perhaps a little tired."

"Have you supped? It was thoughtless of me not to ask."

"I ate on the way, thank you. I have had all I needed. Perhaps—some more wine—"

I half rose, but before I could get to my feet he was on his, and came round the table with the jug and served me himself. While I drank he stayed where he was, near me, sitting back against the table's edge. I was reminded sharply of how he had stood this way that night in Brittany when I discovered him. I remember that I held it in my mind, and in a short while was able to smile at him.

"I am quite well, sir, indeed I am. Please go on. You were giving me the second reason for putting your monument at Amesbury."

"You probably know that it is not far from there that the British dead lie buried, who were slain by Hengist's treachery. I think it fitting—and I think there is no man who will argue with this—that the monument to my victory, to the making of one kingdom under one King, should also be a memorial for these warriors." He paused. "And you might say there is yet a third reason, more powerful than the other two."

I said, not looking at him, but down into the cup of wine, and speaking quietly: "That Amesbury is already the site of the greatest monument in Britain? Possibly the greatest in the whole West?"

"Ah." It was a syllable of deep satisfaction. "So your mind moves this way, too? You have seen the Giants' Dance?"

"I rode out to it from Amesbury, when I was on my way home from Winchester."

He stood up at that and walked back round the table to his chair. He sat, then leaned forward, resting his hands on the table. "Then you know how I am thinking. You saw enough when you lived in Brittany to know what the Dance was once. And you have seen what it is now—a chaos of giant stones in a lonely place where the sun and the winds strike." He added more slowly, watching me: "I have talked of this to Tremorinus. He says that no power of man could raise those stones."

I smiled. "So you sent for me to raise them for you?"

"You know they say it was not men who raised them, but magic."

"Then," I said, "no doubt they will say the same again."

His eyes narrowed. "You are telling me you can do it?"

"Why not?"

He was silent, merely waiting. It was a measure of his faith in me that he did not smile.

I said: "Oh, I've heard all the tales they tell, the same tales they told in Less Britain of the standing stones. But the stones were put there by men, sir. And what men put there once, men can put there again."

"Then if I don't possess a magician, at least I possess a competent engineer?"

"That's it."

"How will you do it?"

"As yet, I know less than half of it. But it can be done."

"Then will you do this for me, Merlin?"

"Of course. Have I not said I am here only to serve you as best I can? I will rebuild the Giants' Dance for you, Ambrosius."

"A strong symbol of Britain." He spoke broodingly now, frowning down at his hands. "I shall be buried there, Merlin, when my time comes. What Vortigern wanted to do for his stronghold in darkness, I shall do for mine in the light; I shall have the body of her King buried under the stones, the warrior under the threshold of all Britain."

Someone must have drawn the curtains back from the door. The sentries were out of sight, the camp silent. The stone doorposts and the heavy lintel lying across them framed a blue night burning with stars. All round us the vast shadows reared, giant stones linked like pleached trees where some hands long since gone had cut the signs of the gods of air and earth and water. Someone was speaking quietly; a king's voice; Ambrosius' voice. It had been speaking for some time; vaguely, like echoes in the dark, I heard it.

"... and while the King lies there under the stone the Kingdom shall not fall. For as long and longer than it has stood before, the Dance shall stand again, with the light striking it from the living heaven. And I shall bring back the great stone to lay upon the grave-place, and this shall be the heart of Britain, and from this time on all the kings shall be one King and all the gods one God. And you shall live again in Britain, and for ever, for we will make between us a King whose name will stand as long as the Dance stands, and who will be more than a symbol; he will be a shield and a living sword."

It was not the King's voice; it was my own. The King was still sitting on the other side of the map-strewn table, his hands still and flat on the papers, his eyes dark under the straight brows. Between us the lamp dimmed, flickering in a draught from under the shut door.

I stared at him, while my sight slowly cleared. "What did I say?"

He shook his head, smiling, and reached for the wine jug.

I said irritably: "It comes on me like a fainting fit on a pregnant girl. I'm sorry. Tell me what I said?"

"You gave me a kingdom. And you gave me immortality. What more is there? Drink now, Ambrosius' prophet."

"Not wine. Is there water?"

"Here." He got to his feet. "And now you must go and sleep, and so must I. I leave early for Maridunum. You are sure you have no messages?"

"Tell Cadal he is to give you the silver cross with the amethysts."

We faced one another in a small silence. I was almost as tall as he. He said, gently: "So now it is goodbye."

"How does one say goodbye to a King who has been given immortality?"

He gave me a strange look. "Shall we meet again, then?"

"We shall meet again, Ambrosius."

It was then I knew that what I had prophesied for him was his death.

10

Killare, I had been told, is a mountain in the very center of Ireland. There are in other parts of this island mountains which, if not as great as those of our own country, could still merit the name. But the hill of Killare is no mountain. It is a gentle conical hill whose summit is, I suppose, no more than nine hundred feet high. It is not even forested, but clothed over with rough grass, with here and there a copse of thorn-trees, or a few single oaks.

Even so, standing where it does, it looms like a mountain to those approaching it, for it stands alone, the only hill at the center of a vast plain. On every hand, with barely the least undulation, the country stretches flat and green; north, south, east, west, it is the same. But it is not true that you can see the coasts from that summit; there is only the interminable view on every hand of that green gentle country, with above it a soft and cloudy sky.

Even the air is mild there. We had fair winds, and landed on a long, grey strand of a soft summer morning, with a breeze off the land smelling of bog myrtle and gorse and salt-soaked turf. The wild swans sailed the loughs with the half-grown cygnets, and the peewits screamed and tumbled over the meadows where their young nestled down between the reeds.

It was not a time, or a country, you would have thought, for war. And indeed, the war was soon over. Gilloman, the king, was young—they said not more than eighteen—and he would not listen to his advisers and wait for a good moment to meet our attack. So high was his heart that, at the first news of foreign troops landing on the sacred soil of Ireland, the young king gathered his fighting men together, and threw them against Uther's seasoned troops. They met us on a flat plain, with a hill at our backs and a river at theirs. Uther's troops stood the first wild, brave attack without giving ground even a couple of paces, then advanced steadily in their turn, and drove the Irish into the water. Luckily for them, this was a wide stream, and shallow, and, though it ran red that evening, many hundreds of Irishmen escaped. Gilloman the king was one of them, and when we got the news that he had fled west with a handful of trusted followers, Uther, guessing he would be making for Killare, sent a thousand mounted troops after him, with instructions to catch him before he reached the gates. This they just managed to do, coming up with him barely half a mile short of the fortress, at the very foot of the hill and within sight of the walls. The second battle was short, and bloodier than the first. But it took place in the night, and in the confusion of the mêlée Gilloman himself escaped once more, and galloped away with a handful of men, this time nobody knew where. But the thing was done; by the time we, the main body of the army, came to the foot of Mount Killare, the British troops were already in possession, and the gates were open.

A lot of nonsense has been talked about what happened next. I myself have heard some of the songs, and even read one account which was set down in a book. Ambrosius had been misinformed. Killare was not strong-built of great stones; that is to say, the other fortifications were as usual of earthworks and palisades behind a great ditch, and inside that was a second ditch, deep, and with spikes set. The central fortress itself was certainly stone-walled, and the stones were big ones, but nothing that a normal team, with the proper tackle, could not handle easily. Inside the fortress wall were houses, of the most part built of wood, but also some strong places underground, as we have in Britain. Higher yet stood the innermost ring, a wall round the crest of the hill like a crown round the brow of a king. And inside this, at the very center and apex of the hill, was the holy place. Here stood the Dance, the circle of stones that was said to contain the heart of Ireland. It could not compare with the Great Dance of Amesbury, being only a single circle of unlinked stones, but it was impressive enough, and still stood firm with much of the circle intact, and two capped uprights near the center where other stones lay, seemingly without pattern, in the long grass.

I walked up alone that same evening. The hillside was alive with the bustle and roar, familiar to me from Kaerconan, of the aftermath of battle. But when I passed the wall that hedged the holy place, and came out towards the crest of the hill, it was like leaving a bustling hall for the quiet of some tower room upstairs. Sounds fell away below the walls, and as I walked up through the long summer grass, there was almost silence, and I was alone.

A round moon stood low in the sky, pale still, and smudged with shadow, and thin at one edge like a worn coin. There was a scatter of small stars, with here and there the shepherd stars herding them, and across from the moon one great star alone, burning white. The shadows were long and soft on the seeding grasses.

A tall stone stood alone, leaning a little towards the east. A little further was a pit, and beyond that again a round boulder that looked black in the moonlight. There was something here. I paused. Nothing I could put a name to, but the old, black stone itself might have been some dark creature hunched there over the pit's edge. I felt the shiver run over my skin, and turned away. This, I would not disturb.

The moon climbed with me, and as I entered the circle she lifted her white disc over the cap-stones and shone clear into the center of the ring. My footsteps crunched, dry and brittle, over a patch of ground where fires had recently been lit. I saw the white shapes of bones, and a flat stone shaped like an altar. The moonlight showed carving on one side, crude shapes twisted, of ropes or serpents. I stooped to run a finger over them. Nearby a mouse rustled and squeaked in the grass. No other sound. The thing was clean, dead, godless. I left it, moving on slowly through the moon-thrown shadows. There was another stone, domed like a beehive, or a navel-stone. And here an upright fallen, with the long grass almost hiding it. As I passed it, searching still, a ripple of breeze ran through the grasses, blurring the shadows and dimming the light like mist. I caught my foot on something, staggered, and came down to my knees at the end of a long flat stone which lay almost hidden in the grass. My hands moved over it. It was massive, oblong, uncarved, simply a great natural stone on to which now the moonlight poured. It hardly needed the cold at my hands, the hiss of the bleached grasses under the sudden run of wind, the scent of daisies, to tell me that this was the stone. All round me, like dancers drawing back from a center, the silent stones stood black. On one side the white moon, on the other the king-star, burning white. I got slowly to my feet and stood there at the foot of the long stone, as one might stand at the foot of a bed, waiting for the man in it to die.

It was warmth that woke me, warmth and the voices of men near me. I lifted my head. I was half-kneeling, half-lying with my arms and the upper part of my body laid along the stone. The morning sun was high, and pouring straight down into the center of the Dance. Mist smoked up from the damp grass, and its white wreaths hid the lower slopes of the hill. A group of men had come in through the stones of the Dance, and were standing there muttering among themselves, watching me. As I blinked, moving my stiff limbs, the group parted and Uther came through, followed by half a dozen of his officers, among whom was Tremorinus. Two soldiers pushed between them what was obviously an Irish prisoner; his hands were tied and there was a cut on one cheek where blood had dried, but he held himself well and I thought the men who guarded him looked more afraid than he.

Uther checked when he saw me, then came across as I got stiffly to my feet. The night must have shown still in my face, for in the group of officers behind him I saw the look I had grown used to, of men both wary and amazed, and even Uther spoke a fraction too loudly.

"So your magic is as strong as theirs."

The light was too strong for my eyes. He looked vivid and unreal, like an image seen in moving water. I tried to speak, cleared my throat, and tried again. "I'm still alive, if that's what you mean."

Tremorinus said gruffly: "There's not another man in the army would have spent the night here."

"Afraid of the black stone?"

I saw Uther's hand move in an involuntary gesture as if it sprang of itself to make the sign. He saw I had noticed, and looked angry. "Who told you about the black stone?"

Before I could answer, the Irishman said suddenly: "You saw it? Who are you?"

"My name is Merlin."

He nodded slowly. He still showed no sign of fear or awe. He read my thought, and smiled, as if to say, "You and I, we can look after ourselves."

"Why do they bring you here like this?" I asked him.

"To tell them which is the king-stone."

Uther said: "He has told us. It's the carved altar over there."

"Let him go," I said. "You have no need of him. And leave the altar alone. This is the stone."

There was a pause. Then the Irishman laughed. "Faith, if you bring the King's enchanter himself, what hope has a poor poet? It was written in the stars that you would take it, and indeed, it is nothing but justice. It's not the heart of Ireland that that stone has been but the curse of it, and maybe Ireland will be all the better to see it go."

"How so?" I asked him. Then, to Uther: "Tell them to loose him."

Uther nodded, and the men loosed the prisoner's hands. He rubbed his wrists, smiling at me. You would have thought we two were alone in the Dance. "They say that in times past that stone came out of Britain, out of the mountains of the west, in sight of the Irish Sea, and that the great King of all Ireland, Fionn Mac Cumhaill was his name, carried it in his arms one night and walked through the sea with it to Ireland, and set it here."

"And now," I said, "we carry it a little more painfully back to Britain."

He laughed. "I would have thought the great magician that's yourself would have picked it up in one hand."

"I'm no Fionn," I said. "And now if you are wise, poet, you will go back to your home and your harp, and make no more wars, but make a song about the stone, and how Merlin the enchanter took the stone from the Dance of Killare and carried it lightly to the Dance of the Hanging Stones at Amesbury."

He saluted me, laughing still, and went. And indeed he did walk safely down through the camp and away, for in later years I heard the song he made.

But now his going was hardly noticed. There was a pause while Uther frowned down at the great stone, seeming to weigh it in his mind. "You told the King that you could do this thing. Is that true?"

"I said to the King that what men had brought here, men could take away."

He looked at me frowningly, uncertainly, still a little angry. "He told me what you said. I agree. It doesn't need magic and fine words, only a team of competent men with the right engines. Tremorinus!"

"Sir?"

"If we take this one, the king-stone, there will be no need to trouble overmuch with the rest. Throw them down where you can and leave them."

"Yes, sir. If I could have Merlin—"

"Merlin's team will be working on the fortifications. Merlin, get started, will you? I give you twenty-four hours."

This was something the men were practiced at; they threw down the walls and filled in the ditches with them. The palisades and houses, quite simply, we put to the flame. The men worked well, and were in good heart. Uther was always generous to his troops, and there had been goods in plenty to be looted, arm-rings of copper and bronze and gold, brooches, and weapons well made and inlaid with copper and enamel, in a way the Irish have. The work was finished by dusk, and we withdrew from the hill to the temporary camp which had been thrown up on the plain at the foot of the slope.

It was after supper when Tremorinus came to me. I could see the torches and the fires still lit at the top of the hill, throwing what was left of the Dance into relief. His face was grimy, and he looked tired.

"All day," he said bitterly, "and we've raised it a couple of feet, and half an hour ago the props cracked, and it's gone back again into its bed. Why the hell did you have to suggest that stone? The Irishman's altar would have been easier."

"The Irishman's altar would not have done."

"Well, by the gods, it looks as if you aren't going to get this one either! Look, Merlin, I don't care what he says, I'm in charge of this job, and I'm asking you to come and take a look. Will you?"

The rest is what the legends have been made of. It would be tedious now to relate how we did it, but it was easy enough; I had had all day to think about it, having seen the stone and the hillside, and I had had the engines in my mind since Brittany. Wherever we could we took it by water—downriver from Killare to the sea, and thence to Wales and still as far as possible by river, using the two great Avons, with little more than a score of dry miles to cross between them. I was not Fionn of the Strong Arm, but I was Merlin, and the great stone travelled home as smoothly as a barge on an untroubled water, with me beside it all the way. I suppose I must have slept on that journey, but I cannot remember doing so. I went wakeful, as one is at a death-bed, and on that one voyage of all those in my life, I never felt the movement of the sea, but sat (they tell me) calm and silent, as if in my chair at home. Uther came once to speak to me—angry, I suppose, that I had done so easily what his own engineers could not do—but he went away after a moment, and did not approach me again. I remember nothing about it. I suppose I was not there. I was watching still between day and night in the great bedchamber at Winchester.

The news met us at Caerleon. Pascentius had attacked out of the north with his force of German and Saxon allies, and the King had marched to Carlisle and defeated him there. But afterwards, safely back at Winchester, he had fallen ill. About this, rumours were rife. Some said that one of Pascentius' men had come in disguise to Winchester where Ambrosius lay abed of a chill, and had given him poison to drink. Some said the man had come from Eosa. But the truth was the same; the King was very sick at Winchester.

The king-star rose again that night, looking, men said, like a fiery dragon, and trailing a cloud of lesser stars like smoke. But it did not need the omen to tell me what I had known since that night on the crest of Killare, when I had vowed to carry the great stone from Ireland, and lay it upon his grave.

So it was that we brought the stone again to Amesbury, and I raised the fallen circles of the Giants' Dance into their places for his monument. And at the next Easter-time, in the city of London, Uther Pendragon was crowned King.

BOOK V

THE COMING

OF

THE BEAR

1

Men said afterwards that the great dragon star which blazed at Ambrosius' death, and from which Uther took the royal name of Pendragon, was a baleful herald for the new reign. And indeed, at the start, everything seemed to be against Uther. It was as if the falling of Ambrosius' star was the signal for his old enemies to rise again and crowd in from the darkened edges of the land to destroy his successor. Octa, Hengist's son, and Eosa his kinsman, counting themselves freed by Ambrosius' death from their promise to stay north of his borders, called together what force they could still muster for attack, and as soon as the call went out, every disaffected element rose to it. Warriors greedy for land and plunder crowded over afresh from Germany, the remnants of Pascentius' Saxons joined with Gilloman's fleeing Irish, and with whatever British thought themselves passed over by the new King. Within a few weeks of Ambrosius' death Octa, with a large army, was scouring the north like a wolf, and before the new King could come up with him had destroyed cities and fortresses clear down from the Wall of Hadrian to York. At York, Ambrosius' strong city, he found the walls in good repair, the gates shut, and men ready to defend themselves. He dragged up what siege engines he had, and settled down to wait.

He must have known that Uther would catch up with him there, but his numbers were such that he showed no fear of the British. Afterwards they reckoned he had thirty thousand men. Be that as it may, when Uther came up to raise the siege with every man he could muster, the Saxons outnumbered the British by more than two to one. It was a bloody engagement, and a disastrous one. I think myself that Ambrosius' death had shaken the kingdom; for all Uther's brilliant reputation as a soldier, he was untried as supreme commander, and it was already known that he had not his brother's calmness and judgment in the face of odds. What he lacked in wisdom, he made up in bravery, but even that would not defeat the odds that came against him that day at

York. The British broke and ran, and were saved only by the coming of dusk, which at that time of year fell early. Uther—with Gorlois of Cornwall, his second in command—managed to rally his remaining force near the top of the small hill called Damen. This was steep, and offered cover of a kind, cliffs and caves and thick hazel-woods, but this could only be a temporary refuge from the Saxon host which triumphantly circled the base of the hill, waiting for morning. It was a desperate position for the British, and called for desperate measures. Uther, grimly encamped in a cave, called his weary captains together while the men snatched what rest they could, and with them thrashed out a plan for outwitting the huge host waiting for them at the foot of the hill. At first nobody had much idea beyond the need to escape, but someone—I heard later that it was Gorlois—pointed out that to retreat further was merely to postpone defeat and the destruction of the new kingdom: if escape was possible, then so was attack, and this seemed feasible if the British did not wait until daylight, but used what element of surprise there was in attacking downhill out of the dark and long before the enemy expected it. Simple tactics, indeed, that the Saxons might have expected from men so desperately trapped, but Saxons are stupid fighters, and as I have said before, lacking in discipline. It was almost certain that they would expect no move till dawn, and that they slept soundly where they had lain down that night, confident of victory, and with any luck three parts drunken on the stores they had taken.

To do the Saxons justice, Octa had posted scouts, and these were wide enough awake. But Gorlois' plan worked, helped by a little mist which crept before dawn up from the low ground and surrounded the base of the hill like a veil. Through this, twice as large as life, and in numbers altogether deceiving, the British came in a silent, stabbing rush at the first moment when there was light enough to see one's way across the rocks. Those Saxon outposts who were not cut down in silence, gave the alarm, but too late. Warriors rolled over, cursing, snatching their weapons up from where they lay beside them, but the British, silent no longer, swept yelling across the half-sleeping host, and cut it to pieces. It was finished before noon, and Octa and Eosa taken prisoner. Before winter, with the north swept clear of Saxons, and the burned longboats smoking quietly on the northern beaches, Uther was back in London with his prisoners behind bars, making ready for his coronation the following spring.

His battle with the Saxons, his near defeat and subsequent sharp, brilliant victory, was all that the reign needed. Men forgot the bale of Ambrosius' death, and talked of the new King like a sun rising. His name was on everyone's lips, from the nobles and warriors who crowded round him for gifts and honours, to the workmen building his palaces, and the ladies of his court flaunting new dresses like a field of poppies in a colour called Pendragon Red.

I saw him only once during these first weeks. I was at Amesbury still, superintending the work of raising the Giants' Dance. Tremorinus was in the north, but I had a good team, and after their experience with the king-stone at Killare, the men were eager to tackle the massive stones of the Dance. For the raising of the uprights, once we had aligned the stones, dug the pits and sunk the guides, there was nothing that could not be done with rope and shear-legs and plumb-line. It was with the great lintels that the difficulty lay, but the miracle of the building of the Dance had been done countless years before, by the old craftsmen who had shaped those gigantic stones to fit as surely one into the other as wood dovetailed by a master carpenter. We had only to find means to lift them. It was this which had exercised me all those years, since I first saw the capped stones in Less Britain, and began my calculations. Nor had I forgotten what I had learned from the songs. In the end I had designed a wooden crib of a kind which a modern engineer might have dismissed as primitive, but which—as the singer had been my witness—had done the task before, and would again. It was a slow business, but it worked. And I suppose it was a marvellous enough sight to see those vast blocks rising, stage by stage, and settling finally into their beds as smoothly as if they had been made of tallow. It took two hundred men to each stone as it was moved, drilled teams who worked by numbers and who kept up their rhythms, as rowers do, by music. The rhythms of the movement were of course laid down by the work, and the tunes were old tunes that I remembered from my childhood; my nurse had sung them to me, but she never sang the words that the men sometimes set to them. These tended to be lively, indecent, and intensely personal, and mostly concerning those in high places. Neither Uther nor I was spared, though the songs were never sung deliberately in my hearing. Moreover, when outsiders were present, the words were either correct or indistinguishable. I heard it said, long afterwards, that I moved the stones of the

Dance with magic and with music. I suppose you might say that both are true. I have thought, since, that this must have been how the story started that Phoebus Apollo built with music the walls of Troy. But the magic and the music that moved the Giants' Dance, I shared with the blind singer of Kerrec.

Towards the middle of November the frosts were sharp, and the work was finished. The last camp fire was put out, and the last wagon-train of men and materials rolled away south back to Sarum. Cadal had gone ahead of me into Amesbury. I lingered, holding my fidgeting horse, until the wagons had rolled out of sight over the edge of the plain and I was alone.

The sky hung over the silent plain like a pewter bowl. It was still early in the day, and the grass was white with frost. The thin winter sun painted long shadows from the linked stones. I remembered the standing stone, and the white frost, the bull and the blood and the smiling young god with the fair hair. I looked down at the stone. They had buried him, I knew, with his sword in his hand. I said to him: "We shall come back, both of us, at the winter solstice." Then I left him and mounted my horse, and rode towards Amesbury.

2

News came of Uther in December; he had left London and ridden to Winchester for Christmas. I sent a message, got no reply, and rode out once more with Cadal to where the Giants' Dance stood frostbound and lonely in the center of the plain. It was the twentieth of December.

In a fold of the ground just beyond the Dance we tethered our horses and lit a fire. I had been afraid that the night might be cloudy, but it was crisp and clear, with the stars out in their swarms, like motes in moonlight.

"Get some sleep, if you can in this cold," said Cadal. "I'll wake you before dawn. What makes you think he'll come?" Then, when I made no reply: "Well, you're the magician, you should know. Here, just in case your magic won't put you to sleep, you'd better put the extra cloak on. I'll wake you in time, so don't fret yourself."

I obeyed him, rolling myself in the double thickness of wool, and lying near the fire with my head on my saddle. I dozed rather than slept, conscious of the small noises of the night surrounded by the immense stillness of that plain; the rustle and crack of the fire, the sound of Cadal putting new wood on it, the steady tearing sound of the horses grazing at hand, the cry of a hunting owl in the air. And then, not long before dawn, the sound I had been expecting; the steady beat of the earth beneath my head which meant the approach of horses.

I sat up. Cadal, blear-eyed, spoke morosely. "You've an hour yet, I reckon."

"Never mind. I've slept. Put your ear to the ground, and tell me what you hear."

He leaned down, listened for perhaps five heartbeats, then was on his feet and making for our horses. Men reacted quickly in those days to the sound of horsemen in the night.

I checked him. "It's all right. Uther. How many horses do you reckon?"

"Twenty, perhaps thirty. Are you sure?"

"Quite sure. Now get the horses saddled and stay with them. I'm going in."

It was the hour between night and morning when the air is still. They were coming at a gallop. It seemed that the whole of the frozen plain beat with the sound. The moon had gone. I waited beside the stone.

He left the troop some little way off, and rode forward with only one companion. I did not think they had yet seen me, though they must have seen the flicker of Cadal's dying fire in the hollow. The night had been bright enough with starlight, so they had been riding without torches, and their night sight was good; the two of them came on at a fast canter straight for the outer circle of the Dance, and at first I thought they would ride straight in. But the horses pulled up short with a crunch and slither of frost, and the King swung from the saddle. I heard the jingle as he threw the reins to his companion. "Keep him moving," I heard him say, and then he approached, a swift striding shadow through the enormous shadows of the Dance.

"Merlin?"

"My lord?"

"You choose your times strangely. Did it have to be the middle of the night?" He sounded wide awake and no more gracious than usual. But he had come.

I said: "You wanted to see what I have done here, and

tonight is the night when I can show you. I am grateful that
you came."

"Show me what? A vision? Is this another of your dreams?
I warn you—"

"No. There's nothing of that here, not now. But there is
something I wanted you to see which can only be seen
tonight. For that, I'm afraid we shall have to wait a little
while."

"Long? It's cold."

"Not so long, my lord. Till dawn."

He was standing the other side of the king-stone from me,
and in the faint starlight I saw him looking down at it, with
his head bent and a hand stroking his chin. "The first time
you stood beside this stone in the night, men say you saw
visions. Now they tell me in Winchester that as he lay dying
he spoke to you as if you were there in his bedchamber,
standing at the foot of the bed. Is this true?"

"Yes."

His head came up sharply. "You say you knew on Killare
that my brother was dying, yet you said nothing to me?"

"It would have served no purpose. You could not have
returned any sooner for knowing that he lay sick. As it was,
you journeyed with a quiet mind, and at Caerleon, when he
died, I told you."

"By the gods, Merlin, it was not for you to judge whether
to speak or not! You are not King. You should have told
me."

"You were not King either, Uther Pendragon. I did as he
bade me."

I saw him make a quick movement, then he stilled himself.
"That is easy to say." But from his voice I knew that he
believed me, and was in awe of me and of the place. "And
now that we are here, and waiting for the dawn, and whatever it is you have to show me, I think one or two things must
be made clear between us. You cannot serve me as you
served my brother. You must know that. I want none of your
prophecies. My brother was wrong when he said that we
would work together for Britain. Our stars will not conjoin. I
admit I judged you too harshly, there in Brittany and at
Killare; for that I am sorry, but now it is too late. We walk
different ways."

"Yes. I know."

I said it without any particular expression, simply agreeing,
and was surprised when he laughed, softly, to himself. A

hand, not unfriendly, dropped on my shoulder. "Then we understand one another. I had not thought it would be so easy. If you knew how refreshing that is after the weeks I've had of men suing for help, men crawling for mercy, men begging for favours ... And now the only man in the kingdom with any real claim on me will go his own way, and let me go mine?"

"Of course. Our paths will still cross, but not yet. And then we will deal together, whether we will or no."

"We shall see. You have power, I admit it, but what use is that to me? I don't need priests." His voice was brisk and friendly, as if he were willing away the strangeness of the night. He was rooted to earth, was Uther. Ambrosius would have understood what I was saying, but Uther was back on the human trail like a dog after blood. "It seems you have served me well enough already, at Killare, and here with the Hanging Stones. You deserve something of me, if only for this."

"Where I can be, I shall be at your service. If you want me, you know where to find me."

"Not at my court?"

"No, at Maridunum. It's my home."

"Ah, yes, the famous cave. You deserve a little more of me than that, I think."

"There is nothing that I want," I said.

There was a little more light now. I saw him slant a look at me. "I have spoken to you tonight as I have spoken to no man before. Do you hold the past against me, Merlin the bastard?"

"I hold nothing against you, my lord."

"Nothing?"

"A girl in Caerleon. You could call her nothing."

I saw him stare, then smile. "Which time?"

"It doesn't matter. You'll have forgotten, anyway."

"By the dog, I misjudged you." He spoke with the nearest to warmth I had yet heard from him. If he knew, I thought, he would have laughed.

I said: "I tell you, it doesn't matter. It didn't then, and less than that now."

"You still haven't told me why you dragged me here at this time. Look at the sky; it's getting on for dawn—and not a moment too soon, the horses will be getting cold." He raised his head towards the east. "It should be a fine day. It will be interesting to see what sort of job you've made of this. I can tell you now, Tremorinus was insisting, right up to the time I got your message, that it couldn't be done. Prophet or no prophet, you have your uses, Merlin."

The light was growing, the dark slackening to let it through. I could see him more clearly now, standing with head up, his hand once more stroking his chin. I said: "It's as well you came by night, so that I knew your voice. I shouldn't have known you in daylight. You've grown a full beard."

"More kingly, eh? There was no time to do anything else on campaign. By the time we got to the Humber ..." He started to tell me about it, talking, for the first time since I had known him, quite easily and naturally. It may have been that now I was, of all his subjects, the only one kin to him, and blood speaks to blood, they say. He talked about the campaign in the north, the fighting, the smoking destruction the Saxons had left behind them. "And now we spend Christmas at Winchester. I shall be crowned in London in the spring, and already—"

"Wait." I had not meant to interrupt him quite so peremptorily, but things were pressing on me, the weight of the sky, the shooting light. There was no time to search for the words that one could use to a king. I said quickly: "It's coming now. Stand with me at the foot of the stone."

I moved a pace from him and stood at the foot of the long king-stone, facing the bursting east. I had no eyes for Uther. I heard him draw breath as if in anger, then he checked himself and turned with a glitter of jewels and flash of mail to stand beside me. At our feet stretched the stone.

In the east night slackened, drew back like a veil, and the sun came up. Straight as a thrown torch, or an arrow of fire, light pierced through the grey air and laid a line clear from the horizon to the king-stone at our feet. For perhaps twenty heartbeats the huge sentinel trilithon before us stood black and stark, framing the winter blaze. Then the sun lifted over the horizon so quickly that you could see the shadow of the linked circle move into its long ellipse, to blur and fade almost immediately into the wide light of a winter's dawn.

I glanced at the King. His eyes, wide and blank, were on the stone at his feet. I could not read his thoughts. Then he lifted his head and looked away from me at the outer circle where the great stones stood locked across the light. He took a slow pace away from me and turned on his heel, taking in the full circle of the Hanging Stones. I saw that the new beard was reddish and curled; he wore his hair longer, and a gold circle flashed on his helm. His eyes were blue as wood-smoke in the fresh light.

They met mine at last. "No wonder you smile. It's very impressive."

"That's with relief," I said. "The mathematics of this have kept me awake for weeks."

"Tremorinus told me." He gave me a slow, measuring look. "He also told me what you had said."

"What I had said?"

"Yes. 'I will deck his grave with nothing less than the light itself.'"

I said nothing.

He said slowly: "I told you I knew nothing of prophets or priests. I am only a soldier, and I think like a soldier. But this—what you have done here—this is something I understand. Perhaps there is room for us both, after all. I told you I spend Christmas at Winchester. Will you ride back with me?"

He had asked me, not commanded me. We were speaking across the stone. It was the beginning of something, but something I had not yet been shown. I shook my head. "In the spring, perhaps. I should like to see the crowning. Be sure that when you need me I shall be there. But now I must go home."

"To your hole in the ground? Well, if it's what you want ... Your wants are few enough, God knows. Is there nothing you would ask of me?" He gestured with his hand to the silent circle. "Men will speak poorly of a King who does not reward you for this."

"I have been rewarded."

"At Maridunum, now. Your grandfather's house would be more suitable for you. Will you take it?"

I shook my head. "I don't want a house. But I would take the hill."

"Then take it. They tell me men call it Merlin's Hill already. And now it's full daylight, and the horses will be cold. If you had ever been a soldier, Merlin, you would know that there is one thing more important even than the graves of kings: not to keep the horses standing."

He clapped me on the shoulder again, turned with a swirl of the scarlet cloak, and strode to his waiting horse. I went to find Cadal.

3

When Easter came I still had no mind to leave Bryn Myrddin (Uther, true to his word, had given me the hill where the cave stood, and people already associated its name with me, rather than with the god, calling it Merlin's Hill) but a message came from the King, bidding me to London. This time it was a command, not a request, and so urgent that the King had sent an escort, to avoid any delay I might have incurred in waiting for company.

It was still not safe in those days to ride abroad in parties smaller than a dozen or more, and one rode armed and warily. Men who could not afford their own escort waited until a party was gathered, and merchants even joined together to pay guards to ride with them. The wilder parts of the land were still full of refugees from Octa's army, with Irishmen who had been unable to get a passage home, and a few stray Saxons trying miserably to disguise their fair skins, and unmercifully hunted down when they failed. These haunted the edges of the farms, skulking in the hills and moors and wild places, making sudden savage forays in search of food, and watching the roads for any solitary or ill-armed traveller, however shabby. Anyone with cloak or sandals was a rich man and worth despoiling.

None of this would have deterred me from riding alone with Cadal from Maridunum to London. No outlaw or thief would have faced a look from me, let alone risked a curse. Since events at Dinas Brenin, Killare, and Amesbury my fame had spread, growing in song and story until I hardly recognized my own deeds. Dinas Brenin had also been renamed; it had become Dinas Emrys, in compliment to me as much as to commemorate Ambrosius' landing, and the strong-point he had successfully built there. I lived, too, as well as I ever had in my grandfather's palace or in Ambrosius' house. Offerings of food and wine were left daily below the cave, and the poor who had nothing else to bring me in return for the medicines I gave them, brought fuel, or straw for the horses' bedding, or their labour for building jobs or making simple furniture. So winter had passed in comfort and peace, until on a sharp day in early March Uther's messenger, having left the escort in the town, came riding up the valley.

It was the first dry day after more than two weeks of rain and sleety wind, and I had gone up over the hill above the cave to look for the first growing plants and simples. I paused at the edge of a clump of pines to watch the solitary horseman cantering up the hill. Cadal must have heard the hoofbeats; I saw him, small below me, come out of the cave and greet the man, then I saw his pointing arm indicating which way I had gone. The messenger hardly paused. He turned his beast uphill, struck his spurs in, and came after me.

He pulled up a few paces away, swung stiffly out of the saddle, made the sign, and approached me.

He was a brown-haired young man of about my own age, whose face was vaguely familiar. I thought I must have seen him around Uther's train somewhere. He was splashed with mud to the eyebrows, and where he was not muddy his face was white with fatigue. He must have got a new horse in Maridunum for the last stage, for the animal was fresh, and restive with it, and I saw the young man wince as it threw its head up and dragged at the reins.

"My lord Merlin. I bring you greetings from the King, in London."

"I am honoured," I said formally.

"He requests your presence at the feast of his coronation. He has sent you an escort, my lord. They are in the town, resting their horses."

"Did you say 'requests'?"

"I should have said 'commands', my lord. He told me I must bring you back immediately."

"This was all the message?"

"He told me nothing more, my lord. Only that you must attend him immediately in London."

"Then of course I shall come. Tomorrow morning, when you have rested the horses?"

"Today, my lord. Now."

It was a pity that Uther's arrogant command was delivered in a slightly apologetic way. I regarded him. "You have come straight to me?"

"Yes, my lord."

"Without resting?"

"Yes."

"How long has it taken you?"

"Four days, my lord. This is a fresh horse. I am ready to

go back today." Here the animal jerked its head again, and I saw him wince.

"Are you hurt?"

"Nothing to speak of. I took a fall yesterday and hurt my wrist. It's my right wrist, not my bridle hand."

"No, only your dagger hand. Go down to the cave and tell my servant what you have told me, and say he is to give you food and drink. When I come down I shall see to your wrist."

He hesitated. "My lord, the King was urgent. This is more than an invitation to watch the crowning."

"You will have to wait while my servant packs my things and saddles our horses. Also while I myself eat and drink. I can bind up your wrist in a few minutes. And while I am doing it you can give me the news from London, and tell me why the King commands me so urgently to the feast. Go down now; I shall come in a short while."

"But, sir—"

I said: "By the time Cadal has prepared the food for the three of us I shall be with you. You cannot hurry me more than that. Now go."

He threw me a doubtful look, then went, slithering on foot down the wet hill-side and dragging the jibbing horse after him. I gathered my cloak round me against the wind, and walked past the end of the pine wood and out of sight of the cave.

I stood at the end of a rocky spur where the winds came freely down the valley and tore at my cloak. Behind me the pines roared, and under the noise the bare blackthorns by Galapas' grave rattled in the wind. An early plover screamed in the grey air. I lifted my face to the sky and thought of Uther and London, and the command that had just come. But nothing was there except the sky and the pines and the wind in the blackthorns. I looked the other way, down towards Maridunum.

From this height I could see the whole town, tiny as a toy in the distance. The valley was sullen green in the March wind. The river curled, grey under the grey sky. A wagon was crossing the bridge. There was a point of colour where a standard flew over the fortress. A boat scudded down-river, its brown sails full of the wind. The hills, still in their winter purple, held the valley cupped as one might hold in one's palms a globe of glass . . .

The wind whipped water to my eyes, and the scene

blurred. The crystal globe was cold in my hands. I gazed down into it. Small and perfect in the heart of the crystal lay the town with its bridge and moving river and the tiny, scudding ship. Round it the fields curved up and over, distorting the curved crystal till fields, sky, river, clouds held the town with its scurrying people as leaves and sepals hold a bud before it breaks to flower. It seemed that the whole country-side, the whole of Wales, the whole of Britain could be held small and shining and safe between my hands, like something set in amber. I stared down at the land globed in crystal, and knew that this was what I had been born for. The time was here, and I must take it on trust.

The crystal globe melted out of my cupped hands, and was only a fistful of plants I had gathered, cold with rain. I let them fall, and put up the back of a hand to wipe the water from my eyes. The scene below me had changed; the wagon and the boat had gone; the town was still.

I went down to the cave to find Cadal busy with his cooking pots, and the young man already struggling with the saddles of our horses.

"Let that alone," I told him. "Cadal, is there hot water?"

"Plenty. Here's a start and a half, orders from the King. London, is it?" Cadal sounded pleased, and I didn't blame him. "We were due for a change, if you ask me. What is it, do you suppose? He"—jerking his head at the young man—"doesn't seem to know, or else he's not telling. Trouble, by the sound of it."

"Maybe. We'll soon find out. Here, you'd better dry this." I gave him my cloak, sat down by the fire, and called the young man to me. "Let me see that arm of yours now."

His wrist was blue with bruising, and swollen, and obvious-ly hurt to the touch, but the bones were whole. While he washed I made a compress, then bound it on. He watched me half apprehensively, and tended to shy from my touch, and not only, I thought, with pain. Now that the mud was washed off and I could see him better, the feeling of familiarity persisted even more strongly. I eyed him over the bandages. "I know you, don't I?"

"You wouldn't remember me, my lord. But I remember you. You were kind to me once."

I laughed. "Was it such a rare occasion? What's your name?"

"Ulfin."

"Ulfin? It has a familiar sound . . . Wait a moment. Yes, I

have it. Belasius' boy?"

"Yes. You do remember me?"

"Perfectly. That night in the forest, when my pony went lame, and you had to lead him home. I suppose you were around underfoot most of the time, but you were about as conspicuous as a field mouse. That's the only time I remember. Is Belasius over here for the coronation?"

"He's dead."

Something in his tone made me cock an eye at him over the bandaged wrist. "You hated him as much as that? No, don't answer, I guessed as much back there, young as I was. Well, I shan't ask why. The gods know I didn't love him myself, and I wasn't his slave. What happened to him?"

"He died of a fever, my lord."

"And you managed to survive him? I seem to remember something about an old and barbarous custom—"

"Prince Uther took me into his service. I am with him now—the King."

He spoke quickly, looking away. I knew it was all I would ever learn. "And are you still so afraid of the world, Ulfin?"

But he would not answer that. I finished tying the wrist. "Well, it's a wild and violent place, and the times are cruel. But they will get better, and I think you will help to make them so. There, that's done. Now get yourself something to eat. Cadal, do you remember Ulfin? The boy who brought Aster home the night we ran into Uther's troops by Nemet?"

"By the dog, so it is." Cadal looked him up and down. "You look a sight better than you did then. What happened to the druid? Died of a curse? Come along then, and get something to eat. Yours is here, Merlin, and see you eat enough for a human being for a change, and not just what might keep one of your precious birds alive."

"I'll try," I said meekly, and then laughed at the expression on Ulfin's face as he looked from me to my servant and back again.

We lay that night at an inn near the crossroads where the way leads off north for the Five Hills and the gold mine. I ate alone in my room, served by Cadal. No sooner had the door shut behind the servant who carried the dishes than Cadal turned to me, obviously bursting with news.

"Well, there's a pretty carry-on in London, by all accounts."

"One might expect it," I said mildly. "I heard someone say

Budec was there, together with most of the kings from across
the Narrow Sea, and that most of them, and half the King's
own nobles, have brought their daughters along with an eye
to the empty side of the throne." I laughed. "That should suit
Uther."

"They say he's been through half the girls in London
already," and Cadal, setting a dish down in front of me. It
was Welsh mutton, with a good sauce made of onions, hot
and savoury.

"They'd say anything of him." I began to help myself. "It
could even be true."

"Yes, but seriously, there's trouble afoot, they say. Woman
trouble."

"Oh, God, Cadal, spare me. Uther was born to woman
trouble."

"No, but I mean it. Some of the escort were talking, and
it's no wonder Ulfin wouldn't. This is real trouble. Gorlois'
wife."

I looked up, startled. "The Duchess of Cornwall? This
can't be true."

"It's not true yet. But they say it's not for want of trying."

I drank wine. "You can be sure it's only rumour. She's
more than half as young again as her husband, and I've
heard she's fair. I suppose Uther pays her some attention, the
Duke being his second in command, and men make all they
can of it, Uther being who he is. And what he is."

Cadal leaned his fists on the table and looked down at me.
He was uncommonly solemn. "Attention, is it? They say he's
never out of her lap. Sends her the best dishes at table each
day, sees she's served first, even before he is, pledges her in
front of everybody in the hall every time he raises his goblet.
Nobody's talking of anything else from London to Winchester. I'm told they're laying bets in the kitchen."

"I've no doubt. And does Gorlois have anything to say?"

"Tried to pass it over at first, they say, but it got so that he
couldn't go on pretending he hadn't noticed. He tried to look
as if he thought Uther was just doing the pair of them
honour, but when it came to sitting the Lady Ygraine—that's
her name—on Uther's right, and the old man six down on
the other side—" He paused.

I said, uneasily: "He must be crazed. He can't afford
trouble yet—trouble of any kind, let alone this, and with
Gorlois of all people. By all the gods, Cadal, it was Cornwall
that helped Ambrosius into the country at all, and Cornwall

who put Uther where he is now. Who won the battle of Damen Hill for him?"

"Men are saying that, too."

"Are they indeed?" I thought for a moment, frowning. "And the woman? What—apart from the usual dunghill stuff—do they say about her?"

"That she says little, and says less each day. I've no doubt Gorlois has plenty to say to her at night when they're alone together. Anyway, I'm told she hardly lifts her eyes in public now, in case she meets the King staring at her over his cup, or leaning across at table to look down her dress."

"That is what I call dunghill stuff, Cadal. I meant, what is she like?"

"Well, that's just what they don't say, except that she's silent, and as beautiful as this, that and the other thing." He straightened. "Oh, no one says she gives him any help. And God knows there's no need for Uther to act like a starving man in sight of a dish of food; he could have his platter piled high any night he liked. There's hardly a girl in London who isn't trying to catch that eye of his."

"I believe you. Has he quarrelled with Gorlois? Openly, I mean?"

"Not so that I heard. In fact, he's been over-cordial there, and he got away with it for the first week or so; the old man was flattered. But Merlin, it does sound like trouble; she's less than half Gorlois' age and spends her life mewed up in one of those cold Cornish castles with nothing to do but weave his war-cloaks and dream over them, and you may be sure it's not of an old man with a grey beard."

I pushed the platter aside. I remember I still felt wholly unconcerned about what Uther was doing. But Cadal's last remark came a little too near home for comfort. There had been another girl, once, who had had nothing to do but sit at home and weave and dream . . .

I said abruptly: "All right, Cadal. I'm glad to know. I just hope we can keep clear of it ourselves. I've seen Uther mad for a woman before, but they've always been women he could get. This is suicide."

"Crazed, you said. That's what men are saying, too," said Cadal slowly. "Bewitched, they call it." He looked down at me half-sideways. "Maybe that's why he sent young Ulfin in such a sweat to make sure you'd come to London. Maybe he wants you there, to break the spell?"

"I don't break," I said shortly. "I make."

He stared for a moment, shutting his mouth on what, apparently, he had been about to say. Then he turned away to lift the jug of wine. As he poured it for me, in silence, I saw that his left hand was making the sign. We spoke no more that night.

4

As soon as I came in front of Uther I saw that Cadal had been right. Here was real trouble.

We reached London the very eve of the crowning. It was late, and the city gates were shut, but it seemed there had been orders about us, for we were hustled through without question, and taken straight up to the castle where the King lay. I was scarcely given time to get out of my mud-stained garments before I was led along to his bedchamber and ushered in. The servants withdrew immediately and left us alone.

Uther was ready for the night, in a long bedgown of dark brown velvet edged with fur. His high chair was drawn to a leaping fire of logs, and on a stool beside the chair stood a pair of goblets and a lidded silver flagon with steam curling gently from the spout. I could smell the spiced wine as soon as I entered the room, and my dry throat contracted longingly, but the King made no move to offer it to me. He was not sitting by the fire. He was prowling restlessly up and down the room like a caged beast, and after him, pace for pace, his wolfhound followed him.

As the door shut behind the servants he said abruptly, as he had said once before:

"You took your time."

"Four days? You should have sent better horses."

That stopped him in his tracks. He had not expected to be answered. But he said, mildly enough: "They were the best in my stables."

"Then you should get winged ones if you want better speed than we made, my lord. And tougher men. We left two of them by the way."

But he was no longer listening. Back in his thoughts, he resumed his restless pacing, and I watched him. He had lost weight, and moved quickly and lightly, like a starving wolf. His eyes were sunken with lack of sleep, and he had mannerisms I had not seen in him before; he could not keep his hands still. He wrung them together behind him, cracking the finger-joints, or fidgeted with the edges of his robe, or with his beard.

He flung at me over his shoulder: "I want your help."

"So I understand."

He turned at that. "You know about it?"

I lifted my shoulders. "Nobody talks of anything else but the King's desire for Gorlois' wife. I understand you have made no attempt to hide it. But it is more than a week now since you sent Ulfin to fetch me. In that time, what has happened? Are Gorlois and his wife still here?"

"Of course they are still here. They cannot go without my leave."

"I see. Has anything yet been said between you and Gorlois?"

"No."

"But he must know."

"It is the same with him as with me. If once this thing comes to words, nothing can stop it. And it is the crowning tomorrow. I cannot speak with him."

"Or with her?"

"No. No. Ah, God, Merlin, I cannot come near her. She is guarded like Danaë."

I frowned. "He has her guarded, then? Surely that's unusual enough to be a public admission that there's something wrong?"

"I only mean that his servants are all around her, and his men. Not only his bodyguard—many of his fighting troops are still here, that were with us in the north. I can only come near her in public, Merlin. They will have told you this."

"Yes. Have you managed to get any message to her privately?"

"No. She guards herself. All day she is with her women, and her servants keep the doors. And he—" He paused. There was sweat on his face. "He is with her every night."

He flung away again with a swish of the velvet robe, and paced, soft-footed, the length of the room, into the shadows beyond the firelight. Then he turned. He threw out his hands and spoke simply, like a boy.

"Merlin, what shall I do?"

I crossed to the fire-place, picked up the jug and poured two goblets of the spiced wine. I held one out to him. "To begin with, come and sit down. I cannot talk to a whirlwind. Here."

He obeyed, sinking back in the big chair with a goblet between his hands. I drank my own, gratefully, and sat down on the other side of the hearth.

Uther did not drink. I think he hardly knew what he had between his hands. He stared at the fire through the thinning steam from the goblet. "As soon as he brought her in and presented her to me, I knew. God knows that at first I thought it was no more than another passing fever, the kind I've had a thousand times before, only this time a thousand times stronger—"

"And been cured of," I said, "in a night, a week of nights, a month. I don't know the longest time a woman has ever held you, Uther, but is a month, or even three, enough to wreck a kingdom for?"

The look he gave me, blue as a sword-flash, was a look from the old Uther I remembered. "By Hades, why do you think I sent for you? I could have wrecked my kingdom any time in these past weeks had I been so minded. Why do you think it has not yet gone beyond folly? Oh, yes, I admit there has been folly, but I tell you this is a fever, and not the kind I have had before, and slaked before. This burns me so that I cannot sleep. How can I rule and fight and deal with men if I cannot sleep?"

"Have you taken a girl to bed?"

He stared, then he drank. "Are you mad?"

"Forgive me, it was a stupid question. You don't sleep even then?"

"No." He set down the goblet beside him, and knitted his hands together. "It's no use. Nothing is any use. You must bring her to me, Merlin. You have the arts. This is why I sent for you. You are to bring her to me so that no one knows. Make her love me. Bring her here to me, while he is asleep. You can do it."

"Make her love you? By magic? No, Uther, this is something that magic cannot do. You must know that."

"It is something that every old wife swears she can do. And you—you have power beyond any man living. You lifted the Hanging Stones. You lifted the king-stone where Tremorinus could not."

"My mathematics are better, that is all. For God's sake, Uther, whatever men say of that, you know how it was done. That was no magic."

"You spoke with my brother as he died. Are you going to deny that now?"

"No."

"Or that you swore to serve me when I needed you?"

"No."

"I need you now. Your power, whatever it is. Dare you tell me that you are not a magician?"

"I am not the kind that can walk through walls," I said, "and bring bodies through locked doors." He made a sudden movement, and I saw the feverish brightness of his eyes, not this time with anger, but I thought with pain. I added: "But I have not refused to help you."

The eyes sparked. "You will help me?"

"Yes, I will help you. I told you when last we met that there would come a time when we must deal together. This is the time. I don't know yet what I must do, but this will be shown to me, and the outcome is with the god. But one thing I can do for you, tonight. I can make you sleep. No, be still and listen . . . If you are to be crowned tomorrow, and take Britain into your hands, tonight you will do as I say. I will make you a drink that will let you sleep, and you'll take a girl to your bed as usual. It may be better if there is someone besides your servant who will swear you were in your own chamber."

"Why? What are you going to do?" His voice was strained.

"I shall try to talk with Ygraine."

He sat forward, his hands tight on the arms of the chair. "Yes. Talk to her. Perhaps you can come to her where I cannot. Tell her—"

"A moment. A little while back you told me to 'make her love you.' You want me to invoke any power there is to bring her to you. If you have never spoken to her of your love, or seen her except in public, how do you know she would come to you, even if the way were free? Is her mind clear to you, my lord King?"

"No. She says nothing. She smiles, with her eyes on the ground, and says nothing. But I know. I know. It is as if all the other times I played at love were only single notes. Put together, they make the song. She is the song."

There was a silence. Behind him, on a dais in the corner of the room, was the bed, with the covers drawn back ready. Above it, leaping up the wall, was a great dragon fashioned of red gold. In the firelight it moved, stretching its claws.

He said suddenly: "When we last talked, there in the

middle of the Hanging Stones, you said you wanted nothing from me. But by all the gods, Merlin, if you help me now, if I get her, and in safety, then you can ask what you will. I swear it."

I shook my head, and he said no more. I think he saw that I was no longer thinking of him; that other forces pressed me, crowding the firelit room. The dragon flamed and shimmered up the dark wall. In its shadow another moved, merging with it, flame into flame. Something struck at my eyes, pain like a claw. I shut them, and there was silence. When I opened them again the fire had died, and the wall was dark. I looked across at the King, motionless in his chair, watching me. I said, slowly: "I will ask you one thing, now."

"Yes?"

"That when I bring you to her in safety, you shall make a child."

Whatever he had expected, it was not this. He stared, then, suddenly, laughed. "That's with the gods, surely?"

"Yes, it is with God."

He stretched back in his chair, as if a weight had been lifted off his shoulders. "If I come to her, Merlin, I promise you that whatever I have power to do, I shall do. And anything else you bid me. I shall even sleep tonight."

I stood up. "Then I shall go and make the draught and send it to you."

"And you'll see her?"

"I shall see her. Good night."

Ulfin was half asleep on his feet outside the door. He blinked at me as I came out.

"I'm to go in now?"

"In a minute. Come to my chamber first and I'll give you a drink for him. See he takes it. It's to give him sleep. Tomorrow will be a long day."

There was a girl asleep in a corner, wrapped in a blue blanket on a huddle of pillows. As we passed I saw the curve of a bare shoulder and a tumble of straight brown hair. She looked very young.

I raised my brows at Ulfin, and he nodded, then jerked his head towards the shut door with a look of enquiry.

"Yes," I said, "but later. When you take him the drink. Leave her sleeping now. You look as if you could do with some sleep yourself, Ulfin."

"If he sleeps tonight I might get some." He gave a flicker of a grin at me. "Make it strong, won't you, my lord? And see it tastes good."

"Oh, he'll drink it, never fear."

"I wasn't thinking of him," said Ulfin. "I was thinking of me."

"Of you? Ah, I see, you mean you'll have to taste it first?"

He nodded.

"You have to try everything? His meals? Even love potions?"

"Love potions? For him?" He stared, open-mouthed. Then he laughed. "Oh, you're joking!"

I smiled. "I wanted to see if you could laugh. Here we are. Wait now, I won't be a minute."

Cadal was waiting for me by the fire in my chamber. This was a comfortable room in the curve of a tower wall, and Cadal had kept a bright fire burning and a big cauldron of water steaming on the iron dogs. He had got out a woollen bedgown for me and laid it ready across the bed.

Over a chest near the window lay a pile of clothes, a shimmer of gold cloth and scarlet fur. "What's that?" I asked, as I sat down to let him draw off my shoes.

"The King sent a robe for tomorrow, my lord." Cadal, with an eye on the boy who was pouring the bath, was formal. I noticed the boy's hand shaking a little, and water splashed on the floor. As soon as he had finished, obedient to a jerk of Cadal's head, he scuttled out.

"What's the matter with that boy?"

"It isn't every night you prepare a bath for a wizard."

"For God's sake. What have you been telling him?"

"Only that you'd turn him into a bat if he didn't serve you well."

"Fool. No, a moment, Cadal. Bring me my box. Ulfin's waiting outside. I promised to make up a draught."

Cadal obeyed me. "What's the matter? His arm still bad?"

"It's not for him. For the King."

"Ah." He made no further comment, but when the thing was done and Ulfin had gone, and I was stripping for the bath, he asked: "It's as bad as they say?"

"Worse." I gave him a brief version of my conversation with the King.

He heard me out, frowning. "And what's to do now?"

"Find some way to see the lady. No, not the bedgown; not yet, alas. Get me a clean robe out—something dark."

"Surely you can't go to her tonight? It's well past mid-night."

"I shall not go anywhere. Whoever is coming, will come to me."

"But Gorlois will be with her—"

"No more now, Cadal. I want to think. Leave me. Good night."

When the door had shut on him I went across to the chair beside the fire. It was not true that I wanted time to think. All I needed was silence, and the fire. Bit by bit, slowly, I emptied my mind, feeling thought spill out of me like sand from a glass, to leave me hollow and light. I waited, my hands slack on the grey robe, open, empty. It was very quiet. Somewhere, from a dark corner of the room, came the dry tick of old wood settling in the night. The fire flickered. I watched it, but absently, as any man might watch the flames for comfort on a cold night. I did not need to dream. I lay, light as a dead leaf, on the flood that ran that night to meet the sea.

Outside the door there were sounds suddenly, voices. A quick tap at the panel, and Cadal came in, shutting the door behind him. He looked guarded and a little apprehensive.

"Gorlois?" I asked.

He swallowed, then nodded.

"Well, show him in."

"He asked if you had been to see the King. I said you'd been here barely a couple of hours, and you had had time to see nobody. Was that right?"

I smiled. "You were guided. Let him come in now."

Gorlois came in quickly, and I rose to greet him. There was, I thought, as big a change in him as I had seen in Uther; his big frame was bent, and for the first time one saw straight away that he was old.

He brushed aside the ceremony of my greeting. "You're not abed yet? They told me you'd ridden in."

"Barely in time for the crowning, but I shall see it after all. Will you sit, my lord?"

"Thanks, but no. I came for help, Merlin, for my wife." The quick eyes peered under the grey brows. "Aye, no one could ever tell what you were thinking, but you've heard, haven't you?"

"There was talk," I said carefully, "but then there always was talk about Uther. I have not heard anyone venture a word against your wife."

"By God, they'd better not! However, it's not that I've come about tonight. There's nothing you could do about that—though it's possible you're the only person who could talk some sense into the King. You'll not get near him now till after the crowning, but if you could get him to let us go back to Cornwall without waiting for the end of the feast ... Would you do that for me?"

"If I can."

"I knew I could count on you. With things the way they are in the town just now, it's hard to know who's a friend. Uther's not an easy man to gainsay. But you could do it—and what's more, you'd dare. You're your father's son, and for my old friend's sake—"

"I said I'd do it."

"What's the matter? Are you ill?"

"It's nothing. I'm weary. We had a hard ride. I'll see the King in the morning early, before he leaves for the crowning."

He gave a brief nod of thanks. "That's not the only thing I came to ask you. Would you come and see my wife tonight?"

There was a pause of utter stillness, so prolonged that I thought he must notice. Then I said: "If you wish it, yes. But why?"

"She's sick, that's why, and I'd have you come and see her, if you will. When her women told her you were here in London, she begged me to send for you. I can tell you, I was thankful when I heard you'd come. There's not many men I'd trust just now, and that's God's truth. But I'd trust you."

Beside me a log crumbled and fell into the heart of the fire. The flames shot up, splashing his face with red, like blood.

"You'll come?" asked the old man.

"Of course." I looked away from him. "I'll come immediately."

5

Uther had not exaggerated when he said that the Lady Ygraine was well guarded. She and her lord were lodged in a court some way west of the King's quarters, and the court was crowded with Cornwall men at arms. There were armed men in the antechamber too, and in the bedchamber itself some half dozen women. As we went in the oldest of these, a greyhaired woman with an anxious look, hurried forward with relief in her face.

"Prince Merlin." She bent her knees to me, eyeing me with awe, and led me towards the bed.

The room was warm and scented. The lamps burned sweet oil, and the fire was of applewood. The bed stood at the center of the wall opposite the fire. The pillows were of grey silk with gilt tassels, and the coverlet richly worked with flowers and strange beasts and winged creatures. The only other woman's room that I had seen was my mother's, with the plain wooden bed and the carved oak chest and the loom, and the cracked mosaics of the floor.

I walked forward and stood at the foot of the bed, looking down at Gorlois' wife.

If I had been asked then what she looked like I could not have said. Cadal had told me she was fair, and I had seen the hunger in the King's face, so I knew she was desirable; but as I stood in the airy scented room looking at the woman who lay with closed eyes against the grey silk pillows, it was no woman that I saw. Nor did I see the room or the people in it. I saw only the flashing and beating of the light as in a globed crystal.

I spoke without taking my eyes from the woman in the bed. "One of her women stay here. The rest go. You too, please, my lord." He went without demur, herding the women in front of him like a flock of sheep. The woman who had greeted me remained by her mistress's bed. As the door shut behind the rest of them, the woman in the bed opened her eyes. For a few moments of silence we met each other eye to eye. Then I said: "What do you want of me, Ygraine?"

She answered crisply, with no pretense: "I have sent for you, Prince, because I want your help."

I nodded. "In the matter of the King."

She said straightly: "So you know already? When my husband brought you here, did you guess I was not ill?"

"I guessed."

"Then you can also guess what I want from you?"

"Not quite. Tell me, could you not somehow have spoken with the King himself before now? It might have saved him something. And your husband as well."

Her eyes widened. "How could I talk to the King? You came through the courtyard?"

"Yes."

"Then you saw my husband's troops and men at arms. What do you suppose would have happened had I talked to Uther? I could not answer him openly, and if I had met him in secret—even if I could—half London would have known it within the hour. Of course I could not speak to him or send him a message. The only protection was silence."

I said slowly: "If the message was simply that you were a true and faithful wife and that he must turn his eyes elsewhere, then the message could have been given him at any time and by any messenger."

She smiled. Then she bent her head.

I took in my breath. "Ah. That's what I wished to know. You are honest, Ygraine."

"What use to lie to you? I have heard about you. Oh, I know better than to believe all they say in the songs and stories, but you are clever and cold and wise, and they say you love no woman and are committed to no man. So you can listen, and judge." She looked down at her hands, where they lay on the coverlet, then up at me again. "But I do believe that you can see the future. I want you to tell me what the future is."

"I don't tell fortunes like an old woman. Is this why you sent for me?"

"You know why I sent for you. You are the one man with whom I can seek private speech without arousing my husband's anger and suspicion—and you have the King's ear." Though she was but a woman, and young, lying in her bed with me standing over her, it was as if she were a queen giving audience. She looked at me very straight. "Has the King spoken to you yet?"

"He has no need to speak to me. Everyone knows what ails him."

"And will you tell him what you have just learned from me?"

"That will depend."

"On what?" she demanded.

I said slowly: "On you yourself. So far you have been wise. Had you been less guarded in your ways and your speech there would have been trouble, there might even have been war. I understand that you have never allowed one moment of your time here to be solitary or unguarded; you have taken care always to be where you could be seen."

She looked at me for a moment in silence, her brows raised. "Of course."

"Many women—especially desiring what you desire—would not have been able to do this, Lady Ygraine."

"I am not 'many women'." The words were like a flash. She sat up suddenly, tossing back the dark hair, and threw back the covers. The old woman snatched up a long blue robe and hurried forward. Ygraine threw it round her, over her white nightrobe, and sprang from the bed, walking restlessly over towards the window.

Standing, she was tall for a woman, with a form that might have moved a sterner man than Uther. Her neck was long and slender, the head poised gracefully. The dark hair streamed unbound down her back. Her eyes were blue, not the fierce blue of Uther's but the deep, dark blue of the Celt. Her mouth was proud. She was very lovely, and no man's toy. If Uther wanted her, I thought, he would have to make her Queen.

She had stopped just short of the window. If she had gone to it, she might have been seen from the courtyard. No, not a lady to lose her head.

She turned. "I am the daughter of a king, and I come from a line of kings. Cannot you see how I must have been driven, even to think the way I am thinking now?" She repeated it passionately. "Can you not see? I was married at sixteen to the Lord of Cornwall; he is a good man; I honour and respect him. Until I came to London I was half content to starve and die there in Cornwall, but he brought me here, and now it has happened. Now I know what I must have, but it is beyond me to have it, beyond the wife of Gorlois of Cornwall. So what else would you have me do? There is nothing to do but wait here and be silent, because on my silence hangs not only the honour of myself and my husband and my house, but the safety of the kingdom that Ambrosius died for, and that Uther himself has just sealed with blood and fire."

She swung away to take two quick paces and back again. "I am no trashy Helen for men to fight over, die over, burn down kingdoms for. I don't wait on the walls as a prize for some brawny victor. I cannot so dishonour both Gorlois and the King in the eyes of men. And I cannot go to him secretly and dishonour myself in my own eyes. I am a lovesick woman, yes. But I am also Ygraine of Cornwall."

I said coldly: "So you intend to wait until you can go to him in honour, as his Queen?"

"What else can I do?"

"Was this the message I had to give him?"

She was silent.

I said: "Or did you get me here to read you the future? To tell you the length of your husband's life?"

Still she said nothing.

"Ygraine," I said, "the two are the same. If I give Uther the message that you love him and desire him, but that you will not come to him while your husband is alive, what length of life would you prophesy for Gorlois?"

Still she did not speak. The gift of silence, too, I thought. I was standing between her and the fire. I watched the light beating round her, flowing up the white robe and the blue robe, light and shadow rippling upwards in waves like moving water or the wind over grass. A flame leapt, and my shadow sprang over her and grew, climbing with the beating light to meet her own climbing shadow and join with it, so that there across the wall behind her reared—no dragon of gold or scarlet, no firedrake with burning tail, but a great cloudy shape of air and darkness, thrown there by the flame, and sinking as the flame sank, to shrink and steady until it was only her shadow, the shadow of a woman, slender and straight, like a sword. And where I stood, there was nothing.

She moved, and the lamplight built the room again round us, warm and real and smelling of applewood. She was watching me with something in her face that had not been there before. At last she said, in a still voice: "I told you there was nothing hidden from you. You do well to put it into words. I had thought all this. But I hoped that by sending for you I could absolve myself, and the King."

"Once a dark thought is dragged into words it is in the light. You could have had your desire long since on the terms of 'any woman', as the King could on the terms of any man." I paused. The room was steady now. The words came clearly to me, from nowhere, without thought. "I will tell you, if you like, how you may meet the King's love on your terms and on his, with no dishonour to yourself or him, or to your husband. If I could tell you this, would you go to him?"

Her eyes had widened, with a flash behind them, as I spoke. But even so she took time to think. "Yes." Her voice told me nothing.

"If you will obey me, I can do this for you," I said.

"Tell me what I must do."

"Have I your promise, then?"

"You go too fast," she said dryly. "Do you yourself seal bargains before you see what you are committed to?"

I smiled. "No. Very well then, listen to me. When you feigned illness to have me brought to you, what did you tell your husband and your women?"

"Only that I felt faint and sick, and was no more inclined for company. That if I was to appear beside my husband at the crowning, I must see a physician tonight, and take a healing draught." She smiled a little wryly. "I was preparing the way, too, not to sit beside the King at the feast."

"So far, good. You will tell Gorlois that you are pregnant."

"That I am pregnant?" For the first time she sounded shaken. She stared.

"This is possible? He is an old man, but I would have thought—"

"It is possible. But I—" She bit her lip. After a while she said calmly: "Go on. I asked for your counsel, so I must let you give it."

I had never before met a woman with whom I did not have to choose my words, to whom I could speak as I would speak to another man. I said: "Your husband can have no reason to suspect you are pregnant by any man but himself. So you will tell him this, and tell him also that you fear for the child's health if you stay longer in London, under the strain of the gossip and the King's attentions. Tell him that you wish to leave as soon as the crowning is over. That you do not wish to go to the feast, to be distinguished by the King, and to be the center of all the eyes and the gossip. You will go with Gorlois and the Cornish troops tomorrow, before the gates shut at sunset. The news will not come to Uther until the feast."

"But"—she stared again—"this is folly. We could have gone any time this past three weeks if we had chosen to risk the King's anger. We are bound to stay until he gives us leave to go. If we go in that manner, for whatever reason—"

I stopped her. "Uther can do nothing on the day of the crowning. He must stay here for the days of feasting. Do you think he can give offense to Budec and Merrovius and the other kings gathered here? You will be in Cornwall before he can even move."

"And then he will move." She made an impatient gesture. "And there will be war, when he should be making and mending, not breaking and burning. And he cannot win: if he is the victor in the field, he loses the loyalty of the West. Win or lose, Britain is divided, and goes back into the dark."

Yes, she would be a queen. She was on fire for Uther as much as he for her, but she could still think. She was cleverer than Uther, clear-headed, and, I thought, stronger too.

"Oh, yes, he will move." I lifted a hand. "But listen to me. I will talk to the King before the crowning. He will know that the story you told Gorlois was a lie. He will know that I have told you to go to Cornwall. He will feign rage, and he will swear in public to be revenged for the insult put on him by Gorlois at the crowning ... And he will make ready to follow you to Cornwall as soon as the feast is over—"

"But meanwhile our troops will be safely out of London without trouble. Yes, I see. I did not understand you. Go on." She drove her hands inside the sleeves of the blue robe, and clasped her elbows, cradling her breasts. She was not so ice-calm as she looked, the Lady Ygraine. "And then?"

"And you will be safely at home," I said, "with your honour and Cornwall's unbroken."

"Safely, yes. I shall be in Tintagel, and even Uther cannot come at me there. Have you seen the stronghold, Merlin? The cliffs of that coast are high and cruel, and from them runs a thin bridge of rock, the only way to the island where the castle stands. This bridge is so narrow that men can only go one at a time, not even a horse. Even the landward end of the bridge is guarded by a fortress on the main cliff, and within the castle there is water, and food for a year. It is the strongest place in Cornwall. It cannot be taken from the land, and it cannot be approached by sea. If you wish to shut me away for ever from Uther, this is the place to send me."

"So I have heard. This will be, then, where Gorlois will send you. If Uther follows, lady, would Gorlois be content to wait inside the stronghold with you for a year like a beast in a trap? And could his troops be taken in with him?"

She shook her head. "If it cannot be taken, neither can it be used as a base. All one can do is sit out the siege."

"Then you must persuade him that unless he is content to wait inside while the King's troops ravage Cornwall, he himself must be outside, where he can fight."

She struck her hands together. "He will do that. He could not wait and hide and let Cornwall suffer. Nor can I understand your plan, Merlin. If you are trying to save your King and your kingdom from me, then say so. I can feign sickness here, until Uther finds he has to let me go home. We could go home without insult, and without bloodshed."

I said sharply: "You said you would listen. Time runs short."

She was still again. "I am listening."

"Gorlois will lock you in Tintagel. Where will he go himself to face Uther?"

"To Dimilioc. It is a few miles from Tintagel, up the coast. It is a good fortress, and good country to fight from. But then what? Do you think Gorlois will not fight?" She moved across to the fireside and sat down, and I saw her steady her hands deliberately, spreading the fingers on her knee. "And do you think the King can come to me in Tintagel, whether Gorlois is there or no?"

"If you do as I have bid you, you and the King may have speech and comfort one of the other. And you will do this in peace. No"—as her head came up sharply—"this part of it you leave with me. This is where we come to magic. Trust me for the rest. Get yourself only to Tintagel, and wait. I shall bring Uther to you there. And I promise you now, for the King, that he shall not give battle to Gorlois, and that after he and you have met in love, Cornwall shall have peace. As to how this will be, it is with God. I can only tell you what I know. What power is in me now, is from him, and we are in his hands to make or to destroy. But I can tell you this also, Ygraine, that I have seen a bright fire burning, and in it a crown, and a sword standing in an altar like a cross."

She got to her feet quickly, and for the first time there was a kind of fear in her eyes. She opened her mouth as if to speak, then closed her lips again and turned back towards the window. Again she stopped short of it, but I saw her lift her head as if longing for the air. She should have been winged. If she had spent her youth walled in Tintagel it was no wonder she wanted to fly.

She raised her hands and pushed back the hair from her brows. She spoke to the window, not looking at me. "I will do this. If I tell him I am with child, he will take me to Tintagel. It is the place where all the dukes of Cornwall are born. And after that I have to trust you." She turned then and looked at me, dropping her hands. "If once I can have speech with him ... even just that ... But if you have brought bloodshed to Cornwall through me, or death to my husband, then I shall spend the rest of my life praying to any

gods there are that you, too, Merlin, shall die betrayed by a
woman."

"I am content to face your prayers. And now I must go. Is
there someone you can send with me? I'll make a draught for
you and send it back. It will only be poppy; you can take it
and not fear."

"Ralf can go, my page. You'll find him outside the door.
He is Marcia's grandson, and can be trusted as I trust her."
She nodded to the old woman, who moved to open the door
for me.

"Then any message I may have to send you," I said, "I
shall send through him by my man Cadal. And now good
night."

When I left her she was standing quite still in the center of
the room, with the firelight leaping round her.

6

We had a wild ride to Cornwall.

Easter that year had fallen as early as it ever falls, so we
were barely out of winter and into spring when, on a black
wild night, we halted our horses on the clifftop near Tintagel,
and peered down into the teeth of the wind. There were only
the four of us, Uther, myself, Ulfin, and Cadal. Everything,
so far, had gone smoothly and according to plan. It was
getting on towards midnight on the twenty-fourth of March.

Ygraine had obeyed me to the letter. I had not dared, that
night in London, to go straight from her quarters to Uther's
chamber, in case this should be reported to Gorlois; but in
any case Uther would be asleep. I had visited him early next
morning, while he was being bathed and made ready for the
crowning. He sent the servants away, except for Ulfin, and I
was able to tell him exactly what he must do. He looked the
better for his drugged sleep, greeted me briskly enough, and
listened with eagerness in the bright, hollow eyes.

"And she will do as you say?"

"Yes. I have her word. Will you?"

"You know that I will." He regarded me straightly. "And
now will you not tell me about the outcome?"

"I told you. A child."

"Oh, that." He hunched an impatient shoulder. "You are

like my brother; he thought of nothing else ... Still working for him, are you?"

"You might say so."

"Well, I must get one sooner or later, I suppose. No, I meant Gorlois. What will come to him? There's a risk, surely?"

"Nothing is done without risk. You must do the same as I, you must take the time on trust. But I can tell you that your name, and your kingdom, will survive the night's work."

A short silence. He measured me with his eyes. "From you, I suppose that is enough. I am content."

"You do well to be. You will outlive him, Uther."

He laughed suddenly. "God's grief, man, I could have prophesied that myself! I can give him thirty years, and he's no stay-at-home when it comes to war. Which is one good reason why I refuse to have his blood on my hands. So, on that same account ..."

He turned then to Ulfin and began to give his orders. It was the old Uther back again, brisk, concise, clear. A messenger was to go immediately to Caerleon, and troops to be despatched from there to North Cornwall. Uther himself would travel there straight from London as soon as he was able, riding fast with a small bodyguard to where his troops would be encamped. In this way the King could be hard on Gorlois' heels, even though Gorlois would leave today, and the King must stay feasting his peers for four more long days. Another man was to ride out immediately along our proposed route to Cornwall, and see that good horses were ready at short stages all the way.

So it came about as I had planned. I saw Ygraine at the crowning, still, composed, erect, and with downcast eyes, and so pale that if I had not seen her the night before, I myself would have believed her story true. I shall never cease to wonder at women. Even with power, it is not possible to read their minds. Duchess and slut alike, they need not even study to deceive. I suppose it is the same with slaves, who live with fear, and with those animals who disguise themselves by instinct to save their lives. She sat through the long, brilliant ceremony, like wax which at any moment may melt to collapse; then afterwards I caught a glimpse of her, supported by her women, leaving the throng as the bright pomp moved slowly to the hall of feasting. About halfway through the feast, when the wine had gone round well, I saw Gorlois, unremarked, leave the hall with one or two other men who were answering the call of nature. He did not come back.

Uther, to one who knew the truth, may not have been quite so convincing as Ygraine, but between exhaustion and wine and his ferocious exultation at what was to come, he was convincing enough. Men talked among themselves in hushed voices about his rage when he discovered Gorlois' absence, and his angry vows to take vengeance as soon as his royal guests had gone. If that anger were a little overloud and his threats too fierce against a Duke whose only fault was the protection of his own wife, the King had been intemperate enough before for men to see this as part of the same picture. And so bright now was Uther's star, so dazzling the luster of the crowned Pendragon, that London would have forgiven him a public rape. They could less easily forgive Ygraine for having refused him.

So we came to Cornwall. The messenger had done his work well, and our ride, in hard short stages of no more than twenty miles apiece, took us two days and a night. We found our troops waiting encamped at the place selected—a few miles in from Hercules Point and just outside the Cornish border—with the news that, however she had managed it, Ygraine was fast in Tintagel with a small body of picked men, while her husband with the rest of his force had descended on Dimilioc, and sent a call round for the men of Cornwall to gather to defend their Duke. He must know of the presence of the King's troops so near his border, but no doubt he would expect them to wait for the King's coming, and could have as yet no idea that the King was already there.

We rode secretly into our camp at dusk, and went, not to the King's quarters, but to those of a captain he could trust. Cadal was there already, having gone ahead to prepare the disguises which I meant us to wear, and to await Ralf's message from Tintagel when the time was ripe.

My plan was simple enough, with the kind of simplicity that often succeeds, and it was helped by Gorlois' habit, since his marriage, of riding back nightly where he could—from Dimilioc or his other fortresses—to visit his wife. I suppose there had been too many jests about the old man's fondness, and he had formed the habit (Ralf had told me) of riding back secretly, using the private gate, a hidden postern to which access was difficult unless one knew the way. My plan was simply to disguise Uther, Ulfin, and myself to pass, if we were seen, as Gorlois and his companion and servant, and ride to Tintagel by night. Ralf would arrange to be on duty himself at the postern, and would meet us and lead us up the secret path. Ygraine had by some means persuaded Gorlois— this had been the greatest danger—not to visit her himself that night, and would dismiss all her women but Marcia. Ralf and Cadal had arranged between them what clothes we should wear: the Cornwall party had ridden from London in such a hurry on the night of the coronation feast that some of their baggage had been left behind, and it had been simple to find saddle-cloths with the blazon of Cornwall, and even one of Gorlois' familiar war cloaks with the double border of silver.

Ralf's latest message had been reassuring; the time was ripe, the night black enough to hide us and wild enough to keep most men within doors. We set off after it was full dark, and the four of us slipped out of camp unobserved. Once clear of our own lines we went at a gallop for Tintagel, and it would have been only the keen eye of suspicion which could have told that this was not the Duke of Cornwall with three companions, riding quickly home to his wife. Uther's beard had been greyed, and a bandage came down one side of his face to cover the corner of his mouth, and give some reason—should he be forced to talk—for any strangeness in his speech. The hood of his cloak, pulled down low as was natural on such a fierce night, shadowed his features. He was straighter and more powerful than Gorlois, but this was easy enough to disguise, and he wore gauntlets to hide his hands, which were not those of an old man. Ulfin passed well enough as one Jordan, a servant of Gorlois whom we had chosen as being the nearest to Ulfin's build and colouring. I myself wore the clothes of Brithael, Gorlois' friend and captain: he was an older man than I, but his voice was not unlike mine, and I could speak good Cornish. I have always been good at voices. I was to do what talking proved necessary. Cadal came with us undisguised; he was to wait with the horses outside and be our messenger if we should need one.

I rode up close to the King and set my mouth to his ear. "The castle's barely a mile from here. We ride down to the shore now. Ralf will be there to show us in. I'll lead on?"

He nodded. Even in the ragged, flying dark I thought I saw the gleam of his eyes. I added: "And don't look like

that, or they'll never think you're Gorlois, with years of
married life behind you."

I heard him laugh, and then I wheeled my horse and led
the way carefully down the rabbit-ridden slope of scrub and
scree into the head of the narrow valley which leads down
towards the shore.

This valley is little more than a gully carrying a small
stream to the sea. At its widest the stream is not more than
three paces broad, and so shallow that a horse can ford it
anywhere. At the foot of the valley the water drops over a
low cliff straight to a beach of slaty shingle. We rode in
single file down the track, with the stream running deep
down on the left, and to our right a high bank covered with
bushes. Since the wind was from the south-west and the
valley was deep and running almost north, we were sheltered
from the gale, but at the top of the bank the bushes were
screaming in the wind, and twigs and even small boughs
hurtled through the air and across our path. Even without
this and the steepness of the stony path and the darkness, it
was not easy riding; the horses, what with the storm and
some tension which must have been generated by the three of
us—Cadal was as solid as a rock, but then he was not going
into the castle—were wild and white-eyed with nerves. When,
a quarter of a mile from the sea, we turned down to the
stream and set the beasts to cross it, mine, in the lead,
flattened its ears and balked, and when I had lashed it across
and into a plunging canter up the narrow track, and a man's
figure detached itself from the shadows ahead beside the
path, the horse stopped dead and climbed straight up into the
air till I felt sure it would go crashing over backwards, and
me with it.

The shadow darted forward and seized the bridle, dragging
the horse down. The beast stood, sweating and shaking.

"Brithael," I said. "Is all well?"

I heard him exclaim, and he took a pace, pressing closer to
the horse's shoulder, peering upwards in the dark. Behind me
Uther's grey hoisted itself up the track and thudded to a halt.
The man at my horse's shoulder said, uncertainly: "My lord
Gorlois . . . ? We did not look for you tonight. Is there news,
then?"

It was Ralf's voice. I said in my own: "So we'll pass, at
least in the dark?"

I heard his breath go in. "Yes, my lord . . . For the

moment I thought it was indeed Brithael. And then the grey horse ... Is that the King?"

"For tonight," I said, "it is the Duke of Cornwall. Is all well?"

"Yes, sir."

"Then lead the way. There is not much time."

He gripped my horse's bridle above the bit and led him on, for which I was grateful, as the path was dangerous, narrow and slippery and twisting along the steep bank between the rustling bushes; not a path I would have wished to ride even in daylight on a strange and frightened horse. The others followed, Cadal's mount and Ulfin's plodding stolidly along, and close behind me the grey stallion snorting at every bush and trying to break his rider's grip, but Uther could have ridden Pegasus himself and foundered him before his own wrists even ached.

Here my horse shied at something I could not see, stumbled, and would have pitched me down the bank but for Ralf at its head. I swore at it, then asked Ralf: "How far now?"

"About two hundred paces to the shore, sir, and we leave the horses there. We climb the promontory on foot."

"By all the gods of storm, I'll be glad to get under cover. Did you have any trouble?"

"None, sir." He had to raise his voice to make me hear, but in that turmoil there was no fear of being heard more than three paces off. "My lady told Felix herself—that's the porter—that she had asked the Duke to ride back as soon as his troops were disposed at Dimilioc. Of course the word's gone round that she's pregnant, so it's natural enough she'd want him back, even with the King's armies so close. She told Felix the Duke would come by the secret gate in case the King had spies posted already. He wasn't to tell the garrison, she said, because they might be alarmed at his leaving Dimilioc and the troops there, but the King couldn't possibly be in Cornwall for another day at soonest ... Felix doesn't suspect a thing. Why should he?"

"The porter is alone at the gate?"

"Yes, but there are two guards in the guard-room."

He had told us already what lay inside the postern. This was a small gate set low in the outer castle wall, and just inside it a long flight of steps ran up to the right, hugging the wall. Halfway up was a wide landing, with a guard-room to the side. Beyond that the stairs went up again, and at the top was the private door leading through into the apartments.

"Do the guards know?" I asked.

He shook his head. "My lord, we didn't dare. All the men left with the Lady Ygraine were hand-picked by the Duke."

"Are the stairs well lighted?"

"A torch. I saw to it that it will be mostly smoke."

I looked over my shoulder to where the grey horse came ghostly behind me through the dark. Ralf had had to raise his voice to make me hear above the wind which screamed across the top of the valley, and I would have thought that the King would be waiting to know what passed between us. But he was silent, as he had been since the beginning of the ride. It seemed he was indeed content to trust the time. Or to trust me.

I turned back to Ralf, leaning down over my horse's shoulder. "Is there a password?"

"Yes, my lord. It is *pilgrim*. And the lady has sent a ring for the King to wear. It is one the Duke wears sometimes. Here's the end of the path, can you see? It's quite a drop to the beach." He checked, steadying my horse, then the beast plunged down and its hoofs grated on shingle. "We leave the horses here, my lord."

I dismounted thankfully. As far as I could see, we were in a small cove sheltered from the wind by a mighty headland close to our left, but the seas, tearing past the end of this headland and curving round to break among the offshore rocks, were huge, and came lashing down on the shingle in torrents of white with a noise like armies clashing together in anger. Away to the right I saw another high headland, and between the two this roaring stretch of white water broken by the teeth of black rocks. The stream behind us fell seawards over its low cliff in two long cascades which blew in the wind like ropes of hair. Beyond these swinging waterfalls, and in below the overhanging wall of the main cliff, there was shelter for the horses.

Ralf was pointing to the great headland on our left. "The path is up there. Tell the King to come behind me and to follow closely. One foot wrong tonight, and before you could cry help you'd be out with the tide as far as the western stars."

The grey thudded down beside us and the King swung himself out of the saddle. I heard him laugh, that same sharp, exultant sound. Even had there been no prize at the end of the night's trail, he would have been the same. Danger was drink and dreams alike to Uther.

The other two came up with us and dismounted, and Cadal took the reins. Uther came to my shoulder, looking at the cruel race of water. "Do we swim for it now?"

"It may come to that, God knows. It looks to me as if the waves are up to the castle wall."

He stood quite still, oblivious of the buffeting of wind and rain, with his head lifted, staring up at the headland. High against the stormy dark, a light burned.

I touched his arm. "Listen. The situation is what we expected. There is a porter, Felix, and two men-at-arms in the guard-room. There should be very little light. You know the way in. It will be enough, as we go in, if you grunt your thanks to Felix and go quickly up the stair. Marcia, the old woman, will meet you at the door of Ygraine's apartments and lead you in. You can leave the rest to us. If there is any trouble, then there are three of us to three of them, and on a night like this there'll be no sound heard. I shall come an hour before dawn and send Marcia in for you. Now we shall not be able to speak again. Follow Ralf closely, the path is very dangerous. He has a ring for you and the password. Go now."

He turned without a word and trod across the streaming shingle to where the boy waited. I found Cadal beside me, with the reins of the four horses gathered in his fist. His face, like my own, was streaming with wet, his cloak billowing round him like a storm cloud.

I said: "You heard me. An hour before dawn."

He, too, was looking up at the crag where high above us the castle towered. In a moment of flying light through the torn cloud I saw the castle walls, growing out of the rock. Below them fell the cliff, almost vertical, to the roaring waves. Between the promontory and the mainland, joining the castle to the mainland cliff, ran a natural ridge of rock, its sheer side polished flat as a sword-blade by the sea. From the beach where we stood, there seemed to be no way out but the valley; not mainland fortress, nor causeway, nor castle rock, could be climbed. It was no wonder they left no sentries here. And the path to the secret gate could be held by one man against an army.

Cadal was saying: "I'll get the horses in there, under the overhang, in what shelter there is. And for my sake, if not for yon lovesick gentleman's, be on time. If they as much as suspicion up yonder that there's something amiss, it's rats in a trap for the lot of us. They can shut that bloody little valley as sharp as they can block the causeway, you know that? And I wouldn't just fancy swimming out the other way, myself."

"Nor I. Content yourself, Cadal, I know what I'm about."

"I believe you. There's something about you tonight ... The way you spoke just now to the King, not thinking, shorter than you'd speak to a servant. And he said never a word, but did as he was bid. Yes, I'd say you know what you're about. Which is just as well, master Merlin, because otherwise, you realize, you're risking the life of the King of Britain for a night's lust?"

I did something which I had never done before; which I do not commonly do. I put a hand out and laid it over Cadal's where it held the reins. The horses were quiet now, wet and unhappy, huddling with their rumps to the wind and their heads drooping.

I said: "If Uther gets into the place tonight and lies with her, then before God, Cadal, it will not matter as much as the worth of a drop of that sea-foam there if he is murdered in the bed. I tell you, a King will come out of this night's work whose name will be a shield and buckler to men until this fair land, from sea to sea, is smashed down into the sea that holds it, and men leave earth to live among the stars. Do you think Uther is a King, Cadal? He's but a regent for him who went before and for him who comes after, the past and future King. And tonight he is even less than that: he is a tool, and she a vessel, and I ... I am a spirit, a word, a thing of air and darkness, and I can no more help what I am doing than a reed can help the wind of God blowing through it. You and I, Cadal, are as helpless as dead leaves in the waters of that bay." I dropped my hand from his. "An hour before dawn."

"Till then, my lord."

I left him then, and, with Ulfin following, went after Ralf and the King across the shingle to the foot of the black cliff.

7

I do not think that now, even in daylight, I could find the path again without a guide, let alone climb it. Ralf went first, with the King's hand on his shoulder, and in my turn I held a fold of Uther's mantle, and Ulfin of mine. Mercifully, close

in as we were to the face of the castle rock, we were
protected from the wind: exposed, the climb would have
been impossible; we would have been plucked off the cliff like
feathers. But we were not protected from the sea. The waves
must have been rushing up forty feet, and the master waves,
the great sevenths, came roaring up like towers and drenched
us with salt fully sixty feet above the beach.

One good thing the savage boiling of the sea did for us, its
whiteness cast upwards again what light came from the sky.
At last we saw, above our heads, the roots of the castle walls
where they sprang from the rock. Even in dry weather the
walls would have been unscalable, and tonight they were
streaming with wet. I could see no door, nothing breaking the
smooth streaming walls of slate. Ralf did not pause, but led
us on under them towards a seaward corner of the cliff.
There he halted for a moment, and I saw him move his arm
in a gesture that meant 'Beware'. He went carefully round
the corner and out of sight. I felt Uther stagger as he
reached the corner himself and met the force of the wind. He
checked for a moment and then went on, clamped tight to
the cliff's face. Ulfin and I followed. For a few more hideous
yards we fought our way along, faces in to the soaking,
slimy cliff, then a jutting buttress gave us shelter, and we
were stumbling suddenly on a treacherous slope cushiony
with sea-pink, and there ahead of us, recessed deep in the
rock below the castle wall, and hidden from the ramparts
above by the sharp overhang, was Tintagel's emergency door.

I saw Ralf give a long look upwards before he led us in
under the rock. There were no sentries above. What need to
post men on the seaward ramparts? He drew his dagger and
rapped sharply on the door, a pattern of knocks which we,
standing as we were at his shoulder, scarcely heard in the
gale.

The porter must have been waiting just inside. The door
opened immediately. It swung silently open for about three
inches, then stuck, and I heard the rattle of a chain bolt. In
the gap a hand showed, gripping a torch. Uther, beside me,
dragged his hood closer, and I stepped past him to Ralf's
elbow, holding my mantle tightly to my mouth and hunching
my shoulders against the volleying gusts of wind and rain.

The porter's face, half of it, showed below the torch. An
eye peered. Ralf, well forward into the light, said urgently:
"Quick, man. A pilgrim. It's me back, with the Duke."

The torch moved fractionally higher. I saw the big emerald

on Uther's finger catch the light, and said curtly, in Brithael's voice: "Open up, Felix, and let us get in out of this, for pity's sake. The Duke had a fall from his horse this morning, and his bandage is soaking. There are just the four of us here. Make haste."

The chain bolt came off and the door swung wide. Ralf put a hand to it so that, ostensibly holding it for his master, he could step into the passage between Felix and Uther as the King entered.

Uther strode in past the bowing man, shaking the wet off himself like a dog, and returning some half-heard sound in answer to the porter's greeting. Then with a brief lift of the hand which set the emerald flashing again, he turned straight for the steps which led upwards on our right, and began quickly to mount them.

Ralf grabbed the torch from the porter's hand as Ulfin and I pressed in after Uther. "I'll light them up with this. Get the door shut and barred again. I'll come down later and give you the news, Felix, but we're all drenched as drowned dogs, and want to get to a fire. There's one in the guard-room, I suppose?"

"Aye." The porter had already turned away to bar the door. Ralf was holding the torch so that Ulfin and I could go past in shadow.

I started quickly up the steps in Uther's wake, with Ulfin on my heels. The stairs were lit only by a smoking cresset which burned in a bracket on the wall of the wide landing above us. It had been easy.

Too easy. Suddenly, above us on the landing, the sullen light was augmented by that from a blazing torch, and a couple of men-at-arms stepped from a doorway, swords at the ready.

Uther, six steps above me, paused fractionally and then went on. I saw his hand, under the cloak, drop to his sword. Under my own I had my weapon loose in its sheath.

Ralf's light tread came running up the steps behind us.

"My lord Duke!"

Uther, I could guess how thankfully, stopped and turned to wait for him, his back to the guards.

"My lord Duke, let me light you—ah, they've a torch up there." He seemed only then to notice the guards above us, with the blazing light. He ran on up past Uther, calling lightly: "Holà, Marcus, Sellic, give me that torch to light my lord up to the Duchess. This wretched thing's nothing but smoke."

The man with the torch had it held high, and the pair of them were peering down the stairs at us. The boy never hesitated. He ran up, straight between the swords, and took the torch from the man's hand. Before they could reach for it, he turned swiftly to douse the first torch in the tub of sand which stood near the guard-room door. It went out into sullen smoke. The new torch blazed cleanly, but swung and wavered as he moved so that the shadows of the guards, flung gigantic and grotesque down the steps, helped to hide us. Uther, taking advantage of the swaying shadows, started again swiftly up the flight. The hand with Gorlois' ring was half up before him to return the men's salutes. The guards moved aside. But they moved one to each side of the head of the steps, and their swords were still in their hands.

Behind me, I heard the faint whisper as Ulfin's blade loosened in its sheath. Under my cloak, mine was half-drawn. There was no hope of getting past them. We would have to kill them, and pray it made no noise. I heard Ulfin's step lagging, and knew he was thinking of the porter. He might have to go back to him while we dealt with the guards.

But there was no need. Suddenly, at the head of the second flight of steps, a door opened wide, and there, full in the blaze of light, stood Ygraine. She was in white, as I had seen her before; but not this time in a night-robe. The long gown shimmered like lake water. Over one arm and shoulder, Roman fashion, she wore a mantle of soft dark blue. Her hair was dressed with jewels. She stretched out both her hands, and the blue robe and the white fell away from wrists where red gold glimmered.

"Welcome, my lord!" Her voice, high and clear, brought both guards round to face her. Uther took the last half dozen steps to the landing in two leaps, then was past them, his cloak brushing the sword-blades, past Ralf's blazing torch, and starting quickly up the second flight of steps.

The guards snapped back to attention, one each side of the stair-head, their backs to the wall. Behind me I heard Ulfin gasp, but he followed me quietly enough as, calmly and without hurry, I mounted the last steps to the landing. It is something, I suppose, to have been born a prince, even a bastard one; I knew that the sentries' eyes were nailed to the wall in front of them by the Duchess's presence as surely as if they were blind. I went between the swords, and Ulfin after me.

Uther had reached the head of the stairway. He took her hands, and there in front of the lighted door, with his enemies' swords catching the torchlight below him, the King bent his head and kissed Ygraine. The scarlet cloak swung round both of them, engulfing the white. Beyond them I saw the shadow of the old woman, Marcia, holding the door.

Then the King said: "Come," and with the great cloak still covering them both, he led her into the firelight, and the door shut behind them.

So we took Tintagel.

8

We were well served that night, Ulfin and I. The chamber door had hardly shut, leaving us islanded halfway up the flight between the door and the guards below, when I heard Ralf's voice again, easy and quick above the slither of swords being sheathed:

"Gods and angels, what a night's work! And I still have to guide him back when it's done! You've a fire in the room yonder? Good. We'll have a chance to dry off while we're waiting. You can get yourselves off now and leave this trick to us. Go on, what are you waiting for? You've had your orders—and no word of this, mark you, to anyone that comes."

One of the guards, settling his sword home, turned straight back into the guard-room, but the other hesitated, glancing up towards me. "My lord Brithael, is that right? We go off watch?"

I started slowly down the stairs. "Quite right. You can go. We'll send the porter for you when we want to leave. And above all, not a word of the Duke's presence. See to it." I turned to Ulfin, big-eyed on the stairs behind me. "Jordan, you go up to the chamber door yonder and stand guard. No, give me your cloak. I'll take it to the fire."

As he went thankfully, his sword at last ready in his hand, I heard Ralf crossing the guard-room below, underlining my orders with what threats I could only guess at. I went down the steps, not hurrying, to give him time to get rid of the men.

I heard the inner door shut, and went in. The guard-room, brightly lit by the torch and the blazing fire, was empty save for ourselves.

Ralf gave me a smile, gay and threadbare with nerves. "Not again, even to please my lady, for all the gold in Cornwall!"

"There will be no need again. You have done more than well, Ralf. The King will not forget."

He reached up to put the torch in a socket, saw my face, and said anxiously: "What is it, sir? Are you ill?"

"No. Does that door lock?" I nodded at the shut door through which the guards had gone.

"I have locked it. If they had had any suspicion, they would not have given me the key. But they had none, how could they? I could have sworn myself just now that it was Brithael speaking there, from the stairs. It was—like magic." The last word held a question, and he eyed me with a look I knew, but when I said nothing, he asked merely: "What now, sir?"

"Get you down to the porter now, and keep him away from here." I smiled. "You'll get your turn at the fire, Ralf, when we have gone."

He went off, light-footed as ever, down the steps. I heard him call something, and a laugh from Felix. I stripped off my drenched cloak and spread it, with Ulfin's, to the blaze. Below the cloak my clothes were dry enough. I sat for a while, holding my hands before me to the fire. It was very still in the firelit chamber, but outside the air was full of the surging din of the waters and the storm tearing at the castle walls.

My thoughts stung like sparks. I could not sit still. I stood and walked about the little chamber, restlessly. I listened to the storm outside and, going to the door, heard the murmur of voices and the click of dice as Ralf and Felix passed the time down by the gate. I looked the other way. No sound from the head of the stairs, where I could just see Ulfin, or perhaps his shadow, motionless by the chamber door ...

Someone was coming softly down the stairs; a woman shrouded in a mantle, carrying something. She came without a sound, and there had been neither sound nor movement from Ulfin. I stepped out on to the landing, and the light from the guard-room came after me, firelight and shadow.

It was Marcia. I saw the tears glisten on her cheeks as she bent her head over what lay in her arms. A child, wrapped warm against the winter night. She saw me and held her burden out to me. "Take care of him," she said, and through the shine of tears I saw the treads of the stairway outline themselves again behind her. "Take care of him . . ."

The whisper faded into the flutter of the torch and the sound of the storm outside. I was alone on the stairway, and above me a shut door. Ulfin had not moved.

I lowered my empty arms and went back to the fire. This was dying down, and I made it burn up again, but with small comfort to myself, for again the light stung me. Though I had seen what I wanted to see, there was death somewhere before the end, and I was afraid. My body ached, and the room was stifling. I picked up my cloak, which was almost dry, slung it round me, and crossed the landing to where in the outer wall was a small door under which the wind drove like a knife. I thrust the door open against the blast, and went outside.

At first, after the blaze of the guard-room, I could see nothing. I shut the door behind me and leaned back against the damp wall, while the night air poured over me like a river. Then things took shape around me. In front and a few paces away was a battlemented wall, waist high, the outer wall of the castle. Between this wall and where I stood was a level platform, and above me a wall rising again to a battlement, and beyond this the soaring cliff and the walls climbing it, and the shape of the fortress rising above me step by step to the peak of the promontory. At the very head of the rise, where we had seen the lighted window, the tower now showed black and lightless against the sky.

I went forward to the battlement and leaned over. Below was an apron of cliff, which would in daylight be a grassy slope covered with sea-pink and white campion and the nests of seabirds. Beyond it and below, the white rage of the bay. I looked down to the right, the way we had come. Except for the driving arcs of white foam, the bay where Cadal waited was invisible under darkness.

It had stopped raining now, and the clouds were running higher and thinner. The wind had veered a little, slackening. It would drop towards dawn. Here and there, high and black beyond the racing clouds, the spaces of the night were filled with stars.

Then suddenly, directly overhead, the clouds parted, and there, sailing through them like a ship through running waves, the star.

It hung there among the dazzle of smaller stars, flickering at first, then pulsing, growing, bursting with light and all the colours that you see in dancing water. I watched it wax and flame and break open in light, then a racing wind would fling a web of cloud across it till it lay grey and dull and distant, lost to the eye among the other, minor stars. Then, as the swarm began their dance again it came again, gathering and swelling and dilating with light till it stood among the other stars like a torch throwing a whirl of sparks. So on through the night, as I stood alone on the ramparts and watched it; vivid and bright, then grey and sleeping, but each time waking to burn more gently, till it breathed light rather than beat, and towards morning hung glowing and quiet, with the light growing round it as the new day promised to come in clear and still.

I drew breath, and wiped the sweat from my face. I straightened up from where I had leaned against the ramparts. My body was stiff, but the ache had gone. I looked up at Ygraine's darkened window where, now, they slept.

9

I walked slowly back across the platform towards the door. As I opened it I heard from below, clear and sharp, a knocking on the postern gate.

I took a stride through to the landing, pulling the door quietly shut behind me, just as Felix came out of the lodge below, and made for the postern. As his hand went out to the chain-bolt, Ralf whipped out behind him, his arm raised high. I caught the glint in his fist of a dagger, reversed. He jumped, cat-footed, and struck with the hilt. Felix dropped where he stood. There must have been some slight sound audible to the man outside, above the roaring of the sea, for his voice came sharply: "What is it? Felix?" And the knocking came again, harder than before.

I was already halfway down the flight. Ralf had stooped to the porter's body, but turned as he saw me coming, and interpreted my gesture correctly, for he straightened, calling out clearly:

"Who's there?"

"A pilgrim."

It was a man's voice, urgent and breathless. I ran lightly

down the rest of the flight. As I ran I was stripping my cloak off and winding it round my left arm. Ralf threw me a look from which all the gaiety and daring had gone. He had no need even to ask the next question; we both knew the answer.

"Who makes the pilgrimage?" The boy's voice was hoarse.

"Brithael. Now open up, quickly."

"My lord Brithael! My lord—I cannot—I have no orders to admit anyone this way . . ." He was watching me as I stooped, took Felix under the armpits, and dragged him with as little noise as I could, back into the lodge and out of sight. I saw Ralf lick his lips. "Can you not ride to the main gate, my lord? The Duchess will be asleep, and I have no orders—"

"Who's that?" demanded Brithael. "Ralf, by your voice. Where's Felix?"

"Gone up to the guard-room, sir."

"Then get the key from him, or send him down." The man's voice roughened, and a fist thudded against the gate. "Do as I say, boy, or by God I'll have the skin off your back. I have a message for the Duchess, and she won't thank you for holding me here. Come now, hurry up!"

"The—the key's here, my lord. A moment." He threw a desperate look over his shoulder as he made a business of fumbling with the lock. I left the unconscious man bundled out of sight, and was back at Ralf's shoulder, breathing into his ear:

"See if he's alone first. Then let him in."

He nodded, and the door opened on its chain-bolt. Under cover of the noise it made I had my sword out, and melted into the shadow behind the boy, where the opening door would screen me from Brithael. I stood back against the wall. Ralf put his eye to the gap, then drew back, with a nod at me, and began to slide the chain out of its socket. "Excuse me, my lord Brithael." He sounded abject and confused. "I had to make sure . . . Is there trouble?"

"What else?" Brithael thrust the door open so sharply that it would have thudded into me if Ralf had not checked it. "Never mind, you did well enough." He strode in and stopped, towering over the boy. "Has anyone else been to this gate tonight?"

"Why, no, sir." Ralf sounded scared—as well he might—and therefore convincing. "Not while I've been here, and Felix said nothing . . . Why, what's happened?"

Brithael gave a grunt, and his accoutrements jingled as he

shrugged. "There was a fellow down yonder, a horseman. He attacked us. I left Jordan to deal with him. There's been nothing here, then? No trouble at all?"

"None, my lord."

"Then lock the gate again and let none in but Jordan. And now I must see the Duchess. I bring grave news, Ralf. The Duke is dead."

"The Duke?" The boy began to stammer. He made no attempt to shut the gate, but left it swinging free. It hid Brithael from me still, but Ralf was just beside me, and in the dim light I saw his face go pinched and blank with shock. "The Duke—d-dead, my lord? Murdered?"

Brithael, already moving, checked and turned. In another pace he would be clear of the door which hid me from him. I must not let him reach the steps and get above me.

"Murdered? Why, in God's name? Who would do that? That's not Uther's way. No, the Duke took the chance before the King got here, and we attacked the King's camp tonight, out of Dimilioc. But they were ready. Gorlois was killed in the first sally. I rode with Jordan to bring the news. We came straight from the field. Now lock that gate and do as I say."

He turned away and made for the steps. There was room, now, to use a sword. I stepped out from the shadow behind the door.

"Brithael."

The man whirled. His reactions were so quick that they cancelled out my advantage of surprise. I suppose I need not have spoken at all, but again there are certain things a prince must do. It cost me dear enough, and could have cost me my life. I should have remembered that tonight I was no prince; I was fate's creature, like Gorlois whom I had betrayed, and Brithael whom I now must kill. And I was the future's hostage. But the burden weighed heavy on me, and his sword was out almost before mine was raised, and then we stood measuring one another, eye to eye.

He recognized me then, as our eyes met. I saw the shock in his, and a quick flash of fear which vanished in a moment, the moment when my stance and my drawn sword told him that this would be his kind of fight, not mine. He may have seen in my face that I had already fought harder than he, that night.

"I should have known you were here. Jordan said it was your man down there, you damned enchanter. Ralf! Felix! Guard—ho there, guard!"

I saw he had not grasped straight away that I had been inside the gate all along. Then the silence on the stairway, and Ralf's quick move away from me to shut the gate told its own story. Fast as a wolf, too quickly for me to do anything, Brithael swept his left arm with its clenched mailed fist smashing into the side of the boy's head. Ralf dropped without a sound, his body wedging the gate wide open.

Brithael leapt back into the gateway. "Jordan! Jordan! To me! Treachery!"

Then I was on him, blundering somehow through his guard, breast to breast, and our swords bit and slithered together with whining metal and the clash of sparks.

Rapid steps down the stairs. Ulfin's voice: "My lord—Ralf—"

I said, in gasps: "Ulfin . . . Tell the King . . . Gorlois is dead. We must get back . . . Hurry . . ."

I heard him go, fast up the stairs at a stumbling run. Brithael said through his teeth: "The King? Now I see, you pandering whoremaster."

He was a big man, a fighter in his prime, and justly angry. I was without experience, and hating what I must do, but I must do it. I was no longer a prince, or even a man fighting by the rules of men. I was a wild animal fighting to kill because it must.

With my free hand I struck him hard in the mouth and saw the surprise in his eyes as he jumped back to disengage his sword. Then he came in fast, the sword a flashing ring of iron round him. Somehow I ducked under the whistling blade, parried a blow and held it, and lashed a kick that took him full on the knee. The sword whipped down past my cheek with a hiss like a burn. I felt the hot sting of pain, and the blood running. Then as his weight went on the bruised knee, he trod crookedly, slipped on the soaked turf and fell heavily, his elbow striking a stone, and the sword flying from his hand.

Any other man would have stepped back to let him pick it up. I went down on him with all the weight I had, and my own sword shortened, stabbing for his throat.

It was light now, and growing lighter. I saw the contempt and fury in his eyes as he rolled away from the stabbing blade. It missed him, and drove deep into a spongy tuft of sea-pink. In the unguarded second as I fought to free it, his tactics shifted to match mine, and with that iron fist he struck me hard behind the ear, then, wrenching himself aside,

was on his feet and plunging down the dreadful slope to
where his own sword lay shining in the grass two paces from
the cliff's edge.

If he reached it, he would kill me in seconds. I rolled,
bunching to get to my feet, flinging myself anyhow down the
slimy slope towards the sword. He caught me half on to my
knees. His booted foot drove into my side, then into my
back. The pain broke in me like a bubble of blood and my
bones melted, throwing me flat again, but I felt my flailing
foot catch the metal, and the sword jerked from its hold in
the turf to skid, with how gentle a shimmer, over the edge.
Seconds later, it seemed, we could hear, thin and sweet
through the thunder of the waves, the whine of metal as it
struck the rocks below.

But before even the sound reached us he was on me again.
I had a knee under me and was dragging myself up painfully.
Through the blood in my eyes I saw the blow coming, and
tried to dodge, but his fist struck me in the throat, knocking
me sideways with a savagery that spreadeagled me again on
the wet turf with the breath gone from my body and the
sight from my eyes. I felt myself roll and slip and, remembering what lay below, blindly drove my left hand into the
turf to stop myself falling. My sword was still in my right
hand. He jumped for me again, and with all the weight of his
big body brought both feet down on my hand where it
grasped the sword. The hand broke across the metal guard. I
heard it go. The sword snapped upwards like a trap springing
and caught him across his outstretched hand. He cursed in a
gasp, without words, and recoiled momentarily. Somehow, I
had the sword in my left hand. He came in again as quickly
as before, and even as I tried to drag myself away, he made
a quick stride forward and stamped again on my broken
hand. Somebody screamed. I felt myself thrash over, mind-
less with pain, blind. With the last strength I had I jabbed
the sword, hopelessly shortened, up at his straddled body, felt
it torn from my hand, and then lay waiting, without resistance, for the last kick in my side that would send me over
the cliff.

I lay there breathless, retching, choking on bile, my face
to the ground and my left hand driven into the soft tufts of
sea-pink, as if it clung to life for me. The beat and crash of
the sea shook the cliff, and even this slight tremor seemed to
grind pain through my body. It hurt at every point. My side

pained as though the ribs were stove in, and the skin had been stripped from the cheek that lay pressed hard into the turf. There was blood in my mouth, and my right hand was a jelly of pain. I could hear someone, some other man a long way off, making small abject sounds of pain.

The blood in my mouth bubbled and oozed down my chin into the ground, and I knew it was I who was groaning. Merlin the son of Ambrosius, the prince, the great enchanter. I shut my mouth on the blood and began to push and claw my way to my feet.

The pain in my hand was cruel, the worst of all; I heard rather than felt the small bones grind where their ends were broken. I felt myself lurching as I got to my knees, and dared not try to stand upright so near the cliff's edge. Below me a master wave struck, thundered, fountained up into the greying light, then fell back to crash into the next rising wave. The cliff trembled. A sea-bird, the first of the day, sailed overhead, crying.

I crawled away from the edge and then stood up.

Brithael was lying near the postern gate, on his belly, as if he had been trying to crawl there. Behind him on the turf was a wake of blood, glossy on the grass like the track of a snail. He was dead. That last desperate stroke had caught the big vein in the groin, and the life had pumped out of him as he tried to crawl for help. Some of the blood that soaked me must be his.

I went on my knees beside him and made sure. Then I rolled him over and over till the slope took him, and he went after his sword into the sea. The blood would have to take care of itself. It was raining again, and with luck the blood would be gone before anyone saw it.

The postern gate stood open still. I reached it somehow and stood, supporting myself with a shoulder against the jamb. There was blood in my eyes, too. I wiped it away with a wet sleeve.

Ralf had gone. The porter also. The torch had burnt low in its socket and the smoky light showed the lodge and stairway empty. The castle was quiet. At the top of the stairway the door stood partly open, and I saw light there and heard voices. Quiet voices, urgent but unalarmed. Uther's party must still be in control; there had been no alarm given.

I shivered in the dawn chill. Somewhere, unheeded, the cloak had dropped from my arm. I didn't trouble to look for it. I let go of the gate and tried standing upright without support. I could do it. I started to make my way down the path towards the bay.

10

There was just light enough to see the way; light enough, too, to see the dreadful cliff and the roaring depths below. But I think I was so occupied with the weakness of my body, with the simple mechanics of keeping that body upright and my good hand working and the injured hand out of trouble, that I never once thought of the sea below or the perilous narrowness of the strip of safe rock. I got past the first stretch quickly, and then clawed my way, half crawling, down the next steep slide across the tufted grasses and the rattling steps of scree. As the path took me lower, the seas came roaring up closer beside me, till I felt the spray of the big waves salt with the salt blood on my face. The tide was full in with morning, the waves still high with the night's wind, shooting icy tongues up the licked rock and bursting beside me with a hollow crash that shook the very bones in my body, and drenched the path down which I crawled and stumbled.

I found him halfway up from the beach, lying face downwards within an inch of the edge. One arm hung over the brink, and at the end of it the limp hand swung to the shocks of air disturbed by the waves. The other hand seemed to have stiffened, hooked to a piece of rock. The fingers were black with dried blood.

The path was just wide enough. Somehow I turned him over, pulling and shifting him as best I could till he was lying close against the cliff. I knelt between him and the sea.

"Cadal. Cadal."

His flesh was cold. In the near-darkness I could see that there there was blood on his face, and what looked like thick ooze from some wound up near the hair. I put my hand on it; it was a cut, but my numbed hand kept slipping on the wet flesh and I could feel nothing. I pulled at his soaked tunic and could not get it open, then a clasp gave way and it tore apart, laying the chest bare.

When I saw what the cloth had hidden I knew there was no need to feel for his heart. I pulled the sodden cloth back over him, as if it could warm him, and sat back on my heels, only then attending to the fact that men were coming down the path from the castle.

Uther came round the cliff as easily as if he were walking across his palace floor. His sword was ready in his hand, the long cloak gathered over his left arm. Ulfin, looking like a ghost, came after him.

The King stood over me, and for some moments he did not speak. Then all he said was:

"Dead?"

"Yes."

"And Jordan?"

"Dead too, I imagine, or Cadal would not have got this far to warn us."

"And Brithael?"

"Dead."

"Did you know all this before we came tonight?"

"No," I said.

"Nor of Gorlois' death?"

"No."

"If you were a prophet as you claim to be, you would have known." His voice was thin and bitter. I looked up. His face was calm, the fever gone, but his eyes, slaty in the grey light, were bleak and weary.

I said briefly: "I told you. I had to take the time on trust. This was the time. We succeeded."

"And if we had waited until tomorrow, these men, aye, and your servant here as well, would still be living, and Gorlois dead and his lady a widow ... And mine to claim without these deaths and whisperings."

"But tomorrow you would have begotten a different child."

"A legitimate child," he said swiftly. "Not a bastard such as we have made between us tonight. By the head of Mithras, do you truly think my name and hers can withstand this night's work? Even if we marry within the week, you know what men will say. That I am Gorlois' murderer. And there are men who will go on believing that she was in truth pregnant by him as she told them, and that the child is his."

"They will not say this. There is not a man who will doubt that he is yours, Uther, and rightwise King born of all Britain."

He made a short sound, not a laugh, but it held both amusement and contempt. "Do you think I shall ever listen to you again? I see now what your magic is, this 'power' you talk of ... It is nothing but human trickery, an attempt at statecraft which my brother taught you to like and to play for and to believe was your mystery. It is trickery to promise men what they desire, to let them think you have the power to give it, but to keep the price secret, and then leave them to pay."

"It is God who keeps the price secret, Uther, not I."

"God? God? What god? I have heard you speak of so many gods. If you mean Mithras—"

"Mithras, Apollo, Arthur, Christ—call him what you will," I said. "What does it matter what men call the light? It is the same light, and men must live by it or die. I only know that God is the source of all the light which has lit the world, and that his purpose runs through the world and past each one of us like a great river, and we cannot check or turn it, but can only drink from it while living, and commit our bodies to it when we die."

The blood was running from my mouth again. I put up my sleeve to wipe it away. He saw, but his face never changed. I doubt if he had even listened to what I said, or if he could have heard me for the thunder of the sea. He said merely, with that same indifference that stood like a wall between us:

"These are only words. You use even God to gain your ends. 'It is God who tells me to do these things, it is God who exacts the price, it is God who sees that others should pay ...' For what, Merlin? For your ambition? For the great prophet and magician of whom men speak with bated breath and give more worship than they would a king or his high priest? And who is it pays this debt to God for carrying out your plans? Not you. The men who play your game for you, and pay the price. Ambrosius. Vortigern. Gorlois. These other men here tonight. But you pay nothing. Never you."

A wave crashed beside us and the spume showered the ledge, raining down on Cadal's upturned face. I leaned over and wiped it away, with some of the blood. "No," I said.

Uther said, above me: "I tell you, Merlin, you shall not use me. I'll no longer be a puppet for you to pull the strings. So keep away from me. And I'll tell you this also. I'll not acknowledge the bastard I begot tonight."

It was a king speaking, unanswerable. A still, cold figure, with behind his shoulder the star hanging clear in the grey. I said nothing.

"You hear me?"

"Yes."

He shifted the cloak from his arm, and flung it to Ulfin, who held it for him to put on. He settled it to his shoulders, then looked down at me again. "For what service you have rendered, you shall keep the land I gave you. Get back, then, to your Welsh mountains, and trouble me no more."

I said wearily: "I shall not trouble you again, Uther. You will not need me again."

He was silent for a moment. Then he said abruptly: "Ulfin will help you carry the body down."

I turned away. "There is no need. Leave me now."

A pause, filled with the thunder of the sea. I had not meant to speak so, but I was past caring, or even knowing, what I said. I only wanted him gone. His sword-point was level with my eyes. I saw it lift and shimmer, and thought for a moment that he was angry enough to use it. Then it flashed up and was rammed home in its housings. He swung round and went on his way down the path. Ulfin edged quietly past without a word, and followed his master. Before they had reached the next corner the sea had obliterated the sound of their footsteps.

I turned to find Cadal watching me.

"Cadal!"

"That's a king for you." His voice was faint, but it was his own, rough and amused. "Give him something he swears he's dying for, and then, 'Do you think I can withstand this night's work?' says he. A fine old night's work he's put in, for sure, and looks it."

"Cadal—"

"You too. You're hurt ... your hand? Blood on your face?"

"It's nothing. Nothing that won't mend. Never mind that. But you—oh, Cadal—"

He moved his head slightly. "It's no use. Let be. I'm comfortable enough."

"No pain now?"

"No. It's cold, though."

I moved closer to him, trying to shield his body with my own from the bursting spray as the waves struck the rock. I took his hand in my own good one. I could not chafe it, but pulled my tunic open and held it there against my breast. "I'm afraid I lost my cloak," I said. "Jordan's dead, then?"

"Yes." He waited for a moment. "What—happened up yonder?"

"It all went as we had planned. But Gorlois attacked out

of Dimilioc and got himself killed. That's why Brithael and Jordan rode this way, to tell the Duchess."

"I heard them coming. I knew they'd be bound to see me and the horses. I had to stop them giving the alarm while the King was still . . ." He paused for breath.

"Don't trouble," I said. "It's done with, and all's well."

He took no notice. His voice was the merest whisper now, but clear and thin, and I heard every word through the raging of the sea.

"So I mounted and rode up a bit of the way to meet them . . . the other side of the water . . . then when they came level I jumped the stream and tried to stop them." He waited for a moment. "But Brithael . . . that's a fighter, now. Quick as a snake. Never hesitated. Sword straight into me and then rode over me. Left me for Jordan to finish."

"His mistake."

His cheek-muscles moved slightly. It was a smile. After a while he asked: "Did he see the horses after all?"

"No. Ralf was at the gate when he came, and Brithael just asked if anyone had been up to the castle, because he'd met a horseman below. When Ralf said no he accepted it. We let him in, and then killed him."

"Uther." It was an assumption, not a question. His eyes were closed.

"No. Uther was still with the Duchess. I couldn't risk Brithael taking him unarmed. He would have killed her, too."

The eyes flared open, momentarily clear and startled. *"You?"*

"Come, Cadal, you hardly flatter me." I gave him a grin. "Though I'd have done you no credit, I'm afraid. It was a very dirty fight. The King wouldn't even know the rules. I invented them as I went along."

This time it really was a smile. "Merlin . . . little Merlin, that couldn't even sit a horse . . . You kill me."

The tide must be on the turn. The next wave that thundered up sent only the finest spray which fell on my shoulders like mist. I said: "I have killed you, Cadal."

"The gods . . ." he said, and drew a great, sighing breath. I knew what that meant. He was running out of time. As the light grew I could see how much of his blood had soaked into the soaking path. "I heard what the King said. Could it not have happened without . . . all this?"

"No, Cadal."

His eyes shut for a moment, then opened again. "Well," was all he said, but in the syllable was all the acquiescent faith of the past eight years. His eyes were showing white now below the pupil, and his jaw was slack. I put my good arm under him and raised him a little. I spoke quickly and clearly:

"It will happen, Cadal, as my father wished and as God willed through me. You heard what Uther said about the child. That alters nothing. Because of this night's work Ygraine will bear the child, and because of this night's work she will send him away as soon as he is born, out of the King's sight. She will send him to me, and I shall take him out of the King's reach, and keep him and teach him all that Galapas taught me, and Ambrosius, and you, even Belasius. He will be the sum of all our lives, and when he is grown he will come back and be crowned King at Winchester."

"You know this? You promise me that you know this?" The words were scarcely recognizable. The breath was coming now in bubbling gasps. His eyes were small and white and blind.

I lifted him and held him strongly against me. I said, gently and very clearly: "I know this. I, Merlin, prince and prophet, promise you this, Cadal."

His head fell sideways against me, too heavy for him now as the muscles went out of control. His eyes had gone. He made some small muttering sound and then, suddenly and clearly, he said, "Make the sign for me," and died.

I gave him to the sea, with Brithael who had killed him. The tide would take him, Ralf had said, and carry him away as far as the western stars.

Apart from the slow clop of hoofs, and the jingle of metal, there was no sound in the valley. The storm had died. There was no wind, and when I had ridden beyond the first bend of the stream, I lost even the sound of the sea. Down beside me, along the stream, mist hung still, like a veil. Above, the sky was clear, growing pale towards sunrise. Still in the sky, high now and steady, hung the star.

But while I watched it the pale sky grew brighter round it, flooding it with gold and soft fire, and then with a bursting wave of brilliant light, as up over the land where the herald star had hung, rose the young sun.

THE LEGEND OF
MERLIN

Vortigern, King of Britain, wishing to build a fortress in Snowdon, called together masons from many countries, bidding them build a strong tower. But what the stonemasons built each day collapsed each night and was swallowed up by the soil. So Vortigern held council with his wizards, who told him that he must search for a lad who never had a father, and when he had found him should slay him and sprinkle his blood over the foundations, to make the tower hold firm. Vortigern sent messengers into all the provinces to look for such a lad, and eventually they came to the city that was afterwards called Carmarthen. There they saw some lads playing before the gate, and being tired, sat down to watch the game. At last, towards evening, a sudden quarrel sprang up between a couple of youths whose names were Merlin and Dinabutius. During the quarrel Dinabutius was heard to say to Merlin: "What a fool must thou be to think thou art a match for me! Here am I, born of the blood royal, but no one knows what thou art, for never a father hadst thou!" When the messengers heard this they asked the bystanders who Merlin might be, and were told that none knew his father, but that his mother was daughter of the King of South Wales, and that she lived along with the nuns in St. Peter's Church in that same city.

The messengers took Merlin and his mother to King Vortigern. The King received the mother with all the attention due to her birth, and asked her who was the father of the lad. She replied that she did not know. "Once," she said, "when I and my damsels were in our chambers, one appeared to me in the shape of a handsome youth who, embracing me and kissing me, stayed with me some time, but afterwards did as suddenly vanish away. He returned many times to speak to me when I was sitting alone, but never again did I catch sight of him. After he had haunted me in this way for a long time, he lay with me for some while in the shape of a man, and left me heavy with child." The King, amazed at her words, asked Maugantius the soothsayer whether such a thing might be. Maugantius assured him that such things were well known, and that Merlin must have been begotten by one of the "spirits there be betwixt the moon and the earth, which we do call incubus daemons."

Merlin, who had listened to all this, then demanded that he should be allowed to confront the wizards. "Bid thy wizards come before me, and I will convict them of having devised a lie." The King, struck by the youth's boldness and apparent lack of fear, did as he asked and sent for the wizards. To whom Merlin spoke as follows: "Since ye know not what it is that doth hinder the foundation being laid of this tower, ye have given counsel that the mortar thereof should be slaked with my blood, so that the tower should stand forthwith. Now tell me, what is it that lieth hid beneath the foundation, for somewhat is there that doth not allow it to stand?" But the wizards, afraid of showing ignorance, held their peace. Then said Merlin (whose other name is Ambrosius): "My lord the King, call thy workmen and bid them dig below the tower, and a pool shalt thou find beneath it that doth forbid thy walls to stand." This was done, and the pool uncovered. Merlin then commanded that the pool should be drained by conduits; two stones, he said, would be found at the bottom, where two dragons, red and white, were lying asleep. When the pool was duly drained, and the stones uncovered, the dragons woke and began to fight ferociously, until the red had defeated and killed the white. The King, amazed, asked Merlin the meaning of the sight, and Merlin, raising his eyes to heaven, prophesied the coming of Ambrosius and the death of Vortigern. Next morning, early, Aurelius Ambrosius landed at Totnes in Devon.

After Ambrosius had conquered Vortigern and the Saxons and had been crowned King he brought together master craftsmen from every quarter and asked them to contrive some new kind of building that should stand for ever as a memorial. None of them were able to help him, until Tremorinus, Archbishop of Caerleon, suggested that the King should send for Merlin, Vortigern's prophet, the cleverest man in the kingdom, "whether in foretelling that which shall be, or in devising engines of artifice." Ambrosius forthwith sent out messengers, who found Merlin in the country of

Gwent, at the fountain of Galapas where he customarily dwelt. The King received him with honour, and first asked him to foretell the future, but Merlin replied: "Mysteries of such kind be in no wise to be revealed save only in sore need. For if I were to utter them lightly or to make laughter, the spirit that teaches me would be dumb and would forsake me in the hour of need." The King then asked him about the monument, but when Merlin advised him to send for the "Dance of the Giants that is in Killare, a mountain in Ireland," Ambrosius laughed, saying it was impossible to move stones that everyone knew had been set there by giants. Eventually, however, the King was persuaded to send his brother Uther, with fifteen thousand men, to conquer Gilloman, King of Ireland, and bring back the Dance. Uther's army won the day, but when they tried to dismantle the giant circle of Killare and bring down the stones, they could not shift them. When at length they confessed defeat, Merlin put together his own engines, and by means of these laid the stones down easily, and carried them to the ships, and presently brought them to the site near Amesbury where they were to be set up. There Merlin again assembled his engines, and set up the Dance of Killare at Stonehenge exactly as it had stood in Ireland. Shortly after this a great star appeared in the likeness of a dragon, and Merlin, knowing that it betokened Ambrosius' death, wept bitterly, and prophesied that Uther would be King under the sign of the Dragon, and that a son would be born to him "of surpassing mighty dominion, whose power shall extend over all the realms that lie beneath the ray (of the star)."

The following Easter, at the coronation feast, King Uther fell in love with Ygraine, wife of Gorlois, Duke of Cornwall. He lavished attention on her, to the scandal of the court; she made no response, but her husband, in fury, retired from the court without leave, taking his wife and men at arms back to Cornwall. Uther, in anger, commanded him to return, but Gorlois refused to obey. Then the King, enraged beyond measure, gathered an army and marched into Cornwall, burning the cities and castles. Gorlois had not enough troops to withstand him, so he placed his wife in the castle of Tintagel, the safest refuge, and himself prepared to defend the castle of Dimilioc. Uther immediately laid siege to Dimilioc, holding Gorlois and his troops trapped there, while he cast about for some way of breaking into the castle of Tintagel to ravish Ygraine. After some days he asked advice from one of his familiars called Ulfin. "Do thou therefore give me counsel in what wise I may fulfill my desire," said the King, "for, an I do not, of mine inward sorrow shall I die." Ulfin, telling him what he knew already—that Tintagel was impregnable—suggested that he send for Merlin. Merlin, moved by the King's apparent suffering, promised to help. By his magic arts he changed Uther into the likeness of Gorlois, Ulfin into Jordan, Gorlois' friend, and himself into Brithael, one of Gorlois' captains. The three of them rode to Tintagel, and were admitted by the porter. Ygraine taking Uther to be her husband the Duke, welcomed him, and took him to her bed. So Uther lay with Ygraine that night, "and she had no thought to deny him in aught he might desire." That night, Arthur was conceived.

But in the meantime fighting had broken out at Dimilioc, and Gorlois, venturing out to give battle, was killed. Messengers came to Tintagel to tell Ygraine of her husband's death. When they found "Gorlois," apparently still alive, closeted with Ygraine, they were speechless, but the King then confessed the deception, and a few days later married Ygraine.

Uther Pendragon was to reign fifteen more years. During those years he saw nothing of his son Arthur, who on the night of his birth was carried down to the postern gate of Tintagel and delivered into the hands of Merlin, who cared for the child in secret until the time came for Arthur to inherit the throne of Britain.

Throughout Arthur's long reign Merlin advised and helped him. When Merlin was an old man he fell dotingly in love with a young girl, Vivian, who persuaded him, as the price of her love, to teach her all his magic arts. When he had done so she cast a spell on him which left him bound and sleeping; some say in a cave near a grove of whitethorn trees, some say in a tower of crystal, some say hidden only by the glory of the air around him. He will wake when King Arthur wakes, and come back in the hour of his country's need.

AUTHOR'S NOTE

No novelist dealing with Dark Age Britain dares venture into the light without some pen-service to the Place-Name Problem. It is customary to explain one's usage, and I am at once less and more guilty of inconsistency than most. In a period of history when Celt, Saxon, Roman, Gaul and who knows who else shuttled to and fro across a turbulent and divided Britain, every place must have had at least three names, and anybody's guess is good as to what was common usage at any given time. Indeed, the "given time" of King Arthur's birth is somewhere around 470 A.D., and the end of the fifth century is as dark a period of Britain's history as we have. To add to the confusion, I have taken as the source of my story a semi-mythological, romantic account written in Oxford by a twelfth-century Welshman,* who gives the names of places and people what one might call a post-Norman slant with an overtone of clerical Latin. Hence in my narrative the reader will find Winchester as well as Rutupiæ and Dinas Emrys, and the men of Cornwall, South Wales, and Brittany instead of Dumnonii, Demetae, and Armoricans.

My first principle in usage has been, simply, to make the story clear. I wanted if possible to avoid the irritating expedient of the glossary, where the reader has to interrupt himself to look up the place-names, or decide to read straight on and lose himself mentally. And non-British readers suffer further; they look up Calleva in the glossary, find it is Silchester, and are none the wiser until they consult a map. Either way the story suffers. So wherever there was a choice of names I have tried to use the one that will most immediately put the reader in the picture: for this I have sometimes employed the device of having the narrator give the current crop of names, even slipping in the modern one where it does not sound too out of place. For example: "Maesbeli, near Conan's Fort, or Kaerconan, that men sometimes call Conisburgh." Elsewhere I have been more arbitrary. Clearly, in a narrative whose

* Or (possibly) Breton.

English must be supposed in the reader's imagination to be Latin or the Celtic of South Wales, it would be pedantic to write of Londinium when it is so obviously London; I have also used the modern names of places like Glastonbury and Winchester and Tintagel, because these names, though medi- aeval in origin, are so hallowed by association that they fit contexts where it would obviously be impossible to intrude the modern images of (say) Manchester or Newcastle. These "rules" are not, of course, intended as a criticism of any other writer's practice; one employs the form the work de- mands; and since this is an imaginative exercise which no- body will treat as authentic history, I have allowed myself to be governed by the rules of poetry: what communicates simply and vividly, and sounds best, is best.

The same rule of ear applies to the language used through- out. The narrator, telling his story in fifth-century Welsh, would use in his tale as many easy colloquialisms as I have used in mine; the servants Cerdic and Cadal would talk some kind of dialect, while, for instance, some sort of "high lan- guage" might well be expected from kings, or from prophets in moments of prophecy. Some anachronisms I have deliber- ately allowed where they were the most descriptive words, and some mild slang for the sake of liveliness. In short, I have played it everywhere by ear, on the principle that what sounds right is acceptable in the context of a work of pure imagination.

For that is all *The Crystal Cave* claims to be. It is not a work of scholarship, and can obviously make no claim to be serious history. Serious historians will not, I imagine, have got this far anyway, since they will have discovered that the main source of my story-line is Geoffrey of Monmouth's *History of the Kings of Britain*.

Goeffrey's name is, to serious historians, mud. From his Oxford study in the twelfth century he produced a long, racy hotch-potch of "history" from the Trojan War (where Brutus "the King of the Britons" fought) to the seventh century A.D., arranging his facts to suit his story, and when he got short on facts (which was on every page), inventing them out of the whole cloth. Historically speaking, the *Historia Regum Brittaniae* is appalling, but as a story it is tremendous stuff, and has been a source and inspiration for the great cycle of tales called the Matter of Britain, from Malory's *Morte d'Arthur* to Tennyson's *Idylls of the King*, from *Parsi- fal* to *Camelot*.

The central character of the *Historia* is Arthur, King of the first united Britain. Geoffrey's Arthur is the hero of legend, but it is certain that Arthur was a real person, and I believe the same applies to Merlin, though the "Merlin" that we know is a composite of at least four people—prince, prophet, poet and engineer. He appears first in legend as a youth. My imaginary account of his childhood is coloured by a phrase in Malory: "the well of Galapas,* where he wont to haunt," and by a reference to "my master Blaise"—who becomes in my story Belasius. The Merlin legend is as strong in Brittany as in Britain.

One or two brief notes to finish with.

I gave Merlin's mother the name Niniane because this is the name of the girl (Vivian/Niniane/Nimue) who according to legend seduced the enchanter in his dotage and so robbed him of his powers, leaving him shut in his cave to sleep till the end of time. No other women are associated with him. There is so strong a connection in legend (and indeed in history) between celibacy, or virginity, and power, that I have thought it reasonable to insist on Merlin's virginity.

Mithraism had been (literally) underground for years. I have postulated a local revival for the purpose of my story, and the reasons given by Ambrosius seem likely. From what we know of the real Ambrosius, he was Roman enough to follow the "soldiers' god."†

About the ancient druids so little is known that (according to the eminent scholar I consulted) they can be considered "fair game." The same applies to the megaliths of Carnac (Kerrec) in Brittany, and to the Giants' Dance of Stonehenge near Amesbury. Stonehenge was erected around 1500 B.C., so I only allowed Merlin to bring one stone from Killare. At Stonehenge it is true that one stone—the largest—is different from the rest. It comes originally, according to the geologists, from near Milford Haven, in Wales. It is also true that a grave lies within the circle; it is off center, so I have used the midwinter sunrise rather than the midsummer one towards which the Dance is oriented.

All the places I describe are authentic, with no significant

* So *fontes galabes* is sometimes translated.
† Bede, the 7th C. historian, calls him "Ambrosius, a Roman." (*Ecclesiastical History of the English Nation.*)

exception but the cave of Galapas—and if Merlin is indeed sleeping there "with all his fires and travelling glories around him," one would expect it to be invisible. But the well is there on Bryn Myrddin, and there is a burial mound on the crest of the hill.

It would seem that the name "merlin" was not recorded for the falcon *columbarius* until mediaeval times, and the word is possibly French; but its derivation is uncertain, and this was sufficient excuse for a writer whose imagination had already woven a series of images from the name before the book was even begun.

Where Merlin refers to the potter's mark A.M., the *A* would be the potter's initial or trade mark; the *M* stands for *Manu*, literally "by the hand of."

The relationship between Merlin and Ambrosius has (I believe) no basis in legend. A ninth-century historian, Nennius, from whom Geoffrey took some of his material, called his prophet "Ambrosius." Nennius told the story of the dragons in the pool, and the young seer's first recorded prophecy. Geoffrey, borrowing the story, calmly equates the two prophets: "Then saith Merlin, that is also called Ambrosius. . . ." This throwaway piece of "nerve," as Professor Gwyn Jones calls it,* gave me the idea of identifying the "prince of darkness" who fathered Merlin—gave me, indeed, the main plot of *The Crystal Cave*.

My greatest debt is obviously to Geoffrey of Monmouth, master of romance. Among other creditors too numerous to name and impossible to repay, I should like especially to thank Mr. Francis Jones, County Archivist, Carmarthen; Mr. and Mrs. Morris of Bryn Myrddin, Carmarthen; Mr. G.B. Lancashire of The Chase Hotel, Ross-on-Wye; Brigadier R. Waller, of Wyaston Leys, Monmouthshire, on whose land lie Lesser Doward and the Romans' Way; Professor Hermann Brück, Astronomer Royal for Scotland, and Mrs. Brück; Professor Stuart Piggott of the Department of Archaeology at Edinburgh University; Miss Elizabeth Manners, Headmistress of Felixstowe College; and Mr. Robin Denniston, of Hodder & Stoughton Ltd., London.

February 1968–February 1970.   M.S.

---

* Introduction to the Everyman ed. of *History of the Kings of Britain*.